To: Briggs John —

From: Clay Lang

Christmas 2000

The Jekyl Island Club

The Jekyl Island Club

A NOVEL BY

Brent Monahan

ST. MARTIN'S MINOTAUR ☙ NEW YORK

Edited by Gordon Van Gelder
Book design by Kate Thompson

Library of Congress Cataloging-in-Publication Data

Monahan, Brent.
    The Jekyl Island Club : a novel / by Brent Monahan.
        p. cm.
    ISBN 0-312-26183-7
        1. Morgan, J. Pierpont (John Pierpont), 1837–1913—Fiction.
2. Pulitzer, Joseph, 1847–1911—Fiction. 3. Capitalists and
financiers—Fiction. 4. Brunswick (Ga.)—Fiction. 5. Rich people—
Fiction. 6. Sheriffs—Fiction. 7. Georgia—Fiction. I. Title.
PS3563.O5158 J4 2000
813'.54—dc21   00-024415

First Edition: May 2000

1   3   5   7   9   10   8   6   4   2

FOR BONNIE

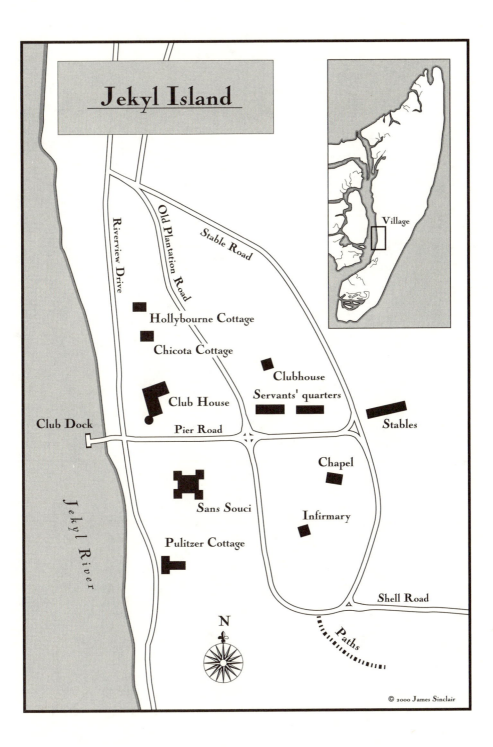

Jekyl Island

Village

Riverview Drive

Old Plantation Road

Stable Road

Hollybourne Cottage

Chicota Cottage

Clubhouse

Servants' quarters

Club House

Stables

Club Dock

Pier Road

Chapel

Sans Souci

Infirmary

Pulitzer Cottage

Jekyl River

N

Shell Road

Paths

© 2000 James Sinclair

A NEW WINTER CLUB

ONE OF THE OLD SEA ISLANDS SECURED
BY A PARTY OF WEALTHY GENTLEMEN

THE JEKYL ISLAND CLUB is the title of an association of wealthy gentlemen who have recently bought the island of this name situated seven miles from the mainland and opposite Brunswick, Georgia.

Jekyl Island, one of the famous Sea Island cotton plantations, is 10 miles long and 2½ miles wide. On the ocean side it has a frontage of hard white sand beach 100 yards wide, affording splendid driving and bathing facilities the entire length of the island, which is composed of a large area of rich cultivatable soil, oak and pine timber, ponds fresh and salt, fine cover for game, for which it is well stocked. The island has been in the undisturbed possession of the family of the recent owner for over one hundred years, and the game preserved, which consists of deer, wild turkey, quail, snipe, woodcock, English snipe, and wild fowl. The fishing is said to be unequaled, and includes an abundance of that excellent fish, sheephead. An oyster bed several miles long occupies the inner shore, from which the epicures of Baltimore and Washington secure their supplies, regardless of cost.

The purchase includes a fine house and grounds, 400 head of cattle, 100 head of horses, 400 hogs, not including several hundred wild ones, which will give the young members of the club a fine chance to hunt the wild boar. The sanitary considerations are valuable as being seven miles from the mainland, and, having a frontage on the sea, the cool breezes make the climate most enjoyable and healthy, and rids the island of the annoyance of mosquitoes. The club was barely in time securing the property, as a company of capitalists were about to purchase, with the object of erecting a large hotel and making it the fashionable resort of the South. The club could sell already at a good profit, but speculation was not its object.

The fifty gentlemen composing the club include some of the highest social and wealthiest citizens, and many members of the Union, Yacht, and other clubs. The facilities for yachting are unsurpassed, and fine shelter and anchorage is a feature of the inner shore of the island. The yachts will be utilized to take members and their families to the island, and affords a secure and cheap place to lay up craft out of commission.

It is predicted that the Jekyl Island Club is going to be the "swell" club, the *creme de la creme* of all, inasmuch as many of the members are intending to erect cottages and make it their Winter Newport. There is already a great demand for shares, which, being all taken by private subscription, are not obtainable. It is not intended that it shall be a selfish and exclusive "man's" club. On the contrary, ladies will constitute an attractive element and will be freely admitted to all the privileges to which their husbands, fathers, and brothers are entitled. They can fish, shoot, ride on horseback, bathe, camp out and enjoy themselves. This new feature of the club will, of course, be popular. The Executive Committee, will, in a few days, make a trip to the island, to determine the nature of the improvements to be made, with a view of having the club formally opened in the Fall. Grounds will be laid out for all the games, including polo, and already the younger members are eager to commence the work of breaking and training the 100 head of wild ponies for that purpose.

The following gentlemen compose the Board of Directors and officers for the coming year: Gen. Lloyd Aspinwall, Erastus Corning, of Albany; the Hon. Wirt Dexter, of Chicago; William B. DeWolf; Lewis Edwards; R. L. Ogden; John Eugene Du Bignon; Oliver K. King; Franklin M. Ketchum; L. M. Lawson; Henry E. Howland; and N. S. Finney. The officers are: President—Gen. Lloyd Aspinwall; Vice President—ex-Judge Henry E. Howland; Treasurer—Franklin M. Ketchum; and Secretary—R. L. Ogden.

—from *The New York Times*, April 23, 1886

M'KINLEY AND REED?

Only Chance Meeting
All the Members of Presidential Party Express Surprise at
Speaker's Jekyl Visit
Of course they may confer

Thomasville, Ga., March 19

THOMASVILLE WAS RIFE with political gossip today. Jekyl Island, the story ran, was to be the scene of a political gathering where the future course of the Republican party would be gone over and settled far from the press and shielded from intrusion by strict enforcement of the no-trespassing regulations of the club.

The sudden appearance of Speaker Reed at Jekyl Island, the authoritative statement that President McKinley, Vice-President Hobart and Senator Hanna would make their trips there on Monday, and the visit of Judge Day, ex-Secretary of State, to Thomasville, though mere coincidences, according to the gentlemen named, who are here, revived at once recollections of the important part in national history born of Thomasville conferences four years ago.

The conference now, said the gossip, were to be transferred to Jekyl Island.

Senator Hanna, Vice-President Hobart and President McKinley himself say positively that there is no politics whatsoever in their present visit South, and that it is undertaken solely for rest and recuperation. As to Speaker Reed's presence at Jekyl Island, both Senator Hanna and Vice-President Hobart said they did not know the Speaker was there.

—from *The World,* page 10, 1899

The Jekyl Island Club

FRIDAY

M A R C H   1 7 ,   1 8 9 9

SNAPPING SHEETS OF RAIN had long since washed the perfume of Golden Isles primrose and honeysuckle from the spring air. It had also washed the good nature from the hundreds of vacationers swelling the population of Brunswick, Georgia. Under the promenade roof of the elegant Oglethorpe Hotel its equally elegant guests paraded back and forth with the aspect of caged cats. The oompah-pah bass of a Verdi overture carried through the saturated air from the nearby L'Arioso Opera House. From the opposite direction, a saloon piano player banged out a ragtime tune. The resort town's nine thousand inhabitants were doing their best to rekindle the dampened spirits of those visitors who had braved the downpour.

The roof of the hotel's veranda vaulted out two stories above the deck, having been created more for ornament than function. When the early evening wind whipped from the east, the rain swept in like a tide. A woman in a black and white silk summer toilette dress yelped in dismay and jumped back from the latest wave. Her derriere collided with the table behind her, creating havoc with the chess game in progress.

"I'm terribly sorry!" the woman's escort apologized.

"So am I," John Le Brun muttered under his breath, as the man and woman hurried away. Those chess pieces that had not been overturned were either off their proper squares or rolling like drunkards on the wooden deck.

"Shall we say quits on the tie-breaker, or shall we begin again?" Le Brun's companion asked, in a Kensington accent.

"No need," Le Brun said, groaning softly as he bent low from his chair to retrieve the fallen pieces. "It was pawn to king four, pawn to king four." He began placing the chessmen on the board. "Knight to king's bishop three, knight to queen's bishop three. Bishop to knight five, pawn to queen's rook three. Bishop to rook four, knight to bishop three. Knight to bishop three, pawn to queen three. Then pawn to queen four and pawn to queen's knight four. Your move."

"Extraordinary!" the Englishman exclaimed. "Do you recall everything in life as clearly, Sheriff?"

"Most things," Le Brun replied, fixing his eyes on the board. He squinted a bit. He had been squinting at things close to him for the past three years, ever since he turned fifty. His tanned, thick-skinned face had borne wrinkles for considerably longer than that. Beneath his derby hat, his coarse black hair was thinning. No stranger would have taken him for anything less than his age.

Geoffrey Moore moved his bishop to knight three. "I hope this rain doesn't fall all night. Transporting my luggage to the train will be a dreadful task."

"Anybody's guess," Le Brun replied, taking Moore's pawn with his pawn. He reached automatically for his cigar, realized it had been jostled out of the ashtray, swore under his breath, and bent again to find it. His eyes caught a flash of bright colors. First blue, then, as he looked up, gold and white. A gaudily uniformed figure had mounted the hotel's grand front stairs and was striding long-legged across the promenade. The man shook glittering droplets of rain from the cap in his gloved left hand, while his right arm was pulled up tightly, so that his hand, wrist, and forearm protected several envelopes tucked under his armpit.

"He cuts a dash, despite the foul weather," the Englishman observed. "Swedish navy?"

"No," the sheriff replied, his eyes no longer squinting as he followed the figure through the hotel's front doors and, via the tall foyer windows, to the telegraph desk. "Jekyl Island navy. His name is Cap'n Clark, although he's probably never been more than a few miles offshore and commands nobody."

Le Brun's sarcastic tone caused Moore to lift his eyes from the board and regard his opponent. The Englishman knew far more than most of his fellow countrymen about American Southerners. He had crossed the Atlantic to buy cotton and indigo for the past five years, primarily from the ports of Charleston, Mobile, and New Orleans. This was his first visit to Brunswick, and he found its inhabitants the same "types" as those of the other port cities. Except for this sheriff. Le Brun stood about five foot nine, with a discernible trace of features from his French heritage. That was common enough. It was clear that he had been a well-muscled youth, but he bore the extra belly of too many hours behind a desk. Of too many whiskeys as well. Plenty of Brunswick men shared those traits. But Le Brun's turns of phrase and subtle remarks belonged more properly to a lawyer than a sheriff, even though it was clear that his upbringing had been as rough-spun as his crash suit. And while other towns' sheriffs played checkers and dominoes—if they played games at all—this sheriff played chess.

Moore had been challenged to a match even before he had met the man. The offer had been transmitted by a bellhop at the Oglethorpe who, earlier in the day, had watched from a discreet distance while Moore defeated another hotel guest. Along with the challenge, the bellhop gratuitously threw in glowing facts about his town's leading lawman. Le Brun was one of them, born and raised in the Golden Isles. A veteran of the War of Northern Aggression, served and wounded with honor. A farmer for many years, and sheriff for the past eight. Scrupulous to a fault. Wholly intolerant of riffraff . . . which was what made Brunswick much safer than Charleston, New Orleans, or the Mardi Gras capital of Mobile. In the bellhop's frank opinion, Le Brun was a major reason why Brunswick had grown to be such a successful resort town. Moore had accepted the proxied challenge, as much to meet this marvel as to while away a rainy late afternoon.

"Jekyl Island," Moore remarked. "I understand there's a fabulous club over there. Recently formed, was it?"

"Depends on what you mean by 'recent.' It was incorporated in 1886. Opened in January of '88."

Moore took the offending pawn with his knight. "Membership strictly limited. And those are the likes of the Rockefellers, Goulds, and Morgans! Titans among men. They might as well have named the club 'Olympus.' "

Le Brun took the knight with his knight. "No, sir. First, the highest point on the island is twenty feet above sea level. Second, their Olympuses are New York, Boston, and Philadelphia. If you ask them, they're here to rough it. Commune with nature. Just be simple folk for a time. Except that the hundred of them control one-sixth of the United States' assets."

"Surely you're exaggerating!" the Englishman exclaimed. "How can only one hundred men—even the richest—have that much wealth in such a big country?"

"They don't. They *control* it," the sheriff said with emphasis. "Power is a great deal more important than land or money." Le Brun massaged his right shoulder absent-mindedly with his left hand, as he had done all through their first games. He lifted the hand and snapped his fingers at one of the waiters, who hurried across the veranda to Le Brun's side.

"Beau, didn't Cap'n Clark visit the telegraph office on his afternoon run?" Le Brun asked.

"Yes, sir. He was here three hours ago. Brought and took telegrams and the regular mail, just like every day."

"They have a telephone over there," Le Brun considered, out loud. "On a night like this, why would they have Cap'n Clark haul his hide all the way back here when they could just as easily have phoned them over?"

The waiter indicated his lack of curiosity with a shrug.

"Go on in and find out what's so special to merit another trip from the island!" Le Brun ordered.

The waiter grimaced. "You know I can't do that, Sheriff. Telegrams are personal. It's against the law to read other people's postings."

Le Brun scowled at the waiter. "Just testin' you. Now, bring me another whiskey . . . and another sherry for Mr. Moore!"

The waiter retreated gratefully.

"They're supposed to be on vacation," Le Brun reflected aloud. "But they can't stop pullin' the strings, even for a week or two."

"You mean the members of the Jekyl Island Club?"

"Precisely."

"They say that no unwanted foot steps upon that island," Moore continued. "That they have a regiment of guards circling its edges, day and night."

"That's what 'they' say," Le Brun answered.

"And when you say 'roughing it', exactly how primitive is that?"

"Their chefs come down from Delmonico's. They have three servants for every one of them during the high season. There's about a dozen homes as well as the clubhouse in the Village. They call them 'cottages.' Each one has ten or twelve large rooms. They have their own golf course. You tell me how primitive it is."

"Have you seen all this personally?"

"Only from the river. Once. That was enough."

"So even you aren't allowed on this island?"

"I know the island very well, from my youth. I have no desire to set foot on it now. Have you considered your next move?"

Though the sheriff's words were gently spoken, Moore knew that his opponent had said his last about the island. "Yes, of course. Sorry."

Even as the Englishman focused on the board, the sheriff lost his concentration. His attention was again diverted by the reappearance of the gaudy gold, white, and blue uniform as Captain Clark exited the hotel and strode down the veranda steps back into the downpour, plowing ahead with as much steam as that produced by the eighty-foot launch he commanded. Le Brun made a few reflective noises in his throat, but they were drowned out by the torrent descending through a nearby downspout.

Moore took Le Brun's knight with his queen. Le Brun responded almost without consideration, moving a pawn to bishop four. The sheriff looked out at the rain and expelled a sound of exasperation.

Across the hotel's puddled front lawn, along the checker-patterned sidewalk, stood a huddle of men. They conversed among themselves from beneath dripping, broad-brimmed hats. Of the five of them, three had rifle barrels showing below the hems of their raincoats. The remaining two wore more stylish hats and had the knots of ties and celluloid collars protruding above their raincoats. Each in turn stole a glance in the direction of Le Brun. The two better-dressed men detached themselves from the group and strode along the curve of the sidewalk and up the promenade stairs, coming to the edge of the table.

"Chief of Police John Le Brun," introduced the younger of the two men, a bull-necked fellow with a heavily waxed handlebar moustache, "I'd like you to meet my peer from the Charleston Police force, Deputy Chief Joel Fraser."

"Chief Le Brun," the dripping lawman said energetically.

The sheriff stood with a palpable lack of energy and accepted the proffered wet hand. " 'Sheriff' is fine with me, Deputy Fraser. This is Mr. Geoffrey Moore, of London, England. Mr. Moore, this is my deputy chief, Mr. Warfield Tidewell."

Moore's eyebrows rose in involuntary surprise as he nodded his hello. If Le Brun did not fit the stock role of Southern sheriff, Warfield Tidewell looked, spoke, and carried himself even less like a deputy chief. This one reeked of university. Perhaps tennis and contract bridge as well. And he was much too young for his position. Fraser was citified, but at least he looked forty, slouched and smiling mechanically through tobacco-juice–stained teeth. Moore half rose, only long enough to shake their hands. He knew he had nothing to do with the conversation and was content to retreat from it as quickly as possible.

"You may recall we met last year, sir, at the law enforcement conference in Savannah?" Fraser prompted Le Brun.

"Sorry, I don't. What brings you into Georgia and our jurisdiction?"

"I have an arrest warrant and extradition papers for a nigger born in these parts . . . calls hisself Thomas Jefferson Bowen."

"What's he done?"

"Kilt a man, or nearly. A *white* man." Fraser cocked an eyebrow dramatically and waited in vain for Le Brun's reply. "Gut-shot him with a pistol Wednesday night. Might be dead by now. We been informed Bowen grew up in Brunswick."

"Why'd he kill the man, or nearly?" Le Brun asked.

The deputy missed the sarcasm in Le Brun's words and plodded on. "This Bowen come into Charleston two years back. Took up with a quadroon girl from one of our good colored families."

The Englishman had picked up enough Southern history to understand that the man referred to Negroes freed before the War of Northern Aggression (as the Southerners generally called the American Civil War). These elite mulatto artisans and craftsmen provided invaluable services to the wealthy white families of Charleston.

"She's real fair," Fraser described. "Got green eyes. She decided to take up with a white man. Bowen shot him point-blank."

"Shameful," Le Brun declared, but without emotion.

"Exactly," Deputy Fraser agreed. "It's like my minister says: before the war the nigger was peaceful and happy and never got in bad trouble. Now, jest about every killin' you see's got a nigger behind it. Without white owners to control them, their natural savagery and hot jungle blood swells up. Now, even if they don't shoot ya, they're all-fired uppity and rude. Demandin'. By the time we're called in, they're too far gone."

"Who's your minister?" Le Brun inquired.

"What?" Fraser returned, unprepared for the question.

"I say, Who is your minister?"

"Oh. The Reverend W. H. Campbell."

"That's not what I was referrin' to when I said 'Shameful,' " Le Brun informed. "I was wonderin' what South Carolina's law is regardin' miscegenation."

"Miscegenation?" Fraser repeated.

"Step away from that downspout, Deputy," said Le Brun. "You seem to be havin' trouble hearin' me. I'm speakin' of racial amalgamation. Sexual intercourse between members of different races. What kind of punishment can the white man expect if he lives?"

"That's not my concern," Fraser declared. "My concern is gettin' the nigger back to justice." He glanced beyond railing and lawn to his well-armed posse. The chances of Thomas Jefferson Bowen's arriving in Charleston alive were nil. "Deputy Tidewell says that you know the particulars on all the niggers in Brunswick, that you'd have a fair notion of where he'd be hidin'."

John Le Brun rubbed his chin with weighty deliberation. "Well, his momma lives over on Carpenter Street. If he's not there, he might be at Auntie Tuesday's place, on the Jessup Road."

"I'd be obliged if you took us there," Fraser said.

John pursed his lips and shook his head slowly. "Sorry, Mr. Fraser. My time is strictly spoken for this evening." He gave a solemn but meaningless nod in the direction of the hotel lobby. "However, Deputy Tidewell will take you over to the boardinghouse where a darkie gentleman named Neptune lives. He'll guide you to Miz Bowen's . . . and Auntie Tuesday's, if need be."

Moore regarded John Le Brun's second-in-command. Warfield Tidewell was studying his superior with narrowed eyes. His jaw relaxed as if he wanted to make a comment, and then he thought better of it.

"Let's go, Mr. Fraser," Tidewell said.

"I wish you good huntin'," Le Brun called out, as the men reached the stairs. The Charleston deputy paused to execute a Southern bow. Le Brun held his place until the deputies and the lethal little deputation disappeared around the corner into the gathering darkness.

"Why am I convinced that Mr. Bowen is not at his momma's, nor this Auntie Tuesday's?" Moore asked, remembering Deputy Tidewell's quizzical look.

"Because he ain't," said the sheriff, taking his seat.

"Where is he?"

Le Brun drew the pocket watch from his vest and consulted it. "Should be almost to Hardeeville by now, in the custody of my most trustworthy deputy, Bobby Lee Randolph. I don't know Thomas Bowen personally, but his momma I do. She's a smart woman. Knew white men would show at her door soon enough and didn't want it to be the wrong ones."

"So she turned in her own son."

The sheriff sat back down in front of the chess game. "Accordin' to the son, it was the white man's gun. There was a struggle, and it went off into his stomach. She hopes, between the ownership of the gun and the testimony of a 'good colored girl,' that her son might could have a slim chance of survivin','"

"Why take him to Hardeeville?" Moore asked.

"First, because the sheriff's a friend of mine. Second, because it's in South Carolina. Thomas will be allowed to say he voluntarily turned himself in before leavin' the state."

"Pardon the ignorance of a foreigner," Moore said, "but couldn't this hurt you when the story inevitably circulates around the dark parts of town? I mean give you a reputation of—as I have heard it put—a 'nigger lover'?"

John smiled softly and returned his attention to the board. "The smart ones'll know what I love is justice. The stupid ones may get bolder, and that'll make it easier to catch them breakin' the law. Do me a favor, Mr. Moore, if you would?"

"Sir?" Moore expected to have to pay for the whiskey and sherry that had just arrived, the price for the box seat he had been given at the farce.

"The next time you happen to be up in Charleston, if you should find yourself there of a Sunday, promise me you won't attend the Reverend W. H. Campbell's church."

Moore laughed. "Of that you can be assured." He noted how intensely Sheriff Le Brun was studying the chessboard and determined to focus hard himself in order to win the critical third game. He was not surprised, however, when he toppled his own king in resignation.

SINCE BEFORE BRUNSWICK'S CHARTER of incorporation, its citizens had had grand dreams. In 1836, they formed and capitalized the Brunswick Canal and Railroad Company, to connect Georgia's southern interior with the coast. The scheme had been to rival Jacksonville to their south and Savannah to their north as the region's vital seaport. The War of Northern Aggression, two epidemics of yellow fever, and several successive depressions had stifled the dream but had not killed it. After decades of exploiting the land and water for indigo, cotton, turpentine, pitch, long leaf pine lumber, and river phosphate fertilizers, the clever folk of Brunswick realized that they could exploit their climate as well. Railroads could transport to the Golden Isles' shores within a day the swelling numbers of middle-class Yankees, those less hardy souls who suffered so from their winter weather. Consequently, Brunswick's railroad station—the gateway to this newly chic winter mecca—had to be built to extravagant proportions. Beneath its slate roof, its six gables and triple chimneys, Victorian gingerbread and scrollwork hung in profusion from its eaves and clung to its smoothly turned columns, both of which were painted a reddish brown to match its brick foundation. The rest of the wood was pastel yellow, the unofficial town color.

John Le Brun skirted the edge of the station, picking his way around a maze of puddles, heading toward the tracks. Beside him walked Geoffrey Moore. Behind them both, a pair of Negro porters followed at a respectful distance, carrying Moore's luggage. The morning sky beyond the neighboring warehouses was dotted lightly with clouds, but the damp was already rising from the ground, making any exertion uncomfortable.

"You really didn't have to accompany me to the train, Sheriff," the Englishman protested.

"Nonsense," Le Brun answered, fetching his watch from his vest pocket and glancing at it. "You have given this town several thousand dollars in new business and have given me several fine games of chess. It's the least I can do. My watch has stopped. Can you tell me the time?"

"Quarter past ten."

"Much obliged." Le Brun carefully wound the watch stem, then pulled the stem out and adjusted the hands.

Le Brun and Moore came to the edge of the station platform. It was crowded with those departing from their week or two of vacation. The men looked anxious to get back to their businesses, the woman seemed generally refreshed, and the children were doing what children always do—inventing noisy games out of their present circumstance. Among the crowd circulated shoeshine boys and women selling picnic baskets for the long rides home. Le Brun revested his watch. Moore held out his hand.

"Thanks again. If you should have a mind to come to London, do drop me a line a month or so in advance, and I'll see that you're welcomed."

"Most kind."

Moore nodded at a train some distance down the track, its stack belching smoke and its safety valves blowing steam. "Shouldn't it have pulled up to the station by now?"

Le Brun shook his head. "Not that one. That's the *Jekyl Island Special.* Not all the club members, millionaires though they be, own private railroad cars or yachts. Nor will they condescend to ride with the common man. That train's the compromise. It runs out to Thalmann Junction, where other private arrangements are made on the main line. The personal handiwork of Mr. J. P. Morgan."

"Ah, yes," Moore said, eager to show his knowledge of American finance. "Your southern railroads were ruining each other with competition. Mr. Morgan stepped in and united them into the smooth-running Southern Railway System."

Le Brun kicked an errant stone off the platform onto the track bed. He spat in its direction. "Morgan saw an openin' and capitalized on it. That so-called ruinous competition was keeping the rates reasonable for the farmer and passenger. If Morgan had stayed out, soon enough the weak and inefficient ones would have gone under. But his deep pockets allowed him to step in and snap up bargains, force the remaining roads to their knees, and gobble them up as well. Now we have no choice. The system runs smoothly, but the farmer and the passenger are forced to pay the only rate there is."

"Is it just Morgan you hate, or are all the members of the Jekyl Island Club on your list?" Moore inquired, recalling several of the sheriff's critical remarks from the previous evening.

Le Brun kept his gaze fixed down the tracks, to where the *Jekyl Island Special* stood alongside the Jekyl Island Club's private dock. "I hate no creature. But when the mosquito lands on my arm for my blood, I swat it. When the rattlesnake takes up residence on my property, I cut off its head. You don't have to hate a thing whose nature is to harm you, even if you have to kill it. Your train *will* be late. Damn the schedule during the Jekyl Island Club's season." Despite the venom in his words, his delivery was mild and matter-of-fact. "Come! Let's see which nabobs are departing paradise this morning. Moses, Buchanan, wait right here!"

The sheriff began a slow ramble toward the train, rubbing his right shoulder as he walked.

"The B. and W. added two tracks here, thanks to Morgan. Once his club opened, it did wonders for the town's reputation," the sheriff reported. "Should we get down on our knees in gratitude, Mr. Moore?"

"I'm not fool enough to answer such a question," Moore replied, trailing the sheriff slightly.

"Shield your eyes, sir!" John suddenly exclaimed. "Mortal man shall not look on the gods and live."

The Englishman narrowed his eyes, to bring into focus the figures ascending from the *Howland*'s deck. He saw an old man in the lead, bald but for a sparse imperial crown of white hair, round-shouldered and bent at the knees. As the patriarch came upon the dock, a throng of waiting children rushed up to him but stopped within a few feet, as if an invisible force repelled them. The man clutched a small leather bag in his left hand. Breaking into a smile, he reached into the bag, pulled out a handful of coins, and tossed them high in the air. Copper glinted briefly in the sunshine before falling to the ground. The children dove heedlessly into the mud, like starving birds for seed, screaming in delight or disappointment.

As Moore came closer, he noted the man's manner of moving over the gravel path with a deliberate lifting of his knees, as if pulling himself out of mud with each step.

"That's John D. Rockefeller!" Moore exclaimed.

Le Brun *tsk*ed. "You looked. Not my fault if you turn to stone."

Right behind Rockefeller came a self-important-looking younger man, his stride almost mincing in his efforts to match that of his employer, his right hand poised above the old man's collar, set to save him from a tumble. The rest of the entourage consisted of a servant carrying a large golf bag and six others—all white—weighted down with matching luggage. No one else debarked from the club launch. Less than a minute after the last servant climbed onto the train, its wheels labored into motion and it chugged out of the station, tooting its whistle to halt traffic at the first of several town crossings.

"And Mr. Rockefeller?" Moore asked his companion. "What do you think about him?"

"As little as possible."

Moore cleared his throat self-consciously. "We should be getting back to the platform. Perhaps we'll only be a few minutes behind schedule."

"Don't count on it," the sheriff replied, holding his ground. "You see the hands waiting by the dock with all those crates? They'd be bringin' them down, and the captain would have come up to deliver the mail by now if all the passengers had come ashore. Someone's still down there. Someone with a . . ."

The blast of a different train whistle caused John Le Brun to glance in the opposite direction. "Yes, I'm right. Someone with his own private train."

About a minute later, another train came backing down one of the tracks, from the landward direction.

"I don't know what you call them in England," John said. "We call these embarrassments of riches 'private varnish.' "

Three exquisite cars, sparkling in the high gloss of multilayered varnish, rolled by the station's collection of gawking passengers. Each car announced its name in stolid gold lettering: *Atalanta, Dixie, Convoy*. Then passed the coal tender and finally the locomotive, a magnificent ten-wheeler tricked out in gleaming brass, its cowcatcher as red and clean as any fire engine. A switch had been thrown, so that the train backed past the sheriff and the Englishman to where the first train had stood. Only after it had shuddered to a stop did a hidden complement of figures appear from the *Howland*.

"Goulds follow Rockefellers in the peckin' order," Le Brun observed. "In New York, where the Four Hundred form high society, the Goulds have clawed their way past the middle. But down here, they couldn't even get membership until the year after the old robber baron, Jay, died. Behold his progeny!"

The station manager and freight master were at the top of the dock stairs, bowing and scraping before the second wave of Jekyl Islanders. Moore saw that the man in the vanguard appeared precisely like his Sunday *New York Times* rotogravure photographs. He walked ramrod straight, as if he had a rifle barrel for a spine. He stood five foot eight and was elegantly slender. His fine, dark hair was thinning at the temples. The height of his forehead made his large, low ears seem all the lower. He sported a handlebar moustache, preserving the image of a young rake in spite of his thirty-five years.

"George Gould," Geoffrey Moore said to himself aloud.

Several paces behind George, sheltered on either side by protective maidservants, walked his ravishing wife, the former New York actress Edith Kingdon. Her voluptuous poitrine and celebrated wasp waist were not concealed by lavish clothing. She wore a simple, full-length skirt and an ecru shawl over a white blouse. Behind her, her brother-in-law Edwin, bearded, solemn looking as one of the cough-drop Smith brothers, stubby-nosed, taller and thinner than his older brother, strolled arm in arm with his wife, Sarah Shrady Gould. The retinue for the four elder Goulds and four children totaled nine servants.

"That's the last of them," Le Brun judged. "We can go back now."

"Maybe those special telegrams were about Mr. Rockefeller and the Goulds leaving this morning," Moore suggested, once again tagging along after the sheriff. Le Brun made no reply, which indicated to Moore that he did not think they were about any such thing.

Soon after Le Brun and Moore reached the station platform, the Gould train lumbered past them. The click-clack of the wheels passing from one rail to the next and the billowing steam from the locomotive overpowered all other sounds for a time. A trainman stood on the rear platform of the last car, holding an unlit brass lantern.

A new noise reached the station, reverberating across the water. The sheriff squinted to make out its source. A grim smile came to his lips. He whirled with the energy of a young man.

"I'll leave you now, Mr. Moore. Have a safe journey home, and be sure to look me up the next time you're in Brunswick!" Le Brun gave an abbreviated wave as he moved toward the dock. Moore opened his mouth to make the promise but found himself addressing the sheriff's back. He was now history to John Le Brun. Something else had captured the man's interest and therefore his very focused attention. Moore shrugged, then pivoted toward the two black men who guarded his luggage, reaching for his billfold.

J OHN LE BRUN MAINTAINED the normal pace of his stride, but the slight lengthening of it indicated his desire to reach the dock without delay. He kept his gaze fixed on the second Jekyl Island boat, a forty-foot naphtha launch named the *Kitty*. The much smaller craft came up too quickly against the opposite side of the dock and struck it with a shuddering groan of wood. Before it could be secured to the pilings, a man in a dark suit jumped off, mounted the stairs two at a time, and set off across the train yard toward the heart of town at an undignified jog. John altered his direction, so that the man must pass him close by.

"Can I be of service, sir?" John asked.

The man slowed. He was small, slight, and in his midthirties. His receding hair created an expanse of flesh that made his slender face look almost full. He appeared simultaneously flushed and pale, his skin pinched around his eyes and the corners of his lips. "Perhaps. Can you direct me to the residence of Judge Tidewell?" he inquired.

"Go to the buildin' with the steeple and one block past it," John obliged. "Then make a left. Third house on the right side of the street. Four thick white columns on a deep porch. And pay no mind to the coon dog that'll be sittin' under it."

"Thank you." The man spun toward the town.

"I'm the sheriff of Brunswick," Le Brun told him, before he could get up any speed. "Are you sure I'm not the one to help you?"

The man's total being seemed to shudder, but he quickly mastered his surprise and continued on his hasty way without turning around. "No, thank you, Sheriff. Thank you much." His *th*'s sounded more like *d*'s.

John watched the man's flight for a few moments, then descended the dock steps to the *Kitty*. He set the toe of his boot on its gunwale and beamed at the lone sailor setting a bumper between dock and boat.

"How you doin', Lemuel?"

"Right fine, John," returned the gap-toothed and scruffy man, who was about Le Brun's age.

"You had about enough of the club for another year?"

"I reckon. Pretty much shuts down week after this."

"Ready to do some plantin'?"

"If you need me."

"I do. Who was it you just brought here?"

"Ernest Grob. Club superintendent."

"German?"

"Swiss."

Le Brun elevated his eyebrows at the unexpected answer. "What's the big emergency?"

Lemuel picked up a waterlogged length of hawser and began coiling it. "I'm not supposed to know, but I believe I heared one of 'em was shot."

"A member?"

"Yep. Shot dead."

"Hmmph!" John stepped down onto the boat's deck. "If that's true, why do you suppose the superintendent would decline the sheriff's offer of assistance and hightail it for the judge instead?"

"Dunno," Lemuel said, his expression as simple as his answer.

"Well, why don't I sit down here and shoot the breeze with you for a while, until he comes back?" Le Brun suggested, moving under the canvas canopy. "Then maybe we'll both find out."

"Have a seat."

Half an hour passed, with the boat rocking gently to the tide and the sun rising smoothly in the morning sky, before Ernest Grob returned to the dock. He looked manifestly unhappy. Behind him came Deputy Chief Warfield Tidewell. Grob gestured for the young lawman to speak.

"There's been a death over on Jekyl Island," Warfield reported.

"Peaceful, in-your-bed death?" the sheriff asked, maintaining his seat in the boat.

"No. A shooting."

Le Brun stood. "Oh. You must get over that passive, lawyerly manner of speech, Mr. Tidewell," he coached. "It's too subtle down here . . . and wastes time. Speaking of wastin' time, why did you not inform me of this when I informed *you* who I am, Mr. Grob?"

Grob's already flushed face suffused with color. "I have been given explicit orders. The circumstances are apparently open and shut, and the club wished to have it declared so immediately."

John shook his head gravely and reached to his vest pocket. "Still can't get around me. Did this shootin' occur last night?"

"No, sir. Early this morning."

"I understand you keep your own physician over there."

"Yes, sir. A very qualified man. From Johns Hopkins this year."

"Then we needn't round up our medical examiner." Le Brun consulted his watch. "Your employers are evidently in an all-fired rush to dispense with this. Let's not keep them waitin'. Mr. Tidewell, does the office know about this?"

"Yes. I said I would find you, and that they should expect you would be gone all day."

Repocketing the watch, John grunted at the words. "Lem, go to my office and inform them that the deputy chief will accompany me to Jekyl Island." He planted a steadying foot on the dock, then hopped up.

"Should I fetch our launch?" Tidewell asked.

Le Brun crossed to the waiting *Howland*. "No indeed! We ride in style for Jekyl Island Club business."

As soon as John Le Brun moved from under the wooden roof of the *Howland* to the nose of the craft, Warfield Tidewell walked up beside him. Both men clutched the rail. The engine had been cranked up to full speed, and the boat plunged through the water like a steeplechase horse.

"Beautiful day," John observed.

"You have not made a friend of Mr. Grob," Warfield stated. "As soon as he entered the house, I informed him that Father has circuit duty every Saturday. He asked how you could not have known that, and I was compelled to admit that you surely did."

John smiled. "He thinks I was not forthright with him."

"Exactly."

"Then why didn't the little son of a bitch tell me the truth of his errand when I gave him a chance? He got what he deserved. And what do you think of the Jekyl Island Club tryin' to get around me by goin' straight to your father?"

"I don't know what to think," Warfield said.

John snorted. "How long have you been deputy chief of police, Mr. Tidewell?"

"Five weeks."

"Don't you think it's past time we got to know each other better?"

Both men stared resolutely ahead at the open water. For a moment, Warfield said nothing. "Yes, sir, I do. In my defense, since I didn't rise through the ranks, I was totally engaged in learning the job the first weeks.

And then again, I am usually on duty when you're off. Your absence defines my presence, and vice versa. Finally, I understood that you are a private man."

"I'm not talking about us knowin' whether the other sleeps on his right or left side. But we need to know enough so we can trust each other and do our respective jobs right. I say again: What do you think of the Jekyl Island Club tryin' to get around me by goin' straight to your father?"

The younger man turned and looked hard at the sheriff. "Mr. Grob told me that the death appears to be accidental. The staff is sensitive to the fact that the club exists to relieve stress from the membership, not to create it. Also, anything out of the ordinary has a habit of turning into scandal because of these folks' notoriety. If it is actually accidental, they want it officially resolved as quickly as possible."

"Fair enough. Let me be frank with you about my reasons for havin' you come along. First, you can give your father and the mayor an objective report, should my actions or motives be questioned. Second, you are a man of polish, with the benefit of university. I am not. We will probably have to question some of the membership about this death, and you will be better received than me. You are, no doubt, far more tactful." John looked at his companion and laughed. "And there is the proof of it. We both know this to be true, but you refrain from comment. Are you acquainted with any of the membership?"

Warfield drew in a deep breath of the sea air that was blowing his sandy hair back off his head. "A few. From my days at Princeton."

"Ever been invited to the club?"

"No."

"Then that's another reason for havin' you with me."

"I look forward to watching you work, Mr. Le Brun. I am told that you are a master at investigation."

"Oh, maybe for break-ins and arson. Murder's another thing . . . if that's what this turns out to be. I've had precious few suspicious deaths to practice on in my eight years. Most of them were clearly motivated. Drunken brawl. Domestic dispute. For all I know, there are a dozen murderers in Brunswick cleverer than me who got off clean without my suspicion."

Warfield smoothed back his hair. "I believe I'll sit with Mr. Grob and see what else I can get out of him."

"I believe that's a good idea, Mr. Tidewell." Only many seconds after his second-in-command had left the rail did the sheriff shake his head.

THE JOURNEY DOWN the Brunswick River, into St. Simon's Sound, and finally into the Jekyl River (which was in actuality only an inland waterway between barrier island and marshes beyond) stretched seven miles. As the *Howland* plunged along, John Le Brun admired the majestic salt marshes, silently mouthing lines he had memorized from the poet Sidney Lanier's "Marshes of Glynn." The tall reeds bent rhythmically in the wind, their susurrations sounding between the rhythmic chugging of the boat engine like the simple melody of a mother's lullaby.

Half an hour into the ride, the *Howland* approached two enormous yachts. The yachts were more on the scale of oceangoing vessels than coastal pleasure craft. Le Brun made his way back to where Tidewell and Grob sat and plopped himself down casually beside them.

"Whose toys are those?" Le Brun called out.

"The one on the left is *Viking*," Grob replied. "It belongs to George Frederic Baker. The other one is J. P. Morgan's *Corsair*."

"*Corsair III,* actually," Warfield corrected, seemingly mesmerized by the sight of the sleek, black giant, its mammoth smokestack raked slightly backward, its pair of tall masts stark against the sky. "He loaned *Corsair II* to the Navy last year for the war with Spain, but he couldn't wait for its return. So he built a slightly larger version. It's two hundred fifty-two feet on the waterline and has a complement of fifty-five officers and crew."

The club superintendent stared askance at the deputy's depth of knowledge. The sheriff showed no surprise at all.

"Why are they anchored so far from the island?" Le Brun asked.

Before Grob could reply, Tidewell said, "Their drafts are too deep for the Jekyl River. You must know how shallow it is, Sheriff, having lived in this region all your life."

John Le Brun said nothing.

Forty minutes after the trip began, the *Howland* chugged closer to Jekyl Island. In the marshes at its northern limits, Negro laborers stood waist-high in water, tending the oyster beds. A little farther south lay the pond where terrapin were stocked. Beyond the marshes, beds, and pond rose the solid ground of the island. Jekyl, the smallest of Georgia's Golden Isles, sat like an emerald centered in a sparkling diadem. Her beauty derived not from contoured elevations but rather from her diversity of trees and her beaches. On the landward side, thousands of Spanish-moss–draped

live oaks competed for space with sweeping stands of palmetto and mag-
nolia. On the Atlantic side, the island was blessed with miles of wide,
gently shelving white beaches. In between, a veritable zoo of animals,
insects, and birds brought the island to vibrant life.

As the boat steamed southward, the wilderness of woods took on
a tamed look. A road could be seen running close to the river. Along
it cantered a guard on horseback, shotgun and binocular cases hanging plainly from his saddle. At last, the circular turret of the clubhouse
came into view, followed by the first of the village's seasonal mansions.
Three smaller yachts lay rafted together, just upriver of the club's elaborate dock.

"You remember the hurricane last October?" Grob said to Tidewell
and Le Brun.

"I wasn't here," Warfield said.

"I was," said Le Brun. "It was vicious."

"It destroyed the dock," Grob went on. "Also the windmill that draws
water from the artesian well. We had to rebuild them both."

"What about that structure?" John inquired, pointing to a three-story,
perfectly symmetrical building with porches protruding on each level.

"Yes, that's new also," Grob said hurriedly. His attention had been
diverted by three men standing on the dock. The superintendent stood
abruptly and threw back his shoulders in a military manner. He fairly
marched amidships. The moment the gangplank was extended, he rushed
down it to report to the waiting group. John rose slowly, giving Grob the
opportunity to say his piece. With a sweep of his hand, he invited Warfield
to precede him.

As John walked down the gangplank toward the waiting trio and the
obsequious superintendent, his attention fixed on the man in the middle.
The figure stood about six feet tall. His hunting outfit, although impec-
cably tailored, could not hide the fact that he weighed 240 pounds. While
the man listened to the superintendent, his gaze fixed on the sheriff. His
soft jowls suffused with pinkness, darkening by the second but never
matching the fierce red of his enormous, misshapen nose. His hair was the
color of linen, his walrus moustache gray, but his eyebrows were unnat-
urally black for a man of sixty-two. Like George Gould, whom he hated,
his ears were unattractively low. Although arresting, all his other features
might have been absorbed and coped with had it not been for the man's
eyes. Their color was hazel, but that had nothing to do with the light that

blazed out of them. They were like the twin headlamps of an oncoming locomotive.

The elderly men on either side of this arresting creature bore auras of wealth and confidence, but in his presence they seemed merely human.

"If the judge is riding circuit, why could the mayor not be found?" the man demanded of anyone who dared to reply.

"He could have been, I'm sure, given a reasonable amount of time," John replied, coming to a stop a few paces from the bellower.

"We do not have the luxury of time," the man shot back.

"And why's that?"

Muscles tightened under the soft skin of the man's jawline. "Because this incident is causing a strain to the membership. I understand that you are the local constabulary."

"I am," John said. He wiped his hand against his trouser in an exaggerated country way, then held it out. "John Le Brun."

The man regarded the proffered hand for a moment, then took it in his bear paw, his fierce eyes measuring the sheriff from crown to waist as he did. "I'm J. P. Morgan," he said needlessly. He nodded right and left, at the gentlemen who flanked him like the buttresses of a great Gothic cathedral.

"Mr. Charles Lanier, president of the club, and Mr. Francis Lynde Stetson, my legal advisor." Morgan did not wait to exchange further pleasantries but made a sharp about-face and strode up the dock. "I have horses waiting," he announced.

At the top of the dock an anonymous guard and a Negro groundskeeper held the reins of eight saddled horses. Morgan clambered onto the largest horse, a magnificent pure-white beast that looked as if it had been bred for medieval warfare. Stetson took the dappled gray next to it. Both the white and the gray had bulging saddle gun cases. As John mounted his horse, he looked to the clubhouse in the near distance. At least twenty well-but-casually-dressed persons stood by the promenade rails, peering in his direction. A few of the bolder vacationers near the dock, pretending to be absorbed by the yachts and the marshes to the west, stole furtive glances at the group. Word of the mishap had spread. The faces were precisely as Morgan had said: strained.

Morgan started off at a trot. A group of Negro groundskeepers hustled to the edge of the road to avoid being trampled. All cast their eyes groundward.

The group cantered past the massive new building and onto a road covered with crushed seashells. John's head was in constant motion, his eyes drinking in the terrain and the vegetation. Rapidly, the manicured lawns and gardens were left behind and the wilderness of the island encroached the party. Japanese holly gave way to wild American holly, hybrid teas to Cherokee roses. Overhead, mockingbirds and thrashers, flickers and kingfishers celebrated life, swooping and darting through the lush green canopy.

Shell Road branched off to a narrower, less traveled path, and this forked after a quarter mile. They veered to the right. Shortly after, they stopped and dismounted. A wagon blocked the party's advance. A mule was hitched to it, its reins held by an old Negro man.

Morgan sidled his girth between the wagon and the underbrush bordering the path. "Stupid nigger!" he fumed, loudly enough so that all could hear. "Doesn't he have the sense to move this out of our way?" No one had the temerity to point out that there was no spot on the narrow path to park the wagon.

Two men stood on either side of a tarpaulin-covered form, thirty feet beyond the mule and wagon. One was clearly an employee, wearing rough denim pants, homespun shirt, scarf, and cane hat. Despite his position as guard, the man had an uncomfortable, out-of-place look about him. The other appeared to be a member or guest, his two-piece suit made of better material and of better tailoring than those worn by the vacationers in the Club Village. He looked to be a robust thirty and had a distinctly British face, with a network of fine veins running beneath his porcelain skin to ruddy his full cheeks and ears that stood out prominently.

Mr. Grob held up both arms, visually linking Warfield Tidewell with John Le Brun. "Sheriff Le Brun, Chief Deputy Tidewell, this is Dr. Thomas Russell."

"A pleasure, gentlemen, circumstances notwithstanding." The physician's words came out softly and swiftly.

"Has the body been moved?" John inquired, taking a step forward.

"No," replied Dr. Russell. "And I've done little more than make certain he's dead."

"Who found him?"

The guard raised his hand halfheartedly, as if being quizzed by a schoolmaster.

John pulled the tarpaulin from the body and tossed it to the Negro holding the mule's reins. "Was he found in *precisely* this position?"

The guard nodded. The body was lying on its back. The man was in his fifties, thin, well-shaven and groomed, wearing a casual suit and low-quarter walking shoes. His eyes were closed. His face looked placid, as if he were sleeping. His white shirt had a good-sized hole in it, ringed with blood roughly the diameter of a silver dollar and exactly above his heart. The right arm lay at his side, hand palm down. The left arm was cast slightly outward, hand palm upward. His left leg stretched straight down from his torso; his right leg was bent at the knee and beneath the left. There was no sign of struggle and no other visible blood.

John knelt beside the body, taking everything in. He gently turned the corpse over. The exit wound, between the shoulder blades, was quite large.

The cloth of the victim's coat had been badly chewed by the projectile as it left, a few tatters measuring almost an inch in length. Little blood had soaked into the damp ground.

John looked up at the guard and received a volley of quick, reflexive blinks in return. "I know you from Brunswick. What's your name, son?"

"Ezekiel Turner."

"Forgive me for not rememberin'. When you found the body, Mr. Turner, were you on the path?"

Turner relaxed a notch. "Yes, sir."

"Have you stepped off the path since?"

"No, sir."

The sheriff pivoted to face Francis Stetson, wincing as he did at the noonday sun. "Would someone mind telling me who the victim is?"

Charles Lanier spoke. "He's . . . he was Erastus Springer. Of New York City."

"A club member?"

"Yes. Of long standing."

"How old was he?"

Lanier looked to Morgan, who had reached inside his jacket. "Fifty-four?" he guessed.

"Fifty-five," Morgan pronounced with certainty, as he produced three hand-rolled cigars, nearly black and more in the proportion of policemen's nightsticks than smokes. "Anyone care for a cigar?" he offered.

"Are they any good?" John asked.

Morgan reared back as if he had been slapped. His black brows beetled. Then he reconsidered what would have been his normal response. "They're the best Cuba offers. From my own plantation in Santa Clara."

"In that case toss one down." John caught the cigar and stowed it in his inside jacket pocket. "Obliged. Won't smoke it now, out of respect for the dead," he declared, in a voice that dared anyone else to light up.

The efficient Mr. Grob had a match already lit for Morgan, who turned his face toward it unruffled and drew the flame deeply into the wrapped leaves.

Le Brun straightened up with creaking knees and a deep grunt. "Mr. Grob was closemouthed about this all to me. All I've heard is that y'all consider it an accident."

Francis Stetson chose to answer the remark, nodding in the corpse's direction. "That's a high-powered rifle wound. What else could it be but a hunting accident?"

John gave him a cold stare. "A high-powered murder."

"Be serious, Sheriff," Stetson replied. "Who would want to murder Mr. Springer?"

"What did he make his money in?" Le Brun asked.

Stetson wheeled and looked to Morgan, as if inquiring whether or not to answer.

"Railroads and mining mostly," Morgan said.

"Then hundreds of gandy dancers and miners, at least. But none of them can get onto this island, can they?" Before anyone could reply to the affront, the sheriff asked, "This is primarily a huntin' club, right?"

Lanier said, "That was the original intent. Now it serves as much for sport as hunting."

"I assume you keep track of your huntin' parties," Le Brun said.

"Definitely," Mr. Grob jumped in, with a proprietary tone. "We have strict rules. Every hunter must sign up the previous day. He must also specify the type of game he'll be stalking and adhere to bagging quotas."

"I'm only concerned with human quarry," John remarked, as his eyes swept the path above and below the body. He shook his head at the traffic that had obscured potential clues. "Mr. Morgan, Mr. Stetson, what were you huntin'?"

"Boar," Stetson supplied.

"Who else was signed up to hunt this mornin'?"

"Only Mr. Borden," Grob answered. "Quail. Not in this part of the island, however." The clipped precision of his replies suggested a Prussian officer at a debriefing.

The sheriff took a step back so that he could regard as one the quadrangle of members and superintendent distributed around the corpse. He cocked his head in Morgan's direction.

"Quail's taken by shotgun, at any rate, so that would mean the bullet came from your rifle or Mr. Stetson's."

Morgan exhaled a thick, pungent puff of smoke and set his free hand on his hip. "Absolutely not! We were neither of us within a mile of here. No one hunts near the paths! And even if we had shot in this direction, the bullet would have buried itself in the ground long before it reached here."

Grob nodded vigorously until the sheriff redirected his attention toward him. "Yes indeed," the administrator insisted. "We anticipated this sort of danger before the club was opened. We keep trees all around the walking and riding paths marked with red blazes." When Le Brun looked into the surrounding woods, Grob added, "You can't see any from here, of course. This is too close. But I assure you they're all around. They start some five hundred feet out."

Le Brun gave his deputy an emotionless look, then shifted his regard again to Morgan. "I'll check later." He walked up to the guard. "Hold out your hands, Mr. Turner!"

The guard obliged. Le Brun lifted one and then the other, examining them and sniffing at the fingertips. "Now, fetch me your weapon!"

"It's a shotgun," Turner protested, nonetheless moving to his horse and unsnapping his gun case. As soon as he had exposed the double-barreled shotgun, Le Brun motioned for him to return it.

J. P. Morgan shifted his weight impatiently. "Now that you've seen the body and the place of the death, let's conclude this in the clubhouse."

"I've just begun here, Mr. Morgan," the sheriff said.

"Well, if you think—"

The lawyer was not about to allow more words between the lawman and his client. Stetson moved forward quickly, placing himself between the two men. "Look, Sheriff, we believe there can be only one explanation for this unfortunate incident: a poacher."

Le Brun's laugh came out like a jackass's bray. "A poacher? You've got at least half a dozen guards circlin' this island day and night. The word in Brunswick is that no uninvited person has set foot on Jekyl Island since you Yankees bought it."

"You know that's nothing but propaganda," Stetson countered. "Not even six guards can keep eleven miles of beach secure day and night."

John shook his head. "All I know is two fellas tried robbin' your oyster beds five years back. Y'all caught 'em and made me hold 'em in my jail until they were sentenced and fined."

The lawyer laid his forefinger against his nose, weighing his words before he spoke. "The point I'm trying to make is that there have been considerably more than two. Our guards only *saw* two and caught them. Those tales about unwanted feet are bruited about precisely to dissuade poaching. However, it definitely continues, despite our precautions. The members never take the number of deer, wild turkey, boar, pheasant, and quail that we stock. And the creatures certainly aren't swimming through those miles of marshes to escape. The risks are well worth the fines a poacher might receive. Within half an hour he might bag what would take him a full day elsewhere."

A large boulder lay embedded in the earth beside the path. Dr. Russell had already eased his posterior onto it. John perched himself alongside and crossed his arms.

"All right. Let's run with your theory. There's a poacher who's ventured all the way to the center of the island undetected. He meets an innocent-looking, unarmed older gentleman strollin' on the path. The maximum fine for poachin' is ten dollars or ten days in jail. You ask me to believe someone would commit murder on the offhand chance he would be identified, rather than pay ten dollars?"

Although he had been resolutely silent throughout Stetson's and Le Brun's disputation, Morgan betrayed his anger with tightly pressed lips and reddening cheeks. At the sheriff's last words, he could no longer maintain his self-control. "No, no, no!" he exclaimed, smoke billowing from his mouth. "The poacher was some distance off. He fired at something and hit Mr. Springer by accident! Didn't even know he'd done it." As he railed, his foot touched the corpse's leg. He sprang back. "Can't we place the canvas over him again?"

"Somebody hit this man squarely in the heart by *accident?*" John said doubtfully. "Speakin' as a man who lives with probability charts, Mr. Morgan, tell me . . . what is the chance of that?"

The Negro driver had taken Morgan's suggestion as command and stepped forward timidly with the tarpaulin. John rushed off the boulder, grabbed the tarp peevishly, and tossed it over the body. "Y'all must think my skull's full of stump water. Mr. Springer had no reason to stray off the path. There are no signs of vegetation on his shoes. If he was in the path and was hit straight on—as the entrance and exit wounds indicate—

where would the shooter have to have fired from?" He spun to face his deputy. "Mr. Tidewell?"

"From the path," Warfield replied.

"And the path is as straight as the proverbial arrow. Now tell me, Mr. Morgan: What poacher stands in the middle of a path?"

Morgan had no reply. Neither did the others among the human rectangle.

John drew up one corner of his mouth in disdain. He looked over his shoulder at the physician. "Do we have a fix on when the man was shot?"

Dr. Russell stood and brushed off the seat of his pants. "Yes, we do. We have a remarkably good fix. Mr. Springer was a man of several neurotic habits. One was living by an unvarying timetable, at least here on Jekyl Island. Every morning, according to what he told me, he arose between six-thirty and six-forty-five, by means of an internal clock. He dressed by seven, had a standing appointment at the barbershop at seven for a shave and moustache trim, then breakfasted no later than seven-fifteen. Always one egg, one piece of unbuttered toast, and a cup of black coffee. The kitchen and dining room staff expected him, so he was never kept waiting and finished no later than seven-forty.

"He kept a standing appointment with me as well, at the infirmary. I took his pulse, listened to his lungs, looked in his eyes, ears, and throat, and pronounced him healthy enough to survive a brisk walk. Hypochondria was another of his neuroses. He was always off for his walk by eight. Even if we were engaged in some discussion on the advancement of medicine, he would table it for the next day once the minute hand on the infirmary clock pointed straight up. He insisted on walking alone, so that his pace would not be disrupted. He walked for thirty minutes, fifteen out, fifteen back, covering—he said—approximately two miles. He always came back past the infirmary, and I cannot recall ever seeing him pass later than eight thirty-five."

"I would agree then that we have an excellent fix," Le Brun said.

"When he was not back by eight forty-five," Grob broke in, "Mrs. Springer, who was breakfasting, became alarmed and came to me. I counseled patience, I regret to say, but knowing Mr. Springer's punctuality, after another ten minutes I sent several of the staff exploring the three paths the gentleman always used." He nodded at the guard. "Mr. Turner found him at approximately nine-fifteen. He returned to the clubhouse to speak to me personally, so as not to arouse general distress among the members and guests."

"A well-trained employee," John allowed. "I estimate that we are about three-quarters of a mile from the village. So, Mr. Springer had to be shot between eight-ten and eight-thirty, unless he was shot at the start or end of his walk and intentionally moved here." He paused to allow anyone to challenge his calculations, but no one spoke. This time he wheeled to face the physician full on.

"Can you corroborate this time by the condition of the body when you found it, Doctor?"

"Corroborate? Yes," Russell answered. "I arrived a few minutes past ten. I had consulted the thermometer hanging outside the infirmary as I left. The temperature was sixty-eight. Using an oral thermometer, I found that the body had lost approximately three and a half degrees of temperature, Fahrenheit. From that, I estimate that he had been dead almost two hours. He still had a degree of color; all the blood had not settled to his dorsal side, as it has now. Since his eyes had been shut, his eyeballs were moist. Gross postmortem changes do not occur in less than three or four hours, so beyond that and the fact that I saw him alive at eight, I cannot fix the time of death more precisely."

John rubbed his shoulder. "What hour were you huntin', Mr. Morgan?"

This time, Morgan curtained his emotions. "From a bit before seven until a little after nine. Just us hunting. Naturally, we took along members of the game staff, to carry back our kill. We left them waiting on the beach, so as not to alert our quarry."

"Did you hear a rifle report about eight-fifteen?"

After looking at Stetson, Morgan said, "We did not."

"Hm! And did the game staff have any kill to carry back for you?"

"Yes," Morgan answered, smiling with satisfaction. "A large boar. It's back at the clubhouse."

"And you, Mr. Stetson? Did you shoot anything?"

"No."

"The rifles on your horses . . . are they the same ones you carried this mornin'?"

"They are," Stetson said.

It had finally occurred to the fascinated chief deputy to take notes. He began scribbling rapidly into a notebook he had been advised to carry by another of the deputies. Stetson glanced his way at the sound of the writing. Tidewell noticed and lightened his usually heavy touch.

"How many shots did you fire, Mr. Morgan?"

"Two."

"Did they both strike the boar?"

"No. The first missed. It was a wily beast."

"And you, Mr. Stetson, did not fire your rifle?"

"That's correct."

"Would you please hold out your hands, sir?"

The lawyer obliged. Le Brun repeated the process he had used on the guard. He nodded his satisfaction at finding no residue of gunpowder. He turned to the guard. "Please bring me the gentlemen's rifles."

With this, Morgan's carefully constructed calm collapsed. He took a step to block the guard, then pivoted his considerable mass toward John Le Brun. He right hand shot out, cigar extended.

"Mr. Lanier, I will not tolerate this man's impertinent questions on the grounds of my own club!"

John thrust his hand up, forefinger not only pointing but waggling. "Mr. Lanier, either Mr. Morgan *will* tolerate my questions or, by the Almighty, he *and* Mr. Stetson will come back with me to Brunswick and be the guests of my jail. This club, which I had assumed belonged to one hundred men and not Mr. Morgan alone, lies within Brunswick's jurisdiction. Its charter does not render it immune to official investigation concerning sudden death, be it accidental or premeditated."

Morgan flung his cigar to the ground. Grob sucked in an audible breath of abject horror. Stetson put himself in front of his client, wordlessly counseling him with wide, pleading eyes.

John Le Brun forged on, unintimidated.

"Now, *somebody* shot this man with a rifle. *Everyone*—includin' poachers—is under suspicion until proven incapable of his murder or until the guilty party is found. Since nobody's come forward or is likely to, we must proceed in a professional fashion, eliminatin' suspects. You gentlemen knew this must happen. That's why you asked for the mayor or judge to be present. I can appreciate that you want this resolved as soon as possible. So do I. But it will be resolved when *I* say it's resolved. Not the mayor. Not the judge. And certainly not any of you."

Morgan blew out a great breath of exasperation, turned, and stalked off several paces. Grob shook his head several times.

John consulted his watch. "Now, Mr. Lanier and Mr. Grob will accompany Mr. Tidewell back to the clubhouse and begin interviewin' all members, family, and guests as to their whereabouts and what they may have chanced to see out of the ordinary. Dr. . . ."

"Russell," the physician supplied.

"Dr. Russell will accompany the body back to the infirmary. I doubt if any of the bullet can be recovered, but I'd appreciate an autopsy."

The doctor nodded crisply and turned to the old Negro. "Mr. Cain," he said, with genuine courtesy in his tone, "will you give me a hand with the body?"

While the doctor and the wagon driver loaded the corpse, John asked Lanier, "Has the widow been informed?"

"Yes. A few members' wives are providing solace."

Le Brun took the rifles from the patiently waiting guard. They were identical, expensive 30-40 Krag-styles, just recently manufactured by Winchester, the first small-bore rifle to handle smokeless powder. He smelled the first barrel and tossed it to Tidewell.

"Think that could make the hole in Mr. Springer?" he asked.

"That . . . and bigger," answered the deputy, as Le Brun sniffed at the second barrel.

John accepted the Winchester back from Warfield and passed them both to the guard. "Mr. Turner . . . remain here and please stay on the path. Misters Morgan and Stetson, would you be so kind as to show me where the boar was taken?"

CHARLES LANIER led the way back toward the Village. Warfield Tidewell and Ernest Grob rode abreast. For a while, each man harbored his own private thoughts. Then the superintendent could contain his outrage no longer.

"What's wrong with your sheriff?" he exploded at Warfield. "Doesn't he know how powerful Mr. Morgan is?"

The deputy had been thinking of J. P. Morgan's power precisely at the moment Grob chose to speak. How Morgan had almost single-handedly saved dozens of railroads from collapse during the past decade and reorganized them into huge systems. How he had shored up the very Treasury of the United States when virtually all its supply of gold was being called in by European lending institutions fearing the threat of a double metal standard. How, as a tycoon sitting on the boards of dozens of corporations, he could and had called together groups of bankers, industrialists, transportation magnates, and insurance company presidents and, within the space of a day, marshaled tens of millions of dollars. If one had no interest in business, he still could not miss reading about Morgan's profligate spending on rare books, paintings, statues, and especially yachts. My God, the man had no idea how to reef a sail, and yet he had bought himself the commodoreship of the New York Yacht Club by offering numerous gold and silver cup prizes!

But John Le Brun had shown J. P. Morgan no respect. Had, moreover, treated him like the prime suspect in a murder. Although Warfield had only worked in the same offices as the sheriff for five weeks, he knew absolutely that Le Brun was anything but a fool. Warfield reflected on the masterly farce Le Brun had executed at the expense of the Charleston deputy only the day before. He wondered if Sheriff John Le Brun was not at work manipulating yet another game to his advantage.

"Even a cat may look at a king," Warfield replied to Grob.

"You mean *wildcat*, sir," Grob declared. "He did more than look; he bared his claws. Mr. Morgan won't need a rifle to finish off your sheriff, if he decides that's what he wants."

Amen, thought Warfield Tidewell.

T HE RIDE ENDED at the club stables. The superintendent swung out of his saddle even before reaching the main doors, whistling shrilly for the attention of a Negro stable boy. As soon as the black teenager had the horse's reins, Grob stalked off in the direction of the clubhouse.

As the club president dismounted, he said to the deputy, "Please forgive Mr. Grob. He takes personally every affront or perceived affront to the Jekyl Island Club or its members. I know your sheriff is merely attempting to do his duty in the best way he can. Mr. Morgan is certainly daunting. If I were in Mr. Le Brun's place I, too, might have gone out of my way to show him I wouldn't be cowed."

"I shouldn't comment," Warfield said.

Lanier patted the young man on the shoulder. "Nor do I expect you to."

Warfield studied the great length of the stable, illuminated by shafts of light pouring in through upper-level windows. "Very impressive . . . especially considering we're on a small island."

Lanier smiled with pride. "Yes. Sixty stalls. Forty-six privately owned or leased by members. Mr. Morgan has four stalls. So does James Jerome Hill."

"Of the Great Northern Railroad," Warfield said, as if finishing Lanier's sentence.

"You know something of our membership, then," Lanier remarked, looking only a bit less surprised than Grob had when the deputy had delivered his speech on Morgan's latest yacht. "These four stalls are leased by James Alexander Scrymser."

"Submarine cable king, owner of several telegraph systems, and one of Mr. Morgan's favorite partners," Warfield stated.

"Correct! And those four are owned by William Rockefeller."

Warfield nodded. "Younger brother of John D. and builder of Standard Oil. Director of the Milwaukee and St. Paul Railroad, of Consolidated Gas Company, and of Hanover National Bank."

Lanier grasped his hands behind the small of his back. "How is it you know so much about us?"

Warfield smiled ruefully. "You mean 'Why should a bumpkin from Backwater, Georgia, know about us?' I was a corporate lawyer in Philadelphia for several years."

Now it was Lanier's turn to nod. He took a new, deeper look at the young man. Tidewell's revelation explained the fine clothes and their "Northern" cut. Beneath the wool, cotton, and celluloid clearly resided a physically powerful human being. Tidewell carried his arms slightly away from his body, as did circus strongmen. His head seemed to rise directly from his chest, so thick were the muscles of his neck. Lanier envisioned the deputy as a football lineman or rugby player during his college days. His hair and moustache were perfectly trimmed, showing pride in his person. Finally, Lanier studied the eyes and mouth, the two features that never failed to reveal hidden personality traits to the experienced businessman. They told him that Warfield Tidewell was a hungry and frustrated young man.

"Interesting," was all Lanier said. After a moment, he turned and pointed to the end of the gargantuan stable. "Those last ten stalls are all owned by Mr. Joseph Pulitzer, the newspaperman. I'll bet you know what makes *that* interesting."

"I believe I do," Warfield answered. "He can't ride a horse. He's legally blind."

Lanier confirmed the statement with a nod. "A number of members will be fascinated to make your acquaintance, Mr. Tidewell. Would you wait here for just a moment? I must speak to the grooms."

While Lanier delivered instructions to the Negro stable hands, Warfield walked to the main doors. On each door was posted an identical sign, permanently set in a wooden frame and under glass. They contained eight proscriptions for the black employees of the island. The first forbade Negroes to stray off the roads and paths. The second forbade Negroes from leaving their cabins after sunset. The third admonished Negroes to speak to whites only when spoken to.

"Sorry," Lanier said, coming up to Warfield and gently guiding him forward by the pressure of his hand on the deputy's shoulder. "In the interest of time, let's get you interviewing the members and the guests— we call them 'strangers'—as quickly as possible."

As they approached the clubhouse, Warfield winced at the homely looks of the building about which John Le Brun had earlier inquired.

"It's called Sans Souci," Charles Lanier replied. "Mr. Morgan named it. He has an eccentric sense of humor, and he loves word games. Or did you know that also?"

"No," Warfield admitted. "I knew neither fact."

"I'm relieved. I suppose he wanted members who hadn't seen it yet to expect a version of Frederick the Great's palace. About as far from rococo as you can get, eh? He bought the last apartment . . . the sixth one. He and the other owners were tired of the limited quarters available in the clubhouse."

"They must be spacious," Warfield speculated.

"Huge. Each suite has three bedrooms and a central parlor. Other than Sans Souci, I don't know what to call it," Lanier said of the first condominium in the United States.

The clubhouse was a much more beautiful affair, built of brick and painted buff yellow. Its four floors plus a fifth-story turret and widow's walk for panoramic views dominated the village. It had sixty bedrooms, three dining rooms, ladies' drawing room, library, offices, barbershop, men's smoking room, game and card rooms. The kitchen, pantry, cold closets, servants' dining room, and butlers' pantry pushed out from the rear of the clubhouse, their utilitarian aspects hidden from the eyes of the members and guests. Beneath the kitchen lay the laundry. All of the service area was concealed by a combination of clever landscaping and modesty walls, which protected the vacationers from the distasteful views of crowded clotheslines.

Tidewell and Lanier entered through the back stairwell to avoid a press of questioners. Ernest Grob was seated in his office, writing out a list of members, family, and "strangers" currently on the island. Lanier entered the office, grabbed the doorknob, and turned back to the deputy.

"Just one minute, Mr. Tidewell, please." He shut the door.

The hallway was too fascinating for Warfield just to stand and wait.

He strolled slowly toward the front entrance, examining the gold-plated coat hooks that lined the walls. Warfield counted as he went. There were exactly one hundred hooks. Ninety-seven had names engraved on brass plates beneath the hooks. The other three plates were blank. He noted that only one name—that of Mrs. Kate A. Papin—was female, and that the club had one doctor of divinity—the Reverend Charles H. Parkhurst.

Warfield swung around, but the office door was still closed. He continued forward and found another list of rules. This set was meant for the hunters. It was lengthy and detailed. All game killed was to be turned over to the club, the members and guests having the first rights, after the kitchen requirements were provided for, to buy a portion of their own shooting. The prices were fixed by the club. No single hunter could bag more than 150 quail per season, sixty quail per week, or twenty in any day. Only club members and their immediate families could hunt pheasant, boar, and deer and only with rifle. No boys under sixteen were permitted to hunt. Shooting on Sunday was strictly prohibited. A penalty of ten dollars was exacted for each violation. Rifles and shotguns were to be registered at the office upon arrival, and under no circumstances were loaded weapons allowed in the clubhouse.

Twice as many rules remained to be read, but Charles Lanier had emerged from the office and trod down the hallway to Tidewell's side. He handed over two neatly scribed pages of names, as well as a fountain pen and a blank memorandum book.

"I saw that you had your own notebook," Lanier said, "but this is in case you wish to keep these notes separately . . . to hand over to Sheriff Le Brun."

"Thank you," Warfield replied, taking the materials. His eyes strayed back to the list of rules. "All weapons are registered."

Lanier shrugged. "Let us say all weapons are *supposed to be* registered. Considering the class of men in the club, we are not about to search them upon arrival. As far as I know, everyone adheres to the rule."

"And why would you feel a need to tell members not to bring loaded guns into the clubhouse?"

"Believe it or not, a member once did such a thing. He was going hunting directly after breakfast and didn't want to have to return to his cottage for his shotgun. He propped it against a dining room chair, and it went off and blew a large hole in the ceiling molding. Caused several ladies to faint."

The club president expected either a smile or a frown but found himself staring into a stone face. The young deputy's no-nonsense persona was just fine with Lanier. He had pretty well made up his mind about Warfield Tidewell. In a town the size of Brunswick, it was safe to assume the deputy was closely related to the judge. Judge Tidewell had been bought and paid for by the club long ago. Then there was the fact that the younger Tidewell had come within a whisker of contradicting his superior when asked about Morgan's Krag rifle making the bullet hole. Lanier could tell there was no fierce loyalty to John Le Brun. Finally, Warfield Tidewell did not know all he knew about the membership merely from local news; he had gone out of his way to learn about the immensely rich. He no doubt had personal aspirations to great wealth. He had gone so far as to earn a law degree and to secure work in a Philadelphia firm. A corporate law firm, where shameful amounts of money could be made by working the laws to the advantage of big business. But something had gone wrong. That was why he had retreated to Brunswick. And why he had a bitter, hungry look about him. He could certainly be used, if the need arose. Lanier decided to send a couple of telegrams of inquiry up to Philadelphia, if only to satisfy his curiosity.

The president saw Grob coming down the hallway and gestured for him to join them. "Let's begin interviewing then," said Lanier. "I—"

"Did anyone besides John Rockefeller and the Gould family leave Jekyl Island this morning?" Warfield interrupted.

The deputy's possession of this information surprised Lanier more than all the other facts had.

"Sheriff Le Brun was at the railroad station this morning," Grob explained to his employer. "He passed this information to Mr. Tidewell on the boat ride here." Then, to Tidewell: "The answer is no. And no one has signed up to leave on the afternoon run to Brunswick."

"What about yachts?" Warfield asked. "Have any sailed?"

"No. No one has left since the shooting. And every visiting member, relative, and guest is on that list. I personally checked it twice."

Warfield counted the names. He was well aware that the club's high season had already passed. Although nominally open from the middle of November until the first of May, it was overwhelmingly patronized within the weeks between New Year's Day and Easter. In another week or two at the most, the Jekyl Island Club would begin another estivation. Nineteen club members, twenty-nine family members, six strangers, and fifty-six personal servants comprised the entire list.

"But this is not everyone on the island during the shooting," observed the deputy to the superintendent. "Including yourself, the entire clubhouse staff, the white and Negro grounds staff, the gamekeepers and guards, the engineers and boat staff, how many support the persons on this list?"

"Oh, *Gott!*" Grob exclaimed. "This will take some time. There are one hundred and sixty full-time employees. During peak season, we have twice that. Today, we have perhaps two hundred and twenty."

"But the whereabouts of each and every one is accounted for," Mr. Lanier assured. "Each has a supervisor and a set schedule. The only ones with the kind of freedom you wish to investigate are the people on that list."

"They're the only ones Sheriff Le Brun has ordered me to interview, at any rate," Warfield said. "Time is flying. Where may I conduct the interviews?"

"My office," Grob said. "This is the luncheon period. I shall have people come in to you as they finish." He escorted the deputy to the office with a sprightly step and shooed out Julius Falk, the bookkeeper. After herding Tidewell behind the desk, he issued a final imperative:

"Please, for the sake of my job, be considerate of these persons' sensibilities and stations!"

Warfield took a final measure of the superintendent. Ernest Grob was as punctilious and precise as a Swiss watch. He might have been as quick-witted as most of the moguls he served. But just a brief acquaintance assured Tidewell that he lacked their daring, inventiveness, and vision. His energies were exhausted perfecting efficient toadying. This would be the highest position such a man could attain. Inwardly, Warfield shuddered at the acknowledgment of different yet equal weaknesses that might keep him as low in life. He could not decide whether to loathe or pity the man.

"I shall be as considerate and concise as they allow me to be," the deputy returned. Grob nodded darkly and began to exit. "Oh, Mr. Grob!" The superintendent faced Warfield again without enthusiasm. "Do you have complete faith in the accuracy of this list?"

"Absolutely, sir."

Warfield shook his head. "You shouldn't."

"Excuse me?"

Warfield held up the second page and pointed to a name. "Mr.

Springer's current wife is not Septima. She died of consumption last year, in May. Mr. Springer's present wife is Chrystie Ward, the former actress."

Grob's eyes went wide with incredulity. "How is it that you have such minute knowledge of our club members?"

"I subscribe to several New York and Philadelphia newspapers," Tidewell answered. "One merely needs to read. Your members are always in the headlines."

"I'm sure the rest of the list is correct," sniffed the superintendent before closing the door.

The first member sent in was Mr. Robert W. DeForest, of New York City.

"Shocking, isn't it?" DeForest enthused. "An accident, what a terrible thing! Well, certainly better than being killed on purpose . . . but only slightly. And they assured me the paths were so very safe. I've only held my membership since last summer, y'know. This is our first visit, and it's been everything we've hoped for. Until now."

Warfield attempted, without success, to ask a question.

"Because they have so much to do, y'know. Safety bicycling, bird-watching, tennis, fishing, and now golf. Have you ever golfed, Mr. Tidewell?"

"No. I—"

"Oh, you must give it a try! It'll be the national rage some day, I predict. Marvelous exercise walking from tee to tee. And the demand of putting a tiny ball into a tiny hole from such a great distance! Now, this course is pretty rough. Not even finished, really. Had some trouble on account of the hurricane last fall, y'know. Had the whole area under water. But this fellow they brought down from Lakewood . . . is it New Jersey or New York? New York. No, New Jersey. Yes, New Jersey! This fellow—Rawlings, I believe his name is—is getting it in hand. It's my passion now. I golf every morning."

"Including this morning?" Warfield hurried to ask, as Mr. DeForest whooped in a breath.

"Yes, indeed!"

"Alone?"

"No, of course not! That would be pitiful, wouldn't it, tramping through the dunes all by oneself. No, I always have at least one companion. Today I golfed with Mr. Pruyn and Mr. Deering. Was a darned sight more fun this morning than yesterday. Yesterday I golfed with J. D. Rockefeller. First of all he hates the course, on account of its roughness.

And only being nine holes, y'know." He rolled his eyes like a vaudevillian. "I can only imagine the old geezer on eighteen holes. He's so slow and methodical. Drove me crazy." He waggled his hand and laughed. "Crazier! He hit one of the balls into the brush and lost it. Now, how much does a golf ball cost?"

"I have no idea," Warfield said, staring at the Regulator clock on the wall behind Mr. DeForest's back.

"Thirteen cents. Of course, being who he is, J. D. negotiates for his balls like a Jew Shylock and gets them by the gross for twelve cents apiece. And yet he couldn't let that ball stay lost. They import little pickaninnies from the orphanage at Hawkinsville to be our caddies, y'know. He hired one of them to look for the ball. The child found it—three hours later—and J. D. gave him a measly ten cents! 'Two cents' profit!' the old bastard crowed. Honestly!" DeForest touched his fingers to his lips in mock alarm. "You won't let anyone know I'm telling tales out of school, will you?"

"Not if you answer a few simple questions with a few simple words," Warfield said, trying to stay civil and wondering if every interview would be so maddening. "Do you golf at the same time each day?"

"Try to. Of course, it depends on demand and the weather."

"What time did you begin this morning?"

The member's forehead wrinkled in thought. "Let's see. Not too early, not too late. With the sun. Almost the equinox this time of year, y'know. Do you mean golfing, or riding to the course?"

"Golfing."

"About eight, I think. Wait!" DeForest rose slightly from his seat. "I remember Mr. Pruyn predicting how long we would take, and he was right, so count backward. Nine holes times the minutes per hole." He did the math on his fingers. "Must have been eight o'clock on the nose."

The deputy wrote in the memorandum book. "You, Mr. Pruyn, and Mr. Deering completed the entire course together?"

"I should hope so."

"At any time this morning did you see anyone carrying a rifle?"

"Can't say that I did."

Tidewell stood quickly. "That's all, Mr. DeForest. You've been most helpful. Thank you."

"May I ask *you* a question?" the member ventured.

"If it's simple."

"It is. Tomorrow's Sunday. Of course. Chapel in the morning. But we leave on Monday morning, and I was wondering if there's to be any kind of memorial something for Mr. Springer in the afternoon."

"I have no idea. You'd better check with Mr. Grob."

The perpetually jovial Mr. DeForest looked quite irritated.

"Because if this weather holds out," he said, "I'd love to get in just one more round of golf."

Several interviews later, Warfield encountered the antipode to Robert DeForest's champagne personality. Mr. Eugene Delano owed his membership directly, but not openly, to Chinese opium. Delano eyed the deputy as if he were a six-winged seraphim come to earth to exact retribution on him for the sins of his fathers. When Warfield invited him to sit, he remained standing.

"Of what am I being accused?" he demanded.

"Of nothing."

"Very well, then: suspected?"

"Again, nothing," Warfield said, mustering what little equanimity he possessed. "We merely wish to verify everyone's whereabouts between eight and nine this morning."

"Regarding the death of Mr. Springer."

"Precisely. Optimally, we hope that you saw something that might shed light on this unfortunate event."

"I understand you are an appointed law officer of this region."

"That's correct."

"Then I refuse to answer any questions unless I have a lawyer present," Delano stated. "There are a few on the island."

Francis Stetson, J. P. Morgan's legal advisor, had just entered the clubhouse and was dragooned to serve as Delano's ad hoc lawyer. It turned out that the man had breakfasted almost the entire hour in question, in full sight of seven other club members, sixteen family members, three guests, and eight dining room staff.

The afternoon dragged on, with those interviewed falling between DeForest's garrulous cooperation and Delano's truculent antagonism. Warfield became convinced that Le Brun had knowingly assigned him a pointless exercise. Even without drawing schematics of the interviewees' whereabouts during the one-hour period, Warfield could see that virtually no one except a woman in her room with "the vapors" had had the opportunity to slip away and back unaccounted for. That woman's location had been corroborated by her maid.

By six o'clock, the deputy had interviewed all but Mr. Springer's wife, three guests, and one club member. The club member was Joseph Pulitzer. At two minutes past six, with Warfield's stomach rumbling and no one offering him a bite of food, John Le Brun swept into the office.

"Well, have you solved it?" he asked Tidewell with a smile.

Warfield tossed the notebook across the desk. "Of course not. Have you?"

"No. But between us, we've narrowed it down." Le Brun threw himself into one of the chairs on the door side of the desk. "Did nobody rub your logic or intuition the wrong way?"

"Nobody," Warfield confirmed.

Le Brun grunted noncommittally. "Did you notice that all the roads leadin' south come to a single bottleneck at Shell Road, just behind the infirmary?"

"I hadn't," Warfield admitted.

"The only other way south is first north and east and then directly south several miles along the beach. Or down by the river and then cuttin' through dense underbrush. Whoever tried the first would have taken the better part of an hour in each direction . . . and that's on horseback. Whoever tried the second would return to the Village cut and torn in a hundred places."

"What about via the water?" the deputy asked.

Le Brun shook his head. "The path Springer was found on is dead center in the island. It would be a quarter mile east or west to water."

"So you're saying . . ." Warfield trailed off, not knowing what Le Brun was saying.

"If it was someone from the Club Village, they either had to go past the infirmary and Pulitzer's cottage—and most likely a Negro work detail just north of the infirmary—or else they had to leave the Village by seven o'clock and return no earlier than nine."

"That leaves Morgan, Stetson, the patrolling guards, and the five people I haven't yet interviewed." Warfield pointed to the list Mr. Grob had prepared. John studied it.

"It also leaves anyone in the Pulitzer cottage or the infirmary," Le Brun noted.

"And possibly an independent staff member, like the boiler house engineer."

"Highly unlikely from what I've learned," the sheriff said.

"And then there's the theoretical poacher," Warfield added. His stomach growled loudly once again.

"Haven't you eaten?" John asked.

"Not since breakfast."

"Well, see if they can't rustle you up somethin'. Then get one of the staff to run you back to Brunswick. I want you to have Bobby Lee go to my house and fetch me another suit and a pair of shoes. Also my holster and revolver. I'm afraid Mr. Morgan is not goin' to get that lightnin' solution he so hankers for."

Warfield had never heard Le Brun sound so Southern. He wondered if the man had been playing the role of the hillbilly sheriff all day and had forgotten to drop it. He rose stiffly from the chair and stretched his arms wide.

"Am I to return tomorrow?" Tidewell asked.

"Yes. You and Bobby Lee. Mr. Morgan wants this solved quickly? I need the both of you if we're to have a chance of satisfyin' him."

"Have they invited you to stay the night?"

"I'm invitin' myself," John told him, picking up the notebook. "You get goin' as soon as you eat. I'll take care of these last five on the list."

Warfield nodded in the direction of the notebook. "Wait until you see Mrs. Springer. She's one of the most exquisite creatures ever to grace the Broadway stage. Have you read a book called *The Picture of Dorian Gray*, by Oscar Wilde?"

Le Brun squinted. "Can't say as I have."

"In it he writes, 'The husbands of very beautiful women belong to the criminal classes.' "

"Are you makin' a point?" the sheriff asked.

Warfield reached for his jacket. "No. It just came to mind."

"Interestin' nonetheless. Have a good ride home, Mr. Tidewell."

"And you have a good night, Mr. Le Brun." Warfield bowed slightly and took himself out of the office and back toward the kitchen.

The sheriff had been studying his deputy's notes for several minutes, nodding at their thoroughness, when the superintendent entered.

"A carriage awaits you in front of the clubhouse piazza," Grob announced.

"Oh? Where am I goin'?"

"To Mr. Pulitzer's cottage."

"I could hit it with a stone from here," Le Brun returned. "Leastways I could have when I was young."

"Indulge Mr. Pulitzer . . . if it's not too much trouble," Grob said coldly.

"Yes," said Le Brun, rising. "I'm sure he's indulged so infrequently. I intend to stay the night. Please see that *I'm* indulged."

Grob bristled. "I shall let you know if that is possible. It's not up to me."

The sheriff flipped the notebook closed with a flourish. "You do that. I'll be back in a while."

The carriage man was black, a friendly gentleman named Eugene who told the sheriff that he had been in Pulitzer's employ for many years and would never leave it so long as Pulitzer spent most of each winter on Jekyl Island. The ride took all of one minute, so that he had little time to say more. However, as John stepped down from the elegant conveyance, the driver waggled a forefinger at him.

"Now, never you mind his mouth, suh; his heart is pure gold."

John prepared himself mentally for a monster.

The Pulitzer cottage was quite grand, built mostly of brick, with long-windowed half-turrets protruding from each corner of its long, rectangular shape. A deep veranda fronted the house, partially shaded by an uncovered, second-story porch. Pairs of French doors flanked the main entry.

John knocked. While he was admiring the palm trees tastefully planted on the front lawn, the door opened. The gentleman who admitted him was in his midsixties, high-cheeked and mischievous looking.

"Welcome, Sheriff! I am Dr. George Washington Hosmer. Known to everyone as G. W. Longtime companion of Mr. Pulitzer." The man noted Le Brun's nostrils flaring. "Oh, I hope you can ignore the odors. Rather pungent, I suppose, when you're not used to them."

John peeked from the hallway into what should have been the living room. The space had been usurped for a makeshift laboratory.

"Are you a doctor of chemistry?" Le Brun inquired.

"No. An MD." Hosmer chuckled good-naturedly. "In fact, what I am is a jack-of-all-trades, master of none. I'm a graduate of New York College of Physicians and Surgeons. I'm also a member of the bar. Practiced both, briefly, but found them boring. Went into journalism and wrote for Bennett at the *Herald*. Then joined Mr. Pulitzer's *World*. He encourages my dabbling in medicinal chemistry as a hobby. I've set up in here since Mrs. Pulitzer's refused to come down this year. I'll get my own laboratory as soon as the back wing and solarium are finished. What I'm *supposed* to do is keep the boss healthy."

"Even though this club has its own physician, in the building just behind us?" John noted.

"Yes. Well, that's not good enough for Mr. Pulitzer." G. W. leaned in toward the sheriff and softened his voice. "He's a mental and physical wreck, you see. I'm his best friend, so I can tell it to you straight. He's neuropathic."

Pulitzer's self-declared factotum reached forward and gave the shoulder of Le Brun's coat a quick pinch, flick, and brush, as though something offensive had lodged there. The sheriff glanced at the fabric and decided to ignore the familiarity.

"Destroyed his nerves ages ago," Hosmer went on, "driving so hard to make himself the world's best newspaperman. Then there are the real problems: asthma, weak lungs, a bad stomach. And his sight. He suffered a detached retina in Italy, nine years back. Totally blind in one eye and sees only colors and shapes in the other."

"Nevertheless, I would like—"

"To see him? Oh, you shall! But let me finish my thought," G. W. said, through an apish grin. "I'm not the only personal doctor brought down to Jekyl Island. Just the only one here right now. These men have pretty much conquered every mortal opponent, but it's taken most of their life spans to do it. Now their obsession's fighting Father Time and the Grim Reaper. They pay dearly to protect their health. That's why they converted that house behind us to an infirmary several years back. And why Dr. Russell's here. From Johns Hopkins no less! They don't dare risk a one-hour boat ride to Brunswick if they become sick, and they wouldn't trust some small-town Southern sawbones even if they made it. No offense meant."

"None taken," John said, anticipating that he would have to ignore multiple offenses from this doctor and undoubtedly from his employer.

"They hired the first staff physician in December of '97, the year after the Reverend Charles Hoffman took suddenly sick on the island and died. Put the scare in them proper, I must say."

"You are on the guest list," Le Brun said.

Hosmer glanced at the notebook in the sheriff's hand. "Stranger list.

That's what they call . . . yes, I should be. I'd take great offense if I were considered a servant." A twinkle came into his eyes. "Then again, he does pay me. I'm sort of in limbo. Just like Russell and the other doctors who've been dragged down here. Neither member nor family, guest nor servant. Certainly not part of the island staff. You give us a name, Sheriff, if you will."

"I'd rather concentrate on Mr. Springer's death," John replied.

Hosmer missed or ignored the hint. "In fact, the situation caused quite a bit of irritation to the man who served in '97 and '98. Dr. Merrill. He wrote a letter of complaint to the officials and stated straight out that a married and experienced physician shouldn't be treated like a hospital intern but rather 'dealt with' . . . how did he put it . . . 'on a more liberal basis.' Be invited to events, private dinners and such, he meant."

"I take it he declined to serve this year," John prompted.

Hosmer rolled his eyes. "No. He was arrested in Rhode Island about a month before he was supposed to come down again. Seems he'd neglected to secure a license for practicing in that state. Straightened it all out last month, I understand, but of course it was too late. Season was half over. Several members have had surgery at Johns Hopkins and contribute donations, so they prevailed upon the school to supply one of their faculty on short notice."

"You assumed I'd met Dr. Russell," John stated simply. "Why is that?"

Hosmer's jaw dropped, drawbridgelike, for a moment. He recovered but looked rather sheepish. "Oh, I've been watching the goings-on out the windows all morning. I have a wonderful view toward the infirmary and Shell Road. You each rode off in the same direction, so I assumed you'd met. Over Mr. Springer's body, unfortunately."

John leaned against the hallway wall. "That's right. Now, exactly who is stayin' in this house?"

"Who? There's himself and myself, his four secretaries and two house servants. All male. Mr. Pulitzer would never allow the slightest potential for scandal by bringing down any of his female servants. He values his shares in the club too highly."

"I see. And then there's the Negro carriage driver."

"Yes, his coachman. Eugene Stewart. Eugene sleeps with the black servants, of course."

"Of course. And where were Mr. Pulitzer, you, the servants and secretaries between eight and nine?"

"Myself, Barnes, Pollard, Ireland, and Dunningham took turns running

back and forth from the clubhouse, fetching him reading materials and
food. He avoids common gathering places. Too much noise. Several persons saw us, I'm sure. There were always at least two of us in the house
with him at all times. By the by, I crossed Springer's path at about ten of
eight. He was headed toward the infirmary. I tried to exchange pleasantries about the clearing of the weather, but he told me he couldn't talk.
'Behind schedule,' he said. I already asked the secretaries if they saw him
later. None had. Naturally, Mr. Pulitzer saw nothing."

As John made notes, he asked, "Did you see anyone else moving toward Shell Road from the Village during that period?"

"I did not. But, as I say, I was in the clubhouse part of the time. And
I was not in this room very much during that time." Hosmer dipped his
head in the direction of the wide windows.

"I'd like to speak with Mr. Pulitzer now," said the sheriff, closing the
book.

"Of course." Hosmer led the way to the staircase. "You may have
noticed no echo whatsoever in here. No outside noises, either. The walls
are about a foot thick and very well soundproofed. As I've said, he hates
loud or sudden sounds. His ears have compensated for his failure of sight,
becoming very acute. It will also irritate him if you move from place to
place."

John noticed that the smell of the chemicals seemed to follow the men
as they climbed. Evidently, Pulitzer's nose was not nearly so sensitive as
his ears. Before reaching the top of the steps, Hosmer turned and dropped
his voice even lower.

"Don't mind his language. He's really a very charming and caring
man, once he gets to know you."

"I've been warned already," John let the doctor know.

The pair trod lightly around a corner into a large bedroom that had a
bay door half opened. A beautiful westerly view past the low palm trees
to the river and marshes beyond presented itself. The pastel room was
bathed in a golden light from the lowering sun. White gauzy curtains blew
languidly from a shifting breeze. Beyond the bedstead, a young man sat
in an overstuffed wing chair, reading from a book. His voice sounded
tired. In the center of the sitting area was a coffee table, a bottle of wine
in an ice cooler, several wineglasses, cups and saucers, plates and utensils,
and the detritus of what seemed to have been a prodigious banquet. On
the opposite side of the coffee table lay a long couch, and here lounged

Joseph Pulitzer, stretched out along its length like an Egyptian prince. His legs rested on the teal-colored couch cushions, but his shoes dangled off. He had rearranged the pillows to bolster his back, which was to the windows. He had his left hand thrown across his eyes, as if the delicate light were still too harsh for him. John's eyes became riveted on the fingers of that hand, long and exceedingly bony. Pulitzer wore a white linen suit, which did nothing to conceal his gauntness. The white suit, the blindness, the marshes of Glynn, and the setting sun brought a moment of déjà vu to John. He closed his eyes and willed the thought away.

The young reader became aware of Hosmer and Le Brun and paused. Pulitzer dropped his hand and sat up erect. His countenance was not one to be quickly forgotten. He had a hooked blade for a nose and an up-jutting jaw that improperly suggested he had no teeth inside his mouth. The jaw was ill concealed by a reddish beard. Beneath it lay the largest Adam's apple the sheriff had ever seen. The rest of Pulitzer's thick hair, including his moustache, was also red and meticulously trimmed. What eventually fixed Le Brun's attention, however, was his eyes. Blue they were, piercing in their effort to find him and gain intelligence through the haze, but ultimately dead in their sockets, perfect companions for his cadaverous fingers. John recorded the fact that the two most influential men he had met this day also possessed the most alert and forceful stares.

Pulitzer stood abruptly. John saw that he was well over six feet tall Slender as he appeared and ill as Hosmer had described him to be, yet he bore no sign of sickness. Rather, he seemed as daunting as a rapier.

"G. W.?" he asked. The question sounded more like a demand.

"Right here," Hosmer said.

"Is that Sheriff Le Brun beside you?"

The physician/lawyer/reporter/chemist/best friend guided Le Brun gently forward. "It is. Sheriff John Le Brun, may I present Mr. Joseph Pulitzer, publisher of the *World*."

Pulitzer smiled broadly and lifted his skeletal hand. John moved forward to shake it.

"An honor, sir."

Pulitzer's face lit up.

"G. W., listen to that voice. What plummy tones!"

John glanced at Hosmer for a clue to his boss's enthusiasm, but the man merely nodded and smiled.

"You're excused, Barnes!" Pulitzer said to the young man in a brusque tone. Barnes seemed to take no offense but looked relieved to hurry himself out of the room, first placing a marker in the book he had been reading aloud, then quietly setting it atop the other reading matter on the coffee table.

"Do you need anything, Andes?" Hosmer asked.

"No, nothing. You'll know if I do. Get on with your experiments!" Pulitzer continued to beam at the sheriff. "Sit!" His hand waggled in the general direction of the wing chair. "I love doctors. My first true friend in America was Dr. Joseph Nash McDowell, of St. Louis. Half my friends are doctors." The words, spoken with only a hint of his Hungarian heritage, sounded to John like those of a true hypochondriac. "I assume you've met Dr. Thomas Russell already?"

"I have."

"Capital fellow!" Pulitzer eased himself down onto the couch, his back once again to the windows. "He reads to me from time to time. I, in turn, am opening his eyes to the important issues of the coming century. But enough small talk. You are investigating the death of Mr. Springer."

"I am."

"And what have you learned so far?"

Even on such brief acquaintance, John was not surprised to have the tables turned on him by America's most celebrated newsman. He obliged Pulitzer in detail, wanting to borrow the mental processes of a man most of the country acknowledged to be a genius.

"Fascinating," Pulitzer remarked. "Shot directly in the heart while on his habitual and solitary walk. Sounds precisely like premeditated murder to me. Am I suspected?"

A laugh escaped John before he could suppress it. Pulitzer reddened.

"I laugh," John hastened to say, "because it's ridiculous to conceive of a person of your moral character committin' such a crime."

"Not to mention my inability to aim a rifle," Pulitzer said. "But perhaps you underestimate me, Sheriff. I have accomplished a great many things in my lifetime, and I dare say if I wanted Mr. Springer dead I could accomplish that as well."

"How?" John asked, indulging Pulitzer's bizarre tack.

"By an overdose of ink. Literally, I don't know. I haven't given it any thought. Come back tomorrow and I'll have an answer for you. Although the man deserved execution."

John settled back into the chair. "Really? Why is that?"

"For never doing an honest day's work in his life, even as he bilked thousands of workers out of the profits of *their* lives' honest labors. I'll deliver you the specifics if you aren't successful within the next day. Those facts not at my fingertips I can have researched within twenty-four hours. I have the largest intelligence-gathering force on the planet.

"Springer's greatest crime," Pulitzer went on, "was in giving nothing back to the public. Many of these men at least seek to justify their avarice by donating to orphanages, libraries, old age homes, universities, and the like. Not old Springer. Unlike Robin Hood, he robbed from the poor and kept all for himself. Of course, if business amorality alone deserves death, this club should resemble the Little Bighorn."

"Yet only one man is dead," John remarked, refocusing his interviewee. "What I came to ask, sir, is if you or any member of your staff saw anything this morning that might help with the investigation. Dr. Hosmer has already accounted for the time when Mr. Springer was shot. However, it is possible that you may have noted somethin' out of the ordinary later. Another member recalled seein' you ridin' in your phaeton at about ten o'clock."

Pulitzer spidered his bony fingers along the table, feeling its contents until he located a banana. "That is true. My driver pointed out Mr. John Kennedy in a fishing boat just offshore. We also rode by that young partner in Mr. Morgan's firm. What's his name, now?"

"One moment," John said, fishing out the notebook. "James Lovell?"

"No."

"Randolph Rasher?"

"That's it. He tore past us on a safety bicycle. Quite an athlete, I understand. Then again, most of 'Jupiter's' junior partners are athletic. Firm of flesh, mighty of muscle, fair of face. They say when God's angels took unto themselves wives among the daughters of men, the result was the Morgan junior partners. He favors them precisely because he's so ugly and out of shape, y'know. As if close association will rub off on him . . . the vain old fool!"

"Is there any chance at all that Mr. Morgan would have shot Springer?" John ventured, making note of the sighting of Randolph Rasher.

Pulitzer continued smoothly peeling the banana. "None. They haven't shared any business for years. Springer had nothing Morgan wanted or couldn't get. Many of these men are either in the Rockefeller or the Morgan camps, but Springer had become an outsider. Millionaire and ruthless as the rest to be sure, but no threat to anyone. Finally, that's not the way these men operate, even with their worst business enemies. If they want someone dead, they do worse than kill him. They ruin him. They have their lawyers sue him, their judges issue injunctions to tie up his business. Their newspapers libel him and muddy his name. They buy his stocks and create panics. Never anything so courageous—or merciful—as shooting him." He held up the banana. "Care for a piece?"

Le Brun declined. He suddenly realized that all the peels, rinds, crusts, and dregs had been created solely by Joseph Pulitzer. The picture of famine incarnate was in fact an eating machine.

"You have a French name. You must know what Frenchmen say whenever mischief's afoot?" Pulitzer asked.

"Cherchez la femme," John said.

A delighted smile broke across Pulitzer's face. "Exactly! A noble voice and brains as well! And what have you learned from his very young and very beautiful widow?"

"Out of respect for her loss, we've been postponing her interview as long as possible."

Pulitzer spit out the tip of the banana. It landed just beyond the table on the carpet. "Oh, bullshit! She's a heartless little gold digger. If ever there was proof that Springer was ready for euthanasia it's his marrying her. They had no guests with them."

John smiled. "That's a statement, not a question. Apparently I'm not the only one investigatin' the shootin'."

"I must stop patronizing you," Pulitzer said through masticated banana. "Yes. I will be conducting my own personal investigation . . . in my own way. I want this murder solved as quickly as possible."

"You *and* Mr. Morgan. Why?"

"Because the club does not deserve stigma. It is a refuge, a shelter against such human folly. We must find the killer and banish him or her from Jekyl Island as soon as possible. My source says the Springers had no guests."

"That's correct."

"And Erastus had only one child . . . a daughter. If it were a son, I'd look to see him and his stepmother married within the year. My stomach has been in knots with the thought that she's behind her husband's murder." He stuffed the remainder of the fruit into his mouth.

"Because of the scandal that would bring," John said.

Pulitzer swiped his hand across his face slowly, melodramatically, as he chewed. "Precisely. This poor club has been tainted enough already. First it was Willie Vanderbilt bringing his wife and Oliver Belmont down here together on board the *Alva*. That same year, Willie allowed Alva to catch him in flagrante delicto. They divorced, and she promptly married Belmont. Nothing was proven to have happened on the island or the yacht, but we allowed neither him nor her to keep their shares. And then there was the disgraceful incident with Pierre Lorillard."

John witnessed the visible conflict on Pulitzer's face and in his voice. The newspaperman hated scandal on behalf of his beloved club, but he also thrived professionally because of exactly the sort of moral turpitude he described with lurid relish. Other people's scandals had made him a multimillionaire. John expected that the man had paused to gauge the sheriff's interest in the topic, that he would momentarily ask "Are you interested in what happened to Lorillard, or have I made my point about scandal?" But he plunged on.

"It's bad enough tobacco is such an evil weed, but that it's made a little shit like Pierre rich through inheritance is almost more than one can bear. He has a yacht, the *Caimen*. Who knows what the hell the name means. Its draft was shallow enough to anchor it near the clubhouse dock. He had six whores on board. Not one or two. Six! They never came ashore, thank the Lord, but the ladies of the club saw them plainly enough parading back and forth on the deck, lying out in direct sunlight! He was given twenty-four hours to be gone. This is a family club, Mr. Le Brun!" Pulitzer's blind eyes flashed. He had worked himself into a righteous high dudgeon. "If I become convinced that Chrystie Springer had anything to do with her husband's death and she somehow eludes punishment by the law, I will make it my personal cause to ruin her in society for all time. She will be blown away in my wind like so much chaff."

The threat, though undoubtedly real, sounded like thin bluster in the heavily insulated room. Pulitzer coughed lightly and sucked in a few shallow breaths. He had set off his asthma. The self-appointed judge, jury, and executioner threw himself against the couch back in frustration, grabbed a throw pillow, and clasped it to his chest. His mouth worked like that of a fish in a bucket.

"If scandal is such a frightenin' threat," John said, "would it not be possible that Morgan found out Springer was holdin' somethin' over his head?"

"What . . . something Springer would actually reveal?" Pulitzer asked.

"Yes."

Pulitzer forgot his asthmatic attack, and miraculously it was over. "On the surface, the Magnificent J. P. Morgan is a very religious man. A family man. Philanthropist, pillar of society. Yet, as Lord Acton has so wisely written, 'Power corrupts and absolute power corrupts absolutely.' Pierpont's financial power has become nearly absolute. If he does what he pleases on Wall Street, perhaps he has begun pursuing dark pleasures as aggressively. But Springer would have been mad to have let anyone know he had something over Morgan. No one in this club is that insane." The newspaperman shook his head vigorously. "No!" He erupted from the couch like a geyser. "But one thing is certain: Springer either stood in someone's way or provoked powerful emotion. This day has almost ended. I recommend that you stay on the island, to begin all the earlier tomorrow."

John stood as well. "I plan to. However, there may be some games played about findin' me space."

"No, there won't. I'll see to that. If you haven't solved this murder by midday tomorrow, by all means come and see me again. Share what you've learned, and by that time my mind may have found connections that you've overlooked."

Le Brun promised as much, without undue confidence in Pulitzer.

"And perhaps, if you've a few minutes, you might read a few passages for me with that mellifluous voice of yours." As he spoke, Pulitzer sidled awkwardly from between the table and couch. He found the crook of John's arm and guided him falteringly toward the bedchamber entrance. "Should you require background information on anyone, remember that I have virtually unlimited resources," he added. His neck craned forward to find the stairs.

"Barnes, you good-for-nothing son of a bitch! Get your ass up here!" Pulitzer screamed. His fingertips pressed the sheriff forward. "Good evening, Sheriff!"

John escaped down the stairs at a brisk pace, back into the full reek of the chemicals. At the sound of his footsteps, Hosmer popped out of his laboratory wearing a rubberized apron and holding a beaker in his hand. He gestured for John to step inside.

"Not a fire-breathing dragon, is he?" Pulitzer's champion beseeched.

John wondered who had recently subjected Hosmer to the critical phrase. "Perhaps just a gargoyle," he generously replied.

Hosmer appeared relieved by the answer. He rushed to the front door, threw it open, and whistled for the carriage. It stood ready at the foot of the turn-around driveway. Eugene leaned back and opened the door.

"Thank you, no," John said, rattling down the veranda steps. "I must visit the infirmary now."

"I can take you, suh," Eugene offered.

Le Brun shook his head. "Give Dr. Hosmer a ride. I need the exercise." As he hurried on, he heard the snapping of reins, the driver's assured call to the team, and then the smart step of horses prancing toward the stables.

The distance from the rear of the Pulitzer cottage to the porch of the infirmary was about three hundred feet, with only a pair of tall trees in between. As he walked across the manicured lawn, John satisfied himself that the curious Dr. Hosmer had an excellent field of view from his laboratory windows. Dusk was setting in. Thomas Russell had lit the gas jets for the infirmary's wall sconces, and John could see him in yellow light through one of the windows, coatless and with shirtsleeves rolled up, writing at a desk. He either caught John's appearance on the porch or heard the tromp of his boots, because he turned, peered out, and rose before John could rap on the door.

"Welcome," Dr. Russell said, pleasantly but without false enthusiasm. He stepped back so that the sheriff could enter.

John paused at the door. He looked its frame up and down. He stared into the hallway with his habitual squint.

"This was the main house on the island when it was purchased," Russell explained. "It was moved, though, to make room for the clubhouse."

"Yes," John said, entering. "I know." He looked to his right. The house's former living room had been converted to a medical facility that was better outfitted than the hospital surgery in Brunswick. Every manner of modern equipment, instrument, and drug lay within John's view. The millionaires were indeed taking no chances with their health. One thing was not in plain view.

"Where is the victim's body?" John inquired.

"I have him in the back room, iced down," Russell answered. "If you've come for the autopsy report, I'm just now transcribing my notes so that they're readable."

John fished his watch out and studied it, giving the stem a few twists. "Will they be ready in an hour?"

"They will."

"I intend to stay the night. Therefore, I'll be dinin' at eight. That is the fashionable hour for society, I understand."

"They dine anywhere from six until nine down here. I'm usually compelled to wait until eight to be seated," Russell revealed. "This time of year, however, there are plenty of tables. I just so happen to have my reservation at that hour. Would you join me for dinner?"

"Delighted." Le Brun cleared his throat. "Perhaps you can offer me another report right now. I have yet to interview Mrs. Springer. I wonder if you know her state."

"I have attended her," the physician attested. "Twice, in fact. The first time I was present when the news was broken to her. There is no doubt in my mind that she was genuinely shocked. She became pale and nearly fainted. Don't take my word for it; Mrs. Lanier was with her at the time. I administered a few whiffs of aromatic spirits of ammonia, and she recovered quickly. Refused a sedative. She's really quite a strong woman. I returned to check on her about half an hour ago. Several of the wives were distracting her with chatter of fashions. She was moderately attentive. I believe she's strong enough to be interviewed."

The sheriff terminated the conversation as quickly as he could with delicacy and headed out the infirmary's front door. The long, hard shadows John had walked through only minutes before were now merging into the cloaking fabric of night. Few persons were out on the paths. Not one of them was a Negro.

John encountered Charles Lanier in the lobby of the clubhouse. He took the proffered hand in his own. Lanier's handshake was an economy of motion.

"I wonder if you might do me a favor, sir," John said. "I regret to say that I have spent little time in the company of ladies these past years. I feel ill at ease havin' to interrogate the new widow alone."

"I would be happy to accompany you," Lanier replied. His smile was more than warm. He had an ingratiating nature, and John could understand how he had been chosen as club president. Together, they climbed the main stairs up to the second floor and down the hall to the third door on the right. Lanier knocked, and a soft female voice bade them enter.

Warfield had been right. Despite puffy eyes and a complexion mottled by emotion, Chrystie Ward Springer was indisputably the most beautiful woman upon whom John had ever laid eyes. Her golden hair was long and luxuriant, cascading unpinned onto her shoulder, a gilt frame for her angelic face. Her periwinkle-blue eyes were enormous and inviting. She bore none of the hauteur which Charles Dana Gibson had validated with his drawings of upper-class beauties of the day. Her figure was less voluptuous than that of Edith Kingdon Gould—the other millionaire's-actress-wife John had viewed this day—yet it was all the more attractive, for John realized how a young man might fool himself into believing that such a fragile beauty might be accessible to a man of mere wealth and not millions.

John blinked at the young woman's image, but not because of her beauty. She wore a simple primrose-yellow afternoon dress with puffed sleeves, trimmed with blue ribbons matched closely to the color of her eyes. It was too much like another dress that had been worn on this island many years before. All through the day, he had endured images that had reminded him of the past, but this final one was nearly too vivid to master.

"Are you all right, sir?" the young widow asked, embarrassing John for the irony of her having to inquire about his mental state.

"Yes, I am. Thank you. It's been a long day," John said, running his left hand self-consciously back along the crown of his head.

Mrs. Springer had been seated among three other women. They excused themselves discreetly after Lanier made introductions. When John was introduced as the local sheriff, Mrs. Springer forced a smile.

"I understand that my husband's death must be completely investigated," she assured him. She patted the divan directly alongside her, inviting John within touching distance.

"My sincerest condolences," John offered as he sat, clutching the rim of his derby with both hands.

Mrs. Springer dabbed the inner corner of each eye with a much-distressed handkerchief. "Thank you." She caught a little sob in her throat. "Mr. Springer was such a vital man. I had looked forward to many years of wedded bliss." She folded her little hands in her lap and stared down at them. Her voice was like a music box, and John wondered how many times this tune had been played during the day. Genuine as her feelings might have been, her gestures and inflections suggested her years of theatrical training and months on the professional stage, challenging John to take her completely seriously. "How shall I tell his daughter?"

"A series of telegrams, perhaps. Each increasingly grave," Charles Lanier suggested. He turned to adjust a chair and offered John a private roll of his eyes, indicating that he believed the woman to be brainless. To John, the question had sounded theatrically rhetorical.

"I shall consider your suggestion," Mrs. Springer assured him.

"How did you meet Mr. Springer?"

"Oh, I was the secondary ingenue in *The Highwayman*." She smiled and touched the back of John's left hand. "It was a musical comedy in New York City last year."

John nodded, then placed his derby next to him on the divan. While he pulled out the book and a pencil and made a note, he echoed, "Only last year. Such a brief time together. Can you tell me where you were between the hours of eight and nine-thirty this mornin'?"

Mrs. Springer lifted her chin and opened her eyes wide. "Certainly. I was right here, still sleeping. Unlike my husband, I stay up late into the night. As an actress, I rarely went to bed before two o'clock. For some reason I could never change my inside clock. I read." She gestured to the double pile of books on the nearby dresser. John was impressed to see Hugo's *Les Misérables*, Hawthorne's *Marble Faun*, and several volumes of Macaulay's *History of England*.

"Are those from the club library?" John asked.

"No. I brought them with me."

John scribbled again. The woman was definitely not brainless. "And what time, then, did you rise?"

"At seven forty-five," the widow said, pointing to the nightstand beside the bed, where sat an alarm clock topped by two enormous bells. "I performed my toilette and dressed so that I was in the dining room for breakfast at eight-twenty." Her face grew desolate. "That way, my breakfast would be ready by the time Erastus returned. My husband sat with me while I ate. We'd make plans and spend the rest of the day together."

"Every morning on the island the same?" John wanted to know.

"Every morning, period. At home or anywhere else. He was a man of . . ."

"Punctuality?" John suggested.

"Exactness."

John set down the word. "His walk was always thirty minutes, on the same path."

Mrs. Springer's smooth brow wrinkled. "Thirty minutes, yes. He told me he used three paths . . . for variety."

"That's understandable. And you have no personal servants."

"No."

John looked up from his notebook. "Isn't that unusual?"

"Well, yes, it is," the millionaire wife allowed. "But I didn't know I should bring any until I arrived. Back home in New York we have six servants."

"Did your husband mention any fears of late?"

"Fears?" the young woman said, clearly confused.

"Of anyone. Enemies, competitors?"

She shook her head, and the wreath of golden curls swayed gently.

"Did Mr. Springer mention having seen anyone on his walk the previous day or two?" John continued.

The actress unfocused her eyes, as if in profound recollection. "No," she proclaimed surely, after a moment. "He might have, of course, but he didn't say anything to me."

John slapped the notebook shut against his knee. "I believe that's all I need." He was rewarded with the brightest yet of the woman's repertoire of smiles. "Unless you have anythin' to add that you feel would be of help."

"I've been wracking my brains, but I can't think of a thing," she confided. Again, she laid her little hand briefly upon his. It was quite warm. "Thank you ever so much for what you are doing."

John rose. "It's my job, ma'am." He was searching for the words to make a graceful exit when Mrs. Springer redirected her attention to the club president.

"When will I . . . we . . . be able to leave, Mr. Lanier?"

Charles Lanier followed the sheriff's example and got up from his chair. "Leave? Not long, Mrs. Springer, I'm sure. I shouldn't be surprised if you could be headed back to New York by tomorrow morning."

"And will my husband's death make it impossible for me to keep a share in the club?"

"No, no, certainly not!" Lanier hastened to assure her. "You may return to Jekyl Island for . . . for as long as you wish."

A knock on the door and another bevy of solicitous wives provided Le Brun and Lanier a graceful exit. In the hallway, John said, "You shouldn't have promised the lady that she could leave so soon. That depends on several things."

"Such as?"

"The autopsy. And whether or not she rose this mornin' at seven forty-five, as she says she did. No one can corroborate that."

"But she was down in the dining room by no later than eight twenty-five," Lanier argued. "I have heard several ladies say so. So how could she have shot her husband and still show up fresh and clean fifteen minutes later?"

Le Brun slapped his derby on his head. "Probably couldn't. But I've seen a magician tied up and put in a trunk, only to emerge from out of the audience a minute later when the trunk was opened. That's theater, and this woman is from the theater. And she has the best motive of anyone. I don't believe she could have done it—not alone—but I don't want her to slip away until I've looked her over from every side."

"Every beautiful side," Lanier commented, as the two came to the bottom of the staircase and stood again in the foyer. "Is there anything else I can do for you, Sheriff?"

"Yes," John said. He pointed to the lengthy list of posted rules. "This rule about the registerin' of guns—won't it tell us exactly who has brought large-caliber rifles onto the island and where they are?"

"Your deputy pursued this earlier in the day," Lanier let John know. "You have to understand something about our members, Sheriff: They love to make rules, but they intend them for others. Some have their own cottages and apartments and see no point in bringing in their weapons here, only to call upon us to unlock them from the cabinets. Others fear the loss of a prized piece. Have you seen the members arrive or depart from Brunswick station?"

"I have."

"Then you know that they travel with huge valises and steamer trunks . . . scores of them. If they've a mind, they could easily smuggle a rifle in without our knowing. So far as I know, that has never happened. But this resort is run for their pleasure, not annoyance. We would never insult them by conducting searches. Finding an unregistered rifle will not necessarily reveal the person who shot poor Mr. Springer."

"Rules for everyone else," the sheriff echoed, moving his head up and down, going once again for his watch and consulting it. "Thanks much. I'm dinin' with Dr. Russell in a few minutes. I think I can survive on my own until then."

Lanier took his leave. John studied the rest of the rules concerning hunting. He moved to another set of requirements and prohibitions under glass. This one concerned lodging and dining. Rooms rented from seven to twelve dollars per person per day, depending on view and size. Children were $1.50 cheaper, and it cost two dollars a day to room and board servants. Indebtedness to the club could not exceed a hundred dollars. Servant gratuities were strictly forbidden. "Strangers" could only be accepted on personal sponsorship and by written request, with two weeks' notice and the approval of the board. They were allowed a two-week maximum stay in the clubhouse. No member could invite more than two guests simultaneously. No more than six persons were allowed at dining room tables, and tables were not to be pushed together. Smoking was strictly forbidden to women, as was the smoking room. Personal servants as well as staff servants had to be in uniform at all times. No dinner jackets were allowed on the island.

"If these people had climbed Mount Sinai, they'd have returned with a hundred commandments," John said, under his breath.

"Excuse me?"

John turned and found himself *nez à nez grotesque* with J. P. Morgan. Standing next to him was a young man with handsome face and form.

"I believe you have yet to interview at least one person, Sheriff," Morgan said. "This is one of my junior partners, Mr. Randolph Rasher."

His face might have been chiseled by Michelangelo as a study for the *David*. Rasher's wavy hair was jet black, except for a white streak that ran just above and parallel to his part. He wore white duck pants and a bulky sweater which did little to conceal the hard musculature of his frame. If this was the prototype for all Morgan's junior partners, Pulitzer had not exaggerated.

"Sorry to have been so elusive," Rasher apologized, reaching down to capture John's unoffered hand and pumping it within a powerful grip, "but they feed you so blasted much down here that I spend most of the day exercising." John apprehended that the man had been briefed by his employer, because he supplied a chronology of his day without prompting. He had arisen at six-thirty. He had checked a touring bicycle out from the Club House at six-fifty and had bicycled until eight-forty. He took breakfast in the servants' dining room so as not to have to change out of his sweaty clothing and then returned directly to the bicycle paths. By the time Mr. Springer's body had been discovered, he was near the other end of the island and had managed to elude the bad news until seven P.M.

"Once I heard the terrible report," he concluded, exuding a strong odor of cigarette, "I quickly showered and changed and looked for Mr. Morgan. For details and because I supposed everyone must be interviewed. To see where we had been and if we had seen anything. I have a rifle, but it's been locked up in the clubhouse all day. Mr. Fisher checked out the safety bicycle for me—a Hawthorne. Real whizzer!"

"You've neglected to say if you did see anythin'," John observed.

"Well, I rode by the clubhouse piazza at around seven this morning and saw the Bakers. Then I went deep into the paths. But north, the opposite of where Mr. Springer was killed. Saw nobody until I got back. Not surprising, you know, there being so many miles of paths. At about quarter past ten, I think, I saw Mr. Pulitzer in his carriage. Then a few other persons to wave at and finally no one for the longest while. I should have suspected there was something amiss. Something that held everyone to the Village."

"You didn't return to the clubhouse for lunch?"

"Rarely take it," he said. "Anything else?"

John had fished out the notebook and found two reports of interviewees having seen Rasher on the bicycle, further corroborating Pulitzer's mention of the young man.

"That's all for now," John said.

"If you need me, I'll be around," said Rasher. He gave a little salute and fairly sprang away toward the piazza. John and Morgan together watched as youth incarnate shoved open the main door and greeted another man in his twenties, who was in the act of tapping a cigarette out of an opened pack. Rasher accepted another of the cigarettes, and the two began an animated discussion by the light of a shared struck match.

"I remember myself that young," John said.

"So do I. All that strength and boundless energy. Now my pastimes must be more sedentary. Do you play chess?" Morgan asked, the last sentence exploding from his mouth as if from a muzzle.

John affirmed that he did, sure that Morgan knew the answer before asking. Such a man would not have made such an assumption about a small-town Southern sheriff. Apparently, Pulitzer was not the only member gathering information.

"I favor the game myself," Morgan declared. "Since you're staying the night, I'd like to invite you to play." He attempted a generous grin, showing large teeth yellowed by years of cigar smoking.

"That would be right nice." John was frankly amazed at the sea change in Morgan's attitude toward him. Even when he had gone with Morgan and Stetson to view the place where Morgan had killed the boar and he had admitted openly that there was no way an errant bullet could have killed Springer from there, Morgan had maintained an air of hostility toward him. They had parted company at the stables on far less than cordial terms. Now, Morgan had accepted his staying on the island with positive equanimity, even though John had not recanted suspecting him of some part in murder.

"I'm expectin' to dine with Dr. Russell in a few minutes. Can you wait?" John asked.

Morgan puffed prodigiously on his cigar. "Certainly. I did not intend to play until later. I'll see that you're found." With that, he turned, hailed another member, and walked off.

John ambled to an easel that that been set just outside the dining room. A beautifully calligraphed notice stated that, due to the day's unfortunate incident, the evening's performance by the Corktown Minstrels had been canceled. John fetched the notebook from his pocket and made notes on his interviews with Mrs. Springer and Randolph Rasher. According to the list tucked into the notebook, only one person remained to be interviewed. His name was James Lovell. The deputy had lightly noted that this man's presence on the clubhouse grounds the entire morning had been affirmed by several interviewees. Also, Lovell had expressed to his peers an intense dislike of any interview that attempted to fix guilt. As a point of fairness to all who had submitted to interrogation, however, John determined to find the man and force him to give a deposition.

"Sorry to be a bit late," Dr. Russell said, from behind Le Brun. "Shall we go in?"

John noted that the dining room was about as opulent as the main dining salon of the Oglethorpe Hotel. The gaslight flickered behind frosted balls. Dentil molding crowned the dark wood walls. Snapping white linen covered each table, and a bud vase on each displayed spring flowers. Crystal, porcelain, and silver twinkled brightly as the two men wended their way through the room to the far corner. Only six tables were occupied. The doctor led the way to a small table closest to the butler's pantry and consequently nearest to the waiter traffic and kitchen noise. As they were sitting, Russell said, "I have to assume that since you're still here, you found nothing damning against Mr. Morgan or Mr. Stetson."

John pulled his chair closer to the table. "That's correct. Morgan definitely shot the boar. The place was more than a mile south of where Springer was shot. There were no signs of travel through the woods. The ground was quite soft from last night's rain. Even a thin man's footprints would have shown."

"And your deputy's interviews with the members and guests revealed nothing?" Russell asked.

"Nothing conclusive in itself."

The physician picked up his menu and studied it. "I see. Then that leaves the staff."

"Very few of them, either," Le Brun went on. "Most have no business south of the Village. If they do, they're with a supervisor. The Negroes are all overseen and very conspicuous when not at work. The three staff members who do roam were conductin' bird-watchin', givin' bicycle lessons, and takin' Mr. Kennedy fishin'."

"What about the guards?"

"Don't you know their patterns?" John countered, watching Russell's eyes sweep back and forth over the evening's selection. Russell blinked and regarded his companion.

"Actually, no. I'm such a prisoner of the infirmary, I rarely have enlightening conversations about the Jekyl Island Club, much less personally view its operation."

John reviewed his own menu, seeing if the silence would compel Russell to greater explanation. When he knew the man would volunteer no more, he said, "There were six guards on duty this mornin', each assigned to a section of the island border."

"Any of them carrying rifles?"

"No. They all have Colt hammerless ten-gauge shotguns. Club issue. Not to say one couldn't have stowed a rifle near the path at an earlier time and used it. Only one, according to corroboratin' evidence, could have shot Springer with impunity: Ezekiel Turner."

"The same man who found the body."

"The same."

"So, he's your prime suspect?"

A waiter arrived, interrupting Russell's interrogation.

"I speak a bit of French," John said to the supercilious-looking waiter, "but this here is beyond me. What's this Consommé Celestine?"

"Consommé à la Celestine," the waiter corrected. "Unsugared pancakes with chicken forcemeat and fines herbes, in a consommé with finely chopped lettuce."

"I've had it up at Delmonico's in New York," Russell told the sheriff. "It's quite good. These are some of their chefs down here. Practically anything on the menu is superb. Would you like me to suggest an order for the both of us?"

John set down his menu. "Go ahead."

The doctor ordered the consommé, a palmette of pheasant à la Torrens, red snapper, ham braised with stuffed tomatoes as their remove, and breast of woodcock à la Diane as entrée. This was to be followed by salad and a dessert of iced biscuits with vanilla and strawberries. Two bottles of white wine, one from the Rhine and one from the Loire Valley, were ordered to lubricate the courses.

The waiter took no notes. He nodded coolly at Russell and disappeared.

"I like to eat, and I'm famished," John revealed, "but that sounds like enough food for an army."

"Just sample each course," Russell suggested. "That's what I do. They're footing the bill, so why not order it all? Almost everyone eats only a few forkfuls. Tremendous waste."

Both men paused their conversation while Randolph Rasher entered the dining room with an older man and woman, a young woman, and Pierpont Morgan's lawyer.

As the group was seating itself, the doctor said, "You know Francis Lynde Stetson. The man and woman are Mr. and Mrs. George Baker. That's their daughter, Frances. And the dashing fellow is Randolph Rasher . . . a Morgan junior partner."

"I've met him also. You have a hint of a British accent," John observed. "London?"

"Manchester. I left for America with my family when I was quite young."

"Any brothers or sisters?"

"Two sisters. Both older and married."

"I understand you're single."

"True. And you?"

John glanced at Frances Baker. "I was married . . . once."

Russell nodded, leaving it at that.

"Your father's business is . . . ?"

"He's a physician also. Or rather was. He's dead these three years. Albert Russell. He was called to be chief resident of surgery at the College of Physicians and Surgeons in New York City. I followed in his footsteps, did my first two years there. Not to change the subject, but I had asked if that guard was your prime suspect?"

"He's one among a dozen or so," John replied.

"Why not the prime suspect?" Thomas Russell persisted.

"Because he was seen by Mr. Kennedy ridin' south along the shore at a little before eight and then north again at eight-thirty. The path on which Springer was killed lies due east of there, and between the two places there's swampland. It would have taken Turner fifteen minutes' hard ridin' to circle up to the path and another fifteen minutes to circle back. He'd have to have timed the shootin' perfectly, including uncoverin' the rifle and hidin' it again. Another of the guards might have done it, but then he would have known that Turner might have chanced upon him."

"Perhaps there was collusion between Turner and one other guard," the young doctor suggested.

"And the person who hired them," John added. "But conspiracy is a risky business. To be sure to get away with it, you have to kill your partners." He had raised his voice to be heard over the clatter of dishes and a loud exchange in the butler's pantry. Le Brun turned in that direction.

"Isn't it subtle how they let us know our place?" Russell asked, gesturing at the many unoccupied tables in better locations. "I suppose I should be thankful I'm not assigned to the servants' dining room. Unless a member happens to have brought along his personal physician, I usually dine alone. The price for being neither fish nor fowl. I'm practically invisible."

"That's more or less what Dr. Hosmer told me," John volunteered. " 'Neither member nor family, guest nor servant.' The man you replaced was particularly upset about it."

"Yes. Dr. Merrill."

"Do you eat with Dr. Hosmer often?"

"No. He usually dines with his employer, unless Pulitzer accepts an invitation to dine at one of the other cottages. Pulitzer never comes in here."

"So I understand." John glanced again around the room. Every few seconds, another pair of eyes stole a sidelong peek at them.

"We may be in the corner, but we're the center of attention," Russell commented.

"It can't be our clothes," John replied. "I'm as well dressed as any of them . . . and you're dressed a sight better."

After sipping from his water glass, Russell said, "There's a strict rule against formal attire. No dinner jackets allowed."

"I read as much in the hallway."

Russell adjusted his napkin. "Everywhere else they're the paragons of high society. Always on display, expected to take the lead in setting fashion. Here, away from all prying eyes and only among their peers, they can relax and pretend that they're just plain folk. The irony is that many of them *were* plain folk, until they invented something or the land their grandfathers squatted on was suddenly found rich with minerals or oil. Jekyl Island is their once-a-year opportunity to stop pretending they're royalty."

"There's more than a hint of disapproval in your words and tone," John said. "Sounds like you wouldn't mind if more than one of them died."

Russell laughed. "Is that your roundabout way of accusing me of Mr. Springer's death?"

The waiter arrived with a basket of rolls, putting a hiatus in the conversation. He had approached with the stealth of a cat burglar and had lingered longer than needed, straightening the bud vase. Neither Le Brun nor Russell said a word all the while.

"He could get five dollars for just one interesting fact . . . the bastard," Russell announced, as soon as the waiter was out of earshot. "Now he'll be forced to make it up."

A major reason for dining with Russell had opened in the conversation, and John was not about to let it escape. "How well *can* you account for yourself during the time in question?"

The doctor picked up his salad fork, dug it into the tablecloth, and started twisting it left and right. "Not very well, I'm afraid. As I say, everyone more or less leaves me alone unless they're not feeling well. I was reading. I saw no one follow Mr. Springer onto Shell Road, but they might have approached it from behind the house. I did see Dr. Hosmer once at his laboratory window. And then one of Mr. Pulitzer's lackeys dashing to the clubhouse for something. It was very quiet." He waved the salad fork in the sheriff's direction. "Of course, if it *were* me and someone had come seeking my professional services, I would have been caught out instantly, right? Do I look so foolish to take that big a risk to kill one of the most toothless of this den of lions?"

"You don't look foolish at all," Le Brun answered.

"Not to mention the problem of getting a rifle."

"You might have brought one with you."

"But why? For target practice from the infirmary porch? I'm practically chained to that house. My leash is only long enough to get me here for meals. I have to post a sign on the infirmary window if I go out of sight of the place. I hope the members don't suspect me. I receive so few visits already; imagine how lonely I'll be if that's the case. And the final irony is that my only faithful patient's dead." His laughter brought more than one table's conversation to a halt.

"Johns Hopkins," Le Brun said, ignoring the lull.

"Yes. A teacher of surgery."

"Fine school."

"The best. We're at the forefront of medical research. The best endowed."

"I would guess you have some of this club's members as patients?"

"Others on the faculty do. Not I."

The waiter returned with the soup.

"And precisely when do you propose to arrest him, Sheriff?" Dr. Russell asked for the waiter's benefit, as the man was almost to the table.

John looked at the waiter, then cocked an eyebrow at the doctor. He smiled grimly in Russell's direction. The waiter set down the bowls, fussed a moment longer, and disappeared once more.

"I take it you have no intention of servin' here again," John said, taking up his soup spoon.

"No, indeed. The dean owes me a considerable favor for this."

"Speakin' of medicine, will it bother you to review Mr. Springer's autopsy while eatin'?"

"Not at all." Russell reached into his inside jacket pocket and produced a printed form that he had completed in neat, backhand print. "I've given a copy to Mr. Grob as well." He opened and consulted it. "Examination revealed a healthy, well-nourished male, with organs in expected condition for a man of his age. Death came as a result of the severing of the superior vena cava by a projectile of considerable size. The bullet was slightly deflected by the sternum upon entry but seems to have exited cleanly between the spinal column and right scapula. Death was almost instantaneous. Most bleeding was internal." Russell handed the report to the sheriff.

"You assume I know what a vena cava and a scapula are," John said, taking the paper.

"You've been a sheriff for some time," Russell answered. "And you're obviously a smart man."

"We'll let the solution of this murder prove just *how* smart," John replied, tipping his chair back so that it rested against the wall. A woman seated in the middle of the room gasped. John fixed her stare with his own. She looked quickly away. "Would you say that the autopsy was an unnecessary exercise?" he asked, refocusing.

"Only in retrospect," Dr. Russell replied. He dug into his other inside jacket pocket and produced a second paper. This was a piece of cream stationery with two circles drawn on it. "Duplications of the entry and exit wounds."

John squinted at the drawings. "Either a thirty- or thirty-two-caliber bullet."

"I'll take your word for it. I have no experience with gunshot wounds. Actually, I've been precious little help to you."

John waved away the apology with one hand as he pocketed the papers. He shifted into recollections of other murders he had investigated, what weapons had been used, and how he had slowly learned to recognize the wounds they made. During the length of the meal, John sampled more than his share of the wines, as well as two glasses of cordial. The more he drank, the more expansive he became about his experiences as an officer of the law. He invited Russell to match him in his experiences as a healer and was rewarded with detailed information on the life of a teaching surgeon. The courses arrived and were lightly sampled by both men. The minutes piled up into nearly two hours by the time the dessert was cleared.

"I believe, between yourself and myself, we have assayed 'life and death' pretty well tonight," John ventured.

Russell drained his cordial glass. "Pretty well."

The sheriff suppressed a belch. "Best meal I've had in years, but not somethin' I'd care to indulge in often. Not only would I become huge, but I couldn't abide the tremendous wastes of time."

The doctor leaned into the table conspiratorially. "It's like this every evening, unless there's an important entertainment. A foolish practice indeed. I'm frequently summoned around midnight to treat stomach discomforts. At least the women don't wear their tightest corsets down here."

While the two were chuckling, Jupiter Morgan entered the dining room and approached the table, as jovial as his nickname.

"Dr. Russell, Sheriff Le Brun. I trust you've dined well."

Both men concurred.

"What say we play that game of chess at eleven?"

"I thought there was a club curfew rule," John said.

"That's for the clubhouse," Morgan assured. "We'll be playing in my apartment. Over in Sans Souci." He waved his unlit cigar behind him. "That way. The attendant will let you in and show you up." He pivoted around without allowing response and strode out of the dining room. Those few diners remaining had lapsed once more into silence.

"I didn't see him in here tonight," Le Brun remarked to his companion.

"Really? I understand he always eats a prodigious breakfast and a light snack such as fruit for lunch. He often dines with the Bakers right over there. Something's thrown him off his routine."

"The murder, me, or both," John replied.

"You may find out later."

"Does he ever play cards or chess in the game room?"

"No. He couldn't exercise enough control in there," Russell judged. "What if someone saw the great John Pierpont Morgan lose?"

"I take it he's high on your dislike list."

The physician dropped his napkin on his dessert plate. "I wouldn't be alone in that. The farther out you stand from the crowd, the easier a target you make. He also invites judgment because he's such a character. Of those members on the island right now, the two most colorful are Morgan and Pulitzer. Both geniuses. Both perpetually driven. Both high on each other's hate list. Both insomniacs. Every time I'm called for a late-night emergency their bedroom lights are blazing. Speaking of emergencies, I've been here too long. Someone will soon throw a fit because my note on the infirmary door said I'd be back no later than ten. Thank you for your enlightening company, Sheriff!"

John dipped his head and allowed Russell to exit the room first. The waiter approached to clear.

"How do I pay for this?" John asked.

"It's been taken care of by the club, sir," he answered without looking up.

"In that case, transmit my thanks to the club," John said, rising. The waiter made no reply. Leaving the dining room, John was fairly fallen upon by Ernest Grob, who had stationed himself in the foyer.

"I read Dr. Russell's report," he said, beaming. "There is nothing in it that says it was murder."

"Nothin' that says it was an accident, either," John pointed out.

"Likewise, Mr. Tidewell learned nothing suspicious from the members and guests," said Grob, undeterred.

"My investigation is not concluded, sir," John declared. "I'll let you know when it is."

"This is terrible!" Grob lamented.

"Yes, death is a terrible thing," John said, knowing full that the man was speaking about the upset that nonresolution was creating within the club. "By the way—I read that all guests must be sponsored."

"That's correct."

"That their stay must be applied for at least two weeks in advance and that your board must approve them."

"Yes."

"How is it I'm approved so quickly, and by whom?"

Grob glared darkly. "This is a special circumstance. You are being accommodated for the good of the club by the board members in residence and by myself. On occasion, rules must be bent."

"On occasion. Yes. May I see my room?"

Grob led the way up to the third floor and to the farthest door from the main staircase. The room was small but well decorated, with the cabbage-rose wallpaper, the oversized Victorian furniture, the doilies, pillows, and flounce, the water bowl and chamber pot, coat tree, and beveled mirror common to the decade.

"I trust this meets with your approval," Grob said.

"It does."

"Then I wish you a good night," he said, handing Le Brun the door key. When he departed, he left the door open. John closed it, then collapsed on the bed. He pulled out his watch and consulted it. Then he exchanged the watch for his deputy's notebook and the papers Dr. Russell had given him, alternating their review with periods of closed eyes.

At three minutes before eleven, John took himself out the clubhouse's front doors and across the dark lawns to the looming structure everyone called Sans Souci. He knocked and was admitted by the promised servant, a white man of advanced years but elegant bearing, who glided up two sets of stairs to Morgan's door. John noted the utilitarian aspect of the central hallways and the quiet of the building.

J. P. Morgan was not in his suite's parlor when John entered, although a chessboard with carved ebony and ivory pieces had been set up. A bottle of wine stood uncorked and chilling in an ice bucket beside it. The room's appointments were hardly less Spartan than the halls, although several well executed oil paintings with hunt subjects decorated the walls. An arrangement of miniature oil portraits was hung above the fireplace mantel, none of which John recognized.

"Please be seated," the servant said. "I'm sure Mr. Morgan will be with you presently." He pulled the outer door closed behind him.

John ignored the suggestion and remained on his feet, strolling slowly and examining his surroundings. He inhaled the pungent and stale atmosphere of long-gone cigars. Several books and magazines lay strewn about, including a journal called *Rudder,* which John picked up. It declared itself to be the premier periodical on yachting and seemed to fulfill its promise. No evidence of business whatsoever occupied the room, not a single clue to its owner's Wall Street might and international banking stature. On a low table in front of the couch were two packs of playing cards, laid out in a half-finished game of solitaire. John studied the configuration of the cards.

Pierpont Morgan entered from a side door, lit cigar in mouth. He still wore his jacket, tie, and vest.

"I appreciate a man of punctuality," he greeted.

"Is this 'Miss Milliken'?" John asked, gesturing to the cards.

Morgan smiled. "Yes. Are you an aficionado of solitaire?"

"It's not a passion," John answered, "but when you're a bachelor, you find yourself with little to do on those nights when sleep comes hard."

"Exactly!"

While he spoke, John marveled that a man who had used his prodigious intellect to best even the treacherous Jay Gould and who compelled the strong-willed captains of commerce, transportation, and industry to yield to his grand concepts would play a game with so little challenge. "Miss Milliken" was played with two packs, so that many key cards were likely to become buried in the course of play. Consequently, when the player had no more chance of winning, he was allowed to "waive" a card by removing it from the foot of the column to get at the next card. The waived card was set aside until it could be "built in," and then another card might be waived. If this tactic alone failed to guarantee success, the game could be made more liberal by waiving an entire sequence until later in the game. The result guaranteed more wins than losses. He tucked the revelation away for future thought.

"Those little portraits are interestin'," John noted, nodding at the wall.

"I'm fascinated by good paintings," Morgan said. "I'm particularly fond of paintings that immortalize great personages. I brought these down with me to be able to enjoy them while I'm here. From left to right, top to bottom, they're Charles the Second, Charles the First, Madame de Pompadour, Marie Antoinette, the Princess de Lamball, the Duchess of Devonshire, and Mary, Queen of Scots. People who achieved greatness or had greatness thrust upon them, welcomed the challenge, and prevailed." He crossed to the chess table, and John noted for the first time that the man had a slight limp. "It has been a difficult day for all of us, Mr. Le Brun, wouldn't you say?" the plutocrat asked, showing both upper and lower yellowed teeth.

"It has indeed."

"Perhaps a spirited game will allow us to relax and find elusive Morpheus, eh?" He sat, groaning softly as he did.

John placed himself opposite. He saw that his host had given him white and the first move. Morgan had either decided to win John over by offering him the advantage, had sized the sheriff up and considered that the only chance for a decent game was to give him the advantage, or both.

John pushed his king's pawn forward to the fourth square, as standard a move as could be made.

Morgan immediately pushed his king's pawn up to the fourth square, so that the pieces were nose to nose. While he did, John stole a quick glance at the titan's nose. It was almost twice the size it should have been, even given that its owner was a large and overweight man. Its overall shape was like that of cauliflower, but its texture and color more like an almost-ripe strawberry.

Not five seconds had lapsed after Morgan finished his move when he snapped his fingers. "What about a glass of wine?"

"Not just yet, thanks," John said, wanting to get his development going.

"It's truly excellent. From the private vineyard of a French comte in the Côtes du Rhône. Only one thousand bottles a year are produced, and I get one hundred of them."

"Why don't you begin without me?" Le Brun suggested.

"I opened it just for you. I don't drink at night."

John looked up from the board. "In that case, please pour me a glass."

Morgan smiled, set down his cigar in a cut-glass ashtray, stretched to the bottle, drew it out of the ice packed around it in the silver serving bucket, and poured some wine into an ornate crystal glass. He handed the drink across the board to his guest and recaptured his cigar.

"I've moved," John announced.

Jupiter stared at the knight now sitting on the king's bishop three square. Again, with only a second's consideration, he moved the queen's pawn to its third square, to defend his first pawn from John's knight. John responded a few seconds later with queen's pawn to queen four, and Morgan soon after thumped down his bishop on knight five, making a threat against John's queen intended to pin his opponent's advanced knight.

"Are you a religious man, Mr. Le Brun?" Morgan inquired, soon after making his move.

"Not particularly. I was raised Roman Catholic, but I've more or less lapsed in practice."

"A shame. A man needs to acknowledge his God on a regular basis. It's a great source of strength."

John nodded, his eyes riveted to the board.

"I'm Episcopalian myself," said Morgan. "A deacon. Delegate to the triennial conventions. Give as much free time as I can."

John nodded again.

"Do much of my charity work through the church," Morgan went on. "Widow's fund. Several orphanages. Missionary fund."

John took Morgan's king's pawn with his queen's pawn, sure that this attack would silence the millionaire for a time. Morgan removed the attacking pawn's protection by having his bishop kill the advanced knight. John knocked off the bishop by moving his queen into its space. About a minute passed before Morgan took John's most advanced pawn with his queen's pawn. Once again, the center of the board had two pawns nose to nose on the kings' row. But John had his queen out, and every one of Morgan's remaining major pieces was still on its home row.

Now the magnate's blazing, beacon eyes shifted back and forth between the board and the sheriff's face.

"Cigar?" Morgan offered.

"Not with the wine, thanks."

"How's that doctor you dined with?"

"A good conversationalist," John said, hoping to return to silence.

"Seem competent?"

"Yes."

"That's good. I like physicians. They tend to be interesting, Christian men."

Le Brun glanced up for a moment. Morgan was leaning back in his chair, sucking with great satisfaction on his cigar.

"You and Mr. Pulitzer share that opinion," John declared, archly determined to throw Morgan off his monologue and his game.

Morgan's black eyebrows knit and his eyes narrowed. "That's about all he and I share. I'm sure he had nothing good to say about me."

John kept his eyes fixed on the board and his lips fixed together.

"Blasted Hungarian waving the American flag! Do you know what a Hungarian is, Mr. Le Brun? He's a man who enters a revolving door behind you and exits ahead of you." He laughed at his own joke. John said nothing. Morgan's lips became tight around his cigar. He puffed forcefully several times. Between the billowing smoke and the brilliant red glow of the cigar tip, he looked like a volcano about to erupt. "It isn't enough that he has grotesque caricatures drawn of me in the rag he publishes, but now he assails me in private. It was unbearable during the gold crisis. Did you see how he depicted me as a dragon and the *World* as Saint George slaying me?"

John moved his king's bishop to queen's bishop four, backing up his queen's threat to the bishop's pawn two space directly diagonal to Morgan's king.

"I don't read the *World*," John said.

"Right. That's one recommendation for living down here all the time," Morgan came back. He slumped in his chair and studied the threat on the table. Unlike the verbal barrage John endured, John's silence allowed the man to think undistracted for several minutes. Finally, with a decisive gesture, Morgan planted his king's knight on king's bishop three, blocking the line of attack of the enemy queen.

"That bastard Pulitzer pretends everything he does is for the public welfare. He's a yellow journalist, pure and simple. Stirs up the people just to sell newspapers. Him and Hearst. And he gets rich on it, feeding them the nonsense and half-truths they want to hear."

"You mean nonsense like you and the others in this club making too much profit off their backs?"

"Precisely."

"But don't you make millions every year, and doesn't the average man make less than five hundred dollars in the North and four hundred here?"

The millionaire looked as if he had just bitten into a fresh lemon. "This is a free country. If they accept low wages, that's their fault. Several of this club's members started as mailroom boys or bobbin runners. Pulitzer paints me as an archconservative, interested only in the status quo. The truth is that I am a *visionary*. Without visionaries, his status quo would be a dreary reality. The average man would be toiling for subsistence on a small farm, wearing homespun clothes, sleeping with the set of the sun, dying for lack of the simplest drug. My efforts create huge enterprises that hire the common man. The railroads I unite can get him from coast to coast fifty times faster than his fathers—not to mention what he produces! I've funded pharmaceutical companies that have created lifesaving remedies and vaccines. Without the bankers' skill at amassing huge pools of cash, we couldn't get any great enterprises off the ground. Just because I control and direct millions doesn't mean that I keep them. And my efforts don't remain solely on Wall Street, I'll tell you. They're personal. I have been supporting Mr. Edison's efforts to harness electricity for years, both publicly and privately. Mine was the first house to be electrified in this country. My house nearly burned to the ground because it had not been perfected. But someday soon every person in this country will benefit from electric power. Think how much better breathing alone will be without fireplaces and gaslights going inside houses day and night!"

Morgan suddenly realized how the pitch and intensity of his voice had steadily risen. He also realized that his opponent had quietly moved his queen to queen's knight three. He made a bearlike grumbling in his throat and settled back to study the game.

Silence ensued. Whatever desire the king of Wall Street had had at the onset of the game to win was now redoubled. He stabbed out his cigar, thought without it for all of a minute, then poked into his jacket for one of its brothers. He lit it and drew in deeply. Finally, after scratching his white hair for a minute, he moved his queen to king two.

" 'Remember the *Maine*' indeed!" Morgan fumed, speaking of Pulitzer without deigning to use his name. "Pretending to have such passion for the poor, exploited Cubans. But he knew the war had to be fought and won, as a key battle in the bigger war."

"What bigger war?" John asked.

"Imperialism, sir. The Germans and English are eating us alive with their colonies. The French as well, and even the Dutch! We must end our isolationism and fully commit ourselves to this war. Have you made your move?"

"No. I'm still thinkin'," John said softly.

"Sheriff, have you ever seen one of those great cyclorama paintings that travel across the country? The one depicting the Battle of Gettysburg, perhaps?"

"I haven't, but I know what you're talkin' about."

"If you stand up close to them, you may see some wonderful detail. You might truly come to know the intent of the artist in that little corner. But unless you can step back a distance, you'll never comprehend the big picture. Let me tell you what that big picture is: Our industries are huge and hungry engines. Products must be sold constantly if our citizens are to remain employed. We're very good at producing, sir; we produce more than Americans alone can consume. If those industries—as well as our agriculture—can't find buyers beyond our borders, we're in trouble. Then the common man will truly find out what poverty is about. It's either expand or explode, and Joseph Pulitzer knows it. He knew before he provoked his little war that Spain is the weakest colonial power, that the most logical place for us to expand is in the New World. That war gave teeth to the Monroe Doctrine. Mark my words: Within a decade, the great powers of Europe—including that sleeping bear, Russia—will be at each other's throats over world domination. We may be able to stay out of it if we concentrate on the New World. Gain domination over our backyard—the Caribbean, Central and South America."

"This big picture is part of that vision of yours, then?" John asked.

Morgan shook his large head solemnly. "This isn't something of my making; it's a reality I must accept and deal with." He looked at the miniature paintings. "I have had greatness thrust upon me, and I have accepted it. I am not only a trustee on corporate boards and for my church; I'm a trustee for this great nation. I hold that trust most sacred of all."

John looked at Morgan's intense face. "I'm sure you do."

His reply seemed to mollify the man long enough for John to finish his turn, moving his remaining knight to bishop three. Counting the long open diagonal from his bishop's home row to his king's rook six, he now had four powerful pieces in play, as opposed to Morgan's two. While his opponent had ranted, he had gained control of the game.

Humphing and grunting, Pierpont Morgan studied his predicament. In an effort to control the central four squares and to prevent Le Brun's knight from advancing, he moved his queen's bishop pawn up to its third square. He did not look satisfied by his move. He folded his arms and puffed furiously.

"Did you know he wanted this island all to himself?" the banker exclaimed suddenly. "He failed. He also wants to be the man behind the making of a president, since he's foreign born and can never hold that office himself. He'll fail at that, too. At least as long as I'm alive."

"Do other members dislike him so intensely?" John asked.

"Not many," Morgan answered candidly. "Then again, he hasn't attacked them as viciously as he has me. But plenty of them know him for what he truly is and don't approve of his style."

"Then why was he allowed to become a member of the club?"

Morgan's grin was like that of Lewis Carroll's Cheshire cat. " 'Keep your friends close, and your enemies closer,' " he quoted.

John declined to comment. He moved his undeployed bishop up to knight five, pinning the knight who protected Morgan's queen.

Instead of answering the threat on that side of the board, Morgan advanced his king's knight pawn to square four, threatening the other bishop and seeking to control the oblique line on his king's bishop two square. This move seemed to satisfy him, but John was not cowed. Morgan had gotten himself hopelessly behind in his development. At least, thought John, behind in his game development. He had certainly presented plenty of information about his personal life, his moral attitudes, and his objectives, and the sheriff was convinced that this had been the main motive for the invitation to play.

"You disapprove of the money I make," Morgan said, "but you can see that I live simply." He spread his arms wide. "Is there anything here that's really ostentatious?"

"Aside from your miniatures of famous people, your rare wine, and the cigars made on your own plantation?"

Morgan bristled. "These are small extravagances compared to the way others throw money around. 'Bet-a-Million' Gates wagers a thousand dollars on which way a drop of water will roll off someone's hand. There are members of the Four Hundred who routinely throw fancy dress balls that cost forty thousand dollars. I never wager. I don't throw balls. I live in an old brownstone house I didn't even build. I spend my Sundays in church. I entertain inside my house. I play chess with people I like. Or respect." He sighed. "I'm trying to show you, Sheriff Le Brun, that I'm not a selfish man. What I do is fundamentally for the good of others. If I'm forceful about dealing with this Erastus Springer business and want it over with in a hurry, it's for a greater good than my own. I need you to understand that."

"I'll take that into account, sir," John answered.

"I hope so. I truly hope so. Did you make your move?"

"I will now." John took Morgan's threatening pawn with his knight.

Morgan hesitated for only a moment, then killed the knight with his king's bishop pawn.

The slaughter was on. John did not hesitate at all in taking that pawn with his bishop and simultaneously putting the banker's king in check.

The second cigar was extinguished in the ashtray. By grunt and facial expression, Jupiter Morgan indicated that he knew how precarious his position had become. For the first time, he spoke while it was his turn.

"I heard that Springer's wallet was still in his coat pocket."

"That's right," John said. He picked up the wineglass and nearly drained it.

"So it wasn't a robber. I'll grant that this seems unlikely on the surface, but the poor fellow must have gotten himself squarely in the path of a poacher's bullet. You said the murderer had to be on the path to have hit him in the heart. Not so. Perhaps Springer had heard the poacher's advance through the brush and turned in that direction. The poacher was still in a thicket and saw only the bulk of Springer's form. He fired, believing it was game. Coming forward a few more feet, he discovered the path and then Springer. A second later, he was hightailing it off the island. This is not my confection. It's the most popular theory among the members by far."

"Murders are not solved by majority vote," the sheriff stated calmly.

"What other theory holds water?" Jupiter demanded.

"Premeditated murder . . . by someone in this village."

"Oh, bullshit! And who thinks that?"

"Mr. Pulitzer."

Morgan thumped on the table, making the pieces jump. "Naturally! Perverse bastard. He takes the negative side from force of habit. He says he loves doctors. But has he supported any medical school with his own money? No! I, on the other hand, took one minute—*one minute*—to decide to spend a million dollars on buildings for Harvard's new medical school! Remember *that* when you decide which one of us to trust." He snorted with the sound of a whale blowing. His glare shifted to the configuration on the board. He moved his undeployed knight onto queen two.

"Aside from the Jekyl Island Club, what do you think of this island?" Morgan asked, his voice uncharacteristically soft and uninflected.

"I think about it as little as possible." John long-castled, bringing his rooks into play.

"Is that true? Will you excuse me for a minute?" the host asked. "I'm prone to headaches, and a fierce one is coming upon me." He rose without the sheriff's by-your-leave and disappeared into the room from which he had first emerged, closing the door hard behind him.

Le Brun studied the board intently. When Morgan had thumped on the table, he had jostled not only the pieces but the board as well. A tiny corner of yellow paper had appeared; protruding from under Morgan's side. It was the sort of distraction that would gnaw at John until it was removed, and he leapt at Morgan's departure to dispense with it. He reached around and eased it out.

It was a telegram. Instantly, the memory of Captain Clark entering the Oglethorpe Hotel came to him. He could not resist looking at its contents. It had been sent from Thomasville, Georgia, to J. P. Morgan on Friday afternoon at 1:56 P.M., which meant that it had been carried to the island on the previous day's late-afternoon steamer run. Any quick response would have to have been carried back specially to the Western Union office in the Oglethorpe Hotel and could have arrived no earlier than six in the evening. Captain Clark had rushed past John at about quarter past seven. The telegram read:

WM AGREES VISIT JIC MONDAY 20TH
HANNA

The sheriff swiftly replaced the telegram, pushing it back to precisely where it had been. Now that he had read its contents, the little corner of yellow no longer bothered him.

"Sorry," Morgan apologized, coming through the door. "I'll be quick to move."

The promise was not kept. Long minutes crept by while the financier worked one possibility after the other, his intense eyes darting back and forth. He massaged his temples continuously. Finally, he moved his queen's rook to queen one, anticipating the attack along that file.

John's rook swept up the file and captured the knight on queen two. Morgan's rook removed and replaced the piece in a twinkling. Diagonally behind it, his king sat pinned in.

John made no hesitation. His remaining rook went to queen one, staring the length of the file at Morgan's last moved piece. There was no way the banker could trade pieces; moving his rook would have left a clear path between John's bishop and his king.

The black queen came forward one square to king three, so that Morgan's knight was free to defend king two without losing his queen to Le Brun's second bishop, so that the sheriff might be invited to trade queens, and so that Morgan's still-undeployed bishop might have a chance to wade into the war.

"Exactly how long do you suppose you must remain on the island before you declare this death resolved?" Morgan asked, still massaging his temples.

"A lot longer than it'll take me to finish this game," John replied. His bishop took the rook on black queen two. "Check," he said softly.

Morgan had no choice unless he wanted to lose his queen. He took the threatening bishop with his knight.

With a speed meant to offend, John clapped his queen down on knight eight, Morgan's back row. There was nothing between it and Morgan's king.

"Check."

"I was hoping to be able to play to conclusion," Morgan said, "but I can tell the medicine won't take effect soon enough. Shall we call it a draw?"

"No need," the sheriff said. "I'll finish it." He moved the black knight. "You have no choice but to remove my queen." He brought his rook across the board, right beside the king, where his bishop not only prevented the rook from being taken but also prevented the king from fleeing. "Checkmate."

"Neatly done," Jupiter praised.

John Le Brun rose. "Thank you, Mr. Morgan. Between the stimulatin' game and the wine, I hope to be asleep soon."

John Pierpont Morgan maintained his distance from the table, staring down at the board. When he glanced up, Le Brun expected him to be grim and red-faced. He was surprised to see the man quite calm. His countenance was, in fact, devoid of emotion, impossible to read.

"Wine and game weren't all that happened tonight," Morgan emphasized. "Think about the things I've said, Sheriff. I know *I* intend to sleep well. And thank you for the lesson in chess. Please show yourself out." He executed one of his abrupt about-faces and headed for the door whence he had made his entrance.

John exited the apartment and descended the wide stairs. He found the same servant on duty on the first floor, seated quite erect on a cane chair, staring vacantly at the bland wallpaper. The man unlocked the door and let Le Brun out into the dark, cool night. John walked quickly back to the clubhouse, which was a near-black hulk against the even darker woods beyond. He climbed the stairs to the veranda, entered the foyer, trudged up to the third floor and back to his room, seeing no one the entire time. He pulled off his outerwear and boots, tumbled into the bed, and pulled up the thick covers. Within two minutes he was asleep.

SUNDAY

JOHN LE BRUN AWOKE with first light, even though he was still tired. Once he saw where he was, he lowered his heavy lids again for several minutes, hoping to submerge again into sleep. But he had lived in his body too long not to know that once the cogs of his mind meshed, he would have to reach near-exhaustion before he could sleep again. His room, the cheapest in the resort, faced the less spectacular eastward view and took the morning sun. He looked out on a sky dotted with compact white clouds, like sheep grazing in a vast meadow. He washed, shaved, dressed, and descended to the dining room.

Few vacationers had arisen. Those who had and were already in the members' dining room made no effort to acknowledge the sheriff, much less invite him to their tables. He reflected that the word "strangers" which the club gave to guests was sadly apt.

While John breakfasted on an exquisitely prepared and presented meal, he watched the ebb and flow of members, families, and the invited. From where he sat, he could see them ascending and descending the bottom steps of the main staircase. It occurred to him that although the clubhouse had a rear staircase, no one used it. Aside from the fact that they might miss each other's comings and goings if they went that way, they might also have been subjected to viewing the maids at work.

John ate his meal with haste, signed for it, and left the dining room to investigate the rear of the clubhouse. The back staircase lay directly behind the laundry, cold closets, and servants' dining room. Yet another reason for the wealthy to avoid it, he mused. It was perfect, however, for anyone not wanting to be seen exiting on the previous morning. John climbed the stairs to the top and looked down on the back side of the clubhouse. Just to the left of the ground-floor exit lay a dense planting of shrubbery; to the right was situated one of the walled-in yards intended for hanging laundry. Despite the early hour, its lines were already half filled with white clothing. John also spied someone he had not seen from his room, the kitchen, or the laundry levels. She was a young Negro woman, and she worked within the maze of drying wash, pinning more of it onto the remaining lines. He hurried down the steps.

As soon as he entered the open gateway through the modesty wall, John heard the familiar melody of the spiritual "Believer I Know," beautifully sung. The woman did not see him for a moment, allowing him to take a good look at her. She was a homely young creature, wearing an ankle-length skirt just short enough to reveal the dime she had on a string around her ankle. Superstition among the Golden Isles Negroes held that it warded off bad luck.

The woman started when her eyes fell on the sheriff. Her hand flew to her mouth. The spiritual vanished in midword.

"Sorry if I frightened you," John said. "What's your name?"

"Binty, suh," she replied timidly.

John drew out his pocket watch and consulted it. The time was 7:47. "Do you hang laundry here every mornin'?"

"Ebbry mornin' what buckra dem be here," she answered. *Every morning that the white men are here.* Her pure Gullah dialect left no doubt that she was a coastal island native.

"This time every mornin'?" John asked. "From when the sun comes up?"

"Yassuh."

"Yesterday, did you see any of the members—not the white servants or workers but the people who sleep up there." He pointed toward the bedrooms. "Did you see any of them come down through this door?"

Binty shook her head. She and John stared at one another for a moment, she in bewilderment why a white man should need any information from her, he in his disappointment. John thanked her, turned, and put his hand on the top of the gate.

"One go *up,*" Binty offered in a tiny voice.

John spun around. "Up? When?"

"Now. He go up yestiddy now, Monday now, Dursday now. Mebbe mo'. I seed him only dose t'ree day."

John struggled to maintain an inner calm so as not to alarm the woman with his excitement. "A man from one of those rooms went *up* the stairs."

The laundress nodded.

"What does he look like?"

She shrugged. "Like una." *Like you all.*

John chuckled. The woman remained wide-eyed and apprehensive. "Is he young?"

The laundress nodded again. "T'in. An' got hair like a po'cat."

Hair like a polecat. Le Brun pictured in his mind's eye the white streak running back through Randolph Rasher's black hair. He needed no more questions. Nevertheless, he made absolutely sure. He touched a shirt that hung upside down from the line nearest him.

"What was he wearing?"

"Clothes like he da go bicycle."

"Did he see you?"

The laundress shook her head. "I be behin' de clothes. Anyway, none dem buckra ebba sees us."

John nodded his understanding. After so many years' practice at looking through servants and "lesser persons," rich white Northerners did in fact forget they were there. Even if Rasher had seen the laundress, he undoubtedly believed that no one would ever question an ignorant black island girl about him. And certainly, because of the club rules, she was not allowed to volunteer what she had seen. Even without the rule of not speaking until spoken to, she would not have come forward, John knew. Little had changed from before the war; the black man distrusted the white man for good reason and offered as little of his knowledge as possible.

John thought of another question. "You didn't see him come back down yesterday?"

Binty shook her head again. "I be gone soon." She nodded at the two baskets of wash. She would have them hung within minutes.

"Did you see him come back down on Monday or Thursday?"

She shook her head yet again.

John thanked her and exited the enclosure. He waited several seconds, until he was certain the laundress would be engaged in her work, and then he dropped a silver dollar over the gate onto the close-cropped grass where she was sure to find it. This way, he had avoided insulting her and violating the club rule against tipping servants. Moreover, should her testimony be required, she could not say that he had offered her money for her information.

John climbed the rear stairs slowly. He encountered no one. The stairs might as well have been a secret corridor—at least at this time of day. He went back into his room, sat at the little writing desk that stood near the window, and took out the notebook Warfield Tidewell had filled with testimony from the people he interviewed. John tore two empty pages from the back of the book and laid them side by side. He drew a map of Jekyl Island, more accurately than most employees of the club could have. In the central section he sketched in the dock and the Village, structure for structure, and all the roads leading out of it. When he was nearly done, he stood and looked out the window to confirm two landmarks. The Negro laundress was gone. He looked at his watch. It was 7:58. Given that the number of members, family, and guests had decreased somewhat over the past week, John estimated that the Monday morning wash might have taken as much as ten minutes more to hang. That would mean that Randolph had probably not come down before 8:10. Mrs. Springer had told John that she entered the dining room for breakfast at 8:20.

John assigned a number to each person his deputy had interviewed. He placed the number on the map for the eight o'clock position and trailed arrows around if the person had moved in the following sixty minutes. After the first dozen testimonies, he wished he had begun with a very large sheet of paper. Yet, no matter how overlapped the numbers became, none of them save Mrs. Springer (who had had no one corroborate her location until 8:20), Randy Rasher, Dr. Thomas Russell, and Dr. G. W. Hosmer and the Pulitzer secretaries seemed to have the slightest opportunity to have shot Erastus Springer on the path far to the south of the Village. Even with the guards added to their numbers as the only employees free enough to roam to that area, the list of suspects was approaching manageability. But then there was the clear fact that no matter how the Jerkyl Island Club bragged that "no unwanted foot sets upon this island," a determined and skilled person could have gotten to the island, to the path, and away with little chance of being caught. If the rich could hire scores of Pinkerton men to shoot strikers, certainly one man could be hired to come South and kill a millionaire who took a solitary walk at the same time and in the same general area every day.

After fifty minutes of meticulous work, the sheriff sighed, folded up his map, and shoved it into the notebook. He looked again out the window, down at the Village's storage and equipment supply building, confusingly called the Club House. He locked the room and took the rear stairs all the way down.

The back lawns still glistened with dew as John crossed them and entered the Club House. A skinny, rheumy-eyed man who wore his uniform as if it were a straitjacket tended the place.

"You're from Brunswick, if I'm not mistaken," John greeted him upon entering.

The man looked him up and down. "That's right. An' I reckonize you, too."

"I'm Sheriff Le Brun."

The tired old face took on an aspect of fear. John was sure he had arrested the man some years before, for drunken and disorderly conduct. He wondered if the fear were for his office or because Ernest Grob had instructed him, on pain of never working for the club again, to tell the sheriff nothing.

"Joe Fisher."

"Mr. Fisher, I'm told you rent bicycles," John said, giving the place a thorough study.

Such public information Fisher was happy to supply. "We have two kinds: the White Star and the Hawthorne. Hawthorne costs twenty-five cents a day more, but in my opinion it's worth it. Better seat. Better gears. Easier to pedal."

"That's what Mr. Rasher said also," John stated. "He suggested I try one out."

"Can't rent it now, Sheriff," Fisher said, solemnly shaking his head. "Sunday, y'know. Can't let any equipment out until after noon. It's a rule."

"No doubt. Rule number seventy-seven. That's fine. This Hawthorne . . . Mr. Rasher took one out yesterday."

"He took one out every morning this past week." Fisher's tone was suddenly not so ebullient.

"Do tell? Startin' which day?"

Fisher's throat worked up and down as he struggled to think how he could not answer such a straightforward question. John determined to help him make up his mind. He tapped his forefinger on the rental book that lay open under Fisher's nose.

"It must be right in there. This club keeps meticulous records about everthin.' Look there and give me an answer, Mr. Fisher!"

"Let's see." The man flipped pages backward. "It was startin' Monday."

"He took the bicycle out at seven yesterday?"

"No, sir. Six-fifty," Fisher supplied. "Do you want me to set a Hawthorne aside for you for this afternoon?"

"That won't be necessary. Thank you," Le Brun said, already halfway out the door and heading back toward the clubhouse. Before he had taken a dozen steps, he was hailed by J. P. Morgan. The titan was leading a contingent at a brisk pace, his limp all but unnoticeable. In his wake trailed Randolph Rasher, Francis Stetson, and Mr. and Mrs. Cornelius Bliss. His pace slowed as he neared the sheriff.

"Glorious morning, isn't it, Sheriff!"

"Yes, sir, it is."

"I assume you're on your way to chapel."

"I had no idea when it was," John evaded.

At that exact moment, the chapel bell began to toll.

"Right now, right now," Morgan said. "Come along!" Characteristically, he started off again at high speed, not waiting for agreement or demurral.

John fell in alongside Randolph Rasher. They exchanged greetings.

"How long have you been on the island?" the sheriff asked his companion.

"I came down with Mr. Morgan and Mr. Stetson on the eleventh. Two Saturdays ago. Why?"

"And when will you depart?" John asked.

"We plan to leave this Friday. Mr. Morgan will then depart for Europe. London and Paris, actually . . . for a month. I return to New York. Why?"

"Just gatherin' facts," the sheriff said.

"Am I suspected of something?" Rasher persisted.

John had slowed his pace, so that the couple coming up behind them were almost on their heels. "Did those sound like suspicious questions?" Before Rasher could answer, he turned and smiled. "Mr. Bliss, Mrs. Bliss. Good mornin'! I am John Le Brun, sheriff of Brunswick and this part of the Golden Isles."

The walk to Union Chapel took less than two minutes. The chapel was a simple wooden structure, much like Georgia up-country churches. Inside, the small space fairly shook with the singing of the waiters, who stopped serving between eight-thirty and ten-thirty so they could provide the music they had learned each week during the periods between meals. Their harmonies were accompanied by J. P. Morgan's bellowing monotone. John tried to imagine the shock to the ears of those directly in front of him as he rendered "The Church's One Foundation." Even from behind Morgan's left shoulder where he stood, the noise was jarring.

L ET'S GO FORWARD," Warfield Tidewell yelled to Judge Iley Tidewell.

They had been sitting right beside the *Howland*'s engine. Not only did protracted conversation strain the throat, but one had to speak so loudly to be understood that anyone within twenty feet might catch snatches of it. Warfield led the way to the Jekyl Island steamer's bow, which had just been vacated by a quadriga of important-looking men who had not seen fit to introduce themselves at the dock.

"I hope your whore is worth it," Warfield said to his father. "Despite what you always say, Mother isn't completely stupid, you know. How often do you fail to return on Saturday nights?"

"She isn't a whore," the judge replied evenly, "as though that's any of your business. Circuit cases sometimes take well into the afternoon to try, and no one expects me to drive back to Brunswick in the dark. Your mother never complains."

"She's trusting as well as stupid," Warfield replied. "But if the word's gotten to me, it may get to her. Wives aren't always the last to know."

"I am a judge," the elder Tidewell said. "I know how to be judicious." The elegantly thin and elegantly dressed fifty-year-old looked with picaresque expectation for a reaction from his son. He got none. "I liked you much better, boy, when you were away," he declared.

"If you had arrived home last night, I'd have been able to finish our conversation in complete privacy," Warfield complained, "instead of out here in the open"—he glanced over his shoulder at Bobby Lee Randolph, who impatiently paced the length of the steamer as it chugged toward Jekyl Island—"with John Le Brun's favorite deputy breathing down our necks."

Judge Tidewell had returned to his home only an hour earlier, and by

that time Bobby Lee had attached himself to the deputy chief, in anticipation of the two returning to Jekyl Island to continue the investigation.
Warfield was able to take his father aside only long enough to fill him in
on the suspicious death of Erastus Springer and on the investigation to
date, and to tell him about the telephone call Warfield had taken in the
Tidewell home from Superintendent Ernest Grob at nine o'clock the previous evening. The guard who had found the body had amazingly discovered abundant evidence just before dusk to prove a poacher had shot
Springer. The moment the judge returned home, Grob instructed, he was
to take whatever transportation he could commandeer over to the island.
He was expected to review the evidence and summarily pronounce the
case closed, compelling the gadfly Sheriff Le Brun to return to Brunswick.

Iley Tidewell had been an influential and affluent lawyer in Brunswick
when he won his first judgeship race in November of 1885. One of the
first acts of his office was accepting a bribe himself and offering bribes to
the other critical officials of Brunswick on behalf of a pack of Yankee
millionaires, to insure that the purchase of Jekyl Island went smoothly.
Ever since, Judge Tidewell had been on the Jekyl Island Club's pay-
roll and in their back pocket. Not that there had been any truly illegal
deeds to do in the past thirteen years. Just the granting of variances and
tax reliefs, the overlooking of certain health inspections, and the like.
Until now.

"This smells like murder, War," Judge Tidewell said, reaching into his
coat pocket and fetching out an alligator-leather, nickel-framed cigarette
case. He offered the contents to his son. "What do you think?"

"If it is, it was a clever murder," Warfield answered, plucking out a
cigarette. "As I said, I didn't hear one suspicious thing in five hours of
interviews with the members and guests. Even the great John Le Brun
couldn't find anything tangible."

The judge snorted. "John Le Brun can't find 'abundant evidence' all
day, but a guard does just before dark. If it don't smell like murder, it
sure stinks like cover-up."

Warfield located the match safe in his coat pocket, opened it, extracted
a match, and struck it on the wooden rail. He held it up near his father's
mouth, where his cigarette dangled. The match blew out. Warfield swore
softly.

Iley laughed. "You ever hear of turnin' downwind?" While his son got
out another safety match, he said, "Did Grob tell you what they intend to
pay me for this service?"

"No."

"Then that's the first order of business, because I won't come cheap. Not when I have no idea how serious this is. And not with John Le Brun involved in it. He has a very special interest in that island and particularly in the men of that club. He might just be willing to drag me down with them if he gets the chance. You don't know about his history with Jekyl Island, do you?"

"No. Tell me," Warfield said, holding up the second struck match and this time getting both his father's and his cigarettes lit.

Iley Tidewell told all he knew.

The story of the Jekyl Island Club began in the year 1860. An adventurous young Yankee had come to Georgia as an engineer for the U.S. Coastal Survey. He had attended West Point Military Academy for a time but had been dismissed for academic reasons. His name was Newton Sobieski Finney, the middle appellation adopted from a novel his mother had read about the romantic Polish king John Sobieski. There was romance in the namesake as well, or so thought the smitten Josephine Elizabeth du Bignon. She was the granddaughter of the dashing Le Sieur Christophe Anne Poulain du Bignon, a much-decorated French naval captain of Louis XVI's who fled his homeland after the French Revolution and settled on Jekyl Island. Through sea island cotton he remade his fortune and re-created his aristocratic family in the New World. Josephine and John were married soon after they met, and her family grudgingly accepted the charming fortune hunter from the North.

The War of Northern Aggression trapped Finney in Georgia, but in 1872 he moved to New York City and, with a bankroll from a shipping business he had formed, began investing successfully in the many new industries and transport systems springing up throughout the country. He was soon a partner in King, Finney and company, railroad financiers and investment bankers. Through Oliver King's social influence, Finney secured membership in the highly exclusive Union Club.

It happened that around the beginning of 1885 many members of the Union Club were looking for a winter hunting resort. They hired several world travelers to seek out sites that would fit their stringent demands. They required a relatively warm locale, with abundant and varied game and salubrious water for drinking and bathing. It was to be not more than a long day's train ride from New York City, preferably close to the ocean, so that those with yachts could sail them there. Most importantly, it had to offer total privacy from the prying eyes of reporters and common gawkers. Newton Finney believed that he knew precisely the place they sought. He contrived to bring a hunting party to his in-laws' island. With him came John Claflin, scion of the country's largest dry goods enterprise; Claflin's brother-in-law, Edward Everett Eames, also a Union Club member; and his partner, Oliver King, secretary of the Union Club. Claflin, Eames, and King were enchanted by Jekyl Island's beauty, impressed by the game, delighted by the mild temperature and the delicious artesian well water, and overjoyed with the fact that the place was totally cut off from the mainland by water deep enough to accommodate yachts. Within days of their return, every member of the Union Club had had the praises of Jekyl Island sung to him.

By that same year of 1885, due to the deprivations of the War of Northern Aggression, the du Bignon family had sold off several parcels of Jekyl Island. The largest and most southern portion, however, was still owned by John Eugene du Bignon. It was to this du Bignon that Newton Finney came on a secret visit. He offered a deal: If du Bignon would sell his portion and convince the other owners to sell theirs, it could be resold to a New York-capitalized venture for several times the price he had paid. Furthermore, he would be given a lifetime membership in the fabulously exclusive club that would be built there. John du Bignon agreed wholeheartedly. His problem was that he lacked the capital to buy out the other owners and to pay off the Brunswick officials whose permission had to be gotten to make the island a private club. This Finney already knew and, before du Bignon could begin worrying about his critical lacking, Finney offered an arrangement. A certain Mr. Lanier, also of the Union Club, had pledged to advance du Bignon what was needed to complete the transaction.

Over the course of the next month, John Eugene set about paying visits to Mr. Martin Tufts, who owned a shoreside parcel, and Gustav Friedlander and Company, who owned most of the northern portion. John Le Brun and his closest friend, Esau Garnix, were Friedlander's "and Company" silent partners.

Everyone thought they knew what John du Bignon was up to. Brunswick was rapidly becoming a popular resort. A gentleman had been inquiring around town of the availability of local islands for a hotel to rival the Oglethorpe. Verbally, at least, he offered "up to twenty thousand dollars for the right location." No one in Brunswick begrudged John du Bignon the opportunity to make a reasonable profit. Times also being recessionary, Tufts, Friedlander, Le Brun, and Garnix suggested fair figures. John Eugene met their asking prices without haggling. The total outlay for the parcels amounted to just under ten thousand dollars. This was wired without question from one of Mr. Lanier's New York banks. The three thousand dollars necessary to "square" the mayor, the judge, and the councilmen in charge of land zoning came from John du Bignon's personal savings.

Once all impediments had been removed in Georgia, a contract was sent to du Bignon, offering to buy the land on behalf of the Jekyl Island Club. The price quoted was $125,000. Du Bignon accepted on January 18, 1886. The day before, he had turned down an offer from Joseph Pulitzer guaranteeing to "top by ten thousand dollars whatever has been offered by the gentlemen of the Union Club." John du Bignon could not accept the deal; he had already sold his soul to the devil and was in no position to consider legitimate alternatives. The same day du Bignon accepted, formal news of the founding of the Jekyl Island Club broke within the best men's clubs of New York, Baltimore, Chicago, Philadelphia, and Boston. The number of shares was strictly limited to one hundred. Within a week, fifty-seven shares had been sold, two to the indefatigable Joseph Pulitzer.

It was not until 1890 that John Le Brun and several other Brunswick officials got all the details of the scheme from a bitter John du Bignon. For three years, he and his family endured the humiliation of virtual exclusion from every special club activity. Each season, dozens of events such as cottage dinners, afternoon teas, tennis round-robins, and beach picnics were thrown, but the du Bignons were lucky to receive more than two or three invitations. John Eugene resigned his membership. For the brief loan of $9,800, he had repaid Lanier more than $60,000. What was more, only $40,000 went into Lanier's pockets; $20,000 was directly paid to Mr. J. P. Morgan. Although no one ever had the temerity to state it plainly and out loud, it was obvious who the invisible author of the underhanded scheme had been. J. P. Morgan had gotten himself the hunting club he had been most desirous of having, had seen that his fellow members were overcharged for the same privilege, and had pocketed part of those charges without ever himself laying out a cent.

"This all came out the year before Le Brun won the election for sheriff. It's undoubtedly why he's treated Morgan with so little respect," Judge Tidewell concluded, "and why he'd love to implicate the man in a murder.

But that's not going to happen." He turned and made sure that Bobby Lee Randolph was heading toward the stern. "In fact, not only will John Le Brun get no satisfaction out of attacking Pierpont Morgan and his precious club, but his behavior may well do him out of his job. If he blesses out the members publicly or insists on continuing the investigation, I will not stop him. And neither will you."

Warfield scowled. "And then what? You think the members will exert the same kind of pressure they do on their factory, mill, and mine workers and force the club staff to vote against Le Brun?"

"Why not? Several hundred workers and their families depend on employment at that club during the winter season. If they're threatened enough, that could turn hundreds of votes against him."

Warfield tossed the butt of his cigarette overboard. "I doubt it. These men don't have the same kind of control they do up North. If I had to guess, more of the workers would vote *for* John precisely because he badgered the millionaires."

"You'd better not hope so," Iley Tidewell said. "Deputy chief was the only available public job when you came slinkin' home with your tail between your legs, boy. But you sure in hell don't have to stay there." He glared at his son and flicked his butt directly onto Warfield's chest. "Don't depend on me and the Jekyl Island Club to make you sheriff. Learn about your opponent; find his weaknesses and secrets. Try to make friends with Le Brun. He won't trust you very far, considerin' how I got you the job over his objection, but he may relax his guard a little. Tell him you hate me. Use that as a common bond. You've got about five months until you have to declare for the November election. If he wins, he's in for another two years. Jesus Christ, do somethin' positive!" Tidewell spat onto the water. "I spent a fortune on your education. Private school, Princeton University, Penn Law School. And you end up back here."

"It wasn't my fault the firm set me up," Warfield said, knowing as he said it that defense was futile.

"The hell it wasn't!" the judge snapped. "They hire three fresh-out lawyers two years ago. If you had proven first or even second most valuable of the group, they would laid that lawsuit on someone else's doorstep. But you were the most expendable."

"I was the Southerner," Warfield argued.

"That's why you should have made sure you were the best of those hired," his father shot back. "Your mother's stupid, all right, and you inherited it from her. Saints preserve me. Time's runnin' out for you to make somethin' of yourself. Keep your wits about you today, boy."

Iley Tidewell pushed himself back from the rail. "I'll see who our mysterious four gentlemen are; you reflect upon your future."

THE JEKYL ISLAND CLUB imported celebrated clerics, both locally and from New York City, to inspire the membership each Sunday. This week the minister was the Reverend Charles Parkhurst, the only person to hold an honorary membership in the club. John was not surprised that his sermon was on the uncertainty of life, the likelihood that more than a few among the congregation would meet their Maker before they had decided it was time. Only constant faith and periodic renewal through the Body and Blood of the Lamb insured salvation.

John glanced around the little chapel during the sermon. Virtually all members, family, and strangers were in attendance. Mrs. Springer was absent. Dr. Hosmer had just entered, slipping unobtrusively into the back row. His employer did not accompany him. Hosmer sat with interlaced fingers during the sermon and stood with and twiddled his interlaced fingers during the following hymn. Directly after placing money in the offering plate, he withdrew from the chapel. Since John sat in the next-to-last row, he dared to follow the man outside.

"Mr. Hosmer!" he called out.

The ex-physician turned. "Sheriff Le Brun! Good morning!"

"Chapel didn't hold your attention today?"

"Never does," he said, waiting for John to catch up. "I'm an atheist."

"Then why—"

"Because Andes asks me to. He's a member of Saint George Episcopal Church. The same one Jupiter Morgan belongs to . . . although Andes's attendance in New York also leaves something to be desired."

" 'Andes.' I heard you call him that yesterday. Is it a nickname between the two of you?"

"Why, you're almost as sharp and inquisitive as he is! Drumfires of questions from you both." Hosmer reached over to John's jacket shoulder and gave it a pinch, flick, and brush, precisely as he had done the previous day. He leaned close and lowered his voice, although no one else was within sight. "It's his code name. The name he's given himself for communication with the *World*."

"I don't understand," John said.

"Joseph's away from New York for several months a year. His stay here alone lasts about three months. He'll never relinquish direction of the newspaper, despite frayed nerves and failing senses. Twice a day he's sent telegrams of breaking stories. He responds as often."

The news interested John greatly. "He didn't send a flurry of telegrams by special launch Friday night, did he?"

"Why do you ask?"

John briefly described the incident with Captain Clark carrying the telegrams through the Oglethorpe lobby.

"That *is* strange," G. W. agreed, "but it wasn't our doing."

"Nevertheless," John prompted, "Mr. Pulitzer does send many telegrams."

"True. But the Goulds control Western Union. We know of several cases of employees reporting telegrams to them, for profit and blackmail purposes. So Andes thwarts them by telegramming everything in code. He's given names to more than twenty thousand people, places, and things. The code book, which is over two hundred fifty pages, is kept in a safe in the chief editor's office."

"And you are the keeper for 'Andes,' " John guessed.

Hosmer's grin had pushed his cheeks up high against his eye sockets. He clearly enjoyed basking in reflected glory, playing Boswell to Pulitzer's Johnson. "There is no code book on this end," he proclaimed. "It's all inside his head. His memory should be studied by science. I'd wager it against anyone else's on the planet." Hosmer veered to the right, jostling his audience. "I'm sorry. I thought we were headed for breakfast together."

"I've had my breakfast," John said. "I was hopin' we were headin' back to the cottage."

"Very well," the agreeable man said. "You want to ask Andes something?"

"I do indeed."

Hosmer stepped off the path and headed in a beeline for the Pulitzer mansion. "I suppose telling you a few of the code words wouldn't hurt, seeing as you'll never use them. He'll change them in a few months anyway. J. P. Morgan's 'Gadroon.' Fat Teddy Roosevelt's 'Glutinous.' William Jennings Bryan is 'Guilder.' Get it? The silver question? President McKinley's 'Guinea,' because he has the wide-eyed stare of a guinea hen. Advertising's 'polish,' as in making something dull shine. He hates Macy's. They think the *World*'s too low-class to spend many advertising dollars with, so he calls it 'Rat.' " He slowed his pace and turned to the sheriff. "He was up late again last night. Insomnia. I hope he's in a benevolent mood."

Hosmer's apprehension was well founded. The instant they entered the cottage they heard a tirade, as loud as if it were being delivered through a megaphone.

"Jesus, Mary, and Joseph, Pollard, you unmitigated moron! How in thunder could you lose the book? Do you want me to get down on my hands and knees and help you?" Hosmer paused at the bottom of the stairs, holding John back.

"It never lasts more than five minutes," he promised. "Not without at least a lull."

"*You're* sorry?" Pulitzer shouted. "*I'm* the one who's sorry! Sorry I ever hired you. Incompetent imbecile. Oh, you've found it? How stunningly clever of you. Take it downstairs and excise the boring descriptions. Whoever told me that James Fenimore Cooper could write is a cretin, pure and simple. Was it you? Well, that doesn't prove you're not a cretin. Now, get out of my poor sight!"

"He's winding down," G. W. assured, holding fast to the fabric of John's sleeve lest he try to escape.

The put-upon secretary came down the stairs shaking his head. He passed Le Brun and Hosmer without comment.

"Let's chance it," the friend decided, tugging the sheriff along behind him.

Pulitzer lounged in the same place John had found him the previous day, except that he now wore a light gray sack suit, cut to the fashion of the day. His head cocked at their approach.

"Good morning, Andes!" Hosmer beamed.

"Morning, G. W." Pulitzer's voice carried no trace of the calumny he had heaped upon the poor young secretary. "Chapel over already?"

"Not quite. I met Sheriff Le Brun there, and he came back with me."

Pulitzer leaned forward to pick John from the gloom near the top of the stairs. "Wonderful! Have you come to read to me, Sheriff, or to hear my solution to how I could have shot Springer?"

"Neither, sir," John said, taking two steps into the room. "I've come to employ your mind."

"Do tell? It's a bit early in the day, but perhaps you'll force me to brush out the cobwebs. Sit, sit! How may I be of service?"

John lowered himself in a chair directly opposite the near-blind publisher. He saw that his host had a long loop of string and was fashioning cat's cradles.

"I was invited to Mr. Morgan's apartment last night, to listen to what a great humanitarian and patriot he is," John began. Pulitzer laughed, which relaxed the sheriff considerably. "When he excused himself for a couple of minutes, I found a telegram he had received on Friday afternoon. It read 'WM AGREES VISIT JIC MONDAY 20th and it was signed 'Hanna.' "

Pulitzer dropped the string. His mouth dropped open. "Son of a bitch!"

"The 'WM' is for William, as in McKinley," John said, "isn't it?"

"Or the initials of his first and last name," Pulitzer answered. He clapped his hands several times and then rubbed them together, as if he were a quarterback preparing to receive a hiked football. "This makes perfect sense. No wonder Morgan, Stetson, and Lanier are so all-fired intent on resolving this Springer business; the president's coming for a visit. Damn me! Why didn't I realize it?" He looked suddenly furious. "Why didn't I hear about it?"

"But the telegram came from Thomasville," John disclosed.

"Yes. It would. McKinley and his neurotic wife, along with Vice President and Mrs. Hobart, are down at the Grocer's summer cottage there right now."

"Mark Hanna," Hosmer whispered forcefully at the sheriff.

John nodded his understanding. Marcus Alonzo Hanna had been the engineer of William McKinley's nomination and election in 1896. Hanna had inherited a flourishing grocery business from his father and used its profits to expand into coal and iron ventures, then shipping and shipbuilding, banking, street railways, and the *Cleveland Herald*. He was the beau example of the late-nineteenth-century capitalist, throwing his money and power at any enterprise that smelled of profit and using any means, legal or illegal, to guarantee that his investment paid off big.

John understood much more about the men of the Jekyl Island Club than his clearly enthralled chief deputy, Warfield Tidewell, could have guessed. He knew that most of the millionaires ignored politics and considered it nothing but an impediment to greater ambition, considered politicians men who masqueraded as the incarnate will of their constituents but who actually bent to the capitalists' will with the proper monetary pressure. Businessman Mark Hanna, however, embraced politics and had often been quoted in both Southern and Northern newspapers preaching that the welfare of all business (and therefore the nation) depended upon rule by the Republican Party. His reward for raising an unbeatable war chest for McKinley's fight with William Jennings Bryan was one of the senatorships of Ohio.

"McKinley was invited down here last year," Pulitzer went on, "but the sinking of the *Maine* stopped him. They'll call this the delayed acceptance of that invitation. But the real reason is John Moore's guest over at Sans Souci: Thomas B. Reed."

"Speaker of the House," Hosmer hissed.

"Christ Almighty, this is a smart man, G. W.!" Pulitzer shouted. "He doesn't need you to tell him who Thomas Reed is."

"But I do need you to explain why Reed is the reason for this visit," said Le Brun. "He's not really a threat to McKinley as next year's Republican presidential candidate, is he?"

"Reed is if the members of the club decide he is," Pulitzer declared. "McKinley will be staying at Solterra with Mr. and Mrs. Bliss." He whirled to face Hosmer. "If you whisper 'secretary of the interior,' I shall take my cane to you, G. W.!" He pivoted back to the sheriff. "They made the offer of their house to the president last year, and he had accepted." Pulitzer snapped his bony fingers. "I *know* what this is about. The Philippines! Reed is opposing McKinley over annexation of the Philippines. Morgan, Lanier, and the rest of the boys are working on imperialism! Shifting our entire world policy."

As if playing charades with his last thought, Pulitzer shifted on the divan and faced the opposite way. "This solves the riddle of those late-night telegrams on Friday, Sheriff. Both Rockefeller and Gould met with Reed before they left, to get in their two cents. They no doubt thought they'd done all that was possible. Lord, they'll piss rivers when they learn what Morgan's pulled off." He brayed. "They'll be barely back to New York when they learn what they missed."

"Do you think they originally invited Reed down here to set this up?" Hosmer asked his boss.

"Why not? Reed as bait. A six-foot-two, two-hundred-and-seventy-pound worm. There's supposed to be an apple on this table, G. W. Hand it to me, will you?"

The upright cadaver was clearly galvanized by the news. More fuel was called for. The morning was not half gone, and already the table held a coffeepot, a dirty and empty coffee cup off its saucer, the waning crescent of an almost-consumed pastry, the scoured-out rind of a pineapple cut in half lengthwise, two fingers of orange juice in a demi-pitcher with pulpy traces nearly to its neck, and a large plate all but licked clean of the remains of scrambled eggs.

Pulitzer snatched the apple from Hosmer's outstretched hand and took a prodigious bite out of it before continuing. "That cunning bastard!" A bit of apple dropped onto his beard undetected. "Do you know why Morgan has named all three of his yachts *Corsair*, Mr. Le Brun?"

"I would assume he fancies himself a buccaneer," John hazarded.

"Very good. Jupiter believes he's descended from the famous Caribbean privateer Sir Henry Morgan. Old Morgan served the British Crown by uniting several bands of independent pirates into an expeditionary force that wrecked Panama. Got rich on booty and blackened Spain's eyes for England at the same time. This one sees himself in exactly the same way. He's stopped the independent capitalists from ruining themselves, their corporations, and the national economy with their price wars. He's created cooperative monopolies instead, skimmed off a handsome profit from the reorganizations, and he's absolutely sure that he's also serving every citizen in the United States of America. Taking on the villains of this era— England, Germany, Spain—and wrecking their plans for world domination. Didn't he tell you something like that last night?"

"Something like that," John echoed.

"The megalomaniac. The yachts are named after him: *El Corsario Supremo!*"

"There were *several* telegrams in Cap'n Clark's hand," John remembered.

"Which means that more Morgan cronies are on the way down here," Pulitzer said. "Probably arrive any minute. It only took one telegram to respond to the one you saw. Let's see. Sent Friday night. Take all day Saturday to get down here. They'd have to overnight at the Oglethorpe Hotel. I'll wager at least four members—all in the Morgan camp—suddenly arrive on the morning run of the *Howland*."

"No bet," Hosmer was delighted to chime in.

Pulitzer tossed the apple down and slapped his hands against his thighs. "You have enriched my morning immeasurably, Sheriff. Is there anything else I can do for *you*?"

"I'd like to speak with you later in the day, sir. Right now, I need to meet that steamer."

Pulitzer stood. "If you do conclude your investigation right away and have some spare time, I'd love to have you read to me with your splendid voice."

"I'd be pleased," John lied.

The physician jabbered at John all the way down the stairs and out the door, praising his employer's "perspicacity and perspicuity." John said nothing, intent on getting himself beyond the Pulitzer property where, hopefully, Pulitzer's human dog would pull up.

"Be sure to report back as soon as something happens," Hosmer called out.

John clapped his derby onto his head, muttering as he walked toward the club dock. He was more than a little annoyed at the ego-centered nature of the newspaperman's sidekick. It took extraordinary nerve for Hosmer to expect him to become a willing "stringer" for their news gathering.

"Sheriff Le Brun!"

Charles Lanier walked with long strides on an intercept course with John's heading.

"Good news!" he called out. "The killer was indeed a poacher!"

"Was he caught?" John asked.

"No." Lanier came up close, puffing lightly. "But abundant evidence has been found."

"What evidence?"

"Blood. Footprints. A skiff."

"That is abundant evidence. When was all this discovered?"

"First light this morning."

"By whom?"

"One of the guards."

"The one who found the body in the first place."

"Yes." Lanier's expression was as wide-eyed and innocent as could be.

John drummed his fingers against his thigh. "Who else has seen this evidence?"

"No one. We're gathering an investigating party right now."

John peered up the Jekyl River. "How long until the *Howland* arrives?"

The club president looked at his pocket watch. "It should be here in ten minutes."

"Very well," John said. "I have time to go to the clubhouse."

"I'll arrange for horses," Lanier said, loping toward the center of the island. He slowed and turned. "Are you expecting that deputy who knows everything about our club?"

"Yes. He's supposed to be on the mornin' run."

Lanier nodded. "I trust you're pleased by this news."

"I'm speechless," John replied. He walked across the still-deserted lawns, into the clubhouse, and up to the main desk.

"I need a sheet of paper, an envelope, and a pencil," John told the man on duty.

"Yes, sir. You're Sheriff Le Brun, aren't you?" the man asked.

"I am."

"One moment." He reached into one of the cubbyholes directly behind him. "I found this on the counter here, under some newspapers." He turned, holding a sealed, cream-colored envelope. "I don't know how long it was there. Sorry." He handed it over.

John tore open the envelope. Inside was a single piece of Jekyl Island Club stationery. Like the envelope, it was cream white and identical to stationery lying freely available in several locations throughout the clubhouse's first floor. When he unfolded the paper, he found four crudely formed, block-lettered words, as if printed by a right-hander's left hand:

SPRINGER DEATH NO ACCIDENT

"Your name, sir," John asked, as he pocketed the message.

"Falk. Julius Falk."

"Mr. Falk, would you write down Mr. Randolph Rasher's room for me?"

Along with the stationery, Falk supplied another scrap of paper with the requested room number. Le Brun thanked him, moved out to the veranda, wrote a brief note, sealed it inside the envelope, and wrote a name on it. He ambled casually down to the River Road and looked north. The *Howland* had just steamed into view. John continued on to the dock. Already waiting there was the black man with the mule and wagon who had accompanied the group to pick up Erastus Springer's body. The wagon was loaded with suitcases, steamer trunks, satchels, and carpetbags. The heap almost buried a hastily carpentered coffin.

"Mr. Cain, was it?" John asked the man.

"Friday Cain, suh."

"Born on a Friday?"

"Yassuh."

The man was another coastal island native. His hair was extremely curly, snow white, and sparse on the crown. His old face looked like a poorly cultivated farm, overrun with deep gullies. He wore a lopsided grin. On several occasions, from a distance John had heard his frequent and distinctive booming laugh. Yet up close his eyes betrayed the pinch of long-term pain.

"This here's my mule," he introduced, with enough possessive inflection that John figured most of the other island's mules must have been owned by the club. "Name's Rhoda."

"Hello, Rhoda," John said, patting her on the neck. In turn, she waggled an ear at him. He turned to Cain. "Expectin' many guests on this run?"

Before the wagon driver could reply, an impolite imperative was shouted at him from the top of the dock. John turned to regard the caller, and the figure pulled up as short as if a gate had been swung in his face.

"Mr. Lovell," Friday said softly, his lips hardly moving. His tone was not a happy one.

"Mr. Lovell, so good of you to hunt me down," John declared cloyingly to the man who had worked so hard to avoid interrogation. "I am Sheriff Le Brun, and I need to ask you a few questions."

James Lovell was no small man. He was about the same height and weight as the formidable J. P. Morgan. He looked at the moment as if his foot had been caught in a bear trap. He glanced up and down the dock and from side to side, but could not decide how or if to move. Finally, he clapped his hands behind his back and drew himself to his full height.

"No, you don't. This whole investigation is damned impertinent!"

Le Brun took several steps toward him. "Where were you between eight and nine yesterday mornin'?"

"I was around the clubhouse the *entire* morning. You or your deputy could easily have verified that from a dozen people. You're simply badgering the members and guests out of Rebel meanness. You know very well that it was one of your flatlanders who shot Springer . . . probably just to see if you could get away with it."

"I know nothin' of the kind," John replied.

"The war is long over, mister," Lovell declared. "Pretty soon it'll be the twentieth century. Why don't you Crackers get civilized? We won't be scared away from the South, and if we must we'll bring *real* law back down here and see that true justice is done." Having unloaded on the sheriff, he retrained his blustering expression on the wagon driver.

"My luggage is still up at the clubhouse. You left too early."

Cain nodded. "No, suh. The wagon was full. I'll get your belongin's as soon as I deal with these."

"See that you do," Lovell said. He spun around and stalked back toward the clubhouse.

"Good riddance," John said softly to the man's back.

The *Howland* had cut its engine and was drifting toward the dock, with a deckhand extending a pole to guide it. It came smartly parallel to the dock and was tied up quickly. The first passenger off the boat was a dapper-dressed but ferret-faced man in his middle forties, carrying his fedora in one hand and his pince-nez in the other. He looked acutely distressed.

"Can you direct me to the nearest washroom?" he inquired of the sheriff, his voice almost a whine.

John pointed to the clubhouse and informed him of the proper door off the lobby. In his haste, the man neglected to give thanks. John watched him cross the road with long, rapid steps. The previous day, the *Howland*'s head had been out of order. John was sure the nearly one-hour trip would be purgatory to an older man's full bladder.

Three other men followed off the boat with less urgency, conversing among themselves in low tones. None had family or guests in tow. None looked as if he had taken the seven-hundred-fifty-mile journey down from New York City for recreation. Each in turn gave John a mildly curious eye but failed to introduce himself. The Negro driver they failed to acknowledge at all.

"John!"

Iley Tidewell walked down the gangplank, followed by Warfield Tidewell and Bobby Lee Randolph.

"Solved the case yet?" the judge wanted to know.

"Apparently it's been solved for me," John said. He repeated Charles Lanier's words. "Quite convenient havin' you show up here in the nick o' time."

"Well, they wanted me to have a look around yesterday, so I'm finally here," the judge said.

"To get it resolved as soon as possible," John filled in.

"Exactly. Just discovered all that at first light, Mr. Lanier said?"

"That's what he said."

"Very interesting."

John gestured inland. "Why don't you and your son move on up to the clubhouse? Horses'll be there any second. Wouldn't be surprised if they happened to bring along two or three extra."

As the Tidewells left the dock, John grabbed Bobby Lee's arm. "Is that my gun and clothes?"

The tough-looking deputy held up the sack he had in his left hand. "No. I'm collectin' here for charity."

John laughed. "I'll take it. Hate to put you right back on the boat, but I have some mighty important work for you to do. First, take this." John produced the sealed message he had written in the clubhouse. "Find L. J. Leavy. If he isn't at the newspaper, seek him out. Don't delay."

"I know where to find him," Bobby Lee attested.

"Next: The president of the United States is about to pay a visit here."

Deputy Randolph looked askance. "Just like that, with no warnin'?"

"Just like that. Startin' tomorrow mornin' everybody's on double duty. I want you, Burt, Harvey, and Redmond over here in two boats, no later than nine o'clock."

"Big doin's on Jekyl Island," Bobby Lee observed.

"You have no idea," John answered, patting his longtime accomplice on the shoulder. The deputy returned to the boat, shaking his head all the while.

John took his holster and revolver from the sack and strapped them on. As he passed Friday Cain, he pressed the bundle of clothing into the driver's hand. "Can you see that this is delivered to my room in the clubhouse?"

"Yassuh, Sheriff."

"By the way . . . who gave you permission to take Mr. Springer's body from the infirmary?"

"Mr. Lanier. He say I should put it on the boat, cover it with a tarp, an' stack the luggage around it."

"Very well," Le Brun said, moving toward the clubhouse with speed. By the time he had neared the veranda, a light cavalry of men and horses were assembled. Among their number, however, were none of the four men who had just left the club steamer. J. P. Morgan sat astride his huge white steed, with Mr. Lanier and Mr. Stetson again serving as customary bulwarks. Mr. Grob was also mounted. The two Tidewell men were climbing into their stirrups, and Warfield clutched the reins of another horse. John accepted the reins and mounted up.

Not a word was spoken during the slow parade out of the Village, onto Shell Road and thence to the path where Erastus Springer had been shot. The group traveled with the solemnity of a funeral procession. As he had done the previous day, John scrutinized the landscape on both sides of the path. The group, led by Lanier, passed the place where the body had been found and traveled on another hundred yards. There, as the day before, the same guard waited patiently beside his horse.

The moment all had dismounted, Ezekiel Turner strode off the path in an easterly, oceanward direction, through a tangle of vegetation so dense as to be almost impenetrable. Presently, where the canopy of the trees made the floor cover sparse, he stopped and squatted down. He pointed to a mossy area stained with dried blood.

"Here's where he took down a deer," Turner said. "He busted a lot of branches, so it weren't hard to find."

"It was difficult gettin' in here, Mr. Turner," John observed. "Wouldn't you agree?"

"I guess so," the guard begrudged.

"With an entire island to wander around on, why would you suppose our poacher would have struggled through all that?"

The guard glanced at Lanier and Morgan. He licked his lower lip and looked back at the sheriff. "I don't know."

"Continue," Judge Tidewell directed the guard.

"We need to turn around and go back out to the path. I'll show you what happened next."

Warfield Tidewell studied his superior. John Le Brun's expression was as grim as a hangman's, but he said no more.

When all were reassembled on the path, Turner faced the group and walked backward two dozen paces, heading south. Finally, he found what he was looking for and pointed to a place several paces to the west of the path.

"Now, he went across here and moved into the brush. Then he musta heard Mr. Springer come along. He threw down the deer—you can see all the blood here—took his rifle, and fired. He probably thought it was another deer. Mr. Springer musta heard him drop the deer he had, so he turned at the noise. That's how he come to be shot square in the chest."

"Poachin' one deer wasn't enough?" John asked. "How was he gonna carry two full-grown deer?"

"I don't know," Turner answered again.

"Then do you know this: It took twenty seconds or less for this poacher to enter the path, walk down it, and get this far into the opposite side," Le Brun said matter-of-factly. "The path is straight as an arrow. But he couldn't see Springer when he entered the path? And Springer didn't see this person carryin' a deer where huntin' is strictly prohibited?"

"Maybe the poacher killed him in cold blood," Turner retrenched.

"And Springer waits patiently for him to drop the deer, raise the rifle, and fire. He just stands there and takes a bullet in the heart."

Turner looked like a first grader who had forgotten his lines in the class play. "I'm only *guessin'* what happened," he declared. He swallowed. "One way or the other, he put down the deer here. He shot Mr. Springer. Then he picked up the deer and continued this way."

"Continue, please," Judge Tidewell exhorted.

The group followed into the marshy woods to the west of the path, being instructed every hundred yards or so to witness crushed weeds and more blood. The silence among the gathering was profound; no one— including the sheriff—made comment, expressed agreement, or offered dissent. All seemed determined to see the reenactment played out to its conclusion. Overhead, mockingbirds supplied plenty of noise, imitating irritated crows.

Sheriff Le Brun got himself to the front of the group, virtually beside the guard as he advanced. When the group halted for the fifth time and the disturbed undergrowth and debris fell silent, the buzzing of many flies filled the air. A fallen tree had created an impasse to the beeline they had been following. Beneath its rotting trunk lay the carcass of a female deer, shot through the neck.

"This dead tree musta been too much for him," Turner speculated. "By now he was tired, panicky, and in a sweat to get off the island. We got to climb over the tree, gentlemen."

The guard pushed on apace, with his silent audience struggling behind gamely, their boots and shoes making sucking noises as they trudged through the soggy ground. Turner pointed left, right, and to his feet at other clues but no longer paused. They plunged and weaved and stumbled for more than a quarter mile, until they at least reached the verge of a vast stretch of marsh, meandering so far into the island that the Jekyl River could not be seen.

"I lost him here," Turner announced. "He went into the water, and I never could pick up the trail again. But he wut'nt too smart, 'cause he lost track of his skiff. I found it over yonder." He plunged into the knee-deep, brackish water, moving to a long, narrow rowboat with a raised centerboard and simple sailing rig, de-stepped and stowed. He grunted as he tugged it to where the party of investigators stood, alternately swatting flies and dabbing their foreheads with handkerchiefs. The skiff had nothing in it except a splinter-edged paddle and a coil of rope so old that it had turned flat gray.

Now that the re-creation had faltered to its conclusion, Iley placed himself so that he could watch John Le Brun's every move. He cocked an eyebrow, waiting for the explosion. He was disappointed.

"What do you think, John?" he finally asked.

"What do you think, Judge?" the sheriff countered.

"I would say the evidence is overwhelming."

John laughed. "It's certainly overwhelmed me." He took a step backward, so that he could address the entire group. "I thought I was pretty good at my job. Yesterday, I searched all around the area where Mr. Springer lay . . . as Mr. Turner can attest. But somehow, I missed all the footprints, the broken twigs, and even two pools of blood."

"I don't think you looked quite far enough south, sir," Turner said, his eyes fixed not on Le Brun but rather on the judge.

"Apparently not. I also fancied myself a pretty experienced hunter. That doe back there looked about fourteen hours dead to me, not twenty-eight. She bled like a split wine cask where she was supposedly shot and was still bleedin' after the theoretical poacher dropped her to kill Mr. Springer. Yet she stopped bleedin' in between, while the poacher toted her several dozen paces down the path."

Morgan slapped at his neck. "Damn it! Can we get out of here?"

"Certainly," John said. He gestured for the group to precede him. The men retraced their steps as if an enemy army were on their heels.

"And why was that doe there to be shot?" John asked loudly. "First of all, it was daylight. She should have been well hidden after her evenin' foragin' and mornin' drink. She should have been sleepin'. Or, if she *was* grazin', it would have been in the grassy areas near the beaches. That's where I always find deer when I hunt on the other islands. If I was a poacher, I'd know that. I sure in hell wouldn't troop like we are, through almost a mile of underbrush."

"What are you saying, Sheriff?" Warfield Tidewell encouraged.

"I'm sayin' what I observed," John answered.

"Are you contradicting all of this evidence?" Charles Lanier asked.

"*I'm* not," John affirmed. "The evidence is contradictin' itself. Now, I'm not sayin' it's impossible. This hypothetical poacher *could* have wandered in that far in broad daylight. Obviously he must be a product of our legendary incestuous breedin', since he left his skiff where he couldn't find it."

"Be careful, Sheriff," Judge Tidewell warned, without slowing his pace.

"I'm bein' very careful, Judge. I figure he must have swum back to the mainland one-handed, holdin' his rifle over his head all the way. If he went straight west, that would be about two miles of marsh and hummock. Alligators. Water moccasins. Other inbred imbecile hunters. Rabid niggers. We'll never hear his side of it, 'cause he's a dead poacher by now for sure!"

This time, Iley Tidewell stopped short, compelling the rest of the group to do the same. "Get to it, Sheriff Le Brun. Say what you mean, plain out."

"I defer to you, Judge. We now all agree that Mr. Springer was murdered. Murder is a very serious crime. Is this case solved or not?"

"Do you believe it is solved?" Tidewell evaded.

"I believe it is *re*solved, if that is the extent of what y'all want," John replied. "However, I also believe that no one here really knows what happened and why Mr. Springer died." He pulled back his jacket and set his hand meaningfully on the butt of his revolver. "That could be very dangerous, in light of the fact that President McKinley and Vice President Hobart are both comin' to this island tomorrow."

The heads of Morgan, Lanier, and Grob did not move. Their eyes remained fixed on the sheriff. Stetson's eyes shifted to Morgan's. The heads of the guard and the Tidewell men jerked back and forth, first with surprise, then in an effort to assess from their faces what everyone else knew concerning the sheriff's revelation.

"You have a point, sir," Charles Lanier granted. "What do you suggest?"

Sheriff Le Brun looked first at Lanier, then at Morgan. "That myself and young Mr. Tidewell stay on the island, with the excuse of bein' the local constabulary and needin' to assure that the president and vice president are safe. We will desist with any overt questionin' concernin' Mr. Springer's death, as that has yielded so little to date and is apt to reveal less as time goes on. We will allow Mrs. Springer to depart, with

Mr. Springer's body. We will encourage normalcy. Without belaborin' it, there is a chance with such a death that aftershocks may occur. I want to be here and not in Brunswick if that should happen. If, by the time President McKinley leaves, nothin' else unusual has occurred, Judge Tidewell can declare this case closed with my blessin'. If my requests are not granted, I shall refuse to sign anythin' attemptin' to resolve this case, and should I be approached by the press I will let them know as much."

Francis Lynde Stetson gestured around the wilderness where they stood. "If we speak of what we've seen here to the members of the club, can we count on you not questioning it and making it sound as if danger still lurks about?"

"You can," John promised.

A collective repose came over the group. J. P. Morgan expelled an appeased grunt. The men continued on through the undergrowth, out to the path, and onto their horses. Iley Tidewell signaled subtly for Warfield to allow the rest of the group to ride away first.

"You are studying under a master," the judge told his son. "He's playing this the way he plays chess. He knew yesterday morning that I was being called in to overrule him. But somehow he learned that the reason for all this haste had to do with McKinley's visit and regained the upper hand." He picked a seed burr off his jacket. "I want you to find out who gave him the information. The second he learned this murder was suspicious, he decided to get back the money they cheated him out of for his land. He's hanging around to be bought out. What he doesn't understand is these men will give away thousands to charities because that's public. But they won't be blackmailed to rectify an old business scheme. Business is business. If you got cheated, they expect you to steal from somebody else. Just to have this done with, I'll try to get John his money . . . although I'm not sure even a murder hanging over the club will move Morgan. One thing I am sure of: I want compensation for my part in this."

"This was a travesty of justice," Warfield declared. "You'll be risking your career taking money from these men to sanction it."

"Not if John Le Brun can be bought off, or if you learn what he proposes to do. Why don't you see if you can pay me back for all my investments in you, boy."

The judge dug his heels into his horse's flanks and set it cantering after the others.

NTERING THE STABLES, Judge Tidewell dismounted quickly and approached J. P. Morgan. "I want to make sure you know precisely who you're dealing with in John Le Brun, sir," he began, indicating with a nod that he and the banker should separate themselves. They walked slowly to the edge of the landscaping that bordered the wilderness behind the Village. Morgan lit one of his cudgel-sized cigars as he listened. Tidewell repeated the back end of the story he had related to his son on their trip to the island.

"Mr. du Bignon let it out that you were the person behind the scheme . . . that you had made considerable money on it . . . without having laid out a cent yourself," Tidewell dared, spooning out the words while he monitored the titan's expression. Morgan kept a poker face the entire time. "So, clearly, the sheriff believes he has an ax to grind with you. I'm sure he's looking for restitution."

"I know all about Mr. Le Brun and the selling of his part of this island," Morgan said. "I purposely invited him to my suite last night to see if he would broach the subject. He did not. I even gave him an opening to speak about it, and he declined to take it. I am not convinced this is the motive behind his doggedness. I certainly will not lower myself to bring up the subject."

"If he *did* broach the subject," Tidewell explored, "is there a chance he could receive a monetary . . . consideration?"

"Not from me," Morgan affirmed. "At any rate, he has set his own limitations on pursuing the death of Mr. Springer. In three days it will all be history."

"Let us hope so," the judge wished, deciding against petitioning for his own compensation.

"*Hope* is a word I reserve only for my resurrection," Morgan said. "All else I deal with personally." Having had his say, he strode back toward the clubhouse, leaving the judge to set his own course.

EING THE LAST TO ARRIVE at the stable, Warfield was compelled to wait patiently for the grooms to care for the others' horses first. When he was finally able to deliver over his animal, he found his superior waiting for him beside one of the stable doors, reading the sign posted on it.

"Have you ever seen so many rules in your life?" John commented, as Warfield approached.

"All because of the Golden Rule," Warfield replied. " 'Them with the gold make the rules.' "

"How true," John said. "I observed your father takin' Mr. Morgan away for a walk. It occurred to me I should do the same with you." He started back toward the Shell Road, in the direction from which they had just come. Warfield fell in beside him.

"We must not let that farce we were just subjected to divert us from the critical question," John said.

"You mean 'Does Mr. Springer's death have anything to do with President McKinley's visit?' "

"Exactly!" John exclaimed. He slapped Warfield familiarly on the back. His deputy smiled reflexively from the praise. "Even though I personally believe it's unlikely."

"I agree," Warfield said. "If someone were planning on doing harm to the president, why would he warn everyone by first shooting someone else?"

"Unless his purpose was to frighten the president off. But such an act seems excessive for the purpose."

"Perhaps it's the only way McKinley could be deterred," Warfield suggested. "These are powerful men inviting him, and he declined their invitation once already."

"So I hear."

"From whom are you getting your information?" Warfield asked.

"Mostly from Joseph Pulitizer. A fascinatin' man."

"One of my heroes," Warfield disclosed.

"Really? In that case, I must introduce you."

"That would be wonderful!" the deputy enthused.

"You keep up on these folk to a remarkable degree. How do you come to know so much about them?"

"I used to hear a lot firsthand, when I worked in Philadelphia," Warfield answered. "But now it's through reading. I subscribe to the *New York Tribune*."

"They have the best society columns," John said.

"Yes, they do. How did you know?"

John smiled. "Just a guess."

Warfield declined to tell John about his other subscription, to *Town Topics*, the favorite gossipmongering rag of New York City, where all the dirt about the rich was exposed unless they paid the editor's steep blackmail fees.

"Not to burst your bubble," John said, "but Mr. Pulitzer appears more ogre than hero in person. I must admit, however, that I don't know much about his background."

"Oh, but you really should!" Warfield encouraged. "He's a complex man. A tyrant and taskmaster concerning the newspaper business and his private life but a generous heart elsewhere. Totally devoted to the American public's good. Let's see. He got the schoolchildren to save their pennies in order to buy the base for the Statue of Liberty."

"That's not much sacrifice on his part," John remarked.

"I'm warming up. He gives every one of his employees two weeks' vacation. Fully paid! And every one of his news butchers gets a fully paid Christmas dinner for his family."

"Better."

"He helped build the Metropolitan Opera, not as a bastion for the rich but as a temple of art for the masses. And have you heard of Nellie Bly?"

"It's a song by Stephen Foster."

"True. That's where the woman took the name. It's the pen name of a female investigative reporter. First one I'd ever heard of. Pulitzer hired her a few years back to pose as a crazy woman. Got herself put into the Blackwell's Island Insane Asylum up in New York. She exposed horrible conditions and got the place turned upside down. Very big news in the North."

"I remember that now. That was Pulitzer's doin'?"

"It was her idea, but he backed her. He backed the war with Spain. Also backed the steelworkers when they struck in Homestead, Pennsylvania . . . although he once fired his employees who were striking for the printer's union."

"So he's a hypocrite."

"He said he's sympathetic to unions in spirit but not when they seek to dictate to management policy. He said, 'Union policy is a form of mob rule.' "

"Still sounds two-faced."

"And a few years back he saved the country a small fortune by embarrassing Morgan over the rate he wanted to charge the Treasury for gold. He and old J. P. have been friendly enemies for more than a decade. Sounds like they're at it again down here."

"True enough."

"And you're in Pulitzer's camp."

"I'm in my own camp . . . and Mr. Springer's," John answered. He stopped walking. "Whose camp are you in?"

"You mean Morgan or Pulitzer?"

"No. I hoped you'd say that you are also in Mr. Springer's camp, possibly in mine, and certainly in your own. I'd like to continue with that discussion we began on the boat yesterday. Are you willin' to let me know you better?"

Warfield threw up his hands. "Certainly. What do you wish to know?"

"Tell me why you returned home and are no longer practicin' law in Philadelphia."

"Very well." The deputy cleared his throat. "I was quite unhappy as a young man. I resented very much being sent away from home at the age of fourteen."

"That's why I never met you growin' up," said Le Brun.

"You've been sheriff since '91."

"That's right."

The crushed shells beneath their feet crunched loudly. The two followed the curve of the road directly eastward.

"I've been gone, except for holidays, since '87. My father insisted it was for my own good and that I had to be educated in the North if I wanted to truly make something of myself. I was able to work off some of my aggression through sports. Lifting weights, throwing the discus and shot put, and playing football in high school. Despite all the athletics, I carried a good deal of anger to college. It's too ridiculous to go into, but I broke another fellow's jaw. Not that he didn't deserve it . . ."

"But you blew your stack and hit him where there were witnesses," John guessed.

"Precisely. I was suspended from Princeton University for a semester. I was too embarrassed to come home, so I stayed in the area and worked at a quarry. I had defended myself during the dean's inquest, and that's when I became interested in law. When I graduated, I went to the University of Pennsylvania Law School. Then I got a job at a large firm that specializes in corporate law. My father's suggestion. He said it was the quickest way in law to get rich." Warfield laughed ruefully.

"What did you do, hit a senior partner?" John asked.

"I should have. Should have taken a crowbar to the lot of them. When

I didn't kill someone, I knew I'd conquered most of my anger. They were overcharging our largest client with hundreds of nonexistent hours. Being *good* lawyers"—the young man laid heavy sarcasm on the word *good*— "they had prepared for the eventuality of getting caught. They made it look quite convincing that I had done the false billing on my own. 'In an attempt to impress the senior partners and try to advance himself more quickly,' their internal report said. Set me up. Didn't give a damn that I was disbarred and they'd ruined my career. I was the only Southerner in the firm. I think they hired me believing I could bring them business and relationships from Atlanta, Savannah, and Charleston. They were disappointed when I failed to carry that kind of influence. So they threw me to the wolves. Actually, in some ways I was relieved to be done with them. In two years, I saw, read, and heard more shady dealings than I thought possible from so few people."

"But you're still fascinated by this kind?" John asked, thinking of Warfield's subscription to the *New York Tribune*.

"I am. The good and the bad alike. There are good ones among them, you know . . . even members of this club."

"I'll take your word on it." John pointed left. "This way." They continued walking side by side.

"Anyway, I had had enough of the North," Warfield said. "So I came home."

"You've been home all of what . . . eight weeks?"

"That's about it."

"Are you ready to head North again?"

"What do you mean?" the deputy asked.

"I mean that you should be prepared for an offer by one of the members to take a job in New York or Philadelphia. In exchange for sellin' me out, of course."

"Would they be so blatant?" Warfield said.

"When it happens," John went on, ignoring the question, "remember this: If you accept the job, they'll know two things. The first is that you can be bought. The second is that you'd sell out your boss. You won't go far."

The pair walked together in silence for a hundred yards. Warfield said, "I must admit that I have thought about turning around . . . that I was too rash in leaving the North."

"Then go back," John advised. "Not on their terms; on your own. You have a good mind. You have plenty of education. You've probably also made good connections over the years. That should be enough to make you the millions you seem to hanker for . . . maybe with no worse than hard work."

"And if I decide to stay?"

"Well, you can't have my job," Le Brun said. "At least not for a while. I'm fifty-three. I've lived frugally all my life, made some good investments. But I sure can't afford to retire yet. I figure five more years. If you want to hang around that long and learn the job, I'm more than willin' to teach you everything I've learned. I'm sure the position will be yours if you want it then. If you keep your nose clean, I'd support you. But I doubt if that would satisfy your father's timetable."

"I hate my father," Warfield said.

John bent and retrieved a long stick that lay in the middle of Shell Road. He whipped it back and forth. "You resolve that your own way. But if you've the backbone to stick out this job, you could use it as a springboard. You're young. Sheriff by thirty-one. Who knows what by forty."

Another silence ensued. They crested the road, and the sea breeze greeted them. John flung the stick away.

"If Springer wasn't killed by a poacher, then why was he killed?" the deputy asked.

"Somethin' he did or somethin' he knew," Le Brun judged.

"How do you find out which?"

"For one thing, we work with Mr. Pulitzer. He claims to have the biggest intelligence-gathering body in the world."

"That's probably true."

They walked along for another few minutes. The road dissolved into white sugar sand. A sea gull swooped low over the sea oats that anchored the dunes. The smell of the ocean came up strong with the breeze. Beyond a line of bathhouses, a lone man dressed in white from head to foot walked toward them from a considerable distance.

"This is a beautiful place," Warfield said after inhaling deeply.

"It always was." John came to a halt and looked north and south. He dug his hands into his pockets.

"Do you regret having sold your share of it to the club?"

John squinted at the panorama before him. "I didn't sell it to the club, but I know what you mean. The answer is no. I had had enough of Jekyl

Island when John du Bignon came to me with his offer. I was watchin' your father watchin' me this mornin'. He's expectin' some sort of vendetta from me. I do believe I am owed somethin' more from the sale of this island, but I would not scruple to use a man's murder to settle the issue. Here."

Le Brun handed Tidewell the piece of Jekyl Island Club stationery with the four block-letter words.

"What do you make of it?" the deputy asked.

"It could just be malicious nothin', made to get me to blow *my* stack, so I'd be easier to shove off the island. I might be accused of plantin' it myself. If it's real, then it may mean that somebody other than Erastus Springer knows the somethin' that got Springer dead."

"Or it may mean that someone saw the killing," Warfield said.

John shook his head. "Unlikely, considerin' where he was shot. Who but he and the killer would be out there so early, and where would they have stood not to have been spotted? That couldn't have been written by any of the staff except those who work in the clubhouse, since it's on club stationery. The only workers who could get that are maids and waiters, and they couldn't get away at that hour."

Warfield shot his superior a look of admiration.

"It's why I bargained to stay on the island," John said, pointing to the note. "Perhaps the person will become desperate once he or she hears about the poacher explanation and leave us somethin' more explicit. Or else he or she will be killed as well for what they know." John squatted, scooped up a handful of sand, and let it run through his fingers. "I do hope it's the former."

"Don't we have anything else to go on?" Warfield asked.

"As a matter of fact we do. That gentleman there." The figure had come within two hundred yards of them. John pulled his much-consulted pocket watch out from its pocket. "We'll be cuttin' this close."

"Randolph Rasher," said Warfield. "I know him."

"On a personal basis?"

"Just slightly. From competition with the Elis. Yale men, that is."

"Yes, I know. Well, that makes things all the more interestin'."

"How did you know he'd be down on the beach?" asked the deputy.

"Because I saw him walkin' this way as we rode back to the stables. You should have, too. Your powers of observation need improvin', Mr. Tidewell. We are here to have a serious talk with Mr. Rasher." Rapidly, the sheriff told his deputy what he had learned about Rasher's back-door visits to the clubhouse when he was supposedly bicycling. He also related what he had gathered during his interview with Chrystie Springer.

"She admitted that Mr. Springer was courting her while she was in *The Highwayman*?" Warfield said, as Randolph Rasher was almost upon them. "Then perhaps she isn't as clever as you believe. That proves he was seeing her before his wife died. I happened to be in New York on legal business the night that show closed. It was in April of last year. I had attended specifically to see the woman, as a friend had praised her to the heavens. I also know that Septima Springer—the *first* Mrs. Springer— died in May last year. Old man Springer must have borrowed time from comforting his consumptive wife to 'backstage-Johnny' Chrystie. So their October wedding wasn't that precipitous after all."

"I may recant what I said about your powers of observation," John said. "You assembled those separate facts like a fourteen-jewel watch."

Warfield nodded. "Thank you."

"And as a reward, I am goin' to allow you to share the questionin' in this interview. Are you up to it?"

"You'll let me know if I'm not," the deputy answered, just as Rasher came close to them, a recently lit cigarette in his hand.

"Good morning again, Sheriff," Rasher exclaimed, flashing his patented thirty-two-tooth smile. His white ensemble looked as if he had plucked it from Abercombie & Fitch's front window. His free hand was stuck with casual calculation into his pants pocket.

" 'Mornin' indeed. Allow me to introduce Mr. Warfield Tidewell."

Rasher took a hard look at the deputy. "I know you from somewhere."

"That's right," Warfield said, purposely not helping the Morgan junior partner, wanting to see if he would remember.

"Sorry. I can't place . . ."

"Princeton," Warfield supplied. "Rowing and debating."

"Yes!" Rasher said forcefully. "We thrashed both your teams . . . more than once, I believe."

"Mr. Rasher was captain of Yale's heavyweight crew and their de- bating club," Tidewell said.

"Mr. Tidewell is now deputy chief of *my* team," John announced.

"Really?" Randolph regarded Warfield with a new look that barely disguised his disdain. It was precisely the catalyst John had hoped to pro- vide to test Warfield's potential. "You were called 'War' in school, weren't you?"

"Yes. And you were Randy," Warfield rejoined, coloring the last word a lascivious scarlet.

Rasher smiled lamely at the sheriff. "I had something of a reputation with the ladies when I was single," he admitted, feigning abashedness.

"But such a reputation is a dubious honor once one is married, with babies," Tidewell remarked.

"We're returnin' to the clubhouse, Mr. Rasher," Sheriff Le Brun said. "Join us, will you?"

"Sure. I'm heading there anyway."

John started off at a good clip.

"You're looking as fit as when you were in college," Warfield commented.

"Thank you."

"I understand from Sheriff Le Brun that you've been doing a lot of bicycling down here."

"That's right." Rasher took a deep drag on his cigarette. A trace of the easy smile and casual pose had vanished. A pinch at the corners of the eyes indicated that the young businessman was wary of the pair of lawmen.

"You also told him last night that you had rented your bicycle at six-fifty yesterday morning. Remarkable memory," Tidewell commented.

"I have several remarkable qualities," Randy returned, "but forbearance is not one of them. Would you mind not beating around the bush?"

"Very well," Warfield obliged. "Speaking of bushes, someone I interviewed thought I might want to know that a Hawthorne bicycle was parked several mornings last week in a concealed place near the clubhouse. Always at the same time."

John raised his eyebrows slightly at his deputy's bold improvisation, but he said nothing.

"You were the only person to have rented a Hawthorne during all of those periods." Warfield continued. "It seems that, while you did indeed bicycle much of yesterday, you were not behind the handlebars when Mr. Springer was being murdered."

"I had heard that was an accident," Rasher said. The cigarette fell from his fingers unnoticed.

"If only that were the case," John lamented. The men's pace, brisk as it was, was not enough to generate a sweat from him or his deputy. Nevertheless, John noted that one was breaking out across Randolph Rasher's forehead.

"This person I interviewed has not put two and two together," Warfield said, "but Sheriff Le Brun and I have. We've also deduced why the bicycle was abandoned for forty minutes or so, the same time each morning."

Rasher came to a halt. "Have you told anyone else about this?"

"No."

"Please don't! I beg you."

"You'll have to beg while you walk," John said over his shoulder. "We really must get back to the clubhouse. The *Howland* docks in Brunswick in about ten minutes. The *Jekyl Island Special* pulls out about twenty minutes after that. Might take a few extra minutes to load that coffin on. At any rate, dependin' on what you do or don't tell us, we may have to make a call to the station and have Mrs. Springer and the body detained."

Warfield turned and walked backward. "What a shame. If Mr. Morgan thought the members of the club were stressed by the murder, wait until he learns about *this*."

John and Warfield resumed their relentless march down Shell Road. Randolph sprinted after them, caught up, and took the lead.

"Do you realize what you're threatening to do? You wouldn't just be ruining Chrystie and me. There's my wife and children. My parents. Even Springer's daughter would be disgraced. Blasted society and their moral hypocrisies!"

"You haven't mentioned what it would do to Mr. Morgan," Warfield pointed out.

Rasher looked ready to weep. "Look, Warfield, you may not be a member, but you understand the implacable standards of this place."

"Even I am aware of Pierre Lorillard's expulsion and that of William Vanderbilt," John chimed in.

Randy nodded wretchedly.

"You fell in love and hired that guard Turner to kill her husband," Warfield accused.

"Are you insane?" Rasher wailed. "It was an affair, pure and simple."

"Not simple anymore," Sheriff Le Brun said. "This is what we believe: You'd hire the bicycle early, then stash it around seven-thirty. By that time punctual-to-a-fault Erastus Springer was in the dinin' room. You'd mount the all-but-unused back staircase and then mount Mrs. Springer. Your room was only two doors down from theirs. You'd knock on their door as you passed. A few moments later, Mrs. Springer would appear in your room. About ten after eight, you'd exit your room first, to be sure the coast was clear . . . sweatin' as if you'd been pedalin' all the while. Then Mrs. Springer would make good use of her stage knowledge of quick changes and appear for breakfast a few minutes later. No need to apply rouge; you'd put a natural blush in her cheeks."

"And what if you're right?" Rasher replied. "All that proves is that we were satisfying a mutual need. She had a husband who was half impotent. I've been away from my wife for weeks. It was nothing more."

Warfield raised a forefinger. "That's what you intended at first, but you fell in love this past week. In love with her incredible beauty *and* her husband's incredible bank account." The chief deputy's words flew from his mouth like bullets from a Gatling gun. "You encountered Turner on one of your many bicycling forays, determined that he was the right man for the job, and hired him with a small fortune to do your dirty work."

"Ridiculous!" Rasher protested. Rather than being further panicked by the accusation, he looked to be regaining control. "If I had hired this guard and expected him to kill Springer on Saturday, I would have taken *great pains* to have been sitting in the clubhouse in plain view the entire time . . . *not* to have been upstairs rutting with his wife.

"Furthermore, the woman I married was a virgin and is totally devoted to me. If I threw her over for Chrystie, I'd be cuckolded by our first anniversary. If she did it with me, she'll do it again.

"Besides," Rasher pressed on, "just because Springer married the woman doesn't mean he'd turn his finances upside down for her. He was only in his fifties . . . smitten, not senile. He had to know she wasn't marrying him for love. I'm sure his daughter gets most of his fortune. Chrystie did *far better* keeping him alive, and she knew it.

"Finally, I wouldn't ask some total stranger to kill for me. I'd be condemning myself to a lifetime of blackmail. If I wanted to kill the man I would have done it myself, on my own time, and in New York City. . . . where the police would have had a *million* suspects rather than the few on this island."

"But even if you didn't arrange for Mr. Springer's murder," John Le Brun said, "there is still the matter of the scandal. Your employer thinks of this club as his; he is its patriarch. Your only salvation would be if he died of apoplexy on bein' told his membership had been revoked for invitin' you as a guest."

"You're right about that," Rasher agreed. "He would ruin me utterly. I wouldn't merely be dismissed from his employ. He would make it his personal and everlasting business to see that I never worked in New York or any other major city in the United States—or England—ever again. With any other employer, I would have the opportunity to start over elsewhere, to accept the wages of my sins and rebuild. Not with Mr. Morgan. If you reveal this, gentlemen, you will be condemning me and those I care for to economic death."

"I see how this man defeated you in debate," John said to Warfield. "He's a sly one. There must be somethin' someone so clever can do for us in return for our silence."

"Name it!" Rasher said.

"Tell us about Mr. Morgan's sexual life," John invited.

Randolph had caught himself on a wild rosebush whose tendrils had crept into the roadway. He yanked his leg and succeeded only in snagging his trousers. He bent and tugged at the vine. His hand came up sharply. "Damn it!" he yelped, flexing his fingers. He pulled his leg again, and this time he came free. The other two men had continued without pause. "Can you stop walking for a moment, or must you make that call to Brunswick?"

John looked at his chief deputy. "I think we can let the woman go . . . as long as Mr. Rasher remains on the island." Warfield nodded. The two came to a halt, close to where Shell Road ended on the club grounds.

Rasher stopped as well, puffing from the exertion of defending himself, from his forced march, and from the terrifying threat of exposure.

"Ever since he built his first yacht, he's used them for entertaining single women. At times he's sequestered mistresses on board. Three, to my knowledge. Mr. Morgan favors physicians as friends, and—"

"Just like Pulitzer!" John exclaimed to his deputy. "It's amazin' how alike they are, considerin' how they hate each other."

"Opposites attract and similars repel," Warfield replied.

"Sorry to interrupt, Mr. Rasher," Le Brun apologized. "Please go on."

Rasher had used the hiatus to suck the blood from his injured finger. He withdrew it and clenched his hand into a fist. "When he's done with each mistress, he gives her a one-hundred-thousand-dollar dowry and then matches her to a young doctor acquaintance. In many ways, he's as obsessive to patterns of behavior as Mr. Springer was."

"And this is the same man who led the campaign to have Lorillard and Vanderbilt thrown out of this club for what happened on *their* yachts," John remarked.

"But he would never bring his mistresses down to Jekyl Island," Rasher said. "That makes his hypocrisy all right."

"What else?" John asked. "There's got to be more."

The junior banking partner looked as if he was swallowing glass. "If there is, I don't know of it." He shrugged. "Of course there are the occasional flower girls. But that's nothing unusual."

Warfield nodded his understanding.

John looked at his deputy. "What's he talkin' about?"

Warfield rocked back on his heels. "Oh, very common down on Wall Street. These pretty street women, usually still in their teens, go from office to office, ostensibly selling paper flowers. They're allowed in to see the big bosses; the doors are closed; they get under the desks for a while; they receive a few dollars; they often leave with all their flowers."

"Except the one they'd already lost," Randy said. He forced a smile and attempted to show by appearance as well as witticism that he was again composed and in control. But then he licked his dry lips. "Look, Mr. Morgan's sex life has nothing to do with this case," he argued. "Furthermore, none of it can be proven by you, so you can't hold it over his head, even if you were insane enough to try. My sex life has nothing to do with it either."

"I know that," John assured him. "I was just testin' to see if you'd be willin' to tell us somethin' private. Now, here's my real question: What does Mr. Morgan know about the circumstances of this killin'?"

"Absolutely nothing," Rasher vowed. "He's as mystified by it as everyone else. All he's concerned about. . . ." He snapped his fingers. "I *can* tell you something of interest!"

"The president and vice president are visitin' tomorrow," Sheriff Le Brun said, having followed Rasher's line of thinking. Before the crestfallen junior partner could regroup, he said, "We have you by the testicles, Mr. Rasher. You have confirmed just how firmly we do. Rest assured that we will require any number of favors, at virtually any hour. Some may be difficult." He gave Warfield a collegial pat on the shoulder and encouraged him to start off again toward the clubhouse.

Randolph Rasher was left speechless at the verge of the road.

John turned briefly. "And, naturally, you will not leave this island without my permission, or I *will* see that you do face economic death. Good mornin' *again,* sir."

A S SOON AS they were out of Rasher's earshot, Warfield asked, "If you were so sure going out that he and Chrystie Springer had nothing to do with the murder, why did you let me act as if you thought they did?"

John reached up to his shoulder and began massaging it. "Oh, there was the slight chance they may have been behind it, just as you described. Smart people have done stupider things than that, especially over great passion. If your old nemesis Randy had sweated just a bit more, I'd have had Mrs. Springer delivered right back here. I also wanted to see your examination skills," John revealed. "Not shabby. They taught you somethin' in law school."

"Thank you. . . . I think."

"You're welcome. I figured Rasher wouldn't trust an accomplice."

"Even Mrs. Springer?"

"She couldn't have returned to the clubhouse in time. She told me that she knew about the several paths her husband took. That would also have dissuaded the two of them. I believe Mr. Rasher has told us the whole truth about his relationship with the woman. It fits such a man's mode of behavior. There was no great passion cloudin' his mind; the only one he's hopelessly in love with is himself. But that's why he'll do almost anything we need him to do . . . provided he believes he won't be caught for it. It's good to have a spy in the enemy camp." The sheriff regarded his deputy full on. "That's why I'm sure your father lectured you to cozy up to me, and why I'm equally sure you'll get an offer of a job up North."

"I'm not interested in betraying you, Mr. Le Brun," Warfield said.

"In that case, start callin' me John."

L IKE A DESERT that lies bleak and barren for months on end but bursts with color a week after a heavy rain, the Jekyl Island Club had miraculously transformed itself. When John and the party of investigators had left to look at Ezekiel Turner's evidence, the members and guests had been hanging around the clubhouse like ghosts haunting a mansion. When Sheriff Le Brun and Deputy Tidewell returned from the beach, the vacationers were engaged in a frenzy of activities. Four bicyclers scorched past. One rider sang at the top of his voice. On the lush lawn before the clubhouse, nubile men and women played a spirited game of croquet, under the matchmaking gazes of lynx-eyed matriarchs. The doyennes and dowagers were ensconced in white wicker furniture, which was in turn placed upon white sheets to prevent the grass from staining the hems of their dresses. They were also well shaded by white and pastel parasols against the rays of a sun just past its zenith. Above on the piazza men smoked furiously and talked at each other with vehemence. Staff members wove in and out among them, festooning the balustrades with red, white, and blue bunting. Tiny American flags had been produced from some patriotic chest and were being secured in semicircles around the piazza posts.

"I see that Mr. Springer's death has been declared a poacher accident," John told Warfield, nodding at the goings-on. "Immediately afterward, the news of President McKinley's visit was announced. I wish that the evidence we were subjected to was as genuine."

"What do we do now?" Warfield asked.

"You catch yourself some lunch. I'll be along presently."

The deputy stroked back his hair, then gave his boss a nod and a smile. He loped away with youthful enthusiasm. John squinted in the direction of the dock, where Superintendent Grob was directing the decorating process. He ambled down the hill and onto the long, white, roof-covered pier.

"Who left on the mornin' run, Mr. Grob?" John asked, his hands clasped casually behind his back, so that his revolver peeked out from under his jacket.

Grob was silent for a moment, mastering his dislike for the sheriff. "Mrs. Papin, Mr. Porter and family, James Lovell, and Mrs. Springer."

"And who is scheduled to leave on the afternoon run?"

"Only Judge Tidewell."

John nodded ponderously. "If that should change, be sure to find me before the steamer leaves."

"I thought your investigation was ended," Grob said.

"Where may I find Mr. Reed?"

"I have no idea of his whereabouts at the moment. He's staying with Mr. John Moore, over in Sans Souci. I said: I thought your investigation was ended," he repeated with an edge in his voice.

"I am here until President McKinley leaves or until Mr. Springer's murderer is found. Get used to the idea," Mr. Le Brun said. He kept his gaze leveled on the club official until Grob looked away. Having won both the verbal and staring matches, John turned and retraced his steps.

When John visited Sans Souci, he was told that Speaker of the House Reed was not there and his whereabouts were not known. Nor was he to be found in the clubhouse. When Le Brun passed by the dining room, he saw his deputy seated at a table squarely in the middle of the room, in animated conversation with his father and club president Lanier. In Warfield's hand lay a piece of stationery, folded precisely as the one with the warning that John had given him on the way to the beach. John moved quickly past the entrance to the servants' dining area, where he ate a light meal in silence, the staff eyeing him as if he were the Grim Reaper.

John reemerged into the lobby just as the Tidewell men were exiting the dining room.

"We were expecting you for lunch, Sheriff," Judge Tidewell said.

"Sorry," John apologized. "Other matters demanded my attention. I need to borrow my deputy, if that's all right."

"Certainly."

John walked along the hallway and down the back stairs, compelling Warfield to follow. "Where's your weapon?" John asked, stopping and pivoting next to the gate where the laundry was hung.

"My revolver? Right here." The deputy reached under his jacket, to the small of his back. Using both hands and by considerable contortions, he produced his revolver six seconds later and handed it over. It was a Young America double-action, .32-caliber, five-shot revolver with a two-inch barrel.

"What did you pay for this?"

"A dollar fifteen."

"More than it's worth. You'd be dead in a fight three times over keepin' it back there," John admonished. "Where's the revolver you were issued?"

"In the office. Its barrel is too long. It keeps poking against my chair when I sit down. This one works fine," Warfield defended. "I've had it since college."

"It was fine for college. It's not accurate more than twenty feet, and you need to have that extra chamber. Get yourself a shoulder holster and carry your Hopkins and Allen like you're supposed to. On duty is not the place to be concerned about looks or comfort," Le Brun lectured. "You could look pretty ugly in the casket with a bullet hole between your eyes. I'll trade you," he said, handing back the gun. "This toy for the letter I gave you on Shell Road."

Tidewell handed back the piece of stationery with no expression.

John started walking south. "We're goin' to visit Mr. Pulitzer now, and he won't give a hoot about your looks."

G. W. HOSMER WAS occupied elsewhere when Le Brun and Tidewell arrived at Pulitzer's cottage, saving them immeasurable time. They were ushered upstairs by the lugubrious-looking Mr. Pollard. Another secretary was reading from a book with a tired-sounding throat. When Pollard announced the two lawmen, Pulitzer welcomed them in a voice that approached song.

"Isn't this the most amazing day?" Pulitzer asked. "Come in, come in! You're dismissed, Ireland!" Both secretaries disappeared downstairs with speed. *"Precaution,"* Pulitzer said, of the book. "Fenimore Cooper's first novel. How any publishing house picked him up after that came out is beyond me. I'm grateful you rescued me. It's like arsenic—if I don't ingest it in small doses it'll surely slay me. By the way, you win the bet, Sheriff!"

"How's that, sir?"

"Only three of the four men who landed today are members: Eames, Claflin, and Fabyan," Pulitzer announced. "The other one is James B. Sage. Do you know him?"

"Can't say as I do," the sheriff admitted.

"I do," the deputy said. "He's a corporate lawyer from New Jersey."

"Good for you, Mr. Tidewell. Ireland!" Mr. Pulitzer bellowed, making a mercurial vocal change. "Lemonade! And see what kind of baked goods they have at the clubhouse!" There was no reply, but a few moments later the front door slammed.

"Yes, indeed. Sage is *the* corporate lawyer from New Jersey," Pulitzer continued. "Do you know what's brown and black and looks good on a lawyer, gentlemen? A Doberman pinscher." He laughed at his own joke. "How old are you, Mr. Tidewell?"

"Twenty-six, sir," Warfield answered.

"Then you're too young to remember the time before the trusts . . . oil, sugar, leather, tobacco, harvester, and so forth. Individual companies combined, both for economies of scale and to crush all other competitors. Soulless, rapacious things they are, and the government rightly stepped in to limit them. But then along came Mr. Sage. He hit upon the idea of perverting the Fourteenth Amendment. Do you know what the Fourteenth Amendment says, Mr. Tidewell?"

"Yes, sir. No state may deny any person life, liberty, or property without due process of law."

"Lord, the lawmen in these parts are uncommonly educated!" Pulitzer exclaimed. "They also all have uncommonly dulcet voices. James Sage got the diabolical idea that a corporation should be considered a 'person' under the law as well. His state's politicians were eager to embrace the idea, passing the New Jersey Holding Company Act. That's why Standard Oil and so many other companies are incorporated there; they can hold large blocks of other company stock and create monopolies with impunity. Sage has been a creator of their legal evasions ever since. He must be down here to help Morgan see just how far McKinley can be pushed. This becomes more interesting by the minute."

"I believe you should know that Mr. Tidewell has a background in corporate law," Sheriff Le Brun dared.

Pulitzer reddened. "You should have said so five minutes ago, instead of letting me rattle on. What sort of background?"

"Rittenhouse and Rogers," Warfield said.

"A Philadelphia lawyer no less! They serve Drexel and Company, I believe. You must be quite enamored of Mr. Morgan and his group."

"They are impressive," Warfield granted.

Pulitzer bristled visibly. The corners of his mouth were downturned as he opened it to reply.

"You promised you'd tell me how you'd have killed Mr. Springer," John prompted, to deflect the newsman's ire.

"Right. Well, I couldn't have. Not without help. And I don't mean because I'm blind and haven't fired a rifle in twenty years, either. Even with a sound body, I'd need an accomplice."

"I strongly agree," Sheriff Le Brun said.

"But it couldn't be servants or island staff. By definition, there are no absolutely trustworthy servants."

"That brings me to the point of this visit," John said. "If I could find the proper motive, I'd be more than halfway home. Eliminatin' the staff and servants and all those who have a sound alibi leaves Mr. Randolph Rasher and Dr. Thomas Russell."

"Morgan's partner I could believe," said Pulitzer. "Dr. Russell would be a shock."

"Would you please jot down a telegram asking for complete investigations of these men by the staff, particularly concerning any affiliation with Erastus Springer?"

"Yes. Of course." Pulitzer gestured to a writing desk tucked into a corner of the room. "There's paper and pen over there. Take down what I say." John hurried to the task. He ignored Warfield's perplexed expressions as he copied what seemed simultaneously to be English and a foreign language. "Now bring it over to me, and I'll sign it and write the account number." When Pulitzer had scribbled his signature, he gestured to the coffee table, which was strewn with a different jumble of edible detritus. "I have six or seven telegrams of my own there. Would you carry them down to Captain Clark for me?"

"Certainly." John collected the telegrams.

"Now tell me all about the tromping through the wilderness to view newfound evidence," Pulitzer bid.

The sheriff reported Turner's tour and performance with detached objectivity. Even when Pulitzer laughed, he maintained his neutrality in delivering the events. Finally, John told him how he had negotiated his continued stay in return for allowing the club to declare the murder an accident perpetrated by an outsider.

"I congratulate you on your good nature in the face of such an effrontery," Pulitzer said.

"Let me appeal to *your* good nature, Mr. Pulitzer," John said. "Did you know yesterday that Mr. Morgan was arranging for evidence to be planted?"

Pulitzer pulled himself erect. Every muscle in his face seemed to stiffen. Then, with effort, he swallowed his anger and said, "Why would you ask such a question?"

"Simply because yesterday you encouraged me to resolve Springer's death as soon as possible and then come and read to you. It was as if you expected resolution by midday."

All anger dissolved in Pulitzer's aspect. "I see. Perfectly understandable. No. That was purely coincidence. If I had learned of this stupidity, I would have warned you. I was truly hoping for early resolution ... on behalf of the club. I was also truly hoping to have you read to me with your mellifluous voice. Now that I hear Mr. Tidewell speak, I would hope the same of him. You are the judge's son, are you not?"

"I am," Warfield affirmed.

"I won't hold that against you . . . if you promise to read to me sometime today."

"I would be honored, sir!" Warfield effused.

"Capital!" Pulitzer's sudden swing of emotion drew him up from the couch. He moved toward the afternoon sun that streamed in through the French doors as a thirsty man to water. When he sensed the jamb, he stretched out his arms and ran his fingertips against the enameled wood. "However, Mr. Tidewell, if you are to do me the favor of reading to me, I must first do you the favor of disabusing your foolish admiration for John Pierpont Morgan." He pivoted 180 degrees, facing into the room, pressing his hands fully against the jambs like Samson preparing to bring down the temple. "He now stands as such a colossus that it's difficult to see his feet of clay. Would you allow me to tell you about this colossus when he was still a mortal . . . both before you were born and when you were still in knickers?"

"Certainly, sir," Warfield said. "I can think of no one more qualified."

Pulitzer beamed. "Let us go back to 1861, at the very outset of our nation's great Civil War. Mr. Morgan involved himself in what became known as the Hall Carbine Affair. The chief of ordnance in Washington had sold six thousand out-of-date carbines to a gun dealer at three-fifty each. After the debacle at Bull Run, it became clear that the Union Army would need to be vastly increased. With small improvement, these same rifles could become minimally serviceable. Due to desperate demand, the dealer was able to command twenty-two dollars per refurbished weapon. Jupiter was the one who supplied the dealer the twenty thousand dollars for the refurbishing, squeezing a sixty-five-hundred-dollar profit for his six-week loan. Worst of all, he forced the dealer to hold up delivery until the government had paid in full, causing uncountable deaths by allowing the Confederacy more days to fortify itself. At the time, he was two years younger than you."

Pulitzer looked over his shoulder. He cocked his head and listened. "Ireland!" he shouted. He got no reply. "If that slug isn't back with baked goods in the next five minutes, I'll have him boiled in oil." He faced the room again, instantly composed.

"Second, in July of 1863, immediately after thousands of brave young men had spilled their lifeblood in the fields of Gettysburg, J. P. Morgan was contacted to serve his nation as a 'draftee held to personal service.' You wouldn't believe it now to look at him, but as a youth he was sickly.

However, by his twenty-sixth year he had become a strapping specimen. Nevertheless, he paid a sum of three hundred dollars—less than he paid a few years later for a prize Guernsey cow—for a 'commutation.' Do you know the term, Mr. Tidewell?"

"I would guess that it relieved him from service."

"True . . . provided another man was willing to serve in his stead. And given all the poor arriving to these shores, he had no difficulty finding his replacement. This two-legged beast who had already earned tens of thousands from the bounty of his motherland hired a substitute to preserve it!"

Pulitzer inched his way forward until he found his couch. He threw himself onto it. "I, a foreigner to these shores, volunteered to serve in the army of my adopted land as soon as I arrived. Not for some wealthy man's money, either. But I effectively replaced Morgan, did I not?" He drew himself erect with pride.

"You did," John chorused, happy to stoke Pulitzer's fire.

"Now, I won't mislead you into believing that this commutation was a scheme used by Morgan alone," Pulitzer told the young deputy. "It was a common practice for the rich. Others who joined Morgan in infamy were Jay Gould, John Rockefeller, William H. Vanderbilt, Andrew Carnegie, and Philip Armour. How much have these scoundrels profited since then by the saving of the Union? I tell you, Mr. Lincoln turns in his grave. He died to free the slaves, and now this jackass McKinley allows the likes of J. P. Morgan to enslave black *and* white Americans."

Ireland entered surreptitiously and placed a tray of tarts on the coffee table. Behind him came another secretary, bearing a tea service.

"About time," Pulitzer fumed, sniffing the air. "Turn on the lights, so we can see what we're eating."

John and Warfield declined the fare, using lunch as the reason.

"We must be leavin' soon, in order not to miss the *Howland*'s afternoon run," John reminded Pulitzer.

"True, true! But allow me one more edifying example concerning that great, misshapen mass of ego. Sheriff Le Brun, you surely recall our discussion about *El Corsario Supremo* and his succession of pirate ships. He considers himself even less beholden to the laws of the land—if that's possible—when he's on board his yachts. In 1885, the Pennsylvania Railroad was trying to muscle in on the New York Central's main territory by buying the defunct West Shore Railroad. The New York Central retaliated by beginning the South Pennsylvania Railroad. Mr. Morgan stood to lose much of his English investors' money in the New York Central, and his partners the Drexels had the same situation with the South Pennsylvania. Morgan was having no luck bringing the two sides to the table. So he invited George Roberts and Frank Thompson, the Pennsylvania's president and vice president, up from Philadelphia to steam around on his yacht. They didn't know until after the *Corsair* had left the dock that Chauncey Depew, the president of the NYC, was on board. They steamed all day—to West Point, down to Sandy Hook, and all around New York harbor—until the men agreed to a settlement. Morgan would not have let them off the yacht if they hadn't."

"But wasn't that a good thing?" Warfield asked.

"Good for whom?" Pulitzer countered. "The previous year, a passenger ticket from Philadelphia or New York City to Chicago cost an average of seven dollars. After the settlement, the price rose to an average of twenty. In the following years, I know of no fewer than five other times he used the same strategy. He'll use it again with McKinley, except that he'll use an island instead of a yacht."

"I understand that he uses his yachts to stash his mistresses," John remarked.

"Absolutely. And he doesn't drop his trousers until he's two miles offshore. That's when he considers he's king of the high seas. He'll never bring a mistress down here because his yacht anchors in St. Simon's Sound, and he's afraid someone might get close enough to take a picture. In the old days, the king relied on a castle. But Morgan relies on his yachts as fortresses. He keeps his most valuable documents on board, because some powerful enemy might just pay a judge to issue a search warrant for his Wall Street offices. His yacht can be away from the pier minutes after being warned."

"Do you really consider Mr. Morgan might be behind this murder?" Warfield asked.

"No, indeed!" Pulitzer trumpeted. "Your boss here is playing with the notion, but it's ridiculous. Why would he jeopardize the president canceling his visit after all his hard scheming to get McKinley and Reed down here at the same time?"

"Unless Springer threatened Morgan somehow *after* the invitation had been accepted and couldn't be canceled," Sheriff Le Brun said.

"With all respect, sir, that's asinine," Pulitzer affirmed.

Le Brun got up from his chair. "Then perhaps it was Mr. Morgan's junior partner, acting on his boss's behalf . . . like the knights murdering Thomas à Becket."

"Good allusion; bad logic," Pulitzer said. "I'm betting Dr. Russell is a dead end also."

"Talk about a hypocritical Hippocratic oath," quipped Warfield.

"What was that? I don't understand your reference," Pulitzer said.

"Youthful exuberance," John said. "It's past time to go. I'll deliver these telegrams right now."

"Excellent! And when will you return to read to me, Mr. Tidewell?"

Warfield looked at the sheriff for the answer.

"How about right now?" John suggested.

"Capital! You have your choice between that dreadfully boring gazette, *The Herald,* and James Fenimore Cooper's excrement on paper, *Precaution.*"

Warfield Tidewell did not look as enthusiastic about the proposition as when he had first arrived.

D ON'T YOU WORRY about anythin', Iley," Sheriff Le Brun called out to the judge as the *Howland* pulled away from the club dock. He had delivered directly to Captain Clark and in full view of the judge the telegrams in a large sealed envelope, as well as another note he had scribbled on a scrap of paper. The departing boat did indeed, as Mr. Grob had guaranteed, hold no other passenger. He had been assured that no one but staff had debarked when the craft arrived. All those who had been invited by the Friday telegrams had apparently arrived, and those already on the island were not about to miss the opportunity to meet the political leaders of the nation.

In answer to the sheriff's call, Judge Tidewell waggled his forefinger in warning. John smiled. As soon as the steamer was out of view, he went directly to the guards' barracks and inquired of the officer where he might find Ezekiel Turner.

"Since he was on duty this mornin'," the man said, "he ain't due back until the midnight shift."

"Doesn't he sleep here?" John asked.

"Sometimes yes; sometimes no," the officer answered. "The men often go off alone to distant parts of the island. They've made their own private camps, away from the paths."

"And all the club rules," John commented.

The officer winked. "You said it, Sheriff, not me."

"And where is Mr. Turner's hideout?"

"Can't say."

"Can't or won't?"

"Can't say," the man repeated. He was not familiar to Le Brun from Brunswick or the near environs, so the sheriff elected not to threaten him with his power.

"The minute you or any of your men see him, have him report to the clubhouse. I want a word with him."

"Will do," the man assured.

Le Brun made the same futile inquiry of several grounds overseers and left the same request. Muttering his annoyance, he returned to the clubhouse. There, no one had any better idea where either Turner or Thomas Reed could be found. He inquired if any more messages had been left for him. None had. He walked into the library and scanned its holdings. He noted that books written by women were kept separate from those written by men. He scanned a recently published volume concerning the jockeying of the major powers for presence and influence in China. He consulted his watch. He returned to the lobby and wrote out two notes, inviting Dr. Hosmer and Dr. Russell to dinner at seven-thirty, then gave them to the desk clerk for delivery. He checked with Mr. Grob that all rifles and shotguns were accounted for and received no resistance. He read all the rules on the lobby and hallway walls. He consulted his watch again. Holding to his promise of keeping a low profile was going to be more difficult than he had anticipated. As soon as he received acceptances to both his dinner invitations, he retreated to his bedroom and lay down until the appointed hour.

T HE MAIN CLUBHOUSE DINING ROOM was more crowded than John had yet seen it. It was as if all the blessed on the island wanted to have dinner over with as soon as possible, to be in bed and asleep early, to wake up refreshed for the president's visit. The energy level of the conversations at each table was markedly heightened over that of the previous evening. Le Brun had changed to the midnight-blue double-breasted wool suit he wore to court trials. He had left his revolver in his bedroom.

The pair of physicians were already at the customary table in the far corner. With them sat Warfield Tidewell.

"I found him, rather hoarse-voiced, with Mr. Pulitzer," Hosmer announced, "and thought I'd rescue him."

The deputy had a rueful, weary look about him.

"Sit, Sheriff!" Hosmer bade. "Dr. Russell and I just realized we could cement each other's alibis. I remembered that when I went over to the clubhouse yesterday morning I had seen the Negro driver's wagon parked behind the infirmary. Just as I had seen it around that time over the past week or so. So routine that both Dr. Russell and I forgot about it."

"The patient is Mr. Cain," Russell supplied. "He has terrible rheumatism and visits me in the morning for treatment."

"Ergo," Hosmer went on, "Dr. Russell had to have been in the infirmary. And I had to be going to the clubhouse."

"When was this?" John asked.

"I think a minute or two after eight," Hosmer answered, shrugging. "Could be off by five minutes either side."

John took out the notebook he and his deputy shared and jotted a few words in it. "Who supervises Mr. Cain?"

"I don't know that anyone does from hour to hour," Russell answered. "He's been here for the life of the club. He performs his routine perfectly, as far as I've observed."

"What are you using on the man?" Hosmer asked his fellow physician.

"A new drug, just sent to the school by a Professor Dreser. It's acetylsalicylic acid. I'll send you over some to analyze. It's truly a wonder drug for curing pain and shrinking swelling caused by inflammation. Mr. Cain's much improved, but of late he's complained about a ringing in the ears. I'm cutting his dosage back."

John exchanged glances with his deputy, who declined to make comment. The four men ordered and verbally braced themselves for a two-hour satiation of the senses.

After the appetizers were cleared, Le Brun said, "Mr. Morgan tells me that Mr. Pulitzer tried to buy this island when he knew members of the Union Club wanted it."

"That's true," Hosmer granted. "He adores the place."

"Had he seen it before making the offer?" John asked.

"No. He had only gotten wind of the excellent reports."

Warfield grinned. "Perhaps he's arranged the murder with his Byzantine mind. The scandal would ruin the club; everyone would relinquish their memberships; he could finally have it all to himself."

Hosmer picked at a water stain on one of the plates. "You misunderstand him completely. If the other members abandoned the island, so would he."

"I was only joking," Warfield defended. "My humor also failed with Mr. Pulitzer."

"Don't take that personally," Hosmer counseled. "He loves his own humor—particularly the sarcastic type—but rarely catches that of others."

"Why would he abandon the island if the others did?" asked Le Brun.

Pulitzer's talkative factotum was uncharacteristically quiet. He continued to rub the stain. Presently, he said, "It cuts right to Mr. Pulitzer's essence. He's a wonderful humanitarian. No other newspaperman in the country has worked so tirelessly for the public good. All the way back in Kansas, when he was still a young man, he took on the local gas company, the lottery racket, the horse-car monopoly. He's campaigned to tax luxuries, inheritances, and large incomes. He's exposed the need to reform civil service. He did this for selfless reasons, but it was also the means he hit upon to become successful. Indefatigable drive is similar in all the Jekyl Island Club members; he merely found a more acceptable means to achieve his goals. But by the very acts of defending and informing the common man, he's made himself rich. Ridiculously rich. Unfortunately, the only people who understand the rich are other rich. Others are too busy being jealous. He loathes many of the men in this club and yet he feels drawn to them. He desires the same things they possess. He enjoys their intellect. On his terms, naturally. He wouldn't really want to be here alone."

"What confounds me is why the founding group allowed him membership," said Warfield. "They'd never let him into the Union Club or Manhattan Club, since he's half Jewish."

"Absolutely true," Hosmer said. "His mother was Catholic and his father was Jewish. I hear they call him Jewseph Pulitzer behind his back."

John folded his arms across his chest. "These men would sooner allow a Moslem into their clubs than a Jew."

"I believe it's to muzzle the snarling dog," Dr. Russell opined. "They finally found something they control that he desperately wanted. They let him have his share—"

"*Two* shares," Hosmer corrected.

"Even better. Two shares. And now if he attacks them with his old fury, they can revoke his membership."

John remembered Morgan's words about keeping an enemy close but declined to share them. He asked Hosmer, "Could such a man be black-mailed that way?"

Hosmer set down the plate. "No. If the issue were important enough, Andes would risk his shares. He supported the Sherman Antitrust Act against J. D. Rockefeller and might have lost his membership over that."

"But has he ever taken on Morgan with that energy?" John asked.

"He would," the physician/friend said. His voice was firm, but his look was not as resolute.

D ID YOU BELIEVE DR. HOSMER when he said Pulitzer would risk losing his membership by taking Morgan on full force?" John asked Warfield, after they had parted company with the doctors and were taking a night stroll down the driveway in front of the clubhouse.

"I wasn't sure," Warfield answered.

"Neither was I," said John. "Which makes me wonder if Mr. Pulitzer would truly pursue this murder if he believed Morgan was somehow in-volved with it."

"Are you saying he's giving us a more subtle version of Mr. Turner's planted evidence?"

"Perhaps." John produced the cigar he had been offered in J. P. Mor-gan's apartment and stuck it into his mouth. "You remind me that Mr. Turner has yet to report to us." He looked back at the veranda, where the Negro workers were carrying in the wicker furniture, storing it from the night dampness. A few of the younger people were engaged in a game of dumb crambo around one of the swings, laughing good-naturedly at their feeble guesses.

"Do you want me to seek him out?" Warfield asked.

John lit the cigar. "No. He has the midnight shift. Let's both be sure to rise early and catch him as he returns to the stable."

Warfield yawned. "Good enough. I'm tuckered out. Mr. Pulitzer alone exhausted me. He has the secretaries cross out the long descriptive pas-sages in novels, but the man still gets impatient and keeps saying, 'Skip ahead, skip ahead!' "

John laughed. "Better you than me. Any closing remarks ... as they say in court?"

"I thought it was curious that both doctors failed to mention their common alibi yesterday," Warfield said. "I wonder if they're somehow in cahoots."

"Considerin' their Hippocratic Oath, that would be a startlin' pair o' docs," John said. The smoke pouring out with his words partially hid the twinkle in his eyes.

"Mr. Pulitzer wouldn't have gotten that one, either," Warfield said. "Other than that observation, I'm at a loss. However, I'm sure you're not saying everything you're thinking."

"Come now, Deputy," John replied. "I thought we had agreed not to hold things back from each other."

Tidewell smirked at his boss. "Trust is a fragile tower, built stone by stone."

"And who are you quotin' now?" John inquired.

"Myself."

"I am impressed."

"Likewise, Sheriff Le Brun." Warfield made a small bow. "If there's nothing else pressing, I'd like your permission to retire for the night."

"You have it." John waggled the cigar in a shooing motion. "You get a good night's sleep, so that I may get a good day's work from you."

Warfield turned.

"Oh!" John exclaimed. "I wrote a note for Bobby Lee to bring your issued revolver to you. With the president comin', we must be alert and prepared."

Warfield nodded, then hastened toward the clubhouse.

John Le Brun stood for several minutes, puffing on the cigar, watching the play of moonlight upon the Jekyl River, listening to the call of a lonely water bird. He kept his back resolutely to the clubhouse and all the other elements of the Jekyl Island Club Village. His hand stole unconsciously to his shoulder as he thought. When the cigar was about halfway smoked, he suddenly plucked it from his mouth and ground it into the earth until it was hardly more than dust. Then he kicked the dust and strode toward the clubhouse.

MONDAY

MARCH 20, 1899

JOHN LE BRUN WOKE, saw where he was, and swore softly. He had been dreaming of his wife, wearing a yellow dress with blue ribbons. The problem was more than meeting Chrystie Springer in her dress; it was returning to the island. He remained in bed for a minute, stretching until his joints broke free of the rust of slumber. Then he shaved, sponge washed, climbed into his good suit, strapped on his holster, put on his derby, and went down the back stairs and over to the guards' barracks.

The same laconic officer sat behind the desk just inside the front door, scratching out a report with an old-fashioned nib pen and inkwell.

" 'Mornin'," John greeted.

" 'Mornin'. I was expectin' you."

The man reached across to the left side of the desk for a rubber stamp.

It was then that John noticed for the first time the raggedly healed dimple just under the angle of the man's jaw. From the sag of the skin on his neck and the depth of his wrinkles, John judged the man as a little older than himself.

"Ezekiel Turner never showed last night?"

"That's right." The officer thumped the paper with the stamp, stood up with it, and crossed to the duty board. He moved with a rolling gait, like a sailor on a pitching ship's deck. When the man cleared the line of the desk, John saw that his right leg was locked from the knee down. He also saw the brace mechanism attached to his boot.

"Canister explosion?" John guessed.

The man pinned the report to the board. "Yep. February of '65. Petersburg trenches." He regarded John over his left shoulder.

"Who'd you serve under?" John asked.

"Who *didn't* I serve under?" the man shot back. "Our officers were killed about every six weeks. Last one was Colonel James P. Simms."

"Fifty-third Georgia, then."

"Yep."

"I wasn't far behind you," John said, patting his right shoulder. "March 25, took a minié ball through here retreatin' from Battery Ten. Captain Joseph P. Carson's sharpshooters, Fourth Georgia."

"So, you were in that hopeless dash on Fort Stedman," the man said, his countenance visibly softening. "One of 'Lee's Miserables.' "

"The same. The ball went clean through. I thought I was lucky. But it's pained me every year from October to April, ever since I came home."

The man held out his hand. "Preston Lefferts."

"John Le Brun."

"I believe Mr. Turner has departed this golden shore," Lefferts said.

"Any idea why, other than that he failed to report in for duty?"

"It's only my humble opinion, but I believe he was paid off for 'arrangin' ' the solution to Mr. Springer's death. He may have been ordered to get himself lost."

John sat on the corner of the desk. "When are your men paid?"

"First and sixteenth of the month, so he didn't lose much by skippin' out."

"And how often do they get leave?"

"Two days together, every two weeks."

"When was Turner's next leave supposed to be?"

"This weekend. Club's all but closed down after that. There will be only four of us guardin' the place until next Thanksgiving."

"Could Turner have signed out one of the naphtha launches on his own?"

"No," the captain of guards replied. "Not him nor any other staff except those specifically charged with their running. Mr. Grob tries like the dickens not to let even the *members* run them around." Lefferts opened his desk drawer and pulled out two hand-rolled cigarettes. "Care for a smoke?"

"No, thanks," John declined. "So he's stuck on the island."

"Unless somebody picked him up."

John scratched the hair on his crown. "Yesterday you said you couldn't tell me where your men camp when they're not here. What about today?"

Lefferts smiled. "You know this island?"

"I do."

"That old tabby house on the north tip . . . the one that was abandoned and someone later set fire to. I hear they have a couple pup tents about a hundred yards east of there . . . and a big fire pit. Only use it after the tourists have retreated to the Village for the night, y'understand?"

"I never heard it from you," John said, rising.

"When Turner failed to show, I sent out a fella named Putnam. Him and Turner are pretty thick. Findin' Putnam may be the key to findin' Turner."

"Much obliged, Mr. Lefferts." John moved to the door.

"You know the worst part of that war?" Lefferts said. "The Yankees won, and they just keep winnin'."

COMING AROUND THE CORNER of the stable, John encountered his deputy. Warfield walked stiffly.

"Hey. Sleep the wrong way?" John asked.

"Something like that," Warfield replied. "You said to get up early. Here I am."

"Well, Turner never showed up for his patrol," John shared. "Let's get some horses and see if we can find him." He clapped his subordinate familiarly on the back, then drew in a deep breath. "What time did you retire?"

"Shortly after we parted company. Why?"

"I required a good night's sleep of you, for a good day's work, remember?"

Warfield smoothed down his moustache. "I do. I'm ready to go."

"Good. Then *you* make the more difficult ride north."

After ordering the hand on duty to ready two mares, John pulled one of the identical sets of rules from its frame on the stable door and drew on the back of it a sketch of the route his deputy was to take. It went east by Shell Road, then for three miles followed the uninterrupted beach north toward the wide curve of land that formed the southern lip of St. Simon's Sound. Jekyl Island was shaped like a gigantic left footprint. Where the fourth and fifth toes would have been was swampland, so that the River Road was compelled to run north, then northeast. From the northern tip of the island, the only way to elude the two lawmen would be via a maze of narrow bicycle paths.

John made a careful note of the tabby ruin that Preston Lefferts had cited. Around it, he sketched smaller landmarks, including a cross.

"We rendezvous at the tabby house," John said.

"Does this cross signify a cemetery or church?" Warfield asked.

"Cemetery." John handed him the map. "It's just below the tabby house. Saddle up. And make sure that pistol of yours is somewhere you can reach in a hurry; I'm sure Mr. Turner is in no mood to be caught."

John set off at a canter. As he rode from the Village, the signs of a special day were already apparent. The Negro landscaping crews were out mowing, trimming, and clipping with added energy. Maids were beating rugs. The wicker furniture was being removed from storage even before the dew was off the grass.

Once out of the Village, John encountered no one. He pushed the docile horse to a fast trot, through soft shadows yet untouched by direct sunlight. The air was heavy, with no breeze. It was as if the island was holding its breath in expectation of the president's visit. John dug his heels into his steed's flanks. It was a woman's horse, not used to being pressed, not used to being ridden alone, and not used to being ridden so early in the morning. John kept it at a canter until a wild orange tree in bloom appeared at the edge of the road. He reined in and brought the horse to a halt directly under the tree. With his pocket knife, he cut three petal-laden overhanging branches. He carefully stuck them under his belt, pocketed his knife, and continued on his way.

The abandoned house had originally been built using tabby, the local cement formula of lime, shells, and sand. Its thick walls had stood strong in spite of the fire that gutted its inner walls and roof. As John approached, he could see directly through the open doorway and windows to the woods beyond. He dropped the orange branches onto the ground in front of the structure and kept his horse moving up the road, then onto a path that ran southeastward. As he crossed a small wooden bridge which vaulted a lazy creek, he heard a faint whinnying close by. He dismounted, knotted his reins around a sapling, and continued down the path. Just around its next turn he found two quarter horses tied to a tree. Attached to their saddles were shotgun cases and binoculars, which identified the animals as belonging to island guards. Just beyond them, a weed-hidden path ran off northeastward, at right angles to the main path. John followed its gentle decline through a patch of tall undergrowth.

Where the path widened to a small clearing, a defiant-looking man in his late twenties, clean shaven and clothed but with a rumpled look about him, faced John. He balanced his shotgun casually over his right shoulder, with his index finger inside the trigger guard.

"You Mr. Putnam?" John asked.

"What's it to ya?"

"I'm Sheriff Le Brun, and I'm lookin' for Ezekiel Turner. I understand you are, too."

"Not anymore."

John set his hand on the butt of his revolver. "Why not?"

With a practiced motion, the guard swung the shotgun off his shoulder. The next instant it was cradled in his left hand, with the muzzles crossing the line of the sheriff's chest.

"Because he's left the island. You drove him off it," the guard accused.

John glanced to his left, where a thick oak stood as possible cover. He would have to throw himself through a mass of unfriendly-looking brambles to get there. Moreover, if the guard were as quick on the trigger as he was with his last maneuver, a load of buckshot would be screaming its way toward him long before he reached the tree. The distance between them might keep the blast from being lethal, but only if it failed to hit him squarely.

"How do you figure I did that?" John asked.

"By not acceptin' the evidence he found. By makin' it look like he had planted it. Which makes it look like he mighta been the murderer."

"This is what he told you?"

"That's right. What the hell are you pushin' so hard for? Nobody gives a damn if that man died. And you don't even belong here."

"You're wrong. Jekyl Island is part of my jurisdiction. I can show you on a map."

Putnam spat in Le Brun's direction. "What good is a map? Hell, a map of the world shows India as its own country, but it's owned by England. This island is owned by Yankees. A Yankee was killed. Why in hell don't you leave it their business?"

"Because it's my business," John said evenly.

"Some people might pay a lot of money if you just—"

The noise of disturbed vegetation to the guard's right caused him to face it. In that moment, Sheriff Le Brun had his revolver in his right hand and pointed at Putnam's chest. He thumbed back the hammer.

"Don't move!" John ordered. "Not a hair."

The guard obeyed. The undergrowth continued to vibrate.

"That you, Deputy?"

"Yes, sir. I found drag marks running into the marsh. Appears to be a . . ." Warfield emerged into the clearing from the guard's right side. He stopped, assessing the scene. ". . . a rowboat," he finished.

"Take out your weapon and relieve this character of his, Mr. Tide-well," John directed. "Now, you were sayin'," he said to Putnam, "that people would pay a lot of money if I what?"

"Just went away," the guard answered with a scowl.

"Or were you about to say 'disappeared'?"

Warfield yanked the shotgun away from Putnam with his left hand and, with his right, delivered a blow that raked his revolver across the man's face. "You threaten the law?" he yelled.

"That's enough, Mr. Tidewell!" John ordered.

"He put his hand on his gun," the guard asserted, of Le Brun. His jaw had begun to bleed, but he refused to explore it. "I was afraid he was gonna shoot me."

"And you were already holdin' your shotgun," John replied. "How do you know Mr. Turner left the island?"

"Like he said," Putnam answered, jerking his head at the deputy, "the boat's gone. We keep an old rowboat for our own use . . . fishin' and such. Zeke musta took it yesterday dusk. That's his horse tied up with mine."

John noted the embers of a small fire, glowing within a stone circle just in front of a grimy pup tent. "You didn't just get here," he said to the guard. "Which means that you've obstructed justice. Which means I could lock your sorry self up in my jail for several months, whether or not Mr. Turner had anythin' to do with the murder." He took several steps forward and held the guard's sullen eyes with his stare. "Now, bein' as you're so loyal to old Zeke, you no doubt know where he resides."

The guard considered his situation for a moment. He sighed. "On the road to Darien, about three miles north of Brunswick. Down the lane just past that barn that's half stone and half timber."

"I know the place. Keep the shells, Mr. Tidewell," John said, "then give the man back his weapon. The president of the United States is ar- rivin' today, and he has patrollin' to do."

While Warfield emptied the shotgun's barrels, Le Brun moved past the pup tent to a fallen wall, the bottom several courses of which still survived. Just past it lay a good-sized pit, filled with bones, flesh, and fur. Although it was liberally sprinkled with lime and lye, the putrefied odor and the maggots and flies resolutely avoiding the chemicals were enough to cause John to exhale violently and spin away.

"Game is all it is," Putnam defended. "Deer, rabbits, a few boar. Just enough to give us a good party now and then and feed a few hungry families on the mainland."

"A regular bunch of Robin Hoods," the sheriff commented to the dep- uty, as he crossed back over the wall. "Who guards the guards?"

"Should we turn him in for it?" Warfield asked.

"No. Let the Jekyl Island Club police its own. We have greater con- cerns." John shook his forefinger at Putnam. "Just remember that we own your ass, so don't give us any more trouble. Make sure that fire's com- pletely out, then get back to the Village!"

The guard swore beneath his breath and began kicking dirt onto the embers.

John led Warfield up the path to where the two horses were tied. Warfield collected spare shotgun shells from saddlebags on each horse and fitted the shotgun into its case.

"Turner may not be the brightest man, but he was smart enough not to tell the truth of what he'd done to his fellow guards," John noted to his deputy.

"He may have taken the boat because he trusted no one," Warfield said. He opened the saddle case on the second horse. "Shotgun's missing."

"That's good," said Le Brun. "We can pursue him for stealin' property. Collect your horse and come around the road to the tabby house." After the deputy had jogged off, stuffing shotgun shells into his pockets, John reclaimed his orange branches and walked down the road to the cemetery. He entered the small, walled-in plot, which contained headstones more than a hundred years old, and went directly to the most recent marker in the graveyard. He removed his derby and dropped to one knee. There he stayed, gazing at the grave for some minutes, heedless of the clip-clopping of the two horses as the guard passed. He muttered a prayer with his head bowed and made the sign of the cross on his chest. Then he lapsed in to a silent vigil.

Warfield came up the road on horseback, searched in vain around the tabby house for the sheriff, and spotted him in the distance. He dismounted and quietly entered the cemetery. When he came close, he saw that Le Brun was ripping off the tops of the tall grass blades over the grave, vainly trying to give it a cared-for look.

"I thought I asked you to meet me by the house," John said softly.

Warfield read the grave marker. It read

CLAIRE LE BRUN
BELOVED WIFE OF JOHN
MAY 12, 1852–AUGUST 19, 1883.

"None of the boys ever mentioned that you were married," Warfield said softly.

"I rarely speak of it," John said, taking the orange branches and arranging them in a fan pattern just below the marker. "It's too painful."

"I'm sorry. Even after all this time?" Warfield asked.

John stood and replaced his hat. "Yes. She died of one of those yellow fever epidemics that are never supposed to touch this island. She was pregnant at the time. My son would be havin' his fifteenth birthday right about now." He regarded Warfield with a pinched expression. His lips were pressed so tightly together that they almost disappeared from view.

"That's terrible," Warfield commiserated. "Is that why you didn't mind selling your part of the island?"

"Partly." He nodded at the burned-out hulk. "We used to live in that house. I got to spendin' too much time here. And then Esau, the fellow who owned the parcel just south of mine, came and asked me to sell. He was nearly blind. Couldn't farm anymore. Needed the cash so he could move over to Brunswick. Ironic thing was that he only lived another six months. He was a good neighbor while we lived here, so it was hard to say no. And then there was my second cousin, Eugene du Bignon, houndin' me. In the end, it turned out to be a blessin'. Made me get on with my life."

"Shall I leave you alone?" Warfield asked.

"No," John answered, slapping at his trouser knees. "We have a great deal to accomplish today. Let's get to it."

JOHN AND WARFIELD entered the clubhouse as the front desk's clock struck the quarter hour past nine. John directed his deputy to get them a table in the dining room while he took a piece of club stationery and jotted down several sentences about Ezekiel Turner's disappearance. He also asked that another person be investigated by Pulitzer's renowned staff. He sealed the paper inside an envelope and penned his signature across the flap, as a precaution against the resort's rife espionage. When he collared a minor staff member and directed him to carry the message directly to Joseph Pulitzer, the young man rolled his eyes and exited the front doors as if he were a condemned murderer leaving his cell for the last time.

Yet again, the law officers were ignored by the members and their guests in the dining room. This time, however, the lack of attention was due to the impending presidential visit. The ultrarich, so accustomed to being the center of attention themselves, were eager to assume the opposite role. They chattered with the intensity of small children, so that John and Warfield hardly had to strain to overhear their surmises about the visitors' agenda or their schemes at shouldering their way into a moment of national history. Doing his best to return the act of ignoring, John used the breakfast to instruct his protégé, by means of several personal recollections, in the art and science of police work.

At ten o'clock, Sheriff Le Brun took his deputy down to the club dock, where officers Bobby Lee Randolph, Harvey Buncombe, Redmond Drayton, and Burt Davenport sat playing penny poker, waiting for their superior to give them direction. They had come in the police launch, a tired, leaky steam vessel that the town had purchased from its third owner. They had towed along a smaller skiff that moved purely by wind and oar. They also brought the news that the president would be arriving after noon, on a navy revenue cutter. None of the men looked especially overjoyed at the prospect of extra duty necessitated by the president's visit. While John dispensed advice on controlling the inevitable party-crashers, the *Howland* came steaming down the Jekyl River.

No guests debarked from the *Howland*, but it rode low in the water from the extra provisions, which were portered ashore in a mild fever by half a dozen Negro workers. Friday Cain, his mule, and his wagon awaited the unloading process, as did another Negro driver, wagon, and mule. Charles Lanier and Ernest Grob had come down to the dock to

supervise. Lanier was issuing commands with the urgency of a battle-
field general when John interrupted to deliver the news of Turner's disappearance. The club president looked genuinely shocked. For a moment,
words failed him.

"All . . . right, all right," Lanier stammered. "Thank you for telling me,
Sheriff. How did . . . ?" He waved the half-posed question away with the
flick of his hand. "We'll have to attend to this later. No time now."

John and Warfield joined the poker game. When Warfield won too
many hands, he was made to "buy" the revolver he had been issued from
Bobby Lee. The lawmen's presence kept the vacationers at a distance, but
as the noon hour arrived, more and more of them appeared along the
river's edge. At last, one woman cried out, "They're coming! They're coming!"

A stream of genteel humanity surged across the club lawns to join
those by the river. Ignoring the rules about simple dress, the woman displayed elegant country frocks of dazzling white and alluring pastels, be-
jeweled and beribboned. The yards of expensive materials swirled and
swayed as the figures within glided at the maximum speed allowable for
their station. Matching parasols seemed to float like demi-balloons above
their heads. The men were dressed in golf attire and flannels and sported
jaunty skimmers, determined to remain the embodiment of the club's rai-
son d'être, even in the face of a presidential visit. The weather was clear,
bright, and warm, a perfect invitation.

One man using binoculars reported on the vessel that held the presidential party. The revenue cutter was named the *Colfax*. Long before the
president could have heard, the crowd began to applaud. More and more
spectators assembled, the presentable element of the staff standing in their
own little groups at a respectable distance from the members. In all, the
crowd totaled almost 150 onlookers, with most of the lesser dramatis per-
sonae gaily waving small American flags above their heads.

When John turned, he found himself standing next to the ferret-faced
James Sage, the man who had asked directions to the rest room the previous day. He looked considerably more composed.

"Great day, eh?" Sage said, peering over his pince-nez glasses when
his eye caught John's stare.

"Yes, beautiful," John said, although he was sure that the lawyer was
not thinking of the weather but rather the thumbscrews he and the members were about to apply to William McKinley's political fingers.

Coming up alongside John was Thomas Reed, flanked by his host,

Judge John Moore. The Speaker's carriage was proud, but his eyes could not conceal the ill ease he no doubt felt at being trapped into the unwanted situation. John looked around and spied Dr. G. W. Hosmer watching from the safe distance of a willow tree. Joseph Pulitzer was not present.

Following a faint grinding noise, the cutter stopped dead dramatically, several hundred yards from the dock. It had caught on a sandbar in the shallow river but swiftly reversed its engines and steamed back into the center of the channel. As it neared the dock, the captain sounded the ship's whistle. The crowd cheered. Mr. McKinley was pointed out by many. He stood on the upper deck, hand resting on the shoulder of his wife, who sat motionless in a deck chair. The president wore a black suit and formal top hat. He began waving slowly and mechanically and did not stop until the ship had docked.

Vice President and Mrs. Hobart debarked first, led by Cornelius Bliss. Thomas Hobart was also dressed in sedate black, wearing a tall silk hat. Behind them walked Senator Hanna, in casual brown, his soft jowls spread by an enormous but thin-lipped smile, cane in hand, large ears pushed out even farther by his bowler hat. John reflected that if he had seen the man walking alone on the streets of Brunswick, he would never have guessed from looking at the genial character that this was the ruthless businessman who had engineered McKinley's rise to the presidency by buying favors from influential politicians when he could and silencing staunch opponents by hiring prostitutes to seduce them and then black-mailing them with hard evidence.

At last the McKinleys appeared. John found the president amazingly short, even though he held himself erect and prouder even than Speaker Reed, thrusting out his barrel chest with unstudied presence. Part of his charisma also came from noble looks, John judged, rather like portrait reproductions of Napoleon. His large, seldom-blinking eyes made his countenance a mask, a genuine ecclesiastical face of the fifteenth century.

Ida McKinley held fast to her husband's left arm, as would a child in strange surroundings. She was not a handsome woman. She parted her curly hair straight down the middle of her head. Mannish eyes peered out of a square face. Though her one good feature, her full lips, were drawn into a smile, her eyes betrayed her uneasiness. While the president was cordial to all, his wife barely acknowledged each introduction. John watched peevish lines creep into the corner of her eyes as she watched the crowd re-form into a long greeting line.

President McKinley paused in front of one of the member's daughters.

He took her chin lightly in his hand. "What a healthy face you have!" he exclaimed. Mrs. McKinley tugged petulantly at his arm and fiercely twisted the material of his sleeve. The president hurried forward.

John smiled, seeing that the great political personages in front of him were fully as human as the Jekyl Island Club millionaires with whom he had been dancing.

As McKinley neared the towering figure of Thomas Reed, John noted that his easy smile tensed. The crowd became expectantly quiet, intent on hearing the exchange.

"How do you do, Mr. President?" Reed inquired, in a warm, loud voice.

"How do *you* do, Mr. Speaker?" McKinley returned. They shook hands in an exaggerated manner. Neither was willing to say more. McKinley moved on. After passing along the entire line, the presidential party climbed into a landau, trimmed for the occasion in red calico. It was led by a small Negro boy fitted out as a footman. John watched as the procession headed for one of the private cottages along the River Road.

While the crowd dispersed, John turned to Thomas Reed and introduced himself. The Speaker was as laconic with the sheriff as he had been with the president.

"I'd like to know if you had a conversation with Mr. Springer this past week, sir," John said.

"I was already interviewed by your assistant," Reed informed.

"I'm following up," John persisted.

"I did not."

"And when was it that you learned of the president's decision to visit Jekyl Island?"

John Moore stepped in front of his guest and glowered at the sheriff. "Since no one else on this island is willing to do it, allow me to put this to you bluntly, Sheriff: Your investigation is closed. We endured an accident here. It is over and resolved. The president would not have visited if it weren't. Is that perfectly clear?"

"Like glass."

Judge Moore drew his guest away, throwing a threatening glance over his shoulder at John for good measure. The sheriff surveyed the spectators who were still near the dock. Dr. Hosmer was hurrying back to the Pulitzer cottage. Dr. Thomas Russell had positioned himself almost directly across from John. He had been hidden by a tightly packed throng, so that John had failed to notice him until this moment. John ambled toward him.

"Was he what you expected?" Le Brun asked the physician.

"Shorter," he replied, "and rather like an owl. You know, that wide-eyed, intent stare that mislead people into believing one of the stupidest birds is one of the smartest?"

John laughed.

"Lincoln was probably the last man to be elected purely on merit," the physician speculated. "I shudder to think what mischief is engendered in this visit. But I'll have to continue my thinking at the infirmary. My time out of the cage has lapsed."

The doctor began walking. John dogged along beside him. "Would you say you like these people even less after your experience down here?" he ventured.

"I don't know any of them well enough to dislike them," Russell replied. "I do know that I wouldn't want many for friends."

"What about for patients? This stay must have provided a number of opportunities to recommend your services."

"Remember, I'm a teaching surgeon," Russell pointed out. "They'll only travel down to Baltimore for surgery at the recommendation of their New York doctors. Most of my time is devoted to Johns Hopkins's charity hospital. At any rate, my stint ends this weekend. Next season's duties, thank God, will fall on some other physician's shoulders. I won't be disappointed never to set eyes on this place again."

When they were almost to the infirmary, John asked, "Have you thought any more about the circumstances of Mr. Springer's death?"

Russell gave a soft expulsion of air from his nostrils. "Other than that it was murder? No."

"But of that you're convinced."

"For such a man, there must be a hundred reasons people would want him dead. I'm waiting for *you* to determine that reason, Mr. Le Brun, and thereby the murderer."

"I'm a sheriff, not a big-city detective," John protested. "I've been waitin' for the solution to reveal itself."

"You'll wait forever if it's to be through me," Russell said.

"Other than Mrs. Springer, you are undoubtedly the person on this island he most shared his thoughts with. Did he talk particularly about any other member or guest?"

Russell bent and picked up a piece of tricolored crepe bunting that had escaped from the clubhouse veranda and was rolling across the lawn in the gentle breeze. "No. He disliked the Goulds and J. D. Rockefeller, but he expressed no fear of them."

"He said nothing about Mr. Morgan and his camp?"

"He expressed no opinion."

"And he gave no hint that he knew anythin' about the president's visit?"

"None whatsoever. Do you think the two are connected?"

"It's temptin' to chew on," John replied.

"Speaking of chewing, might I rely on you for company at dinner tonight?" Russell asked, as they came to the infirmary's front stair.

"Unfortunately, I must decline. I will be attendin' to other business."

"Then we shall leave our next meeting to fate," said Dr. Russell. He bowed slightly and entered the house.

John retraced his path to the River Road. A trocha of boats now encircled the *Colfax* and the dock, with John's officers and some of the island's guards operating them. Of the four patrol boats, three were anchored on the north side, where no fewer than a dozen craft of varying sizes were filled to the point of foolhardiness with Brunswick gawkers. John worked his way to the edge of the bank and waved peevishly at them.

"You've seen all you'll see. Now scat! Go home!"

For his words, John received catcalls and worse. He threw up his arms and returned to the road. Warfield and Bobby Lee stood on the dock, speaking with a pair of officers from the cutter. When they spotted the sheriff, they separated themselves and came to where he stood.

"They're only hanging around for the afternoon," Warfield reported, of the navy men. "They're to pick up the president's party around this time on Wednesday."

"Which means we're expected to protect him?" John asked.

"I suppose so," Bobby Lee answered.

John whipped off his derby and slapped it against his thigh. "You think he'd have his own police assigned to him. We've had two presidents assassinated in less than thirty-five years. Does it have to be three before they take the office's protection seriously?"

"I'd love to know if they've kept Mr. Springer's death a secret from them," Warfield said.

"So would I. Walk with me, Warfield," John said. He started up the dock and onto River Road. "I won't have the president of the United

States killed in my jurisdiction. I'm goin' to climb into a boat with Bobby Lee and soundly discourage those creatures on the water from hangin' around. Then he and I are headin' back to Brunswick to see if Mr. Turner is still alive. I want you to go to the guards' barracks and work out with Mr. Lefferts a plan to patrol the Village, the roads, and the river. And I want one of our people within shouting distance of the president at all times. Any questions?"

"Just one: What did Mr. Reed and Judge Moore have to say to you?"

"They wanted me to know how pleased they both are by our continued presence."

Warfield snorted his amusement.

"A solid front has been thrown up against us here," John said. "That's why seekin' the answer through Turner is so important."

"Will you overnight in Brunswick, one way or the other?"

John put his hand on his stomach. "I plan to. I need a night in my own bed and with my own cookin'. I don't care how healthy the members think this island is; the meals alone can kill you."

"You can depend on me," Warfield said.

"Good. In that case, allow me to depend on you for two more things. First, go over to the infirmary and invite Dr. Russell to supper. He claims to remember nothin' pertinent that Springer said to him, but that doesn't seem right. The man spent ten to fifteen minutes with him every mornin', by Russell's admission talkin' about everythin' from the weather to medicine. Now, accordin' to the notes you set down from your interviews, Springer was thought by the membership to be quite outspoken."

"That's what they said."

"Then why didn't he talk about the members to Dr. Russell?"

"Because Dr. Russell isn't a member?" Warfield hazarded.

"Perhaps," John granted. "Anyway, he's still one of our best hopes. Perhaps he's forgotten somethin' small but critical, or else he's happy to let someone on this island get away with murder and purposely forgettin'. Use your lawyer's skill and worm what you can out of him."

"I'll try," Warfield said. "What else?"

"Before dark go over to the Pulitzer cottage and see if they've received any information about Springer, Russell, or Rasher."

"Must I? You know he'll want me to read to him," Warfield complained.

"Where's your Christian charity?" John asked.

Warfield stopped walking. "It ends at martyrdom. I feel like I'm being fed to the lion."

"Think of the overtime you're accumulatin'," John said. He patted Warfield on the back. "And who knows . . . perhaps while I'm gone, you'll solve the case. You'll become the local hero and trounce me in the election this fall. Mustn't forget your father's timetable." He started back toward the dock with pace, denying Warfield a direct response.

"Bastard," Warfield uttered under his breath when Le Brun was beyond earshot.

THE SHERIFF and Bobby Lee Randolph had not yet steamed out of view of the dock before Warfield was hammering out a plan with Preston Lefferts to seal the Jekyl Island Club Village from outside incursion. When Lefferts volunteered a favorable opinion of John Le Brun, Warfield merely nodded. The chief deputy spent that next hour setting a schedule and passing it on to the three deputies who remained with him. He arranged with Thomas Russell to dine at seven-thirty and then went into the clubhouse and had a leisurely lunch. Sated, he retired to his room and napped until four.

Rising resentfully from his bed, Warfield reknotted his tie, tugged on his jacket, and walked toward the Pulitzer cottage. As he approached, a dark phaeton glided by, with a black coachman at the whip and Joseph Pulitzer the lone passenger behind him. The coachman tipped his hat respectfully as they passed; the newspaperman peered in Warfield's direction but showed no sign of recognition. Warfield heaved a sigh of relief. He knocked on the cottage's front door but did not wait to be greeted. Entering, he heard the clinking of glassware in the laboratory. He investigated and found G. W. Hosmer mixing chemicals. The amateur chemist approached the doorway.

"Ah, Mr. Tidewell! You've just missed Mr. Pulitzer."

"So I saw. Is he taking an afternoon constitutional?"

"No, no. He rarely rides by himself. Always wants someone to describe the countryside, the weather, the people. Eugene's tried it by himself, but he can't drive and shout at the same time. Scares the horses." Hosmer paused as he fought to peel off rubber gloves. "No, he invited McKinley, Hobart, and Hanna to see the island with him, and they accepted."

"What's his real agenda?"

"Agenda?" the physician repeated.

"He doesn't like these men. Surely he's putting in a pitch for the cause of the common man, trying to confound Morgan's agenda."

Hosmer removed his rubber apron and tossed it and the gloves onto a bench. Behind him, several solutions boiled in their glassware. The amateur chemist smiled benignly.

"Actually, I believe his agenda is showing off his island. What brings you here?"

"Sheriff Le Brun wants to know if any information on Erastus Springer, Randolph Rasher, or Dr. Russell has arrived."

"Not yet."

Warfield glanced back at a long Parsons table set just to the side of the bottom of the stairs. On it lay four neat piles of newspapers: the *Journal,* the *Tribune,* the *Herald,* and the *World.* About a week of Pulitzer's and his rivals' editions appeared to be in each pile. The headlines on the top copy of the *World* were "HOTELS BUILT BEFORE '92 CALLED FIRETRAPS," and, in giant type, "THE WINDSOR HOTEL/REVISED LIST SHOWS 66 DEAD OR MISSING."

"Anything else, Mr. Tidewell?" the newsman's friend asked.

"I was going to volunteer to read to him."

"Excellent! We've finished *Precaution.* Have you read Thucydides' *History of the Peloponnesian War*?"

"No."

"Then you'll learn as you read. Why not stop by at six?"

"Sorry. I'm busy."

"Pity. Tonight he's otherwise engaged." The bubbling and frothing in the laboratory had reached malevolent proportions. "Excuse me. I was right in the middle of—"

"I haven't read the *World* for months," Warfield said. "Do you mind?"

"No. Read to your heart's content. Just don't remove it," Hosmer said, even as he hurried to rescue his experiment.

Tidewell picked up the newspaper and read about a fire in New York City that had leveled an old and prestigious hotel. The purple prose of the reporting and the sensationalistic angles chosen struck him immediately. The first three pages were completely devoted to the mishap. The deputy did not linger on them but scanned every subsequent headline until he came to page six. There, toward the bottom of the page, was the one he sought: "ERASTUS SPRINGER KILLED IN SHOOTING." The bank

directly below read: "BRUNSWICK, GA. AUTHORITIES PRO-
NOUNCE SHOOTING ACCIDENTAL."

The deputy smiled, then chuckled. The tenor of the article was passive,
superficial, dismissive. While Jekyl Island was mentioned—once—the
Jekyl Island Club was granted total anonymity. Warfield carefully folded
the newspaper and replaced it on its proper pile. Peeking in and seeing
that Hosmer was frantically preoccupied, he left the cottage without a
good-bye.

Passing Sans Souci, Warfield saw J. P. Morgan seated with his
personal lawyer and the infamous New Jersey corporate lawyer on Morgan's balcony, enjoying the late-afternoon sun. Warfield glanced away
quickly and continued on to the clubhouse.

JUDGE TIDEWELL rode by in his sulky as John Le Brun and Bobby
Lee Randolph passed Brunswick's L'Arioso Opera House on foot.

"I believe you've really ticked off the judge," Bobby Lee said. "He saw
us and acted as if we weren't here."

"He'll be more ticked as the week drags on," John replied.

"Now that you've spent more time with his son, what do you think?"
the deputy invited.

"He's hard to read."

"So are you," Bobby Lee told him. "But he's nicer than I expected. I
mean college boy, lawyer, and all. I thought he'd be a real pissant. Look
down his nose at us. But he seems genuine."

"He's tryin' to win y'all over, simpleton," John countered. "He's out
of his depth in knowledge of the job and aware that I wanted you to fill
the vacancy. You're more generous than I would be, given the situation."

"Give him a break, John," the deputy counseled.

"Rope. What I'm givin' him is rope."

"Then cut him some slack."

"Since you're in a mood to arrange things, how about you go and
arrange deputizin' Frank and Bret for tomorrow," John said, as they
neared the office of the *Brunswick Call*. "I'll meet you at the jail."

The deputy strode off without another word. John ducked into the
newspaper office, eyes roaming the length and breadth of the small space.
He called out to the only man occupying a desk, pecking with two fingers
on a typewriter.

"Marston, where's J. L.?"

"Out gathering news, of course," the veteran ink-slinger snapped back without raising his head.

"Did he leave me any information on that biography I wanted checked out?"

"Nope. He was tickled pink about the lead you gave him on the president's visit, though."

"He should be. Did he get that note I had delivered for him over at the Oglethorpe last night?"

"How should I know?"

"Damn!" Le Brun balled up a promotional flyer that lay on the front counter and winged it at the newsman. It bounced off his head. Marston refused to react. "You know a fellow named Ezekiel Turner, by any chance?"

"A drunkard and chicken thief, right?"

"That's the one. Seen him last night or today?"

"Strike three," Marston said. And then, before John could swear again, "But I did see his wife buying out the dry goods store around the corner."

"Finally you're useful," John said. He opened the front door.

"Let me know when *you* are," Marston riposted.

THE SUN had already dipped below the tree line to the west when the sheriff and his deputy found the Turner farm. It was a scratch subsistence affair. Beside its sagging-roofed barn roamed two scrawny goats, a rooster, a horse, and three hens, all searching for sustenance. The fence had needed mending a decade earlier. Only with difficulty could one discern that the house had once been white.

In front of the farmhouse stood an unhitched wagon. On its bed was a barrel of dried black-eyed peas, a large tin of molasses, and five cans of coal oil. Beyond it, a boy of about five and a girl more than a year younger played on the porch. The boy wore new britches, flannel shirt, and suspenders; the girl had on a new gingham dress. The boy was teaching himself how to spin a spanking new top, and the girl had a fierce embrace on a pristine baby doll with perfect blond curls. Both children had clearly not been washed that day or the day before, so that their new clothing appeared at odds with their dirty hair, hands, and faces.

"Hey," John said, walking up to the children, who had paused in their play to stare slack-mouthed at the stranger. "Is your daddy at home?"

Both heads wagged no.

"What about your momma?"

In answer, a woman appeared behind the screened front door. She looked ten years older than her age, with weariness and care etched deeply into her face. The kerchief knotted at the top of her head held back skeins of long, iron-colored hair, black gone prematurely gray. Her skin tone was hardly less gray than the kerchief, apron, and dress she wore, so that she blended into her drab surroundings like a human chameleon. She was barefooted. Ironically, the Colt hammerless ten-gauge shotgun she held in her hands was the most colorful item about her.

"Whatcha want?" she asked.

"Miz Turner, I'm Sheriff Le Brun from Brunswick," John said, derby in hand. He turned back his suit lapel and displayed his badge.

A pinch came around the woman's eyes. Her arms relaxed, so that the shotgun hung almost at her knee level. "What can I do for you?"

John came a step closer. He looked into the tiny house and spied more provisions sitting on a table in the kitchen area. "You can tell me where your husband is."

"He works over at the Jekyl Island Club."

"He's left that employ, without notice. That's why I'm here."

The woman shrugged. "Can't help you."

John turned and looked at Bobby Lee Randolph, who stood alertly near the wagon. Then he turned back to face Turner's wife. "Would you like me and my deputy to help you bring in the rest of your supplies?"

"No, thanks. I can handle them."

"Musta been tirin', first doin' all that shoppin', and then haulin' it into the house. The fella at the dry goods store said you spent thirty-six dollars in hard cash. Hard to forget the amount when somebody plunks down that much cash in one visit. Then there were the children's clothes and toys. I figure Zeke gave you fifty dollars. That be about right?"

"I don't know what—"

"But the truth is that he got *two hundred* for lyin' about a murder over on the island."

The woman's eyebrows sailed upward, but her lips remained resolutely pursed. John nodded at the weapon in her hands.

"That gun he gave you belongs to the Jekyl Island Club. He stole it, and you're holdin' it. I could haul you down to jail for receivin' stolen property, but I don't want to do that. I just need to talk with him. And I'd like to get you some more of that money before he drinks it away or what not."

John caught the reflection of hard calculation in the woman's eyes. She looked at her children.

"I wouldn't have to give the money back?"

"No, ma'am. He earned it. *How* he earned it is another issue, but the money would be yours, Miz Turner."

"It's Alice." The woman's expression softened. She considered her alternatives for a few more moments.

"When is dinner, Momma?" the boy asked.

"Hush! Soon," she answered.

John gestured for Bobby Lee to take the supplies off the wagon bed. When he turned back, Alice had opened the screen door. She was holding out the shotgun.

"Here. He said he was gonna look for another job," the woman said. "If he was, he'd'a come with us to Brunswick. I figure he went up to Darien to celebrate. I knowed he kept some of the money and that he'd go on a bender for a while. His favorite hangout is the Swamp Fox Tavern . . . on the way into town." She stepped back to allow the deputy to carry in the barrel of dried peas.

"Much obliged," John replied.

"You say *two* hundred dollars?" she asked, incredulous.

"Or thereabouts."

"Well, you find him right quick, 'cause we can use that money real bad."

Le Brun smiled. "We will, Miz Turner. We will."

STARS AND A SLICE of the moon lit the sky over the Brunswick-Darien Pike. The road was straight and smooth, but the lawmen kept their horses reined in to a fast walk. In the distance, the lights of the heart of Darien were barely larger than the stars overhead.

"Think, John!" Bobby Lee encouraged. In a lilting, light tenor, he repeated the melody to the lyrics he had been unable to finish for the past mile.

> *"Just break the news to Mother*
> *She knows how dear I love her*
> *And tell her not to wait for me, for I'm not coming home*
> *Just say there is no other can take the place of Mother . . .*
> *Ta-ta, ta-ta, ta-ta, ta-ta, ta-da-dee-da-dee-da."*

"Why worry about it?" John asked. "Any song with a verse that ends, 'They brought him back and softly heard him say' ain't worth rememberin'. Any fool knows it should be 'and heard him softly say.' "

"Forget about the verse and remember the chorus for me," Bobby Lee requested. "There's the Swamp Fox, in the middle of those buildings." He pointed to the first huddle of structures beyond the sign that indicated the town limits. "You want me to ride ahead and fetch Sheriff Stone?"

"Let's see if Turner's here first," Le Brun replied. "Why don't I go in the front door, since I know what he looks like, and you wait around the back?"

"Fine. Just do me a favor: Before you collar Turner, ask the boys at the bar if anyone can sing the chorus of 'Break the News to Mother.' "

"Not likely," John said. "You count to a hundred and take another stagger at it." He dismounted and handed his reins to the deputy. As he entered the tavern, Bobby Lee had resumed humming the Joseph Clauder tune.

Considering it was a Monday night, the Swamp Fox Tavern was fairly full. Two tables were occupied by cardplayers. A game of darts held the attention of half a dozen others. As John moved toward the bar, his eyes swept the room. Before he was halfway to the brass rail, several of the drinkers were telling their confederates that a lawman had invaded their little club.

Ezekiel Turner was not among the crowd. Le Brun rapped on the bar for the attention of the bartender, who was polishing glasses with a white towel. "I understand I can find Zeke Turner here," he said, in an overloud voice.

The bartender looked around. "He must be out back, straining all the whiskey he's knocked down through his kidneys."

Several men in the room laughed. One raised his glass and declared, "Here's to 'Drinks-on-Me' Turner!" Several shot glasses and mugs rose high.

"Don't let me interrupt you," Le Brun said, moving toward the tavern's back door. As he grabbed its knob, a shot rang out on the opposite side.

John drew his revolver from its holster and threw back the door, thrusting the gun barrel out before he exited. He cleared the doorway and went immediately into a squat, describing an arc with the gun's sight that paralleled his sweeping take of the area.

Bobby Lee was sitting on the ground, wrestling his revolver from its shoulder holster. His face was contorted into a grimace of pain. Fifty feet beyond, near a double-doored outhouse, lay a body. Beyond that, a dark figure was sprinting for the back of the clapboard-sided building closest to the tavern.

John squeezed off a shot, but the man had already rounded the building's corner. John came out of his squat.

"Where you hit?" he called out to the deputy.

"In the leg. Go get him!"

John gave chase. Just beyond the wooden building, the trees closed in thick and dark. He stopped and listened. It was as if the woods had swallowed the man up. John realized that he stood in a wash of light from one of the building's rear windows. He took several steps backward into the mask of darkness, listened again, and retraced his path. When he returned to the alley, he found Bobby Lee being ministered to by half the men from the bar. The other half had gathered around the body.

"It's Zeke," one of them announced, after having turned the corpse faceup. "Jesus!" The ground beneath the corpse was shiny in the moonlight and darker than the surrounding dirt.

John hurried to his deputy.

"I think it needs a tourniquet," the bartender decided. He held out his white towel.

Bobby Lee ripped open the bullet hole in his trousers and studied his wound. "No, it don't. It just caught me a graze, but I'm bleedin' like a stuck pig. Give me that rag!" He looked up at Le Brun. "Little bastard. Skinny. With a dark beard and a dark bandanna."

"Barton Cummins," the bartender said. "He left the tavern almost an hour ago. Musta come back here to wait for Zeke to relieve himself."

"He was goin' through Turner's pockets when I rounded the corner," the deputy reported.

"Was Mr. Turner flashing a wad of money?" John asked.

"Better than a wad. He had a fifty and five twenties," the bartender answered. "Laid 'em out on the bar for everyone to see. Stupid move."

"You were right about the two-hundred figure," Bobby Lee grunted, as he attempted to stand.

"Stay down for a few minutes, until you stanch," John counseled. He turned again to the bartender. "Was this Barton character already in the tavern when Turner came in, or did he follow him in?"

"No, he was already here," one of the crowd answered. Another next to him nodded.

Someone beside the body reported loudly, "He got away with Turner's billfold."

John called out, "Y'all leave him be! Back away! Is he dead?"

"Real dead," the man who had rolled Turner over said. "His throat's cut from ear to ear. I didn't think Cummins had that kind of guts."

"Shit he didn't," another near the body declared.

John whipped off his derby and threw it to the ground. He reholstered his revolver in the silence his anger had created. He squatted beside his deputy.

"Right back to square one," the sheriff lamented.

"Sorry, John," Bobby Lee commiserated. He gingerly lifted the towel and confirmed that the bleeding had slowed to an ooze. The wound required cleansing and stitching.

"How you feelin'?" John asked.

"Then kiss her dear, sweet lips for me, and break the news to her,' " the deputy said softly.

"What?"

"I remembered the last lines to the song," Bobby Lee explained.

John shook his head. "You'll live."

WARFIELD STABBED OUT his cigarette in the terra-cotta urn, careful to avoid the molded *JIC* that had been pressed into the white sugar sand that filled it. He continued from the piazza through the clubhouse doors and up to the front desk.

"Please tell me the time," he said.

"Five minutes after seven," the desk clerk answered. "Are you Mr. Tidewell?"

"I am."

The desk clerk produced a sealed envelope of club stationery. Warfield grabbed it with high expectation, hoping that the writer of the previous message had despaired of the lawmen solving the crime and had provided hard evidence. He ripped the envelope open and dug out the sheet of folded paper. The note was not from the anonymous informer but rather from his expected dinner partner. The doctor wrote that he regretted he had to break their dinner engagement, but he had been called to the black quarters to attend to an emergency and had no idea how long he would be. He counseled Warfield not to wait for him. He signed the note *Thomas S. Russell.*

Warfield was shown to what he had begun thinking of as "the lepers' corner" in the dining room. As he reviewed the menu, he overheard from the disgruntled couple sitting at the adjacent table that Mr. and Mrs. McKinley were dining with Commodore Bliss and his wife at the Baker cottage, Solterra. Before and after the meal, selected visitors would be guided in and out of his presence by appointment, and this pair had received no such invitation. Warfield smiled, thinking that they at last felt like he and the doctors did. The couple dissected the day in excruciating detail, but no mention at all was made of their recently late fellow member, Erastus Springer.

A few moments after Warfield ordered, Charles Lanier entered the dining room and crossed directly to him. He pulled out a chair and sat without being invited.

"How are you this evening, Mr. Tidewell?" he asked.

"Fine. And yourself?"

"Excellent. I've made some inquiries about you up in Philadelphia." He was smiling broadly, so Warfield made no attempt to defend himself. "The people who dealt with you at Drexel and Company thought you were quite competent and found it difficult to believe that you were charging for nonexistent hours."

"I was thrown to the wolves, made to pay for the greed of senior partners," Warfield said. "There wasn't a scintilla of truth to it, but I was disbarred nonetheless."

"You don't have to practice law to put it to good use, you know. I think I've found an interesting position for you at the First Security Company."

"What's it affiliated with?"

"The First National Bank of New York."

"Mr. Baker's bank."

"That's right."

And therefore, Warfield thought, part of the J. P. Morgan confederation. "What are the particulars?" he asked.

"They're still evolving . . . but nicely, I believe." Lanier drew his chair slightly closer to the deputy. "You wouldn't mind giving up this deputy job, would you?"

"Not for the right opportunity," Warfield replied.

"Good. What's Sheriff Le Brun up to?"

"You mean tonight?"

"No. In general. Does he have a firm suspect?" Lanier had lost his smile.

"He does not."

"And that's why he's tracking down Ezekiel Turner?"

"That's right."

Lanier leaned back in the chair and gazed up at the ceiling molding. He expelled his air with a humming noise. He looked again at Warfield. "And he meant what he said about vacating the island once the president leaves, whether or not the person is caught?"

"I can't read his mind, but he *is* a man of his word," Warfield said.

The club president thumped the table with his open hand. "Good enough for me." He rose and reaffixed his smile. "I'll be back to you about that job offer . . . probably Wednesday morning."

Warfield expressed his gratitude. As he watched Lanier walk away, he reflected that Wednesday noon would see the president gone and, shortly thereafter, John Le Brun. Even if the job offer were genuine and already secured, it would not be tendered until Warfield had served his time as informant on his superior.

Charles Lanier paused at one of the tables, where a party of members' sons and daughters, all in their late teens and early twenties, were seated. There were five of them, so that one place at the table was vacant. Lanier bent low and spoke a few words to them, ending his speech by glancing in Warfield's direction. He saw one of the young men smirk and a young woman roll her eyes. Warfield had interviewed every one of them. To a person, they were spoiled, self-centered, vapid creatures, the products of ruthless men and beautiful women and far less than the sum of their parts. He had no desire to be cajoled into their midst by Lanier and was greatly relieved to be rebuffed. He decided to focus his attention on the windows, where the dark of night pressed against the glass and nothing could be seen.

When he had finished his dinner, Warfield strolled to the smoking parlor. He put himself into the enormous leather chair most nearly in the center of the room, damned if someone would try to relegate him to a corner. He lit a cigarette. By the time he had puffed it to a tiny butt, a clutch of the younger men had drifted in. They took a collective look at

Warfield's challenging expression and acknowledged him with grudging nods. The young men's presence invited the older men. Several of the patriarchs began a discussion as to whether or not it was economically feasible to build subterranean railways through the granite bedrock of New York City. This led to speculation on tunnels under the Hudson River and a bridge over the same waterway. The capitalization figures the men quoted staggered Warfield's mind. The numbers reminded club member Henry Elias Howland of an editorial he had recently read in the *Journal* criticizing the thousand wealthiest men of the country for amassing more and more wealth and not sharing it with the millions of workers whose lives they controlled.

"And if we did double their salaries," Howland argued, "who would possess the capital to finance such projects as subways and suspension bridges?"

"Exactly," agreed Mr. James Alexander Scrymser. "How will they get into the city to work? They don't understand that we serve them just as much as they serve us."

Many heads nodded.

"Sheep have shepherds to care for them," Scrymser went on, "but who may care for men but other men? In the old days of physical warfare, the physically strongest naturally took the positions of power. Today, warfare is as much an economic struggle, and those most mentally capable must assume the positions of power. On the surface our fortunes may seem selfish, but the weak and stupid don't realize that they must pay to be protected and provided for. Mr. Darwin's survival of the fittest is not fang and claw among men; it's brains using information."

"Precisely," Mr. H. K. Porter chimed in. "Without us, the lower of our species would starve. If they're no longer needed to plow behind oxen or weave in home looms, then what would they do without the jobs we create?" He looked at Howland. "And if we *did* double their salaries, Henry, what would they do but spend it on liquor, gambling, and other base vices? Would *they* support the great artists? Would *they* donate the paintings and sculptures to museums for everyone to appreciate? Would *they*, like Andrew Carnegie, use their surplus cash for public libraries and books, giving everyone access to information and therefore to the American dream?"

The assemblage shook their heads like a syndicate of hanging judges. Someone behind Warfield's chair said, "I started as a bobbin runner in a mill. Worked my way up from nothing. This is the land of opportunity. Greatest country in the world. If a person wants to succeed, nothing's stopping him but his own sloth and stupidity."

Warfield pushed himself up from the soft cushioning and strode out of the smoke-filled room. Mr. Howland collapsed his paunchy frame into the vacated chair with a grateful sigh.

Out on the piazza, the deputy glanced at his pocket watch. The protracted meal and the time in the smoking parlor had almost killed the evening. He had just enough time to take a stroll around the Village and assure himself that the guards and the other deputies were patrolling as they should be. Then, as he had done the night before, he would enter Sans Souci and report to J. P. Morgan.

THE BRUNSWICK POLICE launch entered the mouth of the Jekyl River at about quarter past seven in the morning. On it were John Le Brun and two of his "emergency deputies," Frank Tarbell and Bret Hunter. Frank had officially retired two years earlier and was interested only in picking up "wild money" policing the odd parade or political rally. Bret was a young farmer who was willing to spare a day here and there in the off season. Both had been dragooned into service by Le Brun. They were replacing Redmond Drayton and Burt Davenport, who had braved the blackness of St. Simon's Sound to navigate home at ten the previous evening, after Chief Deputy Tidewell had determined that there was insufficient justification to keep them circling the cottage where the president stayed.

As the lawmen came within view of the clubhouse turret, they also came within hailing distance of a fishing boat. The craft had been pressed into service to satisfy a crowd of Yankee vacationers eager to catch a peek at the exclusive club and its very important guests.

John brandished the weapon he had taken from Alice Turner. "I am the sheriff of this region. Y'all see this shotgun?" he called to the gawkers, who threatened to capsize the fishing boat by bunching together at the port rail. "I took it off one of the guards. He fired it at someone tryin' to sneak ashore. I can't be everywhere. If you get off the boat, I can't guarantee you won't get filled with buckshot."

The Northerners jeered at his words.

"Damn Yankees," John fumed. A minute later, the wallowing police launch thumped against the club dock. He handed Tarbell the shotgun and sprang onto the dock. "Frank, you walk up and down the road, holdin' this." To Bret Hunter, he said, "You stay in the boat and look menacin'." Seeing John's expression, neither man risked a laugh.

John walked into the clubhouse and directly up to Warfield Tidewell's room. He knocked on the door, waited several moments, and rapped more loudly. When he got no reply, he dug into his front trouser pockets for a ring of keys and also for the key he had been given to his clubhouse bedroom. He surveyed both ends of the hallway and satisfied himself that no one was coming. He compared his room key to one on the ring, then pushed the key on the ring into Warfield's door. It turned slightly but failed to open the lock. John sighed. He selected a thin, bent piece of steel on the end of the ring and fitted it into the lock. Twenty seconds later, he was inside the room. He stayed only long enough to verify that the bed-covers had been turned down for the night but not slept under.

The front desk held copies of the previous day's *Brunswick Call* and the *Savannah Register*. Both newspapers bannered the president's visit to Jekyl Island in enormous letters. John took them into the members' dining room and went automatically to the table in the far corner, his eyes sweeping back and forth across the print. The story in the *Register* was identical to that in the *Call*. It detailed the arrival of President and Mrs. McKinley, Mr. and Mrs. Hobart, and Senator Hanna by train at the Brunswick station, what the party wore, which town worthies greeted them, and their transfer to the cutter *Colfax*. The reporter's byline was L. J. Leavy. Leavy also astutely mentioned that Speaker Reed was visiting the club and that members currently on the island included millionaires J. P. Morgan, William Rockefeller, Frederic Baker, H. K. Porter, and George Fabyan. John laughed out loud, without bothering to look up and see if anyone was staring at him.

"What's so funny?" Warfield Tidewell asked, coming across the room. He walked stiffly and looked at John through slitted eyes.

"I like helpin' nice young men succeed in their chosen professions," John replied, laying the paper out across the opposite side of the table. "One of those nice young men is a cub reporter named Leavy. I fed him the secret of the president's visit as quick as I could, and here it is in black and white. I'll bet Hanna was shocked to see how many people were waitin' at the Brunswick station for them yesterday mornin'."

"That was very thoughtful of you," Warfield granted.

"Not really. I usually ask for favors in return. Young Mr. Leavy is doin' his best to find out if Dr. George Washington Hosmer has any shadows in his variegated past. He's made the correspondin' acquaintance of a reporter with the *Tribune* who may be able to help us."

"Wouldn't be surprised if Hosmer had some dark shadows. The man is strange." Warfield stifled a yawn, then moved his fingers from his mouth to his eyelids to squeeze and massage them.

"Another bad night's sleep?" John asked, drawing in a long, deep breath.

"Yes. Worrying about this case. I woke with a splitting headache."

"Two cups of black coffee," the sheriff prescribed. "That's what cures me."

Tidewell took his mentor's advice. He was finishing his second cup, trying through his headache to digest the sheriff's recounting of Ezekiel Turner's demise, when a man in a very casual crash suit approached the table.

"Excuse me, gentlemen . . ." the man began.

Warfield rose from his chair. "Reverend Parkhurst! Good morning!"

"Good morning."

"Sheriff Le Brun, the Reverend Charles Henry Parkhurst. Club member."

"*Honorary* member," Parkhurst corrected gently.

"I've seen you streakin' around the Village on one of those fast bicycles, with your hair streamin' behind your ears," John noted, even as he also noted that one of the man's trouser knees was damp and soiled.

The minister glanced over his shoulder to judge who sat within earshot. He faced the two seated men again. "I believe I may have found something to do with Mr. Springer's death," he said in a half whisper.

"Please sit," John said.

Warfield pulled out a chair, but the minister remained standing. "I think it's best if I showed you. Can you come with me? Now?"

"Tell me this first," John said. "Have you found physical evidence, such as blood or a shell casing?"

"I believe so."

John snatched the napkin from his lap and tossed it onto his half-finished breakfast. "I shall stop momentarily at the front desk, and then you may command our full attention."

At the desk John grabbed half a dozen of the cream-colored club stationery envelopes. He stuffed them in his jacket pocket and gestured for the minister to take the lead. For a man of advanced years, Reverend Parkhurst moved with long, powerful strides. He exited the clubhouse and cut across the dew-damp lawn, heading almost directly south.

"Are we going to where Mr. Springer was killed?" Warfield asked.

"Very near," Parkhurst replied. "I'm not ordinarily up this early," he revealed, "but I found myself drawn from sleep by President McKinley's visit. I prayed for his divine guidance and then thought, since I shan't be on the island for but a few days more, that I'd go for a quiet morning walk. See if nature would inspire me for my next sermon." As they walked by San Souci, the minister maintained his fleet stride, so that the effort of walking and talking made him puff lightly. "I thought I'd take the path where Mr. Springer was shot, since the time was so early and the visibility not very good. I didn't want to be shot accidentally by a hunter, and I figured nobody with a gun would dare venture close to that spot."

"Sound reasonin'," John lauded.

"Nothing much happened for the first few minutes," Parkhurst went on. "Saw a few birds, a beautiful butterfly on a leaf, a bunny. That was about all."

"And then?" Warfield asked.

"I'll hold the rest until we get there, if you don't mind," the minister said. A long minute later, approaching the infirmary, he asked, "You don't believe the business about the poacher, do you?"

Sheriff Le Brun said nothing, compelling his deputy to respond. "We find it . . . within reason of doubt," Warfield answered.

"Too convenient. Too concocted," Parkhurst judged. He wore delicate wire-rimmed glasses. These he removed and cleaned with the edge of his shirt as he walked. "But aside from the flaws in the guard's explanation, do you have any other evidence to cause your doubt?"

"Precious little," Le Brun admitted. "We've been waitin' for a break-through."

"This may be what you've waited for. I'll say no more."

The old minister pushed on apace. They walked without conversation down Shell Road and onto the path. The air was heavy. The two older men labored audibly for breath. The deputy kept his head lowered against the brilliant morning light, his left hand shielding his eyes. First the crushed shells, then the gravel crunched loudly under their combined motion.

Finally, a white handkerchief came into view, tied to the lowest-hanging branch of a towering live oak. Reverend Parkhurst redoubled his pace until he stood under the handkerchief. He retrieved the cloth, sucked in a fortifying breath, and stepped off the path into the undergrowth.

"I'm trying to step precisely where I walked when I first entered," the minister explained. "You see that gorgeous clump of clematis encircling the trunk? I decided to take a closer look."

Le Brun and Tidewell followed their leader's footsteps as closely as they could, until all three had come up to another live oak.

"Stand over there," Parkhurst directed, pointing at the same time to the far side of the tree. Sheriff and deputy moved gingerly through the vegetation. "Look at the flowers!"

Many of the blue-purple blooms had been crushed and mangled, from about eighteen inches above ground level to a height of about three feet. Above this, the flowers were unblemished. Two of the lower flowers were withered, spattered with a rust-colored substance. Just behind these blossoms the tree's bark was cracked and split.

"Now come closer," Parkhurst directed, removing his glasses. "I think that's a spent bullet in there. And look at the rock just below!"

At the base of the oak lay a rectangular rock, roughly the size and shape of a hassock. Its upper surface was stained with droplets of the same rust-colored substance.

"That's dried blood, isn't it?" the minister asked.

"Let's see," John replied. He produced one of the envelopes and his pocket knife and scraped the substance onto the paper. "I would say it is indeed blood."

"Perhaps Mr. Springer left the path as I did, to admire the flowers," Parkhurst speculated. "Is it possible he sat down to rest on this rock, and someone shot him?"

"But why would his body have been moved to the path?" Warfield wondered aloud.

Reverend Parkhurst's eyes drifted right and downward in thought. His mouth curled slowly into a scowl. "So he'd be found? Otherwise, it doesn't make sense, does it?"

"Maybe this is animal's blood," Warfield said.

"Yes, maybe a deer was standing beside the tree!" Parkhurst said, picking up a skein of the notion. "It was shot and collapsed against the trunk."

The sheriff sealed flakes from the rock and the stained clematis petals inside the envelope. "But this isn't the hunting area. And even if it was the work of a poacher, it must have happened after Friday night. Otherwise that big rainstorm would have washed away the blood. Considerin' Mr. Springer was shot so near here the next mornin', would anyone have the audacity to hunt in this spot?"

Warfield turned his head to survey the surrounding area and met the sun's glare full on. He winced and covered his eyes.

"Maybe three or four cups of coffee," John remarked. He worked for some time with his jackknife, until the bullet was coaxed from the wood. He held it up and studied it.

"Difficult to tell when they lodge in somethin' as hard as a tree, but I'd guess it's the same caliber as went through Mr. Springer. From its shape and depth, I'd say it spent some of its energy and began deformin' in somethin' big. Somethin' like a man."

Parkhurst stroked his full, salt-and-pepper beard. "Or a deer." When John scowled at him, he said, "Just playing devil's advocate. I seldom have that opportunity."

John's scowl transformed to a wry smile. He deposited the slug in a second envelope and peered into the hole he had made. "There's a piece of the bullet missin'. Help me search the ground, gentlemen!"

Their combined and meticulous efforts revealed no sliver of lead. But a small piece of cloth was found, all but hidden in the crevice formed between the base of the tree and the back of the rock. Warfield passed it to John for inspection.

"Looks like cloth from trousers or a jacket," the deputy observed. "Does it look like Mr. Springer's suit?"

"It could be the same material," John granted. He knelt beside the rock. "The exit wound was substantial. There should have been more than that."

"Unless someone removed the other pieces," Warfield said.

John stopped searching. "True. Very true."

Warfield stopped massaging his temples. "If he was killed right here, then somebody moved him to the path, either because they'd shot him by mistake and wanted him discovered as soon as possible or because they shot him on purpose and wanted to keep us from finding this place."

John stood. "If they took the trouble to pick up all the evidence, it's the second."

"Which is supported by their roughing over the footprints," Parkhurst chimed in.

"You'll earn an honorary membership in the Brunswick Police as well, Reverend, if you keep that up," John praised. He sealed the bullet in the second envelope, pocketed it, then dropped the tatter of cloth into a third. "Did you tell anyone else about your discovery?"

"No, sir. I came directly to you."

"Thank you very much. I would request that you continue to tell no one else until I give you leave."

"Certainly."

The sheriff faced directly into the woods. "You weren't over here, were you, Reverend?"

"No, sir."

"The ground is turned up," John reported. "Looks like someone dragged the side of his boot to erase the footprints."

Le Brun took a succession of mincing steps forward, passing through ferns, vines, moss, and mushrooms. He maintained his monotonous advance until he had moved himself forty feet from the oak tree. There he stopped short, at yet another of the forest giants. This oak, however, was long dead. All that remained was the base of the trunk, its rotted and ragged upper surface held about forty inches above the forest floor by the crown of its roots. John investigated in silence for several minutes.

"Come here!" he called at last. The other two men followed in his footsteps. "What do you see that isn't natural?" he asked.

Warfield's eye fell on a single strand of white thread. As he bent for it, Reverend Parkhurst found a second, stubby strand. John placed the two fibers into a fourth envelope. Warfield spotted a third patch of white, well concealed under a broad wild-cabbage leaf. The third discovery was more substantial, large enough to prove that the white threads came from loosely interwoven cloth.

"Was Mr. Springer wearing a tie?" Parkhurst asked.

"No," said the sheriff.

"Then perhaps those are from his shirt."

John shook his head. "The bullet as it entered would draw the pierced cloth in with it, not blow it out. If these were from the back of his shirt, they would have been held together by his jacket, not scattered like this. And why would his shirt material be over here, where there's neither blood nor bullet?"

Deputy and minister exchanged glances, then shrugs.

"What's the answer?" Warfield asked his superior.

"I don't know," John said solemnly. "But I will." He continued his

search, walking back beyond the rotten trunk another fifty feet, then working back and forth in a semicircle toward the path, like a janitor cleaning
up the rows after an event in an amphitheater. He found evidence of the
murderer's trip from oak tree to path. Le Brun determined that the killer
was a man. In many places, he had gracefully stepped from stone to stone
and mossy mound to mossy mound in an effort to conceal his movement—
all the while bearing Erastus Springer's deadweight. In those places where
he had been compelled to step on the rain-softened earth, he had twisted
his foot back and forth to obliterate the exact impression of his footprint.

When the sheriff had returned to where the other men waited, by the
back side of the oak with the bullet hole in it, Warfield asked, "How is it
you failed to find this on Saturday, Sheriff?"

Le Brun pointed south. "Did you see the tall stick I drove into the
ground just to the side of the path?"

"Yes," the deputy answered.

"That's where the body was found. How far away would you judge
that to be from here?"

"About two hundred feet."

Le Brun made a broad sweep with his left hand. "Look at all this
wilderness. You see how long it took the three of us to sweep a hundred-
foot-wide semicircle? I fine-tooth-combed a *full* circle all around the body
for about three hundred feet."

"Missed this area by fifty feet," Parkhurst pronounced. "But I, too,
would have thought your search area should have been sufficient."

"Thank you. Except that somebody made sure it wasn't," said the
sheriff. He hurried his last words, having heard something that brought
him alert. He held up his hand for silence and immobility. All three men
remained motionless. Young voices could be heard approaching.

"How much farther?" a female voice complained.

"Not far. Off to the right. We've already beaten a pretty good path,"
said a male. "Are you scared?"

"No," the female asserted. "Why should I be?"

" 'Cause the poacher is sure to come back for his boat sometime. And
if he shot Mr. Springer just because he caught him poaching, what do you
think he'll do if he sees you around his boat?"

"You're out of your tree!" another female voice sang out.

"*You're* the birdbrain," a second male voice riposted.

The voices drifted away, teasing and goading each other.

"I don't want them comin' out here," John told Warfield.

"How can we stop them?"

"By takin' away their fun. If they want to gawk at the boat, let's move it to the south side of the Village."

"Fine. So you believe Mr. Springer was shot here," Warfield said, pushing the teenagers out of the conversation.

"I do. Dr. Russell would have cut that suit off the body. We must find out if he saved it."

"We can ask as soon as we get to the infirmary," Warfield suggested. "It's right on the way."

John began massaging his bad shoulder. "In good time."

"Do you have a better idea who shot Mr. Springer?" Reverend Parkhurst inquired.

"No," the sheriff replied, "but this gives us leverage that may coax the murderer into revealin' himself."

"That's good. May I continue my walk now?"

"You may . . . with *my* blessin'," John said.

The minister tapped him convivially on the shoulder and tiptoed his way out to the path.

"Now what?" Warfield asked.

"Back to the Village," John answered, giving the scene one final sweep of his squinting eyes.

To Warfield's surprise, the two new deputies were the ones who received Sheriff Le Brun's immediate attention. The words were spoken out of the deputy's earshot, with Tarbell and Hunter saying little and nodding much. They walked off toward the path where Erastus Springer had been shot.

"Getting the boat up here right away, eh?" Warfield asked, as John came again to his side.

"Right away."

"*Now* do we talk with Thomas S. Russell, MD?"

"Yes," John affirmed. "This is what I call 'good time.' "

They found Russell sitting on the front porch of the infirmary, reading. "A medical monograph," he explained as he shook the lawmen's hands. "At least all this free time lets me catch up on my studies. Can I help you?"

"Quite possibly," John said. "When you did the autopsy on Mr. Springer, you cut off his suit."

"Yes, of course. The jacket was ruined, and I assumed the widow wouldn't want the trousers."

"I'm sure you're right. Would you still have the suit?"

Russell's eyebrows furrowed. "No. I threw it in the trash. I expect they've burned it by now."

"Perhaps it's still lyin' around," John said. "I'll do some checkin' directly."

Warfield admired the way the sheriff stuck his hands deeply into his pockets and rocked back and forth slightly on his toes and heels, presenting a relaxed, damned-if-I-care attitude calculated to put his interviewee at greater ease.

"You must have a particular reason for wanting the suit," the doctor probed.

"Didn't give it enough attention," John replied, adding a shrug to his carefree tone. "My fault. I should have asked you to hold on to it."

"Sorry."

"Never you mind." John held his ground, staring hard at the physician, saying nothing but swaying back and forth uninterrupted.

"Is there anything else I can do?" Russell asked.

"Matter of fact. You can tell me how thorough your autopsy was."

Warfield noted the physician changing his posture, setting his legs more widely apart, gripping his monograph with both hands so that it covered his stomach and groin area. He was a larger and stockier man than Le Brun, suggesting to Warfield the immovable object facing the sheriff's irresistible force. "In what way?"

"In examinin' the torso."

"The wound area?"

"No, all around. Bones, large muscles, below the chest cavity . . . into the soft organs and pelvis."

"What are you looking for?"

"A piece of the bullet."

"Why?"

John stopped rocking. "Did you pull Mr. Springer apart, dump the organs back in, and sew him up, Doctor, or might a sliver of the bullet have escaped your examination?"

"It could have," Dr. Russell allowed. "I did not, in fact, 'pull Mr.

Springer apart.' I'd just examined him minutes before and found him quite hale, and the bullet wound was indisputably the cause of death. I saw no need."

John gave a conciliatory grunt.

"You should have asked for both the suit and a complete autopsy at the time," Russell pointed out.

"True. As I said: my fault. I suppose I could wire the authorities in New York and have the body looked at again."

"I have no objections. But you'd better do it soon," Russell advised. "Once someone's in the ground, their families are generally opposed to exhumation."

"Especially young, beautiful widows."

Russell smiled. "Out of sight, out of mind?"

"Somethin' like that."

The doctor turned his attention to Warfield. "I must apologize for standing you up at dinner."

"You already did, in your letter," Tidewell reminded him.

"Professional obligations," Russell went on. "I had to attend to a Negro worker who was badly hurt."

"What happened?" John asked.

Dr. Russell shook his large head gravely. "*Why* did it happen is more important. John Rockefeller owns the mules on the island. He charges the club eighteen cents an hour for their services. The Negroes only cost six cents an hour, so they're generally used to do donkey work. The dock was rebuilt in November, after a hurricane damaged it. It seems that one of the pilings was improperly driven. With so many people standing on the dock when the president arrived, it sagged. I didn't get the whole story, but somebody fell, carrying the new piling down into the water, and the log glanced against this one fellow's shoulder, dislocating it and tearing the muscles. Nasty business. He'll never be the same."

John trained a baleful look on his deputy.

"You're terribly quiet, Mr. Tidewell," Russell observed.

"He's got a powerful headache," the sheriff disclosed. "I played doctor and advised him to drink four cups of black coffee."

"I've got something better than that," said the physician. "Come inside." He led the way into the infirmary and across to one of his two overfilled glass medicine cabinets. He removed a large, amber-tinted bottle and poured some of its white-powdered contents onto a scale. With a small scoop, he ladled measured amounts into two tiny envelopes. As he did, he said, "This is that acetylsalicylic acid . . . the drug I mentioned at dinner the other night. The same drug I'm administering to Mr. Cain for his rheumatism pain."

"The darkie with the wagon," John said.

"The same."

"And it works wonders, does it?"

"Truly. It's just been synthesized," Russell imparted. "Came to us directly from Germany. You can't get it in an apothecary shop yet. I heard a wild story about its discovery. It seems a man with a long moustache who suffered from frequent headaches cured himself regularly with chicken soup. Upon chemical examination, it was found that the straining of the soup through his moustache released this acid." The three men laughed at the unlikely possibility of the story being true. "I'll have to track that one down, but at any rate the drug works for all kinds of pain. We believe it reduces swelling."

Russell returned to the medicine cabinet and fetched Warfield a small bottle. "I'm sure y'all know how to use this," Russell said, approximating a Georgia accent. "Coca-Cola syrup, premixed with seltzer water."

"Co-cola, we say," John corrected.

"Either way, the elixir of the South," the physician pronounced, opening the bottle. "Down the hatch, Mr. Tidewell. If the headache persists, repeat the treatment an hour later."

Warfield expressed his thanks.

"Anything *else* I can do for you gentlemen?" Dr. Russell asked.

"That's all for now, thanks," John said. "I must get back to shooin' away the curious. Good day, Doctor."

When sheriff and deputy had walked well distant from the infirmary, Warfield asked, "You still suspect him, don't you?"

"He's still on the list," John affirmed.

"But where's his motive and his opportunity? He's from Johns Hopkins. In Baltimore. Not New York, or Philadelphia, or Boston, where most of these men live and work. He has nothing to do with them. He's only down here by a whim of fate, because some other doctor landed in jail at the last minute."

"But he volunteered," John reminded his deputy.

Warfield flapped his arms in exasperation. "So what? He's a bachelor.

He wanted some stimulation. He was curious. Furthermore, bachelorhood is also the reason he's a bit strange and secretive."

"I take it that's your excuse."

"It will be from now on if you believe it about him."

"My experience says he's resistin' me. Subtly, but resistin' nonetheless." As John spoke, he reached into his inside jacket pocket and produced the memorandum book with all the notes on the members' interviews. "I've read this over twice." He handed Warfield the book. "I've never seen fewer leads in my life. But we're not without hope."

Warfield suppressed a belch. "No. Reverend Parkhurst's find is very exciting. Do you or I try to locate Springer's suit?"

"You. I'm goin' to see if Mr. Pulitzer is able to fulfill his promise to report on Mr. Springer. He's had two and a half days."

"I'll join you there," the deputy said, heading toward the clubhouse with a distinct lack of energy.

Once Warfield was well away, John allowed himself a grand yawn. By the time he had seen that Bobby Lee was properly doctored and put up at a local hotel, had dealt with the aftermath of Ezekiel Turner's murder, and had gotten himself back to Brunswick, he had been able to catch only four hours' sleep. What was worse was that, between the endless investigation on Jekyl Island and chasing after Turner, both his suits had become dirty beyond wearing. He had had to dig into the back of his armoire for a suit he had retired three years before and barely fit into. As he walked, he tugged surreptitiously at the material around his crotch, vainly seeking to create more room. He was fighting a vile mood, but damned if he'd allow anyone to see it.

John knocked on the Pulitzer cottage front door. No one replied. He found the door open and entered. Dr. Hosmer was not in his laboratory. John checked several of the other downstairs rooms and found them empty. Willing to bide his time, he plucked a few of the newspapers from their piles on the Parsons table near the stairs and carried them out to the cottage's front steps. He read from the same edition of the *World* Warfield had read, scanned the inflammatory writing about the destruction of the Windsor Hotel, found the conspicuously benign report of Erastus Springer's death, and went on to study an article with the headline "FILIPINOS IN FORCE TWICE BEATEN OFF." Its byline gave the place as Manila and the date and time March 19, 8:30 A.M. It told how the battleship *Oregon* had had to be called in with its Marines to quell rebel attacks. It seemed the Filipinos resented American presence about as much as they hated rule by Spain.

All the way back on page ten, John found news of the presidential visit. The headlines read:

M'KINLEY AND REED?
Only Chance Meeting
All the members of Presidential Party Express Surprise at
Speaker's Jekyl Visit
Of course they may confer

What interested Le Brun most was the assumption by the writer that every reader was intimately acquainted with the Jekyl Island Club, as it was referred to generically as "Jekyl Island," with never once a mention that there was a club there. Given his reputation as a genius, the error was only explicable as far as John was concerned by the fact that Joseph Pulitzer was so in love with the island and the club that he could not imagine the whole world not knowing about it. Certainly, John thought, it had to have been dictated by Pulitzer; there was no other reporter available to supply the news.

John read through the competitors' newspapers, observing the variance in style. Pulitzer's child was by no means meant for simpletons, as the sheriff had supposed, but staid and tweedy it was not. As he was finishing the first section of the *Herald,* the secretary named Barnes, whom John had seen on his first visit to Pulitzer, came up the path to the cottage.

"Where is Mr. Pulitzer?" the sheriff inquired.

The secretary reacted with a start. "Isn't he inside?"

"I don't know."

Barnes shrugged. "Go on up . . . if you dare."

John glanced across the lawns and saw that Warfield was hurrying toward him with a more sprightly step than he had had only half an hour earlier.

"Burned," Warfield called out, speaking of Springer's suit.

"Figures," John muttered. "How are you feelin'?"

"Much better. That stuff truly is amazing."

"Glad to hear it." John jerked his head toward the cottage entrance. "Shall we enter the gargoyle's lair?"

"Safety in numbers," Warfield said, falling in behind his superior.

John cleared his throat loudly and stepped heavily as he ascended the stairs.

"Who's that?" Pulitzer cried out.

"Sheriff Le Brun and Chief Deputy Tidewell," John replied.

"Welcome, welcome! Eclipse yourself, Ireland!"

The secretary dropped the magazine he had been reading and fled past the lawmen. Pulitzer lifted himself partway from the couch and then lowered himself as rapidly. In those moments, John saw that he wore a light charcoal suit with thin pink stripes. A matching pink handkerchief protruded gaily from his lapel pocket. His cheeks were nearly the same tint; he looked a particular picture of health this day.

"We're here to learn what you've found out about Mr. Springer," John said. "I believe you said you would have it by this time."

A tic fluttered Pulitzer's right cheek. It was as if he had felt the nick of razored steel upon his face. In a measured and calm voice, he replied, "The gathering of *good, corroborated* information takes time, Sheriff. Especially information on such a secretive man as Erastus Springer. I could have had a truncated version sent by telegram, but there's bound to be so much dross that that seemed silly and a waste. I *was* informed that the information was on its way. It will arrive on one of the two steamer runs today. I can tell you that Morgan and Springer went in on deals together from 1880 to 1886. There will be plenty of facts about those years. Does that satisfy you?"

"It *would* . . ." the sheriff dangled.

This assault did not catch Pulitzer unprepared. Rather, it seemed to even his keel. Unlike J. P. Morgan, he was evidently not a man who would bluster at and then streamroller a man who was strong of will yet weaker in power. Pulitzer clearly enjoyed confrontation and challenge and determined to win by forthright reasoning.

"It would . . . if what?"

"If I hadn't just read the article on Mr. Springer's death in your newspaper."

"It gave no less coverage than the other major New York papers," Pulitzer asserted.

"And you, no doubt, fed their articles to them as well, seein' as they had no one down here. The point is that your paper gave no *more*. I thought you said you were determined to see the murderer punished."

"And how would a screaming headline have accomplished that?" the newspaperman returned. "I've goaded William Hearst into pursuing social issues with headlines, but what would a huge article have accomplished in this case? Other papers' reporters aren't allowed on the island. *My* newspaper's reporters aren't allowed on the island. In truth, as a member of the club, I shouldn't have posted that story at all. *That* indicates my desire to see the murderer punished."

"The question isn't the story's existence in your paper; it's how you soft-pedaled it."

The tic curled Pulitzer's cheek again, but still he maintained his composure. "Let me understand this: You think that because I sought to protect the club and its members by 'soft-pedaling' that story, I will withhold important facts gathered for you on Morgan and Springer collaborations for the same reason." Pulitzer drew himself up to his full height. "I am a man of my word. Nothing will be withheld. Look, Sheriff, the public thirsts for the blood of the rich. I know it; I feed it to them often enough. But this would be innocent blood, wouldn't it?"

"I suppose."

"And your own investigation has proven that there was no great conspiracy here. At the very worst, two members might have plotted to murder the man. The official judgment was 'accidental shooting.' To have suggested anything otherwise would have served no purpose other than to put the murderer on his guard. The minute the *World* appeared to question the death, all the other New York papers would have run with it. These papers are shipped down here to the members. You understand?"

"I do."

"However, *if* we do succeed in unmasking this person and I fail to give that headline its due, then you may truly flagellate me. Until then, have faith." Having said his piece, Pulitzer made a blind, spidery reach for a pillow, found one, and shoved it behind his neck. "Have you been equally as hard on Mr. Morgan?"

"I'm keepin' after him," John vowed.

"Not this morning, though," Pulitzer said, with smug assurance.

"No, not this mornin'."

"And do you know where he is at this moment?"

"Can't say that I do."

His smug expression spread across his face. "I do. Last night the small fry were gotten out of the way. Assistant Secretary of the Interior Bliss served as the host, at the Baker cottage. They gushed their platitudes at

McKinley, presented their petitions, stated their concerns, wheedled for political concessions, and now that's out of the way. This morning, the real game begins. Let me not leave you out, Mr. Tidewell. Can you hazard a guess as to the nature of the big game?"

"I'm sorry. I can't."

Pulitzer threw his feet up on the coffee table. He hit a coffee cup a glancing blow, sending it careening off its saucer. Pulitzer gave it a smart kick, and it exploded against one of the walls. Bits of orange peel and grape stem tumbled off the table and were lost in the Aubusson carpet's riotous colors.

"McKinley, Hobart, and Hanna went on another carriage ride," Pulitzer announced. "I was also to have been gotten out of the way yesterday. Morgan pretended to be oh so gallant in offering me 'Guinea's' first attention. He had no idea I'd suggest a carriage ride to the northwest corner of the island, however."

"How did your interview go?" Warfield asked.

Pulitzer waved the question away. "As I anticipated. Useless. McKinley's an idiot. A puppet on Hanna's strings. We were all pleasant to the point of nausea, but the purpose of the ride was the ride itself! What's in the water just off the northwest shore?"

Warfield's tight lips indicated that he adamantly refused to answer.

"The oyster beds," John volunteered.

Pulitzer laughed heartily. "That's the first stupid thing I've heard you say. Farther offshore!"

John understood. "Morgan's yacht."

"Exactly! I took the politicians that way precisely so they'd have no excuse to drive there again. In fact, I specifically said that if they went on any other carriage rides, they should demand to head over to the Shell Road and the beach. This morning, *two* carriages left the stables. I had my secretaries stationed strategically: near the stables, the clubhouse, Sans Souci, Baker's cottage. The first carriage contained Morgan, Lanier, McKinley, and Hanna. The second held Eames, Claflin, Hobart, and Sage. And which way did they head?"

"To Morgan's yacht!" Warfield ejaculated.

Pulitzer beamed. "Northwest for certain. If not to Jupiter's floating fortress, I'll eat it."

"Why didn't they leave from the club dock?" John asked.

"Because everyone knows that Morgan is engineering earthshaking decisions whenever he takes powerful men out on his yacht. He's no different from you or me; he returns to what has worked best for him. He thought he could hide the excursion from his enemies in the club . . . but I know him too well."

"And we are not to know the specifics," John said.

"Certainly not. Yet I know," Pulitzer declared. "Speaker Reed was not brought down here for nothing. His presence is an implicit threat. One must only ask oneself what issue Reed and McKinley are most at odds over. Keep in mind, it must be the quality of issue that might get Reed nominated by his party over McKinley. I gave you the answer the other day: the battle over the limits of U.S. imperialism. Reed vehemently opposes us extending ourselves into the Pacific Ocean. Specifically, annexing the Philippines."

"I recall what you said," the sheriff replied. "I had a lecture about this broad subject from Mr. Morgan as well, the first night I was here."

"No doubt," Pulitzer said. "It is clearly preoccupying his mind. He frequently solidifies his thinking by talking at people. Did he ask for your opinion?"

"No."

"Of course not. He rarely talks *with* people."

Le Brun worked hard to stifle a yawn, then said, "The news seems to argue on Mr. Reed's behalf. I read in your paper about the problems we're already havin' in the Philippines."

Pulitzer smiled with pleasure. "So good of you to read the *World!* Those problems indicate that Reed is right. It is simply too far away to protect and would require stationing of massive numbers of troops. Ventures to the Far East would also require the creation of two separate navies: one for the Atlantic and one for the Pacific. Now, annexing Hawaii last year was an excellent strategy. Those islands are all by themselves, and we have almost eighty years of history there. But coveting the Philippines is asking to make Spain's mistakes all over again. The countries of the Far East are impossible for any Caucasian peoples to control. Especially with the Rising Sun on the imperialistic rise. You mark my words!"

"I take it that you believe some degree of imperialism is justified?" John asked.

"Of course," Pulitzer came back. "It's been the game since Columbus discovered the New World. It made sleepy Spain a world power. Unless we engage in it, we will lose the world supremacy we deserve. If any nation's commerce and politics need exporting, it is 'the land of the free, and the home of the brave.' However, our natural sphere of influence must be limited to the New World."

"I see," the sheriff said.

Warfield leaned far forward in his chair. "What's the point of positioning your secretaries all over the island, other than curiosity?"

"A very practical point," Pulitzer assured him. "If I'm not mistaken, they had Stetson bring the *Kitty*, *Hattie*, or *Sibyl* up to Bayard Brown's dock. Brown's the fellow who joined the club the first year and built a cottage several miles north of here for his bride-to-be. She jilted him, and he sailed to England, brokenhearted. The cottage, its furniture, and its dock are all rotting away, but I daresay the dock's still sturdy enough to hold this fleet-footed gang of scoundrels. I was so sure Morgan was bringing them to his yacht that I posted G. W. near the Brown cottage before sunup!"

"That doesn't seem particularly practical," John pointed out.

Pulitzer cocked his head and listened. "Oh, but it is. And, if I'm not mistaken, here comes G. W. to assure me it was."

Heavy footsteps tromped up the stairs. Dr. Hosmer entered the room, puffing but grinning madly. The tips of his shoes were caked with mud.

"Just as you predicted, Andes!" Hosmer crowed. "Right to the Brown dock. Two carriagefuls. The *Hattie* was waiting for them."

"Who was piloting it?"

"Stetson."

Pulitzer slapped his knee. "Damn, I'm good." He turned toward the sheriff. "Would you please excuse us now, gentlemen? We have a few private matters to discuss. I'll be sure to have you summoned when the Springer information arrives."

"That's fine," John said, rising. "Mr. Tidewell and I will be in our rooms at the clubhouse, restin'."

A T A LITTLE AFTER NOON, Le Brun roused his deputy from a deep sleep, so that they might dine together. To their surprise, they had each become elevated to the status of persona grata, at least as far as Charles Deering and Samuel Dexter were concerned. The members invited the lawmen to sit amongst them and their wives. All were most cordial.

Mention of the departed Erastus Springer and the subsequent investigation and pseudoresolution was pointedly avoided. The topics of discussion during the meal were the islands in the area, the local commerce and festivals, Le Brun's and Tidewell's reactions to the president's visit and to the president himself. It was pleasant if unmemorable conversation, with the exception of the last subject.

"I noted that you dined the other day with Dr. Russell," Mr. Deering observed.

"That's correct," John answered.

"What has he to say about the members of the club?" asked Deering.

John set down his fork. "Very little. He keeps his own counsel. I believe he's anxious to return to his teachin' duties at Johns Hopkins."

Deering and Dexter exchanged glances.

"Are either of you considering him as a surgeon?" John inquired.

"Certainly not!" Mr. Dexter said, in a bristling tone. "We were wondering why Johns Hopkins would have the bad taste to send him down in the first place."

"What's the problem?" Warfield asked.

"He's a nigger doctor," Deering stated, grimacing with distaste. "When that bleeding-heart-of-Jesus fool Johns Hopkins died, he left a fortune to start his medical school. One stipulation was that qualified women be admitted with the same standards as men. That's laudable." Deering smiled at his wife and Mrs. Dexter. "But he also stipulated that the hospital branch of the school maintain a Negro charity ward! Dr. Russell's in charge of all surgery for it. He volunteered for the job!"

Mrs. Dexter read John's incredulous eyes. "I know it sounds shocking, but I went there for minor surgery. Dr. Kelly, not Dr. Russell. I saw it with my own eyes."

"Don't black people deserve medical attention as much as white people?" Warfield blurted.

It was as if the young man had reached out and backhanded the rest of the table in one vicious swipe. Heads reared back. The women blanched.

"Nobody *deserves* anything in this world, Mr. Tidewell," Mr. Dexter proclaimed. "We all earn it. If Mr. Hopkins saw fit to squander part of his fortune helping the useless and ungrateful, that was his prerogative. If Dr. Russell wishes to squander his talents on these people, that's *his* prerogative. However, the school should have better sense than to send us such a man. The error will not happen again, I can promise you."

"The point is," Deering broke in, "that we pay handsomely to have that man *in the infirmary* and at our beck and call. Last night, my wife had severe cramping, and Dr. Russell was not available for almost an hour." He reached out his hand to comfort his pinch-faced spouse. "What did he do but fly over to the Negro quarters, attending to who-knows-what. Something trivial, no doubt . . . while one of the members could have been having a heart attack!"

"A man had a dislocated shoulder and torn muscles," Warfield answered coolly.

"Really?" Deering said equally coolly. "Well, that man should have been brought to the infirmary, so we wouldn't have to hunt all over creation for our doctor. On at least one other occasion since we've been here he left a note on the infirmary door, stating that he was with the black servants. I tell this to you because one is sometimes unfortunately unaware of the poor company he keeps."

"How true," John said.

"And there you sit dining with this nigger lover," Dexter added. "A simple word to the wise can rectify matters."

"Precisely," Warfield said. "A word is all I need."

John glanced at his watch. "Speaking of matters, we must take our leave. We are, after all, also here to serve the club. Thank you so much for this enlightenin' conversation."

John rose and bowed deeply to each of the women. They beamed. The men, however, offered no hands for shaking.

As the Southern men left the dining room, Warfield said, "You know, Princeton, New Jersey, is a very white, colonial town. And yet a sizable section on the western edge is inhabited by Negroes. It's the result of many of the young students' servants being freed before the war. Princeton, you see, was as far north as Southern gentlemen cared to send their sons for a fine education. The minister teachers were quite persuasive about the rights of all Americans to be free."

"I take it the tradition continues," John said.

"It does."

"And what does your father have to say about your sympathies toward our dark brothers?"

"He's never asked, and I've never told him."

"It's a good thing," John said. "He's not exactly been zealous in pursuit of our citizens who wear white sheets and pointed hats." He stopped at the front desk for messages. None had been left. John turned to his waiting chief deputy.

"I want you to find Mr. Rasher and rattle him. We may be askin' him for a great deal soon, and I want him considerin' afresh how we can destroy him with a word."

"It will be my pleasure. Asking him for what?"

"I'll tell you in good time," the sheriff replied, smiling as he used the phrase for the second time that morning. "When you're done, come back here," he directed. "I shall be hauntin' the library or game room."

WARFIELD FOUND RANDOLPH RASHER on one of the three clay tennis courts, giving a workout to the club pro, Frank Bowman. Warfield sat patiently, watching Rasher's combined skill and natural athleticism, observing what the women so admired in him. No matter how sharp the angles of Bowman's shots, the former Yalie was able to reach them, moving with feline quickness and grace. He had evidently been playing for some time, as his shirt was soaked and clinging to his chest and back. Magically, his hair seemed as dry and neat as ever. Finally, he concluded the set in triumph. He jumped the net to thank his opponent, grabbed a towel off the net cord, and walked over to Warfield's bench.

"Got a cigarette?" Rasher asked.

"Sorry."

"Only bum them, eh? Do you play?" he asked, twirling the racquet around his forefinger.

"A little. Too little to be humiliated by you, if that's what you had in mind."

Rasher walked away, heading south. "I take it this is not a social call."

Warfield stood and followed. "I want to know what you've learned regarding Springer's death."

The Morgan junior partner's head swung quickly right and left. "For Christ's sake, lower your voice! I need to cool off. Let's walk someplace shady where we won't be overheard."

"Very well."

"You seem to know so much about my women," Randy said softly. "Tell me about yours."

"I have none."

"What?"

"I did have a serious girlfriend when I was up in Philadelphia," Warfield defended. "That ended along with my employment. As for down here, it's only been a few weeks."

"A few weeks without a woman can be an eternity at our age," Rasher said. He cocked an eyebrow. "Unless one is of the Oscar Wilde ilk."

"One doesn't have to pursue women night and day to have a healthy interest in the opposite sex," Warfield returned.

"Touché."

The two had passed behind Sans Souci and were closing on the infirmary. "Are we far enough away now to suit you?" asked the deputy.

"Another two minutes."

The two minutes brought them to the Shell Road.

"All right," Warfield said. "Time's up. What about Springer's death?"

"The evidence about the poacher was created," Rasher reported.

"By whom?"

"The guard who found the body."

"Ezekiel Turner."

"The same."

"Nothing we don't know already. Who put him up to it?"

"Mr. Morgan. But not because he himself did anything wrong," Rasher hastened to add. "He's still convinced it was a poacher."

"Really?"

"That's what he told me. He just needed the mess cleared up as quickly as possible."

"Because of the president's visit."

"Exactly."

"Turner disappeared," Warfield said.

"I heard. He was paid roughly what he'd earn in an entire season working here. I'm sure he did what's predictable of men of his class. He went to unspeakable places to squander his sudden wealth as quickly as he got it."

Warfield passed on the information about Turner's demise that Sheriff Le Brun had supplied him that morning.

"You see? I was right on the money!" Rasher exclaimed, with no pause to deplore Turner's death.

"What are you grinning about, Randy?" Warfield said, in a tone that was almost a growl. "With Turner dead, the burden of moving this case forward now falls squarely on you."

"That's unfair!" Rasher protested. "I have nothing else to give you. I took a great risk coaxing the information about Turner from Mr. Morgan. They call Mr. Baker the 'Sphinx of Wall Street,' but J. P.'s not far behind."

Warfield turned onto the path where Erastus Springer had been shot. "You took a much bigger risk seducing Mrs. Springer. If you're convinced that Morgan and Stetson had nothing to do with the murder, then look elsewhere. The old bastard didn't shoot himself! And it wasn't any damned poacher."

For all his strength, Rasher sidled away from the even more powerful deputy. There had been vague reports of Warfield Tidewell's temper back in college. He could see now that passion rose rapidly in the man. Such passion, teamed with prodigious muscle power, was nothing a prudent man would ignore.

"Perhaps you should employ your charm on one or two other foolish wives," Warfield suggested.

"Not on your life," Randy returned. "I might ask among the member children what they've heard. All right?"

"Not all right unless you get us answers," Warfield said.

Rasher paused. "I've cooled off enough. I'm going back."

Warfield kept walking. "No, you're not. I want you to see something."

"What?"

"Follow me."

Rasher remained several steps behind the deputy, no longer interested in dialogue. Every minute or so, he swore under his breath and beat the air with his racquet.

When Chief Deputy Tidewell was almost to an enormous live oak, he pointed silently to the vegetation to his right, indicating that Rasher was to leave the path. The businessman obeyed, but swung viciously with the racquet at the low plants that threatened to touch his bare legs.

"Hold it there!" a voice commanded.

Both Tidewell and Rasher came to abrupt halts. A man appeared from behind another live oak, around which curled clematis vines. In his hand was a shotgun.

"Frank!" Warfield exclaimed. "What are you doing out here?"

"John told me to wait here . . . see who showed up. He didn't say what to do if it was you."

"What's this all about?" Rasher asked.

Warfield studied the junior partner's face. It showed patent confusion. He was convinced there was no dissimulation in the expression.

"A bit of a return to the scene of the crime," Warfield blurted, in his embarrassment.

Rasher's expression changed to annoyance. "This isn't the scene of the crime. That's out on the path, somewhere ahead." Then he blinked, and a new look of hard calculation came over his face. His eyes darted around the area. "Isn't it?"

"Never mind," Warfield said. He turned and started out to the path.

"Should I stay put?" Deputy Tarbell called out to Warfield.

"John put you out here," the chief deputy answered. "He'll let you know when he wants you to leave."

"Well, tell him the no-see-ums are eatin' me alive!"

"What happened here?" Rasher demanded, plunging through the undergrowth after the chief deputy.

Having gotten nothing from the Eli and knowing that he had ruined some plan of his superior, Warfield Tidewell's mind was roiling with mixed anger and fear. He wheeled around on Rasher. "I ask *you* questions!" he shouted. "Don't you damned ask me anything else until you can give me some answers. And don't let me see your face again until *I* cool off!" Rasher's mouth gaped open in shock. Warfield whirled again and entered the path at forced-march speed.

SHERIFF LE BRUN was lounging on the clubhouse piazza, reading a magazine and drinking an iced tea with a sprig of mint in it, when Warfield came up to his side.

"I need to speak with you," Warfield hissed, painfully aware of both the heat of his face and the quizzical looks being given him by several people on the piazza.

"I take it from that tone of voice that you mean us to move," John replied.

"Yes."

The sheriff sighed, shut the magazine, took a final sip of the drink, and struggled up from the white wicker fan chair. "Which way?"

"Perhaps we should head south," Warfield suggested in a low voice. "Frank wants to know if he can leave his post."

John Le Brun's eyes went wide. He held his chief deputy's stare with his own. He walked toward the Jekyl River.

"I just embarrassed myself with Randolph Rasher," Warfield said. "You told me to rattle him. He was like a clam, so I thought I'd use the place Reverend—"

"If I asked Reverend Parkhurst not to say anythin' about the place, why would you take Rasher there?"

"To look for a sign of recognition in his eyes," Warfield argued. "I wasn't going to let him search around. And we'd taken every piece of evidence anyway. I don't understand. Did you put Frank there on the off chance that the murderer would return, after four days?"

Le Brun kept walking, veering north on a diagonal that would soon intercept the road. "You certainly *do not* understand. Who have we talked with today who would have gone there if he was the murderer?"

Warfield lowered his head in thought. He knew he had declined in his boss's opinion, and he was determined to sink no farther. At last he had it.

"Dr. Russell."

"Why?"

"Because you asked him about the suit and mentioned a missing sliver of bullet."

"And."

"The murderer had been carefully picking up little pieces of cloth and might want to look in the oak for the bullet."

"And, by leading Mr. Rasher there, you have most likely made Frank's presence useless. You no doubt paraded right by the infirmary."

Warfield stopped. "How can you blame me?" he complained. "All you needed to do was let me in on it." His cheeks reddened as John stopped and looked back at him. "*Why* didn't you let me in on it?"

The sheriff walked up to within inches of his deputy. In a calm, quiet voice, he said, "Because, for the past two days, you have reported to me smelling of the aroma of cigars. Not just any cigars, but the particular ones rolled at Mr. J. P. Morgan's private plantation in Santa Someplace, Cuba."

Warfield's flush drained rapidly.

"That you have been working for Mr. Morgan is beyond doubt," John continued. "In what capacity, I rely on you to confess."

The deputy dug his boot toe into the dirt. He looked to the sky for a moment, as if some deus ex machina would momentarily descend from the clouds to save him.

"As his bodyguard. Nothing more," Warfield said. "The man is frightened to death that the murderer is still on the island, and that he's his next target."

"And what were you supposed to do?"

"For the past two nights I went to his apartment and stood guard from ten until seven. When I say 'stood guard' I'm not exaggerating. He allowed me to catch some sleep, but I had to do it on the couch in the parlor. That's why my back has been killing me." He threw up his hands. "It was purely for the money. He paid me fifty dollars each morning. Cash. One night got me what five weeks as a chief deputy does. After all my expenses defending myself in Philadelphia, then moving my belongings down here, I had virtually nothing, John. You ask me to consider my job seriously? I am. I want to put down roots here, and three or four lousy nights guarding that old bastard would get me the down payment on a little house." He dug into his trouser pocket and hauled out a roll of bills. "Here! Count it. One hundred dollars."

Le Brun eyed the money, then turned in a slow, full circle.

"I'm not bought, Sheriff," Warfield protested. "In fact, I even thought it might loosen Morgan up, that he might believe I was on his side so he'd let down his guard. Reveal who he feared and why."

John gave his deputy a sidelong glance. His look was softer. "I know a right pretty little house on the edge of town. A hundred might just do it."

Warfield laughed with relief.

"Do you feel as beat as I do?" John asked.

"You have no idea."

"He didn't tell you spit, did he?"

"Morgan? Naw. But he also didn't sleep, either. Hiring me gave him no peace of mind."

"That's good." John pinched the bridge of his nose hard. "Damn, that man throws money around! First Turner gets two hundred. Then you get a hundred. When do I get some?"

"I'm sure all you'd have to do is ask," Warfield said.

"Which you know is out of the question." They had passed Baker's cottage, Solterra, on their walk. Just beyond it, well back from the road behind wide lawns and artfully placed bayonet palmetto, lay a house that combined the clean lines of modern architecture with Spanish roofs and whitewashed stucco. Two long rectangles ran away from the road, bookending a high-ceilinged central structure at right angles to them. Three French doors were set equidistant in the central area, topped by lunette windows. Despite the fact that Brunswick had nine thousand inhabitants and was a well-to-do town by Georgian standards, there was not one home so grand on its streets.

"Whose is that?" John asked, nodding at the vacation home.

"It belongs to David H. King, Jr.," Warfield supplied. "He's a successful New York contractor."

"Very pretty," John said admiringly. "So, if I wanted to build me a copy of that, what would it run . . . fifty thousand or so?"

"Probably sixty," Warfield judged. "You're looking at a giant U shape. Inside the U is a swimming pool. Add another ten thousand to furnish it."

John blew out his breath in awe. "I don't think even J. P. Morgan, much as he enjoys throwin' around his cash to have things his way, would give me that much to leave him alone." He nodded in the opposite direction, where other enormous "cottages" fronted the River Road, beyond the clubhouse lawns. "Let's see if the gargoyle disguised as a newspaperman has the background on Springer that he promised."

"I'm sorry about taking Rasher to the oak."

Le Brun waved the apology away. "It was a long shot. Russell's probably innocent, and if he isn't he's too smart to fall for so bald a trick. You might have made up for it by guardin' Morgan. Never know what you might pick up, bein' so near."

Warfield nodded. A degree of care had slipped from his face. It was noted by the sheriff.

A pair of bicyclers whizzed past the men. Farther along the road, several older vacationers paraded by the dock. The president's visit had encouraged most to stick close by the Village. As the lawmen came to the turnaround driveway to Pulitzer's cottage, they noted that a group of young people had gathered around the planted "poacher's skiff" that the deputies had moved out of the swamp. Among them stood Randolph Rasher.

"You've got him scared," John noted to Warfield. "Good for you."

When they entered the cottage, they were greeted by Dr. Hosmer.

"The information you want has arrived," he reported, "but you'll have to wait until late tonight to get it."

"Why's that?" the sheriff asked.

"Because Andes is sleeping. Resting for the big dinner being thrown by Frederick Baker this evening. Over at Solterra. Andes was invited and told that he could not bring a guest. They were counting on his unwillingness to go out unescorted, especially to noisy affairs. He skunked them. Please come back at around ten. He said he wouldn't stay for the whole affair."

John thanked Pulitzer's self-appointed appointment secretary and led his chief deputy down the steps. "Why don't you fetch poor Frank out of the woods, then go back and catch a nap?" he said. "We have a long night ahead of us. As well as hearin' what Mr. Pulitzer has to say, we will take turns watchin' Solterra. If the president is in danger, tonight is the time it will most likely occur."

"Mr. Morgan expects me to watch him," Warfield said softly.

"You may tell him that I require you on duty from eleven to two. If he wishes your services after that, you are free to provide them . . . naturally without sayin' I know anythin' about it."

"Very well."

John raised a hand. "Why don't I make a reservation to dine at eight? There should be tables available."

"There had better be. We won't be invited to anyone else's," Warfield returned.

"And I am crushed." John waved his deputy off and set a tack for the clubhouse.

CONSIDERING THE VISIT of the president, Jekyl Island had become an even more sedate place. Decorum reigned. Although each table in the members' dining room sported a brilliant arrangement of flowers instead of the usual bud or two, the conversations at those tables were especially subdued. John and Warfield decided that everyone was waiting for something momentous to occur. The lawmen worried that the momentous event would be an attack upon the presidential party. Redmond Drayton and Burt Davenport had reported to the clubhouse just before eight, to replace the other, exhausted deputies. Sheriff Le Brun had directed them to patrol constantly around Solterra.

After checking that the Jekyl River was free of strange boats and assuring themselves that the two fresh deputies were alert and prepared for mishap, John and Warfield strolled over to the Pulitzer cottage. Dr. Hosmer greeted them. The hour was precisely ten o'clock, but the newspaperman had not returned.

"Come upstairs and let's wait together," Hosmer invited. "We have a stock of excellent Château Margaux in the cellar. We mustn't end the season without finishing it off."

Tidewell and Le Brun waited on Pulitzer's second-story balcony. The physician appeared without his rubber apron, bearing an uncorked wine bottle and three glasses. He sat on one of the chaise longues and poured himself half a glass.

"Please," he bade. While John and Warfield filled their glasses, he said, "I was hoping you'd come before he returned. I wanted to speak to you about your attack on Andes's ethics today, Sheriff."

"Is that how he phrased it?" John asked.

"Well, no," the publisher's staunch defender admitted. "However, he was quite upset at what you said *and* implied. He holds your opinion in high regard, you know. No small accomplishment on your part, considering the brevity of your acquaintance. He esteems both of you, in fact." He set one heel atop the balcony railing. "It's not so simple, the position he's put in here. Thomas Carnegie of Pittsburgh bought all of Cumberland Island, just to the south, as you may know."

"We do," John said, speaking for Warfield in spite of their bare acquaintance.

Hosmer nodded. "When Andes heard the report on this island, he wanted to do the same. Buy Jekyl outright. Unfortunately, he was frozen out by a previous deal. He determined to retain some part of the island for his enjoyment, even if it meant sharing it. Because he's a journalist and the others are all so newsworthy, he's constantly put into awkward situations." The apologist stopped, as his words should be sufficient explanation.

"Give us a for-instance," Le Brun invited.

Hosmer cleared his throat as he weighed his words. "Andes has a collective name for the members of this club. He calls them 'the wolves.' What is most important is that he divides them into two classes. The first are the 'noble wolves.' They achieve great things and give more to society than they get, in spite of getting much. The second he calls the 'rabid wolves.' These were born with an aggressive instinct and further damaged, he believes, by some childhood calamity. Abject poverty, lack of parental love. Something terrible in their formative years that compelled them to claw, bite, and maul their way to the top."

"The problem is that security can be as much a mental issue as a physical one," John said.

"Exactly," Hosmer agreed. "They continue their fierce ways because they never feel secure. If having ten million is good, having twenty million is better." He made his peculiar pinch, flick, and brush motion, removing seemingly nothing from his chair. "One club, two kinds of members. Here's your 'for-instance,' Sheriff: Andes realizes that he could seriously damage the club's reputation with what he knows about this political visit. Perhaps he could give the place such a notorious reputation that half the members would resign. It fails and closes, which might even allow him the opportunity to buy the island for himself. But at what price? Would that be fair to the innocent members, who only come for relaxation?"

"No, it wouldn't," Warfield said forcefully.

"Just as importantly," Hosmer went on, "there's an understanding at work here. A social contract. Morgan, Lanier, and the others allowed Andes to join because, his journalism notwithstanding, they respect him. Their only condition was that he take a vacation from his work."

"But *they* don't," John pointed out.

Hosmer poured himself another two inches of wine. "Precisely. And therein lies the dilemma. Oh, everyone talks business on the golf course or over dinner. But that's member to member. *Entre nous* stuff. This bringing Reed down and pitting him against McKinley, like throwing two game cocks into a ring, goes far beyond that."

"So, what has your boss done about it?"

Hosmer grinned. "I won't steal his thunder. He must tell you." He jumped up from the longue. "In the meantime, let me reveal one more of the talents I've picked up over my many years: card tricks. I'll get a pack and show you a few."

Warfield shot John a weary glance.

"Wait! Here he comes now!" Hosmer said, leaning over the balcony. He rushed into the house. The phaeton came up River Road and turned into the driveway. The elegant coachman brought the horses to a halt, hopped out, and held the door open for his employer. By that time, G. W. was in the driveway, prattling and soliciting at the same time.

John and Warfield retired into the overlarge bedroom and closed the French doors against the rising night damp. Joseph Pulitzer entered, resplendent in a vanilla-colored suit and white, patent-leather shoes. If Hosmer professed to know card tricks, Warfield reflected, Pulitzer looked like the master magician Harry Kellar about to perform his first illusion, dumping his gloves into his hat and then crisply handing it to his assistant/ physician.

"So good of you to wait for me," Pulitzer declared, addressing a coat tree near the French doors. "And how are you both this evening?"

Le Brun and Tidewell replied together, thoroughly confusing the near-blind man. He retreated to his couch. He seemed to be in too good a mood to be vexed by anything. He belched.

"And I am more than fine. I am excellent, thank you. Except for this blasted stomach of mine. Should I begin with news of the dinner party or of Mr. Springer?"

"The dinner party!" Hosmer cried out, before either of the lawmen could respond.

"That's what I'd prefer," Pulitzer said, clinching the decision.

"Start with who was there," Hosmer coached.

Pulitzer threw his arms along the back of the couch. "It was thrown by Mr. and Mrs. Baker. The guests were myself, the McKinleys, the Hobarts, and the Thomas Pages."

"None of the Morgan gang," G. W. pointed out.

"Will you shut your mouth?" Pulitzer snapped. He reaffixed his genial expression. "The Morgan gang, as G. W. so aptly calls them, were absent. So much for the cast of characters. The setting: Solterra. The style: You tell me when I'm finished. Act One: Pulitzer's Entrance, fashionably late. They all rush to embrace me. Picture them acting as if the poor, blind Joseph were their long-lost brother. Solicitous to a fault. Inquiries about the particulars of my health. And of Kate and the children. Even knew their names. Well rehearsed. But I was forgotten in a corner in no time."

"What?" Hosmer bristled.

"Calm down!" Pulitzer commanded. "It was exactly what I wanted. Act Two: Ida McKinley Throws a Fit . . . even before the appetizers. It came up like a sea change. No one was sure what set her off, but I'll wager it was Mrs. Page's attentions to the president."

"Maybe she was just upset over the trial next month," G. W. posited.

"What trial?" John asked.

"It's a scandal in Ida's family," Hosmer said, "about to come to a head."

Warfield leaned toward the sheriff. "Her brother, George Saxton, was a notorious libertine. He was shot several times as he exited the house of a widow named Eva Something."

"Althouse. And the murderer's name is Anna George," Hosmer broke in, as Warfield was taking a breath. "She's pleading justifiable homicide, because Saxton had promised to marry her shortly before."

"His affair with the widow Althouse was one indiscretion too many," Warfield added.

"Excuse me," Pulitzer said, finally looking annoyed. "May I continue?" His audience encouraged him.

"Thank you. Ida is a jealous viper, pure and simple. She wasn't upset over the trial back in January, when she accused Secretary Alger's wife of trying to steal McKinley away from her. And they were her guests, in the White House no less!"

"It's like having the *World* come alive, isn't it?" Hosmer enthused.

"Act Three: The Dinner," Pulitzer plowed on. "I am seated between Mrs. Hobart and Mrs. Bliss. More like between ignorance and Bliss. They both declared that they did not read my newspaper, but they adored 'what they had heard' about our reporting on the recent Wells Fargo stage holdup and on Jumbo the elephant. Phonies. Their prattle was uncanny, but I did manage to focus my attention on other areas of the table. A greater effort at avoiding politics was never on this continent attempted. Only an imbecile could have come away convinced that this side trip from Thomasville was indeed purely for recreation."

"Only an imbecile," Hosmer echoed.

"When I want a Greek chorus, I'll ask for it," Pulitzer said. "Act Four: The False Alarm. Just as we were about to take dessert, a report came in. It said that John Sherman had died." Everyone in the room understood that this was the brother of Union general hero William Tecumseh Sherman and also able senator from Ohio. He had been duped into accepting the position of secretary of state so Marcus Hanna could grab the senatorship as his reward for winning McKinley the presidency.

"The women retired at this news. We stayed on and smoked, waiting for more intelligence. It turned out he's not dead at all. Just wishes he was, probably. But it gave me a wonderful opportunity to turn the topic to the embarrassing subject of politics. Everyone vowed that the presence of Speaker Reed had nothing to do with the visit. To a man, they swore that next year's election was the farthest thing from their minds."

"And did you say anything about the trip out to Gadroon's yacht?" Hosmer asked.

Pulitzer set his hands on his stomach and looked as jolly as Falstaff. "I did not."

"Why not?" John asked.

"Because I'm waiting for something to develop."

Both Hosmer and Pulitzer burst into forceful laughter, clearly a private joke.

"I told you two I'd sent G. W. to the Brown cottage to spy," Pulitzer shared, when he had recovered. "What I didn't say—and you must forgive me for not trusting you—is that he had with him one of Mr. Eastman's wonderful inventions."

"A box camera!" Warfield exclaimed.

"Yes. You both must have seen the many photographs on the club-house walls. Most were taken by members. The club has two cameras for rent. They'll even have the exposed film developed for you. We can't trust their services, however."

"We'll keep the film cool until we return to New York," revealed Hosmer, the proud coconspirator. "Mr. Pulitzer's photographic experts can develop it."

The newspaper mogul bounced lightly on the couch in his glee. "And even if G. W. did a terrible job and ruined every shot, we can still point to the fact that the camera was rented last night and returned tomorrow. If it's one thing they do here, it's keep meticulous records of every penny laid out and brought in."

"I took six photos in all," Hosmer reported. "One of them getting out of the carriages, two of them on the dock, and three boarding the *Hattie*. I tried to capture the *Corsair* in that last picture, but it was far away. What a miraculous age we live in!"

"Tell me if I'm correct in this," Warfield said. "You will let President McKinley and his party depart without saying a word."

"That's right," Pulitzer affirmed.

"And when will you reveal that you've taken photographs?"

"We won't reveal it," Pulitzer said. "We'll mail copies to McKinley and Morgan. No message; just the pictures."

"And the purpose?" John asked.

Pulitzer threw up his hands. "Whatever we need it to be. Right now, I'm thinking it will be to move McKinley toward Mr. Reed's way of thinking. We do not need to annex the Philippines, no matter how big Jupiter's appetites are."

"Once again, the pen has proven mightier than the sword," Hosmer proclaimed.

"Inapt cliché, G. W.," Pulitzer chided. To the other two, he said, "So, you see that this play I describe had a prologue. And now, gentlemen, you may name its style."

"Vaudeville," Le Brun supplied.

"Nothing so clever," Pulitzer came back. "It is *la comédie rustique Américaine*. They planned a political dinner, whose invitation I would refuse. When I surprised them, they changed the script and improvised a completely apolitical evening. All for naught. Steaming secretly to the silence of that enormous yacht. Getting their cuffs and shoes soaking wet. All for naught. Is there anything here to eat?"

"An apple," Warfield answered.

"Hand it to me, if you would." Pulitzer accepted and polished it, then took a large bite. "And now to the business of Messrs. Springer, Rasher, and Russell.

"Springer first. Almost all his enterprises of late have been free of questionable methods. Like many of the members, he made a good part of his early money through railroads. Oh, the capital wasted on expansion then! He started in 1880, as an agent for the Denver and Rio Grande Railroad. The D and RG was one of those bottomless pits that went from nowhere to nowhere, capitalized mostly with British money. The Morgan family was involved in it at the beginning but wisely pulled out before it went bust. That's the first connection of Springer with a member, albeit tenuous.

"The second is from 1886, when the military district of New Granada, South America, was organized into the Republic of Colombia. Mr. Springer was involved with Jim Hill in providing the money to put certain people in power. In exchange, they got exclusive rights to build the country's railroads. That year, Springer also worked as J. P. Morgan's front man, putting Henry Ives's Vandalia line out of business by calling in his loans.

"The third also involves Morgan and loans. There was a silver mine near Leadville, Colorado, called the Seventh Heaven. It was doing well, but the miners struck. After four weeks they were near starvation. Then a thousand-dollar gift came to them, from a group that called itself the

Miners' Guild of Montana. There was no such group. It was Springer and Morgan supporting the strike through a front, so that it went on long enough to beat the owners. Their loan was about to be called in by the bank, so they sold to the Springer/Morgan syndicate for two-thirds of what they normally would have gotten. Springer made up the thousand-dollar gift by lowering the miners' wages by two cents an hour.

"Lastly, Springer teamed up with Jay Gould in stealing away the Little Kanewha mine. Different method. Same result. After that, he didn't have to use partners. He went into semiretirement when his first wife died. Had a fifty-thousand-dollar policy on her."

"But even he couldn't create consumption," Warfield said.

"Don't bet on it," Hosmer commented. "He might have convinced her to do charity work in the tuberculosis wards."

"All right," John said, anxious to make something of the information. "What about Jim Hill?"

"He's a member, but he wasn't on the island when Springer was murdered," Hosmer said. "And Jay Gould was never a member."

"His son, George, was part of the Kanewha scandal," Pulitzer assured.

"But he would have needed wings to kill Springer and get onto the *Howland*," John pointed out. "What bothers me is that in all of these cases he was working *with* members of the club, not against them. And I can't see any of them fearing that Springer would reveal anything. It would only implicate him as well. Finally, all these cases are so old. That's everythin' about Springer?"

"That's it," Pulitzer said.

"What about Rasher?"

"Born with a silver spoon, and he's been sterling ever since. Father a Hartford insurance man. Mother's family dates back almost to the *Mayflower* and is rich from real estate. Attended Yale. Top honors. Captain of—"

"We know his college history in detail," John broke in.

"Very well. Married money. Two small children. Specializes in Morgan's foreign dealings other than those with England and the European continent. Which is another clue that Morgan's trip down here was specifically made to work on annexation of the Philippines. As deep as my investigators dug, Rasher never had any intercourse with either Springer or his second wife. Never any arrests. Belongs to no hunting or shooting clubs. As far as we can tell doesn't even own a weapon. No displays of

violent temper. A very careful, controlled young man. Cautious in everything but the ladies."

"And Russell?" John asked.

Again, without consultation of notes, Pulitzer said, "Dr. Thomas S.
Russell. Age is twenty-nine. Attended Saint George's Episcopal School in
Manhattan."

"Your church, Andes!" Hosmer exclaimed. "Are his parents members
of the congregation?"

"Were," Pulitzer said. "Both dead. Will you all let me go on? He first
enrolled at the age of thirteen. No record of transfer. Columbia University
with honors. Then College of Physicians and Surgeons for two years." He
glared in Hosmer's general direction. "Your school. We all know. Graduated sixth in his class. For the past five years he's been a teacher and
resident surgeon at Johns Hopkins Medical. Has charge of the black charity wards as well. Commendable, I say. Is a member of no clubs. Drinks
from time to time at his local bar. Takes his meals in three local restau-
rants. He has no arrests and is known to be a mild-mannered, generous
gentleman. No church affiliation. Expresses no public opinions that are
anti-American or even antirich. Apparently completely devoted to his
teaching and the charity wards."

"What about his parents?" John asked.

"Arthur and Winnifred Russell. Came over from London in 1876. That
would have made Thomas only six when they arrived."

"Isn't his accent rather strong, considering he's been in this country so
long?" Warfield asked.

"Accents are largely formed by that age," Pulitzer declared. "After that,
it's a question of a good ear and desire to accommodate."

"Perhaps he had a governess and British tutor in the house," G. W.
postulated. "It would explain why he didn't enroll at Saint George's until
age thirteen."

"You just said that they came over from London," John noted. "Didn't
Dr. Russell tell us he came from Manchester, Mr. Tidewell?"

"Did he?" Pulitzer asked.

"It's in your notebook," John directed. "Take a look!"

Warfield pulled out the notebook and found the right page. "That's
what he said, all right."

"No wonder we haven't tracked down his early life in England," Pulitzer said. "We've been researching in London. That's the second inter-

esting fact. The first is that Arthur was fifty in 1870, when Thomas was born. Stranger is that his wife was forty-four. We got both from their obituaries. Thomas is listed as their surviving son. Bearing and delivering a healthy child at such an advanced age is a rarity, even for a doctor's wife." He laughed at his witticism, and Hosmer followed in support.

"Arthur and Winnifred were both buried under the auspices of Saint George's. I don't mix with the parishioners as much as I should, I suppose, so I had one of my employees who is also a member speak with the sexton. He goes back thirteen years. There are two sisters in the family, quite a bit older than Thomas. They married and moved out of town. The Russells had moved uptown—haven't we allow all—about ten years ago. We couldn't track down any of the former neighbors. As far as we can divine, none of the Russells had anything to do with Morgan or Springer."

"Can you have your people make some inquiries in Manchester?" John pursued.

"Certainly, although I can't fathom what value there is to it. What about from your side, Sheriff?" Pulitzer asked. "Any breakthroughs?"

"Not a one."

Pulitzer took a second bite of the apple and, from his expression, decided it was not to his liking. "Then, to borrow another of G. W.'s clichés, we may be as dead in the water as the *Corsair* is right now. You should have raced to the beach side, G. W. Might have caught a picture of the old pirate's ship steaming by. I'll bet a yacht can be a marvelously quiet thing, especially if built right. Maybe I'll build one, G. W. Make it one foot longer than Morgan's."

The group laughed, needing the humor to pull them out of their collective dejection.

Pulitzer stood. "His is black. Mine shall be pure white. I'll call it *Liberty*. But that's for another day. Good night, gentlemen. Better hunting to you on the morrow!" He extended his hand. Warfield moved forward quickly with an open palm. Pulitzer pressed the apple into it. "Throw that away for me, won't you?"

JOHN WAS STILL CHUCKLING when they hit the night air. "I wager you'll never meet such an interestin' character as long as you live," he told Warfield, speaking of Pulitzer.

"Does that include yourself?"

"I'm not interestin'," Le Brun protested.

"Not from where you stand, perhaps," his protégé said. "I *am* on your side, John. I want you to know that."

"Buildin' that tower of trust stone by stone, eh?"

"Exactly."

John scratched his nose. "Well, you shall have your opportunity to prove your loyalty tomorrow."

"How?"

"By doin' somethin' desperate," said the sheriff. "Mr. Pulitzer did not come through as I had hoped. That probably isn't his fault. But I am now compelled to desperate measures. And if you are truly on my side, then you are also desperate to solve this crime. Tomorrow we shall be politely ejected from Jekyl Island. There will be opportunity for only one more gambit."

"You don't care to share that with me right now?"

"Not because of a lack of trust," Le Brun said, "but because I want at least one of us to get some sleep. Go do your tour of duty. I will relieve you at two. At least when the president climbs back on that navy boat, one of our worries will be over. No, two. I can send all the boys back to town. I keep havin' this wakin' nightmare: Bobby Lee's commandin' a skeleton crew on a wounded leg, and some gang's cleanin' out every bank in Brunswick while we're runnin' in circles over here. I should have sent you back to take over the office this mornin'."

"Why didn't you?" Warfield asked.

"Because there are too many valuable lessons for you here. Keep your eyes open." With those words and a light pat on the back, the sheriff was off for the clubhouse, leaving his chief deputy standing in shadows.

Warfield watched Le Brun retreat for a time. Few lights were on in the Village. Only the upper floor of Pulitzer's cottage and J. P. Morgan's bedroom in Sans Souci blazed with light. Warfield reached to the small of his back for his revolver. Holding the weapon down by the side of his leg, he advanced on Solterra.

WEDNESDAY

MARCH 22, 1899

JOHN LE BRUN QUIT his surveillance of the Village at first sunlight. He returned to his room with the intent only of changing his
underclothing and shirt, washing, and shaving. The bed, however,
beckoned, more to his weary legs even than his sleepy head. He rolled
onto it and stretched out atop the covers. The next thing he knew, someone
was knocking on the door.

Warfield Tidewell stood with his back against the opposite side of the
hallway, droop-shouldered.

"You'll be overjoyed to know that Mr. Morgan is safe and still sleeping," he said.

"What time is it?" John asked, yawning.

"Half past seven. Maybe I shouldn't have—"

"No. It's time to be up." John retreated for his shoes, leaving the door
open. "You as ravenous as I am?"

"Probably more so," Warfield answered. "You had me convinced that
a regiment of kidnappers was coming for the president last night. I was
more nervous than a long-tailed cat in a room full of rocking chairs, and
moving like it."

"Then let's stoke up," John said. "It's probably our last meal on the
joint."

While the pair were waiting to be seated, Ernest Grob approached
them. Without introductory pleasantries, he announced, "The president

has decided to depart ahead of schedule. The time will be ten this morning."

John duplicated the club superintendent's ramrod posture. "Very good," he said, also matching the Swiss man's clipped words.

"And then you will be gone," Grob said.

"Is that a question or a statement?"

"A statement. I may not be a member, but this is *my* club. Members come and go, but this club is my life. You have created a major disruption, and I am convinced you did it with perverse pleasure."

"Mr. Springer's death created the major disruption," John countered. "Be assured that I dislike you at least as much as you dislike me. My reason is your lack of compassion. I pray that someday I shall have the perverse pleasure of hearin' that you've been replaced by an elaborate Swiss watch."

Grob turned on his heels and strode away.

"Their pancakes are very good, John," Warfield said, in an overloud voice.

"Remind me again why he isn't our main suspect," John said.

"He was identified in the clubhouse by more than a dozen people," Warfield answered.

The sheriff snapped his fingers in mock frustration. "To hell with the waiter. Let's go. We know where he'll seat us, anyway."

Following breakfast, the lawmen left the clubhouse by a less direct route than the front doors. John had expressed an interest in viewing more closely the photographs Joseph Pulitzer had referred to the previous evening. There were pictures of successful boar and quail hunts, elaborate picnics on the beach, a spirited doubles tennis match, ladies enjoying tea on the front lawn, bathing on the beach, exploring the shell of the old tabby house, and a new photograph of the president's arrival. De rigueur for every picture was several people having enormous fun.

"The good life, eh?" John asked his deputy.

"One type of good life," Warfield returned.

On the way out, they encountered Reverend Parkhurst, entering from his last walk of the season. John released him from his promised silence, in fact suggesting that the minister tell a few select people. A few moments later, they spied Randy Rasher heading toward the clubhouse in his tennis outfit.

"Win again?" Warfield called out.

Rasher paused, tousling his hair with a towel, as the lawmen approached. "I lost, matter of fact. Sometimes, depending on who you're playing, you can win more by losing."

"You have another chance to win," Le Brun told him. "I require information that will seal our lips forever concerning your relationship with Mrs. Springer."

Rasher's eyes showed expectation of a monumental request.

"I would not ask this except that I believe it has a good chance of exposin' Mr. Springer's killer."

"Name it," Morgan's junior partner said, an edge in his voice.

"I need a detailed layout of the *Corsair*. According to Mr. Pulitzer, your employer keeps his most private papers there. If he can't—or won't—tell us what went on between him and Springer, his records might."

"And what do you intend to do, board his yacht and overpower more than fifty men?" Rasher asked. He looked as if he had been accosted on Wall Street by a mental patient.

"Never you mind that. I require you to diagram precisely where the papers are kept, if they're locked up, and how to get at them."

"I can't do that," Rasher said, aghast.

"Well, you must," Le Brun insisted. "Come, Mr. Tidewell."

"I mean I can't! I don't know where—"

"Then find out. One of us will knock on your door between one and two this afternoon. Have the information ready."

"You might as well tell everyone about me and Chrystie," Rasher said in a defeated tone. "If Mr. Morgan links me to this, my career's over."

"But only with him," John pointed out. "You won't have ruined his reputation at this club, so he won't bedevil you to your grave. I don't want my career ruined either. I assure you, I have devised a way to prevent him from findin' out."

"There is no such way," Rasher said.

The sheriff shrugged and turned toward the clubhouse. "You'd better hope so, Mr. Rasher. One o'clock in your room."

As they rounded the clubhouse, Warfield said, "How can you trust him? What if he tells Mr. Morgan what you're up to?"

"When I need to know what my opponent will do, I always put myself in his shoes," John answered. "It's not as easy an exercise as it seems; most people are too lazy to work at it. You'll need to as a lawman. Become

Randolph Rasher for one minute, then tell me whether he'll risk what I'm askin' in exchange for his freedom or whether he'll go to Morgan."

It took the chief deputy only half the allotted time. "He'll give you what you want."

"If he can, he will," John asserted. "Let's get down to the dock."

T HE TRICKLE of vacationers leaving the clubhouse became a flood as the sound of the navy cutter *Colfax*'s horn blasts ripped through the morning air. John and Warfield walked down to the place on River Road where it intersected with Pier Road. G. W. Hosmer, who had donned a straw skimmer with red, white, and blue bunting and who displayed an effervescent mood, had staked out a prime location and offered its remains to the Southerners. Around them, the servants were supplying their charges with the same tiny American flags they had waved two days earlier.

Two of J. P. Morgan's servants, one the old fellow who had admitted John to Sans Souci on the night he played chess with Morgan, stretched out a red ribbon between themselves, reserving space at the corner of the road and lane extensive enough to hold half a dozen persons. Presently, Morgan came strolling across the lawn, flanked by Stetson and Rasher. They moved up to the red ribbon like racehorses entering their starting gates. Directly across from them stood Judge Moore and Speaker Reed. The acknowledgments of each other's presence carried barely enough energy to vault the lane between them.

"I want you positioned on the opposite side of the lane," John directed his chief deputy in a low tone, "but first go down and tell Harvey to cover the bottom of the dock." Deputy Harvey Buncombe had arrived piloting the Brunswick Police launch a minute before and was tying up to the downstream side of the pier. "Both of you keep your hands near your revolvers when the president arrives. Ignore the politicians and watch the crowd for hidden hands. You understand?"

Warfield nodded and threaded himself slowly through the crowd toward the end of the dock.

As the sheriff studied those around him, he saw Morgan pivot and himself survey the crowd and the lawns beyond. "Where's Sage?" he asked peevishly. He consulted his pocket watch. "For that matter, where's Scrymser?"

No one had an answer. Morgan reached into his coat for a cigar, thought the better of lighting it in such crowded conditions, and returned it to its inner sanctum.

At last, the presidential party appeared, emerging from Solterra, just to the north of the clubhouse. The cheering, applause, and flag waving buoyed them from cottage steps to carriage and thence the short distance to the mouth of the dock. John overheard the intelligence that, to please those half-dozen members and the numerous guests who had not been granted an audience with McKinley, Marcus Hanna had been cajoled into giving a farewell speech.

The president stood directly behind Hanna in support, looking well tailored but not fashionable. The "Grocer" looked much more approachable, a plump man in his late fifties, with a mobile face that looked as beatific as an old Irish priest's. When he spoke he twitched his upper lip and mouth sideways like an old horse, which made him appear anything but a politician. The theme of his short speech was predictable: As soon as McKinley had assumed the presidency, the long recession had ended.

In the middle of his talk, Hanna said, "It's taken some time, but we've gotten this country back on the track. Who can complain? Furnaces are glowing. Spindles are singing their song, and the song is prosperity. Happiness will come to every American as we continue to grow. Our ancestors—and yes, not a few of the very men who stand here—have fought for our freedom, and now we reap the benefits."

George Washington Hosmer leaned in to John Le Brun's ear. "And this from a draft dodger. He'd get more applause if he asked all his fellow draft dodgers to take a bow."

The speech ended with more thinly veiled exhortations to reelect McKinley and thus ensure another four years of prosperity. By this time, John was hardly listening to the platitudes. What held his attention was the growing perplexity and annoyance of J. P. Morgan. Every half minute or so, the man jerked his head toward Sans Souci. Just as the speech was concluding, his face became fixed in that direction. John followed his stare and saw James Scrymser standing in front of the apartment house, almost hidden in the shade of a tree.

The presidential party boarded the *Colfax* to much fanfare. As the boat steamed away, it blew its powerful horn several times. Waiting in the channel to dock was the *Howland*. Quite a few among the crowd hurried toward the clubhouse and their cottages to direct the transport of their belongings to the dock. President McKinley's departure had symbolically, if not officially, signaled the season's end.

Warfield ascended the lane, heaving a theatrical sigh of relief. John and Hosmer remained where they had stood for the speech, John ignoring a rain of inanities pouring from the genial doctor/reporter/chemist. The sheriff's attention was instead riveted on James Scrymser intercepting the Morgan contingent, delivering a few hasty words, and continuing directly toward the lawmen. Whatever he had said had frozen Morgan, Stetson, Lanier, and Rasher. As Scrymser neared, John registered the barely controlled panic in his eyes. John closed the distance between them, leaving the garrulous G. W. talking to himself.

"I need to speak with you, Sheriff," Scrymser said, in a tense voice. "Right away."

Signaling to his chief deputy his still-uninformed state, the sheriff allowed himself to be led to the privacy of a nearby weeping willow. He listened to Scrymser's words for a full minute, glancing twice during that time at the large apartment building. When the millionaire had stopped talking, Le Brun reached out his hand and guided Scrymser toward the Morgan group. At the same time, he crooked his index finger at his chief deputy.

"What's happened?" Dr. Hosmer asked.

"We'll get back to you," Warfield said.

"Do you know what's happened?" Hosmer repeated.

"Stay at your cottage, and we'll come to you," Warfield promised. He jogged up to Le Brun's side.

Le Brun leaned close to Chief Deputy Tidewell's ear. "There'll be a lot of people wantin' to get on the steamer. Go down and tell Harvey not to let 'em."

"What's happened?" Warfield asked.

"Another murder. He's not even to let their luggage go on until you or I tell him personally it's all right, y'hear? Just let the servants stack it all along the dock. No boat is to leave the island!"

"What excuse does he give them?"

"The *Howland* is experiencin' rudder problems. You tell Cap'n Clark that he's to corroborate this. Mr. Lanier's orders."

"There'll be chaos," Warfield warned.

"There already is," John rejoined, heading back toward the waiting group of millionaires. "Get Mr. Lefferts and have him put some of his guards on this!" he called. "Then come up to Sans Souci quick as you can!"

J. P. Morgan, Charles Lanier, Randolph Rasher, Francis Stetson, and James Scrymser formed a defensive huddle before the main entrance to the huge condominium. Close by stood the two servants who had held the red ribbon.

"I don't suppose anyone cares to confess to Mr. Sage's murder?" the sheriff asked.

No one spoke.

John yanked at his tie. "Does anyone *suspect* who killed him? Hello? Y'all look like an oil paintin'."

"We have no idea, Sheriff," Lanier answered.

"All right, then. I'll say this slowly, so it has time to sink in. As you are all convinced, it *is* possible to sweep one murder under the rug. It's possible to mis*judge* one as an accident, with the help of manufactured evidence. I'm not in the mood to debate whether or not this happened here recently. Let me just say for the record if any of you have not yet heard that Mr. Ezekiel Turner, the guard who found the deer and the old skiff, is dead. His death was precipitated by the payment of a large amount of money to him. If it turns out that that obstruction of justice allowed Mr. Sage's death, woe to the person who paid Turner off. And sure as hell there will be no obstruction with this second murder."

No one opened his mouth to comment.

Le Brun stuffed his tie in one of his jacket pockets. "A man shot on the property of a huntin' club is only mildly suspicious; a second man stabbed to death in the seclusion of his bedroom is another matter altogether. The president, thank the Deity, has come and gone." He leveled his stare at Morgan. "He and his party no longer need to be insulated from scandal. I have two deputies on this island, and I will not be threatened or bribed into givin' up this investigation. Is that clear?"

"We won't impede you, Sheriff," Charles Lanier hastened to affirm. "We only request that this be kept amongst the smallest number of persons possible."

"Now, how are you goin' to do that, considerin' that everyone wants to get off the island?"

"I believe we can let anyone Mr. Sage didn't know leave," Scrymser answered. "You'll see when we go upstairs."

"Then let us hasten upstairs. Mr. Scrysmer, you found the body."

"Yes, sir. Mr. Sage was staying in one of my spare bedrooms."

"Lead the way. Those with weak stomachs would best remain in the hallway."

Scrymser spoke as the group entered the hallway, the sheriff at his side, Morgan and his retinue next, and the servants in the rear. "I knocked on Mr. Sage's door about seventy-five minutes ago, in case he had overslept. I got no answer, so I went to breakfast. I didn't see him there, either. Neither had anyone else. I came back here and knocked again, to no answer. Finally, when I saw from the window that Senator Hanna was about to speak, I opened Mr. Sage's door. I found him lying on the floor with . . . well, you'll see in a moment."

The group entered Scrymser's apartment living room and followed him through it into the spacious guest bedroom. The men fanned out in a semicircle from the doorway. Some immediately went for their handkerchiefs, to shield their noses and mouths from the smell of excrement. James Sage lay next to the bed, facedown. Protruding from between his shoulder blades was the hilt of a moderate-sized knife.

"Did you touch anything?" John asked Scrymser.

"Nothing except the doorknob. You should know that all doors inside the apartment were unlocked."

Le Brun approached the body and moved around it in a C pattern several times. Sage was dressed in suit pants, a white shirt, and suspenders. His hair was neatly parted and pomaded. His left profile was exposed. The sheriff got down on hands and knees and laid his face on the carpet parallel to that of the victim. He pressed his palm to the corpse's forehead, pulled back one eyelid, opened the mouth and probed into it, then put his nose close to the mouth and inhaled.

"This man wore pince-nez glasses," John stated. "Where are they?"

"Here, on the writing desk," Scrymser said.

John continued studying the corpse. Both arms lay by its side. He examined both hands and attempted to move the arms up and down. He probed the area around the knife wound. The shirt had absorbed blood to roughly the size of a playing card. The depth of the knife and its place of entry left no doubt that the wound had been fatal.

"This is outrageous," J. P. Morgan said, but his words carried little energy. Dread was stamped on the face of every man in his group.

Warfield entered the room gasping for air. Half the men already in the room started with surprise.

"Catch your breath, Mr. Tidewell. You have missed little," John told him.

The sheriff walked to the only other door in the room, which opened onto a balcony overlooking the front lawns. He tried the doorknob. It was locked. He examined the locking mechanism, turned it, and pulled back the door. Its hinges squeaked softly. He walked outside, returned a few seconds later, and said to his chief deputy, "I want to be sure I can lock myself out. Let me in if I can." He released the spring bolt and stepped outside. His rattling of the doorknob proved what had been obvious: The killer could have locked the door on the way out. The hinges spoke again as he swung the door shut. Finally, he left it open.

"Let's get a little fresh air in here, shall we?" Le Brun said.

"He must have left that door open and been surprised," Stetson declared.

"You would not agree, Mr. Scrymser, would you?" John asked.

"No, sir."

"And why?"

Scrymser nodded toward the desk. Behind Sage's eyeglasses and a nest of splayed-out documents sat two drinking glasses, each containing about a finger's depth of the same color liquid that filled five-sixths of an opened bottle of whiskey.

Le Brun stuck his hands deeply into his trouser pockets and began rocking slowly from his heels to his toes and back.

"Mr. Sage was still in his street clothes," John said, "except for his coat. His shoes were still laced. I would say he was quite awake and alert when he was stabbed. If a sudden breeze from the door's openin' wouldn't inform him that someone had intruded, those hinges certainly would have. He might have been overpowered, but then he wouldn't have been stabbed in the back. There's no sign of struggle. His hands have no cuts. Most damnin' to your theory, Mr. Stetson, are those drinkin' glasses on the writin' desk."

John crossed to the desk and picked up first the bottle, then one of the glasses. With the Henry system of fingerprint detection yet to be introduced at Scotland Yard two years hence, he had no thought of destroying vital evidence.

"Looks very much like a drinkin' buddy was the killer," John said. "Or perhaps it's been made to *look* like a drinkin' buddy was the killer. Whether it was poured down his throat by himself or his killer, Mr. Sage does have whiskey on his lips. Was there a domestic on duty last night?"

"Yes," Morgan spoke up quietly. "My man, Isherwood. He's just out in the hall."

"Ask him in, someone," John ordered.

Randolph Rasher rushed to summon the servant. Isherwood turned out to be the same man who had let the sheriff into Sans Souci on the night he played chess with Morgan, the same man holding the red ribbon near the dock less than an hour before. The servant tried not to look at the body, but his morbid curiosity compelled him to cast his eyes downward. His pale complexion grew chalky.

"Mr. Isherwood, this nearly filled bottle of whiskey in my hand . . . did you bring it to Mr. Sage last night?"

"No, sir. He carried it in himself."

"Last night?"

"Yes, sir."

"When was that?"

The old servant pondered the question sincerely. "Between quarter to ten and ten."

"Was he alone?"

"Yes, sir."

John nodded. "Is there always someone on duty in the downstairs hallway at night?"

"Between the hours of eight and six in the morning there is." Isherwood cast another baleful glance in the corpse's direction.

"No one goes in or out of the buildin' without you or someone replacin' you seein' him?"

"I suppose that must be true. . . . at least through the main doors. Where I sit, I can see them. It's a straight hallway and quite wide."

The sheriff, noting the servant's discomfort and inability to avert his eyes, stepped into his line of view with the body. "Were you on duty all that time?"

"No, sir. I'm on from eight until midnight. Then I'm relieved by one of two younger men. The one who served last night is most likely asleep now."

"I see. But their shift is probably quite dull. I understand everyone is in bed by eleven on Jekyl Island."

Mr. Isherwood cast a fearful eye in J. P. Morgan's direction. "Well, no one comes *in* after midnight, but sometimes those already inside leave. Mr. Morgan has had guests leave later."

"Rarely!" Morgan insisted.

"Yes, very rarely," Isherwood hastened to agree.

"And occasionally I send whoever's on duty then over to the clubhouse," Morgan expanded, "for food, drink, or whatever. I require little sleep."

John sauntered over to the writing desk's wooden chair, over which the suit jacket that matched Sage's trousers neatly hung. "Did you send Mr. Isherwood to the clubhouse at any time last night?"

"No, I did not," Morgan replied.

"You were on duty continually from eight until midnight, Mr. Isherwood?"

"I was."

John lifted the jacket off the chair. His fingers explored the back of the article of clothing and found no rent. "And you stayed in the hallway until your replacement showed."

"I did."

John felt in the jacket pockets. He found a handkerchief, which he dropped onto the floor, and, in a side pocket, a blue jay feather. He replaced the jacket over the chair and set the feather carefully on the desk. Despite the tedium and the droning tone of the sheriff's questions, none of the men spread out along the room's inner wall made restless motions or sounds. None attempted to interrupt, to speed along the process. All seemed fascinated by Le Brun's methodical analysis of the crime. The atmosphere was charged with anticipation.

"Now, you say Mr. Sage came in between nine forty-five and ten o'clock."

"Yes, sir," said Isherwood.

"Did he go out again?"

"Not before I went off duty, for sure."

"Who was inside the building when you went off duty?"

"Everyone."

A few men laughed lightly, relieved for even the slightest excuse to break the oppressive tension.

"Can you tell me their names?"

"Yes, sir. Sorry, sir. On the first floor, no one. Mr. Stickney's apartment's closed up tight for the season. Mr. Anderson's is also unoccupied. Judge Moore and Mr. Reed were together on the second floor. Mr. and Mrs. Rockefeller's, across from them, was vacated last weekend. Mr. Morgan and Mr. Stetson were on the third floor and Mr. Scrymser and Mr. Sage were in apartment six."

"No extraneous guests?"

"No, sir."

In the silence following the servant's words, Warfield Tidewell's pen could be heard furiously scribbling notes.

"Did anyone else come in durin' the night?"

Isherwood nodded at Warfield. "He probably did."

"Right," said the sheriff in a casual tone. "With my blessin', he's been providing protection to the person I suspected would be the next target."

J. P. Morgan's black eyebrows rose in surprise.

Warfield Tidewell continued to scribble, head down.

"When did you enter the buildin', Chief Deputy?"

"It was just after two, Sheriff," Warfield said, as casually as he could.

"And I know you saw no one."

"Other than the young man on duty."

"We'll have an autopsy done presently, but if I'm any judge of time of death Mr. Sage was dead well before two o'clock. His corneas are milky; he's more than cool to the touch, and rigor mortis has fully set in. Good deal of the blood is dry. Mr. Isherwood," John went on, "you've already said you can see whoever comes and goes on the lower floor. What about the upper two floors?"

"If I'm standing, perhaps I may get a glance of someone in the upper hallways. Usually, however, not. I can hear them, but I don't see them."

"So, someone could go from one apartment to another to another quietly, and you might never know."

"I suppose."

J. P. Morgan remained uncharacteristically silent. When the sheriff's eyes locked with his, he merely shook his large head solemnly.

"Mr. Scrymser, when was the last time you were in this room before Mr. Sage's death?"

"Late yesterday afternoon. Mr. Sage and I were looking over some paperwork."

"The papers on the desk now?"

Scrymser crossed to the desk, slid Sage's eyeglasses carefully aside, and studied the papers. "Yes."

"Does it appear that anythin' has been removed?"

"Stolen?"

"If Mr. Sage had somethin' that belonged to the killer, it wouldn't be stealin'. Has anythin' been removed?"

"Not so far as I can see. There wasn't very much in the room."

John picked up the glasses and peered through them. He looked around the room and out past the porch. He set them down and went to the nightstand beside the bed. He took up a billfold that lay there and nosed through it. Plenty of paper currency protruded from the back fold. Simple theft was out of the question. He looked under the bed, threw back the covers, crawled around the carpet a bit, examined the contents of the armoire, and peeked behind the bedroom door.

"All right, then," the sheriff said. "That ends the initial inquiry. You said you'd like this murder hushed up as well." His last words were directed at Lanier.

"It's our earnest wish."

"Very well. Anyone who had nothin' to do with Mr. Sage may depart. I believe it is clear enough that the murderer was invited into this bedroom."

Morgan, Scrymser, and Stetson nodded agreement in unison.

"Mr. Lanier, please come down to the dock with Mr. Tidewell and myself. It's time now for the physician," said the sheriff.

Morgan turned his fiery eyes on Isherwood. "Hobart, would you fetch—"

"Excuse me, Mr. Morgan," John interrupted. "I'll fetch Dr. Russell myself. Would someone like to volunteer to stay in the room while I'm gone, to see that nothin' is touched or removed?"

Rasher, Stetson, Scrymser, and Morgan looked at each other.

"We'll all stay," Morgan announced.

Once the lawmen had accompanied Charles Lanier to the dock and heard him countermand John's order to hold the *Howland*'s departure, they headed for the infirmary. A formation of ducks winged noisily overhead.

"This is so strange. James Sage wasn't even on the island when Erastus Springer was killed," Warfield noted.

"But he had already been summoned," John returned. "Telegrams were sent the night previous to Mr. Springer's murder."

"You know now who did it, don't you?"

The sheriff shook his head. "You think because I've been doin' this job for so long that I should know? I'm a small-town sheriff, pitted against not only somebody smart but also a bunch of people who seem as eager to cover up these murders as the murderer himself. *You're* the one with the high-powered education. You know everythin' I do. I should be askin' you for the solution."

"I'm completely baffled," Warfield admitted.

"Because we still don't have the key information," John said emphatically. "That's why we must get onto Morgan's yacht and into his records. All right, here we are." They had reached the path leading to the infirmary's front door. "Set yourself so you can watch the doctor's face when I break the news about Sage."

"He's still on your list?" Warfield asked, incredulous.

"He still not off my list," John replied.

Thomas Russell answered the infirmary door dressed much as he had been the previous day. "Good morning, gentlemen."

"Not really," John returned. "You know James Sage, don't you?"

There was no sign of recognition on the doctor's face. "No. Should I?"

"He was stayin' at Sans Souci. He's dead."

Russell's eyebrows elevated slowly. Otherwise, he seemed unmoved. "Shot?"

"Stabbed," John revealed.

"That's terrible. And who did it?"

"Probably the same man who murdered Erastus Springer."

Russell sucked in his cheeks a bit and made a small sound in the back of his throat. "I'll make the back room ready for the body."

"Not this time," Le Brun said, halting the physician in midturn. "We're gonna keep this one under our hats for as long as possible. I want you to do the autopsy in the room where he was murdered."

"But I require quite a bit of equipment, and it will get messy," the doctor argued.

"That notwithstandin'." Le Brun began moving. "We'll help you carry whatever you need. Hang a sign on your door, Doc; this will take some time."

IT WAS AS IF time had stood still in James Sage's bedroom. Morgan, Lanier, Stetson, Scrymser, and Rasher remained by the inner wall, silent and serious as a dead pharaoh's golden sentinels. Warfield noted, however, that the pile of papers on the writing desk had not only been neatened but was also visibly lowered.

Dr. Russell acknowledged the formidable group with a nod as he entered, then went directly to the body. From one of his black bags he produced an angled pair of medical scissors and began cutting the dead man's shirt away, from tail to collar. When he was done, he stripped down the suspenders and opened the shirt like a book, exposing the victim's back.

As a child, Warfield had become inured to the carcasses of dead mammals when he often visited a friend whose father owned a meat packing plant. He assumed that the sheriff had witnessed too many bodies in his youth as well, on half a dozen battlefields. But he was surprised that not one of the businessmen beside them seemed in the least degree squeamish. He thought wryly that it was because they had all had so much practice figuratively stabbing men in the back.

"One stab wound," the doctor announced. "Between the third and fourth ribs, right scapula and spine. May I remove the weapon?"

"Go ahead," Le Brun invited. "Then roll him over." He stage-whispered to his chief deputy, "Neatly done. Just one stab, up where Sage'd have a hell of a time pullin' it out. And it looks like a bullfighter did it."

"What do you mean?" the chief deputy asked.

Le Brun lifted a finger. "Wait a second, Doctor! You see how the blade is parallel to the line of the ribs, instead of at right angles to it? Most people would stab a victim with a downward, overhand thrust that would put the handle at an angle and the blade parallel with the spine. Not this killer. Haven't you ever seen pictures of the way a matador thrusts? He holds the sword so that the blade has a better chance of penetratin' the bull without lodgin' in a rib. Same here."

"Excellent observation," Morgan praised.

"What's more," Le Brun went on, "the handle bottom faces right. The attacker either held the knife the normal way in his right hand and kept his elbow out or else used his left and held the knife upside down. And he was probably a tall fellow."

"Because the knife went in so high?" Charles Lanier wanted to know.

"Exactly. And I say 'fellow' because the weapon was driven to the hilt in one stab. You may remove it now, Doctor."

Dr. Russell handed the knife to Sheriff Le Brun.

"That's one of the club's steak knives," Randolph Rasher noted.

"Yes, we noticed that while you were gone, Sheriff," Morgan added. "We forgot to mention it." Even though the word "sorry" was missing, his tone was apologetic. The second murder had taken much of the bark from the watchdog of the club.

"How many knives like this would you say there are, Mr. Lanier?" John asked.

"I'd have to check with the staff, but I'd venture to say two hundred. Virtually anyone could lay his hand on one, even if he weren't eating meat."

"We might take the weapon as a message," John remarked, setting it on the writing desk.

Dr. Russell turned the body over, into a supine position. The sheriff squatted at the feet.

"Doesn't look like he met his maker as peacefully as Springer did," John observed.

Sage's face was frozen into a death mask of horror. His eyes were wide open, his lips drawn back so far that his teeth looked like fangs.

"He also hasn't shed much blood," John observed.

The little amount of blood was dried on the corpse's lips and teeth and trailed down the cheek that had rested against the carpet. Only a small burgundy stain sullied the ornate, Victorian Oriental rug.

"There shouldn't be much blood," Russell stated. "Guessing from the position of the wound, the knife pierced his heart. It would have stopped beating within seconds." He examined the staring eyes, turning the head back and forth, then closed the eyelids.

"How long has he been dead, do you think?" Le Brun asked.

"I'll stick a thermometer in him in a moment. I can also get a good fix if someone knew when he last ate. Should I cut open his abdomen?"

"Not yet," John said. "If he was killed during the sleepin' hours, it shouldn't make a difference. Not at the Jekyl Island Club." He snorted out a sudden burst of air. "All right. I have somethin' else to attend to. Should take about an hour. When I get back, I want to speak with the fellow who was on duty from midnight to six."

"What about Judge Moore and Mr. Reed?" Lanier asked.

"They can be left alone for the time bein'," John said. "We know they were inside the buildin', and if either of them is guilty they won't say more just because they're asked. The fewer people brought into this the better." All heads nodded, including the doctor's.

John stood and ran his hands together. "What you gentlemen *can* set your minds to is gettin' somethin' large and waterproof to put Mr. Sage in, and then start bringin' ice over a bit at a time. He might be here in seclusion until tomorrow. Does anyone expect him home soon?"

"No," Morgan answered. "He wasn't married."

"Too selfish," Randy Rasher judged, his antipathy toward the man just as visible in his expression. "Maybe one of his whores might ask."

Jupiter Morgan shot his junior partner an intimidating look.

"He has a sister in Hackensack," Morgan added.

"A sister can wait." John nodded for Warfield to precede him out the door.

As they exited the building, Warfield looked back at the separate verandas for each bedroom.

"Someone could easily have come up the outside set of steps and been let in by Sage," he noticed.

"If that's the case, whoever it was took the trouble to lock the door on the way out."

"Focusing the crime on Mr. Morgan and his group."

"Just as was done the morning Morgan went huntin'. In fact, it looks so clearly like J. P. Morgan did it that I've pretty near ruled him out. If someone inside the buildin' did kill Sage, the outside door would likely have been left unlocked and possibly ajar."

"So, who did it?"

"Who indeed. Maybe Mr. Pulitzer can help."

H E'S EDITING COPY for tomorrow's edition of the *World*," Dr. Hosmer apologized to the pair of lawmen in the Pulitzer cottage's foyer. "Have a seat. I'm sure he'll see you in a few minutes."

Warfield grabbed the latest copy of the *World* from off the pile. "Shall I be your gazette?"

"By all means," John invited.

"Murderess Mrs. Martha Place is going to the electric chair at Sing Sing. The other main headline wonders if the Windsor Hotel horror was the work of thieves." He turned the page. "Ah. Ex-Secretary Sherman is improving. In Kingston, Jamaica, on the American Line steamer *Parks*."

"If I was in Kingston, Jamaica, I'd be improvin', too," John quipped.

Warfield turned another page. "This is interesting. The headline reads, '$21,000,000 IN CUBAN CLAIMS.' Goes on to say, 'More than two hundred persons on the island have filed demands for damages against Spain which must be settled by the United States.' Why would we agree to pay millions of dollars that Spain owes?"

John sat on the stairs and extended his legs. "Part of the deal, I suppose, for now bein' the virtual controller of the island. Sounds like Morgan's and Pulitzer's U.S. imperialism at work."

The chief deputy turned the pages again. "Here we are: 'M'KINLEY PARTY OFF FOR JEKYL TO-DAY.' " He looked at the front page. "This is Monday's paper."

"And what will tomorrow's paper say, I wonder," John remarked.

"He's ready for you now," Hosmer called down the stairs.

As expected, Mr. Pulitzer had his mouth full when they entered. He allowed his hand to be pumped up and down but continued chewing in an unhurried fashion until he had swallowed.

"What's all the fuss up at Sans Souci?" Pulitzer asked.

"You know that Mr. James Sage is here," Warfield began.

"Yes, the lawyer who wields Morgan's political hatchet," the newspaperman said.

"He's been taken ill," Le Brun said. "They thought he might have been poisoned by the same man who shot Mr. Springer."

Neither Hosmer nor Pulitzer showed that they suspected the lie.

"That was why you fetched Dr. Russell," Hosmer concluded.

"Exactly," said the sheriff. "I see your back windows still work."

"Who was close enough to the man to poison him?" Pulitzer asked.

"Unfortunately, almost everyone."

Pulitzer smiled broadly. "Except G.W. and I."

"Have you received anything about Dr. Russell and Manchester?" John inquired.

"Heavens, no! We only shot off that telegram this morning! It will take at least another day."

"I fear we don't have that much time," John said.

"I'm a journalist, not a magician," Pulitzer said with some annoyance.

John made a slight move toward the stairs. "We do appreciate whatever you can do, sir."

"I'm sure. Keep us informed about Sage, will you?"

On the way from Pulitzer's cottage, the sheriff remarked, "With the first murder, nobody could have done it. Now, between it bein' night and with that door into Sage's bedroom from the veranda, everyone could have."

"Maybe it was two different murderers," Warfield suggested.

"Not likely. It takes a great deal to get someone to murder in cold blood. Statistics discount two. But we'll keep our minds open, shall we?"

John looked up. Light, white clouds were being pushed eastward by dense, gray ones. The temperature and barometer were slowly dropping. The weather seemed to be mimicking the collective mood on the island.

Friday Cain and his mule-drawn wagon passed the two men on the road.

"How many departed on the *Howland*, Mr. Cain?" John called out.

"Twelve, sir," the wagon driver replied, on the move. "I 'spects about that number this afternoon. Hope they not stuck in Brunswick, with the schedule shifted back." The wagon continued toward the more hidden buildings of the Village.

"Pretty soon, it'll be just us and the staff," John told Warfield, "unless we make ourselves a break." He drew his watch from his vest pocket and consulted it. "Time is flyin'. Let's take care of the rest of our business and get to lunch. You locate the servant that was on duty from two until eight; I'll make sure Mr. Morgan stays put tonight. Then we'll both visit Mr. Rasher."

After John trudged into the apartment building, Warfield hunted down the servant, who had to be roused from sleep. The young man swore that no one except Warfield had moved in the hallways the entire night. He would not admit that he had slept during part of the time, but as the chief deputy passed at two A.M. he had witnessed the red marks on the man's cheeks from having slept in the same position for some time. While returning from the servants' house, Warfield found the sheriff hailing Joseph Pulitzer's carriage. Droplets fell sporadically from the clouds.

"Goddamned rain came purely because I wanted to get outside," Pulitzer fumed. "How long will it last, Sheriff?"

"If it's like most March storms in this region, I believe it will continue 'til sunset."

"Shit. Lot of good that will do me. I'm leaving Friday morning. The idiot editors are running my newspaper into the ground." The horses stamped impatiently and strained against Eugene Stewart's reins.

"Mr. Pulitzer, I require another favor from you," John said, as Warfield walked up to his side.

"Name it."

"I'm about to return to Brunswick to pick up some information. Your staff could no doubt use it to dig up more information and maybe solve this murder. It makes no sense to bring it all the way here to you only to—"

"I understand. You want me to sanction a telegram from you to authorize another investigation."

"That's right."

"Very well. Stop by in half an hour or so. I'll have G. W. draft something the idiots in New York will accept. Get going, Eugene! I'm about to wash away!"

The horses started off smartly for the Pulitzer cottage.

"Nice gargoyle," Le Brun commented to his chief deputy.

"I could use his newspaper right now . . . as a hat." Warfield turned up his collar. "What happened in Sans Souci?"

"Surprise. Dr. Russell pronounced Sage's death a murder. Knife through the heart." Le Brun and Tidewell started walking.

"And what did you say to Mr. Morgan?"

"You mean what did he say to me? He thought he should have back the money he paid you for the past two nights, seein' as how I said I had put you up to guardin' him."

"What did you say?"

Le Brun reached into his pocket and produced a twenty-dollar bill. "I told him that you did the job he hired you to do, so he was obligated. Furthermore, he owed you for your work from two to seven today, and that he might possibly be alive only because of your presence. He gave me this for you. Wanted you back tonight as well."

"But I'm going with you to the yacht."

John tugged his derby forward against the rain that now starting to pelt down.

"Of course. I told Mr. Morgan that you had served too many shifts and were goin' home but that I would put one guard in his hallway and one circlin' the buildin' for him . . . for the measly sum of sixty dollars. He agreed. When I walked in, servants were packin' his trunks. He wanted to sail tomorrow, but I told him it was out of the question."

Warfield laughed. "How good did that feel?"

"Like a million dollars. He blustered and complained about how I did not treat him with dignity. I countered by informin' him that his fly was unbuttoned."

"At some point the dog must let go of the tiger's tail," Warfield warned. "And then it's in trouble."

"But this dog is enjoyin' the ride immensely," replied the sheriff. "And now let us enjoy torturin' Mr. Rasher."

A MAP AWAITED Sheriff Le Brun on Randolph Rasher's bed. The precise location belowdecks of J. P. Morgan's private study was meticulously drawn. In the corner of the paper was also sketched a larger version of the study, with two *X*'s marked on it.

"This one's his desk," Rasher explained, poking his finger at the map. "He keeps it locked, but he hides the key in the hollow base of a big piece of rose-colored beryl."

"He really does love to play mental games," Warfield commented, as he took a seat at Rasher's writing desk.

Rasher stared at him. "What do you mean?"

"How do you know it's beryl?"

"He told me."

"What he evidently didn't tell you was the inside joke. Its common name is morganite."

"How fascinating," Rasher said, in a bored tone.

"Did Mr. Morgan show you this hidin' place?" John asked.

Rasher flicked the butt of his cigarette out the half-opened window into the rain. "No. I noticed the gem was frequently turned, whereas nothing else on the desk was. So I looked once when he was in the crapper. There it was. Of course, I've never used it."

"Of course not. What about this other *X*?" John asked.

Rasher made an indecisive move toward the door. "Could you both keep your voices lowered, please? That's the wall safe. Behind the Dutch landscape. I don't think what you're looking for could be in there."

"Why?"

"Size. It's stuffed with money, contracts, bills of sale, and agreements. His most valuable documents. There are a couple of ledger books, but they're small. The safe's only about two cubic feet. It's rather unique-looking on the outside. There's a silver dollar set in the middle of the dialing cylinder."

"A recently minted dollar?" asked Warfield.

"Yes."

"Another private joke." Warfield folded his arms, and a smug look came onto his face. "The man who designed that coin is named Morgan. To distinguish it from the old one, some people call it the 'Morgan silver dollar.' "

"Really. Well, good luck turning such useless knowledge to your advantage," Rasher said, picking up his map and folding it. "I think you can rely more on what I'm risking my neck to supply you."

"Has he entrusted you with the combination?" Le Brun asked.

Rasher handed him the map. "No. But I've caught part of it." A guilty look swept onto his face. "I've done it for the good of the firm. He's not a young man anymore. His heart could give out on him any day. As far as I know, nobody but he knows the combination. The thing is built like a fortress. One might have to dynamite it to get it open, and that could destroy everything inside. So, twice I got close enough when he was opening it to see something. It's a three-number combination. The first number I've never seen, but he gets there circling to the right. The second is back around a full turn and then to somewhere around fifteen. Maybe fourteen or sixteen. I saw only the longer line of the fifteen above his thumb. The last is to the right again, and that's definitely four. You'd better pray what you're looking for isn't in there."

"We could be trying combinations all night," Warfield told the sheriff. John shrugged.

"Promise me on your honor as a Princeton man that no document leaves the ship," Rasher insisted.

The chief deputy looked at the sheriff, who nodded his agreement.

"Very well," the Eli said. "And now we're even. I've paid in full for your silence regarding Mrs. Springer."

"Unless you've crossed us," Sheriff Le Brun said, pushing the map into his trouser pocket. "One last thing. I assume the study door has a lock."

"It does."

"Do you have the key?"

"Certainly not."

"But you've seen Mr. Morgan unlock the door on several occasions."

"Yes."

The sheriff dug into his other trouser pocket and produced his ring of keys. "Which of these shapes is like the key that fits that door?"

Rasher studied the keys for a moment. He touched one. "Like this."

"You're sure?"

"*Like* it, I said," Rasher growled. "I never thought I'd have to memorize its look, you understand. Not like this, this, this, or this." He rejected one key after the next. "That's the best I can do."

Le Brun put away the keys. "Thank you."

Morgan's junior partner walked to the door, opened it, and checked that the hallway was empty. "You'll forgive me for not accompanying you downstairs," he said. "I'm not feeling well."

DURING THEIR LATE LUNCHEON, in the familiar corner of the all-but-deserted members' dining room, Warfield said, "In a way you've won, no matter the outcome, Sheriff."

"And how is that, Chief Deputy?" John asked.

"Because of the second murder. If you solve these crimes, you're a hero, and the Jekyl Island Club is deeply beholden to you. If you fail, the word still gets out how you were impeded, and the blame for Mr. Sage's death falls squarely on Mr. Morgan and the board."

"Mark my words, War," John said. "The Jekyl Island Club will manage to survive this nicely."

"I imagine you're right."

"Still desire a membership?"

"As long as Reverend Parkhurst and his kind have memberships, I must say I would. Does that surprise you?"

"If they offer me eatin' rights and huntin' rights as a thank-you, I'd accept. Does that surprise *you*?"

"No. The barrel is not made rotten by a few bad apples."

"Forget about apples," John said, tipping his soup bowl to get the last spoonful. "Finish your soup. You are about to be quite cold for quite some time."

AFTER ASSURING Deputy Buncombe that replacement officers would relieve him within a few hours, Le Brun and Tidewell took the police launch and headed for the mainland. Cloud cover made the midafternoon hour seem like dusk. The rain abated to a steady mist, reducing visibility to two hundred feet. It did not fall against the surface of the river but rather settled onto it like a sheet thrown upon a bed. The sheriff, huddling under the cover of a tarpaulin, guided the craft with assurance, refusing to be fooled into believing a few wide stretches of marsh water to the west were the mouth of St. Simon's Sound. Waterfowl, hiding among the reeds along the channel, hunkered their heads down under their wings.

Shortly after John changed course in a westerly direction, the images of two huge yachts emerged from the gray-white haze: Morgan's black *Corsair III* and Baker's *Viking*. No sound other than the chugging of the launch's little engine carried across the water. The two yachts rode on the water's calm surface like ghost vessels, silent for all their size, indicating life only by the light of several lanterns.

As they approached Brunswick, commerce on the water picked up. Buoys dinged; boat whistles blew; bells clanged. Le Brun found the dock with uncanny assurance.

"You still haven't told me the details of the plan," Warfield said as he stepped onto the wooden planking.

"If I don't, then you're not an accomplice until it actually happens," John returned. "Meet me here at ten-thirty sharp. Bring your memo pad and somethin' to write with. Sorry to hurry, but I want to see if young Mr. Leavy has found out anythin' on Dr. Hosmer." He headed off before Warfield could reply, leaving him to shake his head in wonder and annoyance.

T HE GRAMOPHONE WAS SCRATCHING out a rough approximation of Jean De Reszke's voice in the parlor when Warfield came through the Tidewell back door. The tenor's wailing would have been enough to let him reach his bedroom undetected, except that Trooper, the family coon dog, gave him away. His father intercepted him with newspaper in hand in the kitchen.

"About time you showed up your face," Judge Tidewell said. "Have you caught the murderer?"

"Not yet," Warfield answered, moving toward the back stairs.

"Don't walk away from me, son," his father ordered. "Has John Le Brun gotten himself in Dutch with the members of the club?"

Warfield turned. "As a matter of fact, he's earned their respect."

Iley peered coldly over the tops of his half glasses. "Well, that doesn't help you much, does it?"

"Don't worry. He's about to do something that could end his career," Warfield said.

The judge's hard countenance softened. "Do tell!"

"And I'll be on hand to witness it."

"What's he doing?"

Warfield set his hand on the stair banister. "I only know a piece of it. Now let me catch some sleep. I've been up the last three nights guarding J. P. Morgan."

The judge put the newspaper down on the kitchen's butcher block table. "That's even more interesting! Securing the right connections, eh?"

"I've had a soft offer from Charles Lanier. Supposedly a good job. First Security Company. Part of First National Bank of New York."

Iley Tidewell pantomimed clapping. "Well, well. Maybe you don't need the sheriff job after all."

"Maybe I don't," Warfield said, moving up the stairs. "Can you refrain from playing that opera music? You don't even like it."

"Yes, sir . . . boss," the judge said. He picked up his newspaper and headed back toward the parlor.

FOG HAD REPLACED RAIN, rolling silently over the town of Brunswick and into St. Simon's Sound. The night was moonless, reducing the visibility to less than a hundred feet. Few people walked the streets. Warfield held a lighted dash lantern high with his left hand and kept his right hand behind his back, fingers touching the grip of his revolver as he moved. It was the sort of night that begged for mayhem.

John Le Brun waited at the top end of the dock. Except for the muffler he had wound around his neck and an open mackintosh, he wore the same clothes and derby he had during the day. In his right hand he held a double-barreled shotgun. In his left, he carried a white cloth bag. He turned as Warfield came down the stairs.

"Did you bring your wits, Mr. Tidewell?" he called.

"I believe so."

"Good." Le Brun led the way to the end of the dock. There, tied to the police launch, floated an old rowboat. Bobby Lee Randolph sat in the launch holding the tiller, wearing a black rubber coat and a black round-crown rubber hat. A railroad lantern with a Fresnel lens at one end glowed at his feet.

"Hey, Bobby Lee. I thought you were shot," Warfield said, stepping into the launch behind the sheriff.

"Only a graze," the wiry older deputy said, in a dismissive tone. "The time I got hit in the rib, *that* was bein' shot."

"You must tell me about that someday." Warfield pivoted to face the sheriff. "Did you find out about Dr. Hosmer?"

"A little. First, about eight years ago he started goin' to a lot of Socialist and Communist meetin's. Never joined, but wasn't just a quiet listener, either. Had plenty to say, and much of it was against the very rich. He hasn't been seen at them of late, though. Second, he's a member of the Bear Mountain Hunt and Gun Club. Third, a few people in the journalistic profession think he's strange. Neurotic."

"Like that habit he has of brushing invisible things off other people's collars," Warfield recalled.

"Or spendin' so much time peerin' out at the world through windows," John said. "Interestin' that he's so quick to speak of his employer's neuroses."

"Birds of a feather."

"But whether he's a harmless cuckoo or a bird of prey remains to be seen."

"Given what you've learned about him, do you still want to board the *Corsair*?" Warfield asked.

"Most definitely."

"Then may I finally know the plan?"

"You may know the *story*," said the sheriff, stepping into the launch and stowing his shotgun and bag. "Or, better yet, let's make it a three-act play, like Mr. Pulitzer would do. Act One: According to your uncanny wealth of information, the *Corsair III* has a complement of fifty-five officers and crew. You know from experience that the captain allows about a third to take shore leave each day. They come in on a longboat at about two and go back at ten. If you'll listen carefully, you'll hear them shovin' off right now."

A series of utterances drifted across the water through the blanketing fog.

"They're late," Warfield noted. "And not as noisy as usual."

"True on both counts. They're preoccupied. One of their group is missin', and they can't find him. He and two others were in the Dixie Tavern this evenin', doin' what sailors do best. Then Jim Wiley, Joe Decker, and Bill Lloyd came in."

Warfield whistled. The sheriff had just reeled off the names of the toughest wharf rats in the town, three longshoremen who could be counted on to spend at least a few days each month in the town jail.

"We suggested that some of their future mishaps might be forgiven if they did what *they* do best," Bobby Lee said.

"It was a nasty mixture," John reported. "Morgan's men accounted well for themselves, but not before a good deal of damage was done . . .

to them and to the tavern. Our thugs let two of 'em escape. The other one they knocked unconscious. They're holdin' him right now for us."

"And this is going to get us on the *Corsair?*" Warfield asked, incredulous.

"Yes, indeed. Act Two: We come to arrest three men for public drunkenness, disorderly conduct, assault and battery, destroyin' private property, and fleein' the scene of a crime. Only two will be found. The ship will need to be searched from stem to stern to insure that the other one isn't avoidin' arrest by hidin'."

"But we won't be allowed to search all by ourselves," Warfield argued.

"No, of course not. I will insist that the captain accompany me. I will see that the area of the boat with Mr. Morgan's study is searched first. Five minutes later, you will tell the second-in-command that you intend to follow behind us, to catch the crewman emergin' in case he eludes our initial inspection."

"It might work," Warfield deemed.

"It had damned well better, for all our sakes," John answered. "How long do you think it would take to inspect the entire yacht if I drag my feet?"

"It's big. Forty minutes?"

"Then you shall have thirty minutes. Act Three: You enter the study."

"But it will be locked."

John reached for the white bag. He set it on his lap. From inside, he produced three metal mechanisms and laid them across his knees on the bright material. "These most nearly resemble the locks for the key that Randy Rasher pointed out." He produced a ring with three keys and two picking devices on it. "Now, while we wait for the crew of the *Corsair* to get ahead of us, I am gonna give you a crash course in pickin' a lock. You, Warfield Tidewell, are the star of Act Three."

After twenty minutes of intense work and with the sheriff's expert guidance, Warfield had opened each lock three times.

"Cast off, Bobby Lee," John said, taking his seat. "The play has begun."

Bobby Lee brought the engine to life, backed out, and carefully maneuvered into open water, with the rowboat trailing behind on a short line. They traveled slowly, with Warfield training the focused Fresnel beam on the water ahead of them. Bobby Lee consulted a compass every minute or so. The fog hung densely over the unusually calm water. Every once in a while, some denizen of the deep broke the surface of the water, but otherwise only the launch's engine disturbed the deathly quiet.

"We must be gettin' close," Le Brun said. "Cut the engine!"

The rhythmic chugging faltered and died. The three men listened as the launch continued on with its momentum. Presently, there was a splash off in the distance, about as loud as a young boy dropping into a deep creek from a tree swing.

"Dumpin' garbage?" Bobby Lee guessed.

Le Brun pulled two oars from the bottom of the launch. He handed one to Warfield and pointed. "Just so long as it isn't dumpin' another body. Let's head that way. Quietly."

They paddled on either side of the launch for a minute. Gradually, the running lights of the yachts emerged from the fog. Le Brun signaled for his chief deputy to stop paddling. With another quick gesture, he indicated that Bobby Lee should transfer himself to the old rowboat. The deputy first doffed his rainwear, then eased himself across and took up the rowboat's oars. The sheriff cast off the line that held the two boats together. Then he started up the launch's engine and had Warfield steer in a long, curving course to the port side of *Corsair III*.

"Ahoy!" John called out, when they were within a hundred feet of the yacht. Warfield cut the engine back to idle and let the launch half drift toward the ship's ramp that hung down almost to the water. A motorized longboat was tied to its handrail.

The crewman on watch appeared at the edge of the deck. He held a pistol in his hand. John stood and trained his shotgun on the man. "Police!" he shouted. "Set down your weapon!"

Warfield brought the launch up to where John could hop onto the ramp, then tied it fast alongside the longboat.

"What do you want?" the man on watch called down.

John ascended, holding his badge in one hand and the shotgun in the other. Warfield followed, with his revolver drawn.

"I am the sheriff of Brunswick, and I am here in search of three men from this vessel. Fetch me your cap'n!"

"He's sleeping, sir," the watch said.

"Then go and wake him!" John ordered. "Oh, forget it. I'll do it myself." He lifted the shotgun and fired a blast into the air.

The watch jumped, then hurried below deck. A few moments later, Bobby Lee appeared from the bow of the yacht, limping gamely along.

He winked at the sheriff and the chief deputy as he hurried past and descended the ship's ramp as quickly as he could.

A second later, men began pouring from two hatches, until ten stood on the deck. All of them were dressed in shore attire. Behind them came the captain, wrapped in a silk dressing gown.

"I am Captain McKay," the officer announced, with a dignity commensurate to his position. "What is the meaning of boarding this ship in the middle of the night?"

"The meanin' is justice," John fairly barked, matching the captain's outraged mien inch for inch. He flashed his badge. "I am John Le Brun, sheriff of Brunswick. A couple of your men have experienced the hospitality of my jail in the past weeks. Tonight, the town's forbearance has been exceeded. We had a drinkin' establishment broken up by members of your crew. Three members, to be precise. You will please produce them immediately."

The captain turned to the officer next to him. "Mr. Raines, would you question the men about this and see if it is true?"

"True?" John cried out. Warfield patted his shoulder and theatrically counseled calm.

Bobby Lee appeared at the top of the ramp, again wearing his foul-weather gear. The man on watch saw him and did a double take. Bobby Lee held his stare until the man looked away.

"These are my deputies, Mr. Tidewell and Mr. Randolph. They will stay here while I have a look around," Le Brun announced. He proceeded to walk toward the stern of the yacht on the port side. Half a minute later, he appeared again, walking forward along the starboard. Half a minute after that, he called out for the captain.

Warfield walked with Captain McKay while Bobby Lee hung back. When they found Sheriff Le Brun, he was peering down over the rail.

"Does that rowboat belong to this vessel?" he asked.

"That? Certainly not!" the captain bristled.

"Well, what's it doin' tied to your anchor chain?"

"I have no idea."

"I do," John said. "Let's see if your first officer has rounded up the culprits." He stalked aft, with the chief deputy and the captain in his wake. When they reached amidships, all hands were on deck. The first officer was conducting a count. He finished and pivoted smartly.

"All but one accounted for, sir!"

"And who is that?"

"Orrey, sir. He went ashore today, but he didn't report to the longboat at ten. We checked the Dixie, the Salt, the High Tide, and the jail, but he wasn't to be found."

"Was he in a brawl tonight?"

"Yes, sir. But our men didn't start it."

"Never mind that! Who tied a rowboat to the anchor chain?"

The entire complement of men, standing in two rows and dressed in various combinations of uniform, mufti, and sleepwear, was silent.

"Your man stole that rowboat and made his way back here, Cap'n," Le Brun accused.

"Row all that way? In this fog? Impossible."

"What other explanation is there?"

"I have no idea," Captain McKay replied, looking over his shoulder toward the bow. "The men who were in the fight step forward!" he ordered, after recovering. A pair of sailors complied with obvious reluctance. "You may have these two, and if the other is on board we shall deliver him to you in the morning," the captain stated.

"No, sir. I want him tonight. I demand a thorough search of the ship before we leave." John started off for the hatch that led most directly to J. P. Morgan's study.

"Oh, for God's sake!" McKay exclaimed. "Very well. Let's be done with this as swiftly as possible. All hands into the lounge!"

Everyone filed into the glass-enclosed lounge that ran between the yacht's twin masts. None but Bobby Lee had the temerity to take a seat. Warfield paced back and forth in front of the yawning, scowling, scratching crew. When he had silently counted to three hundred, he turned to Bobby Lee and, in a loud voice, said, "I'm going below after them. If the man was able to elude the sheriff and the captain, perhaps he'll lower his guard once they've passed, and I can catch him."

"Good idea," Bobby Lee said, cheerfully smiling at the first officer.

Warfield swiftly descended to the third and bottom deck, where lay the private cabins and Morgan's study. As he turned into a gangway, he heard the captain and Sheriff Le Brun coming nearer from above. He found the oak door that separated the study from the corridor and tried the knob. It was locked tightly. He studied the lock and compared it in his mind's eye to the three locks John had tutored him on. He selected one of the keys and inserted it. It fit in easily but would not turn. He eased it back out a fraction, as the sheriff had taught him, simultaneously lifting it up and then pushing it down, twisting slightly side to side. Suddenly, the lock turned. A moment later, he was inside, throwing the bolt.

Considering that he was on a yacht, Warfield thought the study seemed enormous. He oriented himself with his memory of the map Randolph Rasher had drawn. The beryl paperweight was precisely where Rasher noted it would be. Warfield lifted it and found the key. The desk drawers opened with little noise. In the center drawer he found an abundance of stationery with *On Board the Corsair III* embossed across the top. He opened his shirt and slid several sheets down the front. Other papers were tied up in a black ribbon, but they had to do with recent purchases of art. The three side drawers were filled with notebooks, ledgers, and folders of paper. Minutes swept by as Warfield pored over them. His mind staggered at the schemes, manipulations, and deals detailed by the documents, but none seemed to have anything to do with Erastus Springer or James Sage. He replaced everything as he had found it, relocked the desk, and replaced the key.

Warfield grimaced with disappointment. He consulted his watch. He still had seventeen minutes. He stared at the Dutch landscape on the wall. He crossed to it, found the releasing spring, and swung the painting and frame aside. Recessed into the wall lay the safe. It was small, just as Rasher had described, and dead center in its dial was the Morgan silver dollar. To Warfield's surprise, the reverse side of the coin was the one exposed. It had been secured so that its top exactly aligned with the zero line of the dial.

As Warfield looked at the coin, he became convinced that it had not been placed there merely as a symbol of what lay behind. This was the safe of the man who loved games, a man who in his youth had almost been convinced to teach mathematics by his mentor at the University of Göttingen. Warfield became convinced that the coin held the secret to the safe's combination. He studied it carefully. There were no extraneous marks on it. Around its edge ran the words "In God We Trust." Money and God, Warfield reflected: J. P. Morgan's two great passions.

The answer hit Warfield like a charge of static electricity: a three-number combination. Unknown; fourteen, fifteen, or sixteen; and then four. If a number were assigned sequentially to each letter of the alphabet, the word *God* would be seven, fifteen, four. Warfield spun the dial right, fully around left, and back right. The safe popped open at his first pull.

Atop the rest of the safe's contents sat four banded piles of money. The denominations of two piles were twenties, and the other two were fifties. At fifty bills per band, Warfield calculated the total to be seven thousand dollars. As much as most laborers in Brunswick made in twenty years.

Warfield pushed the money aside. He reached for the two small record books on the bottom of the pile, brought them to the desk, and sat. The top book had only four numbers written on it: 1888. The one beneath read 1860–1887. He riffled through the top book and saw that, despite its small-ness, it had only been half filled. The writing was aggressively angular and a challenge to read. It agreed with samples of J. P. Morgan's hand-writing Warfield had seen in the desk. He set the book aside and took up the other. To the left of it he set his pocket watch, and to the right he placed his pen and memo pad.

The date preceded each entry, so it was not difficult to find 1880. This was the year Pulitzer had said Springer was first involved with the Denver & Rio Grande. Warfield saw nothing of Springer's name through the entire year (which required only six pages of Morgan's shorthand). It was the name Sage that Warfield noticed first, on October 2, 1880. The phrase was *"Sage booked to arrive NYC 10/15."* The g of the name was not quite closed, but Tidewell ascribed it to the aggressive penmanship or a slip of the hand. He determined not only to copy the notes but also to attempt to duplicate the handwriting. Under October 9 were the words *"Involve Sage."*

The first entry of 1881 read *"B&M incorporated NJ, 19 Wall,"* fol-lowed by *"deal set w/Springer."* Warfield wracked his brain for several moments, trying to recall a defunct or absorbed railroad. He remembered the quaintly named Belfast & Moosehead Lake Railroad. It certainly could not be the Boston & Maine, which had been running long before 1881. On January 8, an entry noted that *"D&RG on public offering @ 92 p. 20,000."* January 11 had *"D&RG @ 93 1/2 p. 10,000,"* and January 14 *"D&RG @ 94 p. 6,000."*

The chief deputy's eyes fell on what he took at first to be a mistake. Directly after the date 1/17 came the words *"Sage meets Saye."* It dawned on him that the October 2 entry of the previous year had not been an error of penmanship. There was a person named Saye who figured heavily in the Denver & Rio Grande affair. Through the next three months he continued to see the name Saye, frequently beside the cryptic "B&M." In

February, March, and April he found Sage's name once more, and Springer's twice. On May 2, D&RG stock had evidently climbed to 107. On that same day, Morgan had noted *"B&M p. 8,000; hold 44,000."* Morgan was acquiring blocks of stock.

Warfield admired Morgan's talent for patience. Month after month, the slow edge-ups of D&RG stock were carefully recorded. In that same time, he knew the financier must have conducted hundreds of transactions. This book recorded only the schemes, the dirty dealings that were not meant for the public records of his company.

Suddenly, Sage and Saye seemed to have disappeared from Morgan's world. During the following months, notations indicated that Morgan had transferred much of his 44,000 shares of D&RG into other controlled corporate entities. The machinations of this were handled by Oliver King, one of Morgan's Union Club confreres and one of the foursome who had later visited Jekyl Island on the celebrated hunting trip. Warfield knew that King had died soon after the club opened.

In mid-August of 1882 came several notations that could only mean Morgan's shares of D&RG were being dumped. In the following three months, shares plummeted in value from 108 to 40, where they bottomed on November 16. It seemed as if the fate of the mysterious B&M had been inextricably intertwined with that of the D&RG. Warfield shrugged, figuring it was one of scores of short lines, feeder lines, and blackmail roads that had emerged and just as quickly been absorbed or perished in the decades before and after 1880.

Glancing at the vanishing minutes, Warfield leafed more swiftly through the book, searching for other mentions of Sage and Springer. He found precious little. In 1886, he located the proof of Erastus Springer's fronting for Morgan in the ruin of the Vandalia Railroad, but there was no mention of any involvement by Sage. Similarly, shady holding companies often had Sage's name linked to them, but Springer's name was never listed in these operations.

With three minutes left to spare, Warfield snatched up the second book and turned to Morgan's most recent notations. He jotted down an occasional interesting name or figure, working backward. When he had reached February of the previous year, he found a particularly notorious name. Beside this were words and figures that took away his breath. His heart came pounding up into the base of his throat. For a long moment, he simply stared at the entry. His breath returned, ragged and quick. He set about copying the notation into his memo book. Then he thought the better of it, ripped out the page, and stuffed it into his inside jacket pocket.

With no time remaining, the chief deputy scooped up the books and shoved them back into place under the other documents and the money, closed the safe, replaced the painting, and exited the study. He worked for a full minute trying to use his skeleton key to relock the door but found it impossible. His hands were already slick with perspiration and shaking, and the more he fumbled the more he shook. Swearing, he raced for the nearest stairs.

"Where have you been, Mr. Tidewell?" John Le Brun asked, as the chief deputy emerged on deck, reining in his speed precipitously.

"Looking for you," Warfield replied, gripping his hands together behind his back to conceal their trembling.

"No matter," Le Brun said dismissively. "We've only just come back ourselves."

"Did you find him?" Warfield asked.

"No. I don't know what to make of it," the sheriff said, addressing Captain McKay. "We shall search Brunswick again."

"I'll send a boat over in the morning to learn what has happened," the captain said coldly. "In the meantime, please take that rowboat back with you."

"It isn't ours," Le Brun told him.

"Well, it certainly isn't ours!"

John headed casually toward the ramp. "Fine, fine. Mr. Tidewell, Mr. Randolph, let's get home and see what more we can learn. Show our two guests to the launch."

L E B R U N , T I D E W E L L , and Randolph all maintained somber "officer of the law" expressions on the long ride home, softening only so far as to commiserate with the crewmen's protests that they had not started the fight. The sheriff assured them that if their story was borne out by various witnesses they would likely not spend more than the one night in jail and more than a week's pay in restitution. By the time the two were safely inside a cell, the crewmen were considering the officers of Brunswick to be fine, fair fellows.

The moment the cell door was locked, Le Brun and his deputies hastened to the sheriff's office.

"I want to thank you, John, for trusting me," Warfield said, as soon as the door was closed. "Between my father's encouragement for me to go after your job, the job offer from Charles Lanier, and all the time I've spent with Mr. Morgan, you could easily have believed I would double-cross you."

"And how could you have done that?" John asked, winking at Bobby Lee. "I was only on the yacht to find a fugitive from the law; you were the one who broke into Mr. Morgan's study."

Warfield's head snapped back.

Bobby Lee laughed, slapped his bad leg out of habit, swore, and took a couple of short hops across the office. When he recovered, he said, "You'll learn eventually, War . . . ain't nobody craftier than John Le Brun. I'd even bet on him against that fox J. P. Morgan."

"Let's say I trusted you ninety-five percent," John told his chief deputy. "And look at it this way . . . did you ever have such excitement as a lawyer?"

"No," Warfield admitted.

"Stick with us," Bobby Lee said. "It's never dull for long."

"While you two are congratulating each other, Captain McKay didn't buy the business with the rowboat," Warfield said.

John settled back in his chair and propped his feet on his desk. "He didn't have to. Let him think we planted it there as an excuse to search the boat. It'll keep his mind off more subtle schemes. If anythin' aroused his suspicion, it was you comin' back on deck lookin' guilty as hell. You have to find a better possum face. Ah, screw Cap'n McKay; there ain't nothin' he can do. What did you find out, Warfield?"

The chief deputy related his break-in and the first few minutes inside the study. He allowed himself a grin of pride as he told how he had cracked the secret to the safe.

Bobby Lee whistled in appreciation.

"Very impressive!" the sheriff said admiringly. "But was there anythin' worth seein' in it?"

Warfield took out his memo book and slowly read off his notes.

"You mean not a single person vacationin' on that damned island had anythin' to do with Morgan, Sage, and Springer?" the sheriff asked, unbelieving, when Warfield had concluded.

"If they did, I didn't notice their name," Warfield replied.

"Lucifer!" John massaged his right shoulder. "That whole melodrama for nothin', and my shoulder's killin' me from that damp. Let me see your book." When he had it, he said, "You even copied your notes to look like his handwritin'? That seems like a waste of time."

Warfield slumped. "Sorry."

"Did you tear a page out at the end?"

Warfield leaned over and looked at the book. "Well, you tore out a few pages. Oh, that was for a note I left Dr. Russell," he said, looking up and giving the sheriff his very best possum face.

"I see." John turned back to the beginning of the notes. "B and M. Strange."

"I couldn't recall a single railroad with those initials," Warfield said.

"Maybe it's not—" John paused in midsentence. His eyes blinked as if he had been smacked between the shoulder blades with a board.

"What?" Bobby Lee asked.

"Hush up! I'm thinkin'." John sat up, moved the memorandum book closer to his banker's lamp, and studied it carefully, every so often making inarticulate sounds in his throat. He paged forward, then back to the first entries.

"I believe you may have done it, Warfield," John declared.

Warfield took a step toward his notes. "Done what?"

"Solved the case, of course."

"How?"

John snapped the memo book closed and stood. "Diligence."

"No, really."

The sheriff moved to the door, clutching the book. "I don't want to appear a fool, so I'd rather get verification before I speak." He opened the door. "Bobby Lee, you see if the sailor is still lyin' where they were supposed to dump him. I wouldn't want him catchin' his death of cold. Find him at any rate and bring him back here. Warfield, go home and get some sleep. Soon as you wake, take the launch back to Jekyl Island. Let the boys bring it back. Don't let anyone in Sans Souci or Pulitzer's cottage leave. In your spare time, skillfully ask Dr. Hosmer about his affiliations with various antidemocratic groups and the Bear Mountain Hunt and Gun Club. I'm off to send a telegram to the *World*. I will come over to the island as soon as I get an answer."

Le Brun left the room. A second later, he was back in the doorway. "Oh, and the rest of the time, don't let Morgan out of your sight." He hurried toward the police station's front door.

Warfield swung out of the office. "Is he the murderer?"

Sheriff Le Brun passed out into the night without replying.

"The man be damned!" Warfield exclaimed.

Bobby Lee limped toward the front door, chuckling as he went. "But you have to love his flair for the dramatic."

THURSDAY

MARCH 23, 1899

WARFIELD TIDEWELL WOKE from a fitful sleep to the reveille of a tin plate slapping across jail cell bars. One of their more frequent guests knew his rights and was demanding breakfast. The third sailor involved in the bar brawl had not been discovered and deposited with his buddies until after two in the morning. This disturbed the other inhabitants of the cells so that the station for a while assumed a barnyard character. After silence was restored, the chief deputy had neither energy nor desire to walk across town to his father's house. He was certainly not anxious to face the inevitable barrage of questions regarding John Le Brun's act that "could end his career." He had appropriated a cot in an open cell for what turned out to be less than five hours' sleep.

Warfield kept a change of shirt and tie in the office. He dressed and shaved, then visited his favorite eatery in the hope of shoveling down enough food and drinking enough coffee to quiet the churning in his stomach and the pounding at his temples. Inquiry and inspection proved that Sheriff Le Brun and Deputy Randolph were nowhere in the neighborhood. Brunswick itself seemed to be getting a slow start to its day. Warfield staggered down to the wharves, into a fresh breeze.

The police launch still had the white bag of locks stowed under one seat. He tossed these onto the dock, cast off, and set the boat chugging toward Jekyl Island. The time, according to his fogged pocket watch, was a bit after eight-thirty. The sun was rising directly into his eyes, making his headache all the worse. He lowered his gaze and steeled himself for the fifty-minute ride over increasingly choppy waves.

As Warfield steered toward the Jekyl Island Club's dock, he saw that a number of vacationers were prepared to leave. Friday Cain and another Negro were helping the deckhand move volumes of luggage up the gangplank while the privileged took pains not to notice them. Warfield reached for his memo book and realized the sheriff had it. He cast his mind back and calculated that, of the one hundred and ten members, family, "strangers," and personal servants he had on his original list, only about twenty-eight would remain on the island when the *Howland* made its morning run. The season was definitely drawing to a close. Warfield could see that it was not a mass exodus due to flight over the second murder. In fact, those on the dock seemed very much at ease, chatting among themselves, smiling. The secret of James Sage's murder had evidently been contained among a few.

As the chief deputy was securing the police launch, he noticed that the boat next to it was a longboat from the *Corsair III*. The implications made his head pound all the more. Sheriff Le Brun had forbidden Morgan from leaving the island. The longboat's presence meant one of two things: Either Captain McKay had come to report the searching of the *Corsair III* the previous night, or else J. P. Morgan was preparing to flee the island against Le Brun's orders.

The prospect of facing down J. P. Morgan over either scenario worsened Warfield's mental state. Added to all this was the shocking notation he had found from February of 1898. He headed for the infirmary, anxious to receive another dose of the wonder drug Dr. Russell had given him on Tuesday. From a distance, he looked for the note on the front door, the telltale sign that the physician was out on a call. To his relief, there was none. He knocked on the door. Dr. Russell appeared, tugging on his jacket.

"Good morning, Mr. Tidewell!" he exclaimed.

"Could be better, Dr. Russell."

"From the way you're squinting, may I guess that you have another headache?"

"The big brother of the other one," Warfield lamented.

"Come in," Russell bade, stepping aside. "I'm running rather low, but I believe I can spare you one dose. I also have the Coca-Cola extract."

Warfield followed the doctor into the treatment room and sat. A silence ensured. To fill it, he decided to resolve the question of Russell's youth as best he could without letting the man know it had been investigated.

"You said you were from Manchester, not London?"

"That's correct."

"Did you mean originally born in Manchester and later moved to London?"

Russell looked up from measuring the acetylsalicylic acid powder. "London? Ah, yes. We moved to New York from London."

"When you were how old?"

Russell paused again. "Quite young. I was eight, I think."

The reply sounded wrong to Warfield. His hand reached automatically for his memo book, but he caught himself.

"The reason I ask is because you've maintained quite a bit of an accent. Older folk tend to keep theirs," Warfield noted, "but children hang around with other children and pick up the accent of their new country. Did you have a private English tutor for several years in New York?"

Russell began mixing the Coca-Cola syrup. "Yes, exactly. Two tutors, actually. The first was a woman named Miss Brimstone. Scary name, eh? But a lovely lady. The second was a man. Mr. Smyth-Davies. Real taskmaster. Made me long for a schoolhouse education." He handed Warfield the powder and the drink.

"Thanks," Warfield said, after knocking the medicine back. "If it works like last time, I'll be fit as a fiddle in half an hour."

Russell looked at the clock on the wall. "Check your watch at ten-twelve and see. As long as you're here . . . what's to become of James Sage?"

"I suppose they'll try to keep him on ice until Saturday," Warfield answered, "when most of the people have left."

"No definite suspect?"

"Sheriff Le Brun has one," Warfield said, "but he's keeping it close to his vest."

"I see. Come Sunday morning, my tour of duty is over." Dr. Russell wiped his hands on a towel. "I may never learn who did it."

"Give me your address in Baltimore," Warfield offered. "I'll write to you."

"Most kind of you." Russell found a piece of paper and jotted down his address.

Warfield placed the paper in his billfold and stood. "I'll be on my way. A few errands to do before Sheriff Le Brun arrives."

"Perhaps I'll see you for lunch," Russell said, moving with the chief deputy toward the front door.

Warfield said his good-bye and thank-you and walked directly west, retracing his path toward the dock. As he neared the Pulitzer cottage, he spotted G. W. Hosmer watching him from one of the laboratory windows. A moment later Hosmer turned and vanished into the darkness of the room. The man was definitely strange, Warfield thought. Interviewing him about the facts Sheriff Le Brun had uncovered was almost as unpalatable to the chief deputy as facing J. P. Morgan.

After Warfield hurried to the River Road to be sure the *Corsair*'s long-boat was still tied up at the dock, he decided to allow the aspirin to do its work before he confronted anyone. He sat on a bench placed under an ornamental cherry tree, shut his eyes, and waited for the drug to take effect. Five minutes later, he jerked upright with a start. He had fallen asleep and had nearly relaxed into a tumble. He had more than burned his candle at both ends over the investigation. If John Le Brun did not solve the case this very day, he knew he would have to excuse himself for at least eight straight hours to be of any further value.

One of the guards on horseback came riding up River Road. Warfield got off the bench and hailed him.

"You know who I am?" he asked the man.

"Brunswick Police."

"That's right. I have an important job for you. I'm going to be in that cottage for a few minutes." Warfield pointed to Pulitzer's mansion. "I need you to stay here and make sure no one gets into that longboat over there. If anyone tries, you fetch me on the double, you understand?"

"Yes, sir."

The guard dismounted and headed for the same bench Warfield had been using.

Tidewell inhaled deeply, fortifying himself for his interview with Hosmer. He took stock of himself and thought that his head felt a little better. He climbed the cottage stairs and knocked on the front door. One of the secretaries answered and led him to the laboratory. The air stunk of sulfur.

"Good day, Deputy!" Hosmer greeted, an empty test tube in his hand. "How is Mr. Sage feeling?"

"About the same."

"Too bad. Any idea who poisoned him?"

"Unfortunately not."

"You have more questions for Mr. Pulitzer, I expect."

"No. This time they're for you."

Hosmer laughed. "For me? Harmless old me?"

"Are you harmless?" Warfield was glad the test tube was empty. The laugh lines vanished suddenly from the man's face. "What about the Socialist and Communist clubs?"

Hosmer closed the door between the hallway and the laboratory. "Andes and I have a bet whether or not you'd uncover my past. I won."

"Tell him we got the information from a small-town newspaperman. We are not completely without resources in Georgia."

"I never thought you were." Hosmer crossed to his workbench and set the tube in a rack. He sat on a stool and invited Tidewell to do the same.

"Tell me about your affiliation with these groups," Warfield said.

"There's not much to tell. Yet another depression was on. Any fool could see that the capital of the country was being controlled by a few hands and that they were manipulating the economy for their own selfish ends. Both the Democrats and the Republicans were in their control as well. All of Washington, one way or another. I read Karl Marx's treatise. It seemed rather utopian to me, relying too much on the goodwill of men and their willingness to pull together. Nevertheless, I thought I'd see if it could work. Started with the various meetings. If it couldn't work there, I figured it couldn't work on a grand scale. For a time, I was caught up in spirit of the common man shaking off the bonds of his capitalist oppressor. But then I began hearing conflicting messages."

"Such as?"

"Workers who wanted to loot the homes of the rich and murder their children. Others who demanded that the Constitution be abandoned. Many had no idealism behind their participation, no empathy for their fellow workers. They just wanted more for themselves." Hosmer looked suddenly weary. He threw up his hands and let them collapse into his lap. "There seemed to be no champion of a sane middle road. And then I hooked up with Mr. Pulitzer. What a brilliant man. His concept is to enlighten the common man, little by little. Educate him toward humanitarian feelings, make him see and feel for the plight of others. Show that democracy, difficult as it is, is the least bad of all political methods." Hosmer looked up, as if he could see through the ceiling to where his hero sat. "Ever since I hitched my wagon to his star, I've had a great deal more inner peace."

"You're a member of the Bear Mountain Hunt and Gun Club," Warfield noted.

"That's true. What of it? Oh! I know how to shoot a rifle. Yes, I do. Quite well, in fact."

"The club has no record of your bringing one with you."

Hosmer's hand swept out to take in the equipment in the laboratory. "They have no record of all this, either." He stood. "I packed it in with this stuff and never used it."

"May I see it?" Warfield asked.

"Certainly." Hosmer opened a closet and removed a rifle case. He opened it, extracted a Remington No. 3 32-30 hunting rifle, and handed it to the chief deputy.

Warfield smelled the rifle muzzle. He examined the loading chamber. "When did you clean it?"

"Before coming down here. I've been too busy with Andes and my experiments to hunt deer, much less humans. Am I high on your list of suspects?"

"Not mine," Warfield answered. "On John's list, evidently. When we got the news about the Socialist and Communist clubs, he asked me to sound you out." He returned the rifle.

Hosmer sat, swung the weapon toward one of the rear windows, and sighted it. "If I'm a prime suspect, then Mr. Springer's murder will never be solved." Suddenly, he swung the rifle back and aimed it at Warfield's heart.

The chief deputy thrust his hand to the small of his back, groping for his revolver.

Hosmer lowered the rifle and laughed. "Relax! You saw that it's empty." He took up the case and pushed it inside.

"You're a bit strange, Dr. Hosmer, if you don't mind my saying," Warfield fumed.

"If I weren't, would I be here?" Pulitzer's friend countered. He stood up. "If we can help you in some productive way, please let us know. Otherwise, Mr. Tidewell, I'm sure that your time would be better spent elsewhere." All the while he spoke, Hosmer held a genial smile.

"Just being thorough," Warfield muttered.

"And I for one applaud you." Hosmer pushed ahead to the front door and threw it open. "Good day!"

Warfield exited with relief. As he descended the cottage stairs, he realized that his headache was nearly gone. He glanced at his watch. It was not even twelve minutes past ten. He broke into a smile.

And then he saw J. P. Morgan.

Jupiter Morgan sat astride his beautiful white horse, gruffly supervising the movement of several trunks and a few wooden crates toward the longboat. Alongside him, Francis Lynde Stetson sat on the same dappled gray horse he had ridden on the morning of Erastus Springer's death. On the far side of them stood Captain McKay. Stetson noticed Warfield first, when the chief deputy was only a dozen long strides from them. He leaned toward Morgan and said something. Morgan turned and glowered at Warfield with his intense stare.

Taking his lead from John Le Brun's undaunted attitude toward the man who dictated to senators, judges, and even the president, Warfield forced his feet forward.

"Are you going somewhere, Mr. Morgan?" Warfield challenged.

"I'm moving my belongings back to my yacht," Jupiter replied. "Have no fear; I'm not leaving your jurisdiction. I simply prefer to sleep there."

"I see. You are not going there before nightfall, though?"

Morgan patted his horse's neck. "Do I look like I'm going there? Do you see wings on this horse?"

"No, sir."

"I have a few matters to discuss with you, Mr. Tidewell. Francis, would you be so kind as to get down and let him use your horse?"

Stetson dismounted without a word. Warfield took his place.

"Pick me up at nine o'clock sharp, Captain McKay," Morgan directed. "Come with me, Mr. Tidewell!"

Rather than follow the River Road south, Morgan took a shortcut toward Shell Road, guiding his horse along a footpath not intended for animals. Warfield had no choice but to do the same. A Negro gardener, down on his knees weeding the edge of the path, saw the huge white horse coming with only enough time to fall flat forward. The horse took a small leap over the man's feet. Warfield had the time to guide his horse off the path briefly, leaving large divots of sod with their passing.

The two rode in front of the infirmary and headed down Shell Road. Morgan dug his heels into his steed's flanks, encouraging it on at a good pace. His intention was clearly not to engage in conversation while they rode. Warfield was not surprised when Morgan took the path Erastus Springer had chosen on his last morning alive. As Shell Road had been,

the path was devoid of walkers and riders. Again, Warfield was not surprised when Morgan stopped in front of the oak to which Reverend Parkhurst had tied his handkerchief.

Grunting from the effort, Jupiter lowered himself from the saddle and
tied his reins around a sapling. Warfield followed suit. Morgan took the
time to light one of his cudgel-sized cigars. He did not offer one to the
chief deputy but headed abruptly for the oak with the clematis flowers
and went around its far side. He waited for Warfield to join him.

"Reverend Parkhurst found interesting evidence here," Morgan said,
puffing vigorously.

"That's right," Warfield said. "This is where Mr. Springer was shot."

Morgan explored the bullet hole in the tree with his forefinger. "Have
you reasoned out precisely what happened?"

"He must have been unconscious and propped up here."

"But there was no bump on his head," Morgan argued.

"Perhaps there was a small one in his hair. I'm sure Dr. Russell didn't
think to look for a contusion. Certainly, it's unlikely Mr. Springer came
in, sat down, and watched while someone aimed a rifle at him from over
there."

"That fallen tree."

"Yes. That's where the shot was fired from. Whoever it was had plenty
of time to put one bullet squarely through the man's heart. It would require no less than five or six seconds to get into position. By that time,
Springer would have been on his feet and running for the path and could
only have been shot in the back. After he was killed, he was carried far
down the path, to conceal this place." Warfield pointed in the direction
where the body was found. "Deliberate murder and deliberate cover-up.
Which means that the guard was paid for nothing. It was not, as you
assumed, a poacher who killed Mr. Springer."

"Why was I not informed by you of this find?" Morgan demanded.

Warfield's headache had vanished. Moreover, his oblique attack on
the multimillionaire had not set the man into a rage. He determined to
stand his ground against any assault. "Because you are not part of the
investigating party. Facts have rather suggested that you may have had
a hand in the murder."

Morgan thrust his shoulders back. "Those 'facts' were circumstantial,
and you know it! You had an obligation to inform me of all the matters
concerning this investigation."

"Why's that?"

"You know why."

"Because you paid me to guard you? Because Charles Lanier has dangled a job offer under my nose?"

"It's no wonder they decided to pin the blame on you in Philadelphia," Morgan said, allowing himself a tiny smile.

Warfield took a moment to regroup from the verbal sting and from the knowledge that Morgan had taken the trouble to learn the truth about his disbarring. He determined not to lose the upper hand by asking who Morgan's informant had been.

"You have chosen poorly, declaring allegiance to John Le Brun," Morgan continued. "So well educated, so much promise, and you will never get a good job in the North now."

"Save your jobs for toadies," Warfield said evenly. "I find I prefer the South. And I much prefer serving under a man who is straight with everyone . . . provided they're straight with him."

"Straight, you say? What was that slimy business of you and your hero boarding my yacht?" Morgan went on.

"We were pursuing fugitives from justice."

"Jesus Christ! You were bumbling through a pitiful ruse in search of information. You contrived that bar brawl as an excuse to board the *Corsair*." He held up his left hand and proceeded to tick off his proof on his fingers. "You brought a rowboat to abet your story. You had the deputy in the black slicker tie it up and somehow get to your launch afterward. Le Brun got Captain McKay away to search the boat. You followed soon after, once they had left the stateroom level. You managed to get into my study, but you were unable to lock it again. What did you hope to find?"

"The answer to the murders, of course. Springer and Sage worked together at least once, and that was with you." Warfield put one foot on the rock where Springer had been deposited. "The Denver and Rio Grande Railroad."

The cigar went limp in Morgan's mouth. He recovered and plucked it from his lips. "Pulitzer's been feeding you information, hasn't he?"

Warfield felt no need to deny it. "Yes, he has."

"Don't you think I've been wracking my head trying to link people on this island with Springer and Sage? There has been *no one here* in the past three weeks who was ever hurt by them."

"What about over the B and M Railroad?" Warfield asked.

"B and M?" Morgan repeated. "I never heard of it. What's it stand for?" He stuck the cigar back between his teeth.

"Never mind. Then what about somebody named Saye?"

Before Morgan could reply, a rustling noise came from the undergrowth to the west. Both men turned toward it. Warfield planted both feet on the ground. Morgan looked at the chief deputy. Just as he turned his head, a bullet hit his cigar, blowing the wrapped leaves apart. The bullet smacked into the live oak. An instant later, the crack of a high-powered rifle resounded through the woods.

"Get down!" Warfield cried, pushing the tycoon backward.

Whirling around, then bending low, Morgan hurled his considerable mass toward the shelter of a large rock. As he did, his hand dug under his vest. By the time he reached the rock, Warfield's Young America revolver was in his hand.

Another rifle slug tore through the vegetation, clipping leaves.

Warfield looked up at the new wound in the tree and made a rough judgment of where the sniper hid. He tore the Hopkins & Allen service revolver from its holster and snapped off a hip shot as he ducked around the back of the oak.

"Throw the gun to me and run for your horse!" Warfield cried out to Morgan.

Morgan ignored him and fired his first shot wildly into the vegetation. In quick succession he squeezed off two more.

"Throw me the gun!" Warfield yelled.

The millionaire fired a fourth and fifth shot, then turned and dashed for the path. Warfield aimed into the distant undergrowth and sent two slugs flying at two thick patches, some twenty feet from each other. Morgan dashed like a wild bull through the brush, grunting as he went. He trailed his gun hand behind him and squeezed the little pistol's trigger again. The hammer fell on an empty chamber.

"Get help! I'll hold him!" Warfield called out.

Bushes wavered about a hundred feet from the oak. Warfield aimed and fired. A few moments later, he heard the pounding of hooves behind him.

Warfield snapped open the revolver cyclinder. He had fired four bullets. He silently thanked John Le Brun for forcing him to carry the six-shot revolver. The damned titan of Wall Street had taken the revolver he had given him three nights earlier to make him feel more secure and had emptied it to no more purpose than covering his retreat.

"This is Chief Deputy Tidewell," Warfield called out. "I am well armed and determined to bring you in. There will be many men here within minutes. Throw down your arms and come out with your hands up!"

The woods were silent for long seconds. Then a rustle of leaves and a thump sounded near the fallen tree. Soon after, another thump came from farther behind it. Warfield was having none of it. The sounds were too much like falling stones. He put himself in the sniper's place and figured that the person meant to draw him south while he made a break north to the Village.

Warfield picked up a stone and flung it as hard as he could in the direction of the fallen tree. As soon as it was in the air, he dashed to his right, heading for the rock Morgan had hidden behind. He came down hard on his knees and cried out in pain. Morgan had evidently broken an exposed tree root, and the sharp end now penetrated the muscle just below Warfield's knee. He rolled over in pain, clutching the knee with his free hand.

A flurry of motion happened in the distance. Warfield clambered up along the stone and cautiously peered out. The woods had fallen silent just as suddenly. He ducked again and selected a route north that wended from tree trunk to rocky outcropping and again to tree trunk. He caught several quick breaths, then exploded from cover and raced to the first tree. He paused there for a count of ten and started for the rocks. The wound below his knee felt as if it were on fire. He ducked down and listened. He heard nothing. But at least, he figured, he had flanked the sniper. Now the person had to move west through the woods—which would bring him rather quickly to the swampy section that merged with the Jekyl River— or else he had to travel south and then detour even farther south to another path that wended back to the Village. Either way, the escape routes were long and improved the chances that the person would be caught before he could return to the Village.

Warfield checked behind him. He could just make out the shape of the gray horse. It was still tied to the sapling. He popped his head up once or twice a minute like a prairie dog, studying the woods all around him. He took the watch from his vest. Its crystal cover had been cracked when he had thrown himself to the ground. He thumbed it open and set it on a tuft of moss. After ten minutes of silence, he was fairly convinced that the sniper had escaped west or south. With his knee bleeding and swelling, he was not about to venture from cover to find out. Another five minutes dragged by. Warfield swore under his breath. In all, seventeen minutes passed before three guards on horseback came pounding down the path.

"Here!" Warfield called out. "Two of you ride south, and keep your eyes open! I think he's gone that way."

Hoofbeats trailed off into the distance. One of the guards came running toward Warfield.

"Careful!" the chief deputy cautioned. "He might be playing possum." When the hard-bitten-looking man was beside him with shotgun in hand, he said, "You go off that way. I'll circle over there. Let's move one at a time and cover each other."

The guard moved forward first. From protective position to protective position they advanced, until it became clear that the shooter had escaped. Warfield returned to the rocks to reclaim his watch. A precious thirty minutes had elapsed since the first bullet. The sun was nearly overhead. Warfield gave the guard instructions to return to the Shell Road and stop anyone trying to reach the Village from the east.

When Warfield came in front of the infirmary, he eased himself off his horse, tied it to a porch post, and hobbled up the steps. His eyes fell on the piece of paper tacked to the door. He swore for the second time that morning. The note was in Dr. Russell's hand, saying that he had gone to the clubhouse to attend to a sick guest. Warfield was contemplating what to do next when G. W. Hosmer emerged from the back of the Pulitzer cottage and hailed him from a distance.

"He's gone!" Hosmer called out.

"I know," Warfield called back. "He's over at the clubhouse."

"No, he's not. I saw him walking south almost an hour ago. He was carrying his physician's bag and moving quickly. Right after you and Jupiter rode by."

Warfield stood riveted to the spot for a moment. He crossed the porch and tried the doorknob. The door was locked.

"What's the sign say?" Hosmer asked.

"That he's at the clubhouse."

"How could that be?"

"Do me a favor, Doctor," Warfield said. "Go to the clubhouse and see if he's there."

"What happened to your knee?"

"A riding accident."

"I could attend to it."

"Please. Get Dr. Russell," Warfield said.

Hosmer controlled his curiosity and walked quickly away with a sprightly stride. As soon as he was out of sight, Warfield limped down to the dock. His objective was to find out if one of the small club boats was missing. To his relief, all were bobbing on the water. He glanced south.

"Son of a bitch!" he cried out, causing the young man who assisted at the dock to stare at him with surprise. "What happened to the rowboat that was down there at the end of the lawn?" Warfield demanded.

"The rowboat?" the teenager said.

"The one that's been there for the past few days, just in front of those trees."

The teenager looked for the boat. His head bobbed back. "It was there an hour ago."

"Did you see anyone down by it?"

"Sure didn't. I didn't see no one." The young man stepped backward from Warfield's furious, accusing expression.

"Go to the guardhouse and get Mr. Lefferts and every guard there! Bring them here! Run, damn it!"

The dockhand tore across the lawns. Warfield moved slowly up the lane. He turned south on River Road and walked to where it curved inland at the limit of the Village. The grasses beyond its verge were slowly rebounding from the dragging of the rowboat to the Jekyl River. There was nothing for Warfield to do but limp back to the dock and wait for the captain of guards to arrive. He sat, rolled up his trouser leg, and ministered to his wound as best he could with his handkerchief.

Preston Lefferts was not long in arriving. A lone guard accompanied him, and both were on horseback. Their shotgun cases bulged, and the butts of revolvers protruded from their holsters.

"Mr. Morgan's throwin' a fit," Lefferts let the chief deputy know. "He wanted us to stay near him. What's happenin'?"

"I sent your men chasing off in the wrong direction," Warfield answered. "The man who shot at us is Dr. Russell, and—"

"What?" Lefferts exclaimed.

"You heard me. He's gotten away in the rowboat that was down there. Where are the rest of your men?"

Lefferts threw up his hands. "One's still with Mr. Morgan. Two are off on leave. Six are out on normal patrol. You already got three to command. And I'm a man down because of Turner. It's just Erskine and me."

"Take one of the naphtha launches and head south down the river as quick as you can, Mr. Lefferts," Warfield directed, "but be careful! He has a high-powered rifle. I'll do what I can to round up your other men. Let me take your horses."

Lefferts wasted no time in getting himself and his guard into a boat and onto the river. As Warfield moved north, G. W. Hosmer came puffing along River Road.

"Never reported to the clubhouse. And nobody called for him. I told you he went south," Hosmer said peevishly. "What's going on?"

"He's our murderer," Warfield told him.

Hosmer took the news with no reaction for a moment. "And I kept telling myself I was crazy to suspect him. Are you sure?"

"He's lied about the clubhouse; you saw him walking south with his bag; the rowboat that we dragged out of the swamp is missing."

"It's him, then." Hosmer looked at the deputy's knee. "In that case, you'd better accept my invitation to attend to you."

While Hosmer tied the two horses' reins to a post, Warfield said, "By any chance do you know the waterways directly west of here?"

"Not me. I hear the duck hunters say it's a maze. Can you walk to the cottage?"

Warfield put his arm across the old physician's shoulders and hobbled along. At the cottage, Hosmer took his time gingerly cleaning the wound and bandaging it. While he did, the chief deputy related the shooting attack on J. P. Morgan.

"Now, how are they going to keep *this* quiet?" Hosmer asked, as Warfield tried his leg and found the doctoring first-rate.

"That's their business," Warfield said. "Mine is to catch Russell. Thanks much, Doctor."

"I'm coming with you," Hosmer said. "Wait!" He pulled his rifle and a box of shells from the closet and began loading.

Warfield headed for the front door. "I think you should stay here."

"Like hell!"

Hosmer had no trouble catching up with the deputy. Warfield had stopped upon reaching River Road. He was staring upriver.

"Here comes Sheriff Le Brun," Chief Deputy Tidewell said, in a husky, unhappy voice. "Now I'm in for it."

Hosmer wisely made no comment. Again, he offered his shoulders to help the deputy to the dock.

John read trouble on Warfield's face from the moment he stepped onto the dock. He shoved the memo book he had been carrying into his pocket and automatically patted the revolver in his holster. Bobby Lee came up behind him.

"You, too?" John called out, pointing to Warfield's limp.

Warfield made no reply until he was close enough to speak in a subdued voice. "Dr. Russell's our murderer," he said.

"How do you know?" John asked. The sheriff's tone spoke volumes.

"You knew it last night, didn't you?" Warfield said, feeling the anger rise out of the pit of his stomach.

"Not for sure. Not for sure." The second time he said the words, each one was emphasized. "Tell me what's happened."

Warfield related the events beginning with Morgan's invitation to ride south and ending with Preston Lefferts and one of his men boarding the *Hattie*.

"All right, Warfield. Just relax," John counseled, watching the artery pulsing on his chief deputy's neck. "No more talk for now. Let's just find him." He turned to his veteran deputy. "Bobby Lee, he sure in hell didn't chance comin' north past the dock and the Village. The guards have gone south along the river. You go west past Latham's Hummock. Dr. Hosmer, you're officially deputized. You good with that rifle?"

"Excellent."

"Don't hesitate to use it. Dr. Russell has killed twice already."

"Twice?" Hosmer said.

"Later. Warfield, you will accompany me."

THE MARSHES of Glynn were indeed a maze of tiny, irregular islands. Warfield marveled at his sheriff's expertise in navigating from one channel to another, dead-ending only once. The police launch covered miles of winding waterways in the next few hours. Once, rounding a turn, they came upon Bobby Lee and G. W. Hosmer chugging along, but otherwise, they saw no sign of human life. Toward four, Le Brun steered out to the Jekyl River and crossed into the swamps that edged Jekyl Island just south of the Village. Again, they found nothing. When they finally quit the search and came once more into the river, they spied Preston Lefferts motoring north in the *Hattie*. There was no third man on board. Lefferts cut his engine back to an idle as he pulled alongside the police launch.

"We raced south to the bottom of the island," Lefferts reported. "Would certainly have overtaken a rowboat if he had headed that way. Then we waited in hidin' for a while, thinkin' he might have hid from us as we passed." He shook his head. "He's either still on Jekyl Island or else he went west into the marshes."

"He gets out of that boat too soon and he's a dead man," Le Brun judged. Lefferts nodded his agreement.

"All right. Let's head for the dock and parley," the sheriff said.

Bobby Lee and Dr. Hosmer had already returned. It was agreed that the river and the marshes had been quite thoroughly combed. One of the guards who had been in the group J. P. Morgan sent after Warfield was also at the dock. His story was that the guards had concentrated on the lower half of the island, combing it in a coordinated sweep. No one, he estimated, save a trained woodsman or soldier could have escaped their search.

"Maybe I mortally wounded him, and he's dead on one of those hummocks," Warfield hazarded.

"Then where's the rowboat?" Hosmer asked.

"Maybe he scuttled it after a while and tried to walk the rest of the way out. Maybe he drowned."

"Maybe we forget about maybes," Le Brun said. He turned to his veteran deputy. "Take the launch and get back to town. Round up as many of the boys as you can and set up a dragnet to the west of the marshes. Right through the night if need be."

Bobby Lee took his orders in silence and departed in silence. Le Brun did not wait to watch him depart. He pointed to Pulitzer's close friend.

"I need your help, Dr. Hosmer. Do you keep any hypodermic needles in Mr. Pulitzer's cottage?"

"I do."

"And do you have a microscope?"

"That I do not."

"Never you mind. I can find you one. Fetch your needles, please, and meet us at the infirmary."

Hosmer followed Deputy Randolph's example and hurried away to do the sheriff's bidding.

"Come with me, Chief Deputy," John said. He strode up the dock lane, giving no accommodation to Warfield's bad knee. "Do you know why Dr. Russell would take such rash action after all his careful and cautious plans?"

"I may have inadvertently warned him," Warfield replied. "But you—"

"How did you come to warn him?"

"I had a terrible headache, and I went to him this morning for more of that medicine. While I was there, I took the opportunity to ask him the questions we had posed among ourselves: whether he came from London or Manchester, and whether or not he had private tutors . . . because of his accent. But," Warfield rushed on, "I certainly wouldn't have said anything if you had only told me you suspected him last night. You *did* suspect him, didn't you?"

"Yes. However, I gave you specific instructions of who you were to approach today, and Dr. Russell was not one of them."

"But I had a *headache*!" Warfield cried out, limping gamely behind his boss. "Just like the goddamned headache I'm getting right now. You won't push this on me."

"I'm not tryin' to push anythin' on you."

"Yes, you are. Slow down, dammit!"

Le Brun stopped dead. "I'm sorry," he said softly. "I am not blamin' you. I am also not blamin' myself, just because I did not choose to speak out and then perhaps find myself wrong."

"That's a problem of yours, isn't it?" Warfield asked, shaking with pent-up anger. "You're afraid to be wrong."

"I do not enjoy bein' wrong, it's true."

"You also still don't trust me," the chief deputy accused. "Do you?"

"Not completely. You yourself must admit that the tower we are buildin' together, stone by stone and course by course, has barely risen above the ground. The other night, you apologized for keepin' your guard duties with Mr. Morgan a secret from me, and I accepted your apology. Now I apologize to you. Do you accept it?"

Warfield exhaled. "Yes."

"Then unball your fists. We are both to be blamed and neither to be blamed. Now that we agree, let us keep it to ourselves and present a united front to the very powerful forces we will be addressin' in the comin' hours." Having said his piece, John moved on. His pace, however, was more accommodating.

When they came to the infirmary door, Sheriff Le Brun gently removed Russell's note, folded it, and stuck it in his inside jacket pocket. He turned the doorknob.

"I already tried it," Warfield said. "It's locked."

John raised his foot and gave the door a vicious kick, just beneath the knob. It sprang inward with a sharp report of cracking wood.

"Not anymore," said the sheriff. He walked inside half a dozen steps, then paused and surveyed the interior.

Signs of hasty departure could be seen in the examining room and in the front closet. Books, medicine, and clothing lay strewn on the floor.

"I'm here!" Dr. Hosmer called, from the walk leading to the infirmary.

"Check upstairs," John told his deputy. "I'll find that microscope."

Warfield found more evidence of precipitous flight on the second floor. He also found an empty box that had held a bottle of gun oil on one of the beds. By the time he brought it downstairs, Hosmer had left.

"You can leave it here," John said. "We don't want to cause undue stress to those few blessed ones who remain on this island paradise. Heavens forfend one of the ladies should as much as see a picture of a rifle at this point. It's about the time they take in the wicker furniture, isn't it?"

"I believe so," Warfield answered.

"If your leg can stand it, I'd like you to accompany me to the clubhouse."

Warfield smiled. "That's how you control people. You tantalize them with a provocative question, fail to explain it, then invite them to do something—with the unspoken promise of resolution."

"It's *one* of my tricks," Le Brun admitted. "You're very quick. I imagine you'll know all of them within a year."

IN THE EARLY MORNING and early evening, before and after the members' luggage and the club's provisions needed transport to and from the dock, Friday Cain was expected to use his time to move the white wicker furniture out of and back into the clubhouse cellar. This part of his work had not gone unnoticed by the sheriff. He was performing the tedious task of gathering up and storing the chairs, tables, and lounges when John and Warfield descended the steps beneath the laundry and found him. Sheriff Le Brun flashed his badge at Cain's white boss and asked him to leave them alone for a time. When the boss had gone, Warfield eased himself down into one of the chairs and regarded the black man in silence. John stood just to the side of the doorway with his arms folded. A soft rectangle of reflected daylight ran a dozen or so feet along the floor, providing precious little illumination to the rest of the cellar. Friday stood in the shadows.

"Come out into the light, Mr. Cain, please," John said. "I need to talk with you about Dr. Russell."

"Yassuh."

"He's been very good to you, curing your rheumatism."

"Yassuh."

"Did he ever take money from you?"

"No, suh."

"I understand he's helped quite a few colored folk on the island."

"Yassuh."

"Even got himself in trouble for leaving the infirmary to do it."

"Don't know 'bout dat . . . but I spects so." With each question, Cain's downcast face grew more and more anxious. His eyes were fixed on the floor, as if he longed to follow the light to freedom.

"I wonder if he's told you how he also helps many colored folk up in Baltimore, at his hospital," John went on.

"Yassuh." Cain nodded several times. "Saved my brudah's life."

"Your brother?"

"Yassuh. He gone up Baltimo' since ten years. Got a tumor in he stomach big's a baseball, but couldn't pay to get it took out. Dr. Russell take it out fo' nuthin.' Saved my brudah's life."

John shot Warfield a look that warned him to pay careful attention.

"You believe Dr. Russell is a good man."

"Da best man," Friday asserted.

"And you owe him a great deal."

"Yassuh."

"If he asked you for a favor, you would surely do it."

Friday was silent, staring at the fading light.

"Look at me, Mr. Cain!" John ordered.

Cain lifted his head and fixed his gaze on the sheriff's chin.

"You would do him a favor . . . as long as it wasn't against the law. Wouldn't you?"

"Yassuh."

"I'm sure you remember last Saturday. You went to the infirmary right after you'd put out the furniture. Just like you'd been doin' for several days. To get the medicine for your rheumatism. Isn't that right?"

"Yassuh."

"Except that on Saturday Dr. Russell asked you to be sure to bring your wagon and mule. He also asked you to be sure to be there at eight o'clock sharp. Am I right?"

Cain sighed.

"Am I right?" John repeated.

This time the "yassuh" was slow and mumbled.

"Dr. Russell gave you your medicine very quickly and hurried you out the door. You left your mule and wagon with him."

Cain nodded.

"What reason did he give you for wanting to borrow your wagon?"

"He say he has to move some equipment. I tol' him I would hep him, but he say no."

"He also told you to come back later, I'm sure. At what time did he ask you to come back?"

"Ten minute befo' nine."

"You didn't know at the time, but now you know he used your mule and wagon to help him kill Erastus Springer."

"I don' know dat fo' sho'," Friday asserted.

"But you suspected it, when no one else was accused."

Again, the black man said nothing.

"You didn't tell anyone about Dr. Russell borrowin' your wagon," John pointed out.

"Nobody done ask me," Friday returned.

"You're not a stupid man, Mr. Cain. You were right there on the path in front of the body when Dr. Russell told us about Mr. Springer's daily walks. When he gave us the very precise times of those walks. You must have wondered why Dr. Russell rushed you out of the infirmary, why he was so insistent that you arrive by eight, that you not help him with his chores, and that you return at ten minutes before nine."

"I don' ask no questions, suh," Cain answered. "Keeps me out of t'ouble."

"It might not keep you out of trouble this time. You are what the law calls 'an accessory to murder.' You could hang for it, Mr. Cain."

Cain's eyes grew wide and blinked rapidly, although he continued to stand like a cigar-store Indian, left hand clamped to his thigh, right hand balled into a fist, just above his trouser line.

"You could hang," Sheriff Le Brun repeated. "Especially since you never came forward afterward with what you suspected. That is what the law calls 'obstructin' justice.' But I don't want any harm to come to you. Dr. Russell used your friendship to protect himself. You had no idea he intended to kill Mr. Springer until after he'd done it."

Finally, Cain looked directly into the sheriff's eyes. "No, suh! I had no idea."

"Nothin' will happen to you"—John raised his forefinger and waggled it—"*provided* I can be sure no one else will talk about this. Did you speak with any of the other colored folk about it?"

"No, suh!"

"If you're lyin' and they talk around, it'll come out. I'll have to see that you're arrested and hanged."

"I done tol' nobody," Friday vehemently declared.

"Let's hope so." John lowered his arms. "Did Dr. Russell talk to you about Mr. Springer afterward? On Saturday or the past few days?"

"No, suh."

"All right. You can finish your work. Just make sure you keep your mouth shut."

"Yassuh. Thank you, suh!"

John exited the cellar, with Warfield close behind.

"I hope we can keep him out of it," John remarked. "It'll depend on what the club wants."

"So, Mr. Pulitzer was right," Warfield said. "Dr. Russell did need an accomplice, even if the accomplice was unwitting."

Le Brun stopped at the corner of the modesty wall that hid the laundry. He leaned against it. "Russell is a good judge of human nature. He counted on typical Negro silence and on Mr. Cain's friendship to protect himself."

"But why did he want Springer, Morgan, and Sage dead?" Warfield asked. "Did it have to do with the D and RG and the B and M?"

John smiled. "Yes. And I'll tell you everythin', but right now I need to invite an exclusive group for a confab tonight. You need to get off that leg for a time." He nodded toward the back stairs. "Up you go."

IN SPITE of his desperate need for sleep, Warfield had gotten none when John knocked on his door at six-thirty. Over one arm, John held the chief deputy's jacket and trousers, which he had earlier sent a servant up to collect.

"Here. Get decent," John said, handing over the clothes.

As Warfield dressed, John dug out the memo book and squinted at its pages. Warfield asked, "What now?"

"We have an early dinner. They're still searchin' the island for Dr. Russell, but I doubt they'll find him."

"I agree. And after dinner?"

"A cozy little get-together in Mr. Scrymser's apartments."

"And, in between, you're going to tell me everything," Warfield prompted.

"Most everythin'." John waited until Warfield had stabbed his feet into his shoes and stood up before cocking his head in an appraising stare. "Amazin' what a sponge cleanin' and pressin' can do," he remarked.

Warfield realized for the first time that day that Le Brun had arrived on the island wearing his go-to-court suit. Considering all the hours in the police launch, wending through the marshes, he still looked dapper. The suit indicated clearly that the sheriff had crossed to the island this day with the intention of tying up the case.

The deputy ran a comb through his sandy-colored hair, applied a bit of wax to his moustache, and gestured for the sheriff to lead the way.

The maître d' led them into the dining room and paused at the most central table. "Is here all right, gentlemen?" he asked.

John looked around. Only Mr. Deering and Mr. Dexter and their wives had been seated, and they were at an adjacent table. The sheriff and chief deputy were greeted with artificial smiles but smiles nonetheless.

"We're happy with our usual table," Le Brun told the maître d'. He bowed slightly to the two couples and moved on to the corner near the waiters' preparation area. As soon as he and Warfield were seated, he said, "It's hard to believe, but they don't know about Dr. Russell. If they did, considerin' how they lambasted him over bein' a 'nigger lover,' we'd have seen it on their faces."

"There's no way they won't eventually know," Warfield said.

"But what's important is that the knowledge will be unofficial. If the members can speak of it in private and yet be ignorant of it in public, then the Jekyl Island Club will be spared the scandal."

"Completely two-faced," Warfield said, grimacing with disgust.

John opened his linen napkin with a flourish and spread it across his lap. "Welcome to high society. Let's begin fillin' you in. First, I want to see the power of your ratiocination."

"Big word for a Cracker sheriff," Warfield quipped.

"That British businessman I was playin' chess with last week taught it to me. Here goes: Why did Thomas Russell need to borrow Friday Cain's wagon and mule?"

"Shouldn't we begin with *why* he killed Springer?"

"We'll get back to that. What about the wagon?"

"Because Mr. Springer was already dead at eight o'clock. Russell had killed him in the infirmary," Warfield answered confidently.

John leaned in toward his chief deputy. "What about the bullet in the oak and the white cloth in front of the fallen tree?"

"Done to throw us off."

"Didn't he worry about the noise of the gunshot inside the Village?"

"Perhaps he muffled the gun. What do you think?" Warfield invited.

"Dr. Russell had plenty of ways to kill the man in his infirmary, but he couldn't take a chance on some medical murder. Not with Dr. Hosmer on the island and the possibility that the county coroner might be called in. He had to make it look like the kind of death that could have been caused by the average man. Even better, caused by J. P. Morgan. He could read on the posted schedule when Morgan was huntin'. He could also read *what* Morgan was huntin' and, consequently, where the huntin' would occur. He knew that Springer had an inflexible schedule, that he always walked alone, and that he wouldn't leave the Village grounds until he had been checked by the resident physician. All that worked in his favor. The main problem was that Springer randomly used three different paths. He could not have declared the man healthy, then snuck out the back door and run like hell to an exact spot in the woods, where he would have his rifle stowed."

"I agree," Warfield said. "Which is precisely why I believed he had to kill him before he left the infirmary. Then what—" His eyes unfocused to infinity. "I have it! He listens to Springer's heart and tells him he doesn't like the sound of it, or something like that. He tells him that he'd better drink this elixir or take this shot. Since the man is a hypochondriac, he's overjoyed to comply. Russell's victim is rendered unconscious almost immediately. The doctor loads him into the wagon, which is behind the infirmary and pretty much out of view of the rest of the Village. Now, if he's seen with Springer he's not transporting a corpse. Instead, he can boldly call out to the witness and show him Springer's body.

" 'Look!' Russell says to the witness, 'I told Mr. Springer his heartbeat was irregular this morning, but he insisted on walking anyway. I had a Negro patient directly after, for rheumatism. I was so worried about Mr. Springer that I borrowed the Negro's wagon and went out in search of the man. I found him, collapsed, and now I'm trying to find a place to turn this damned wagon around so I can get him back to my medicines at the infirmary.' "

Warfield flung out his hands in triumph. "The witness would even be invited to see that Springer was breathin'. Naturally, the old boy would later die of his alleged attack. Dr. Russell would inject him with some lethal drug, and the witness from the path would swear to the doctor's wonderful extra efforts to protect the foolish man."

"That's a good stagger at it," Le Brun praised. "My thinkin' too, more or less. So, now Russell carts the unconscious Springer out to the path, as close as possible to the area where he knows Mr. Morgan is huntin'. No one has seen him all the way there, so he carries Springer over to the oak, seats him on the rock, and props him against the oak. He takes out his rifle from hidin', walks back to the fallen tree stump, wraps some bandage cloth around the muzzle to muffle the report—"

"That's what that loosely woven cloth was!" Warfield exclaimed.

"—aims and fires. Little pieces of white cloth are scattered near the stump. Far more and more far than he thought." Le Brun's eyes twinkled at his wordplay. "He manages to pick up most of it, but he's in a hurry and misses the few we find. The bullet wound is fatal. The bullet fragments, but Dr. Russell can't see that because the slug is buried in the tree. If we bothered to have another autopsy done—which we won't—I'll bet they'd find the sliver lodged in a rib or the spine.

"Russell also cleans up most of the cloth that shreds off Springer's back. He throws his bandage material over his shoulder to protect his suit, burdens himself with the corpse, and carries it out to the path, as far away from the oak as he can manage with such a deadweight. He dumps the body, takes a few moments to obliterate the footprints made in the soft earth, gets atop the wagon, and hightails it back to the infirmary. Again, luck is on his side, and he isn't spotted. He puts the wagon close to the back door, where trees and bushes almost conceal it. Mr. Cain fetches the wagon. There's no blood on the wagon's flatbed, nothing to suggest its nasty use. The most delicate and time-sensitive part of Dr. Russell's work is finished."

The hovering waiter spotted the pause in the conversation and darted in to take their order.

"What about the rifle and the bloody bandage material?" Warfield asked, once they were again alone.

"Probably shoved under leaves and moss halfway back to the infirmary. Clearly, someplace that Russell remembered and could get to with little trouble."

Warfield's mouth was dry with the excitement of revelation. He sipped from his water glass. "After the body is discovered, Russell is found sitting in the infirmary, as everyone expects him to be—even when he isn't—and is brought out to pronounce the man dead."

"Correct."

Warfield thumped the table with satisfaction. "And now you'll tell me why Dr. Russell wanted Mr. Springer dead, and why he wanted to blame Mr. Morgan for it."

"I will," Le Brun agreed. "But I will only do it with the others in Mr. Scrymser's apartments, unless you can fit together the clues yourself. I will give you this one hint." He produced the memo book, opened it to a particular page, and pointed to one of Warfield's notations. "Here's your imitation of Morgan's handwritin'. What's that say?"

"B and M," Warfield replied.

"Did you see the word 'of' in either record book?"

"I don't think so. He left out little words like that."

"Could that perhaps be Morgan's shorthand form of 'of'?"

"You mean 'B of M'?"

"That's right."

Warfield looked askance at the sheriff. "What the hell is B of M?"

While Warfield was thinking, John added, "And what is the significance of the phrase 'booked to arrive'?"

Their appetizer arrived while Warfield continued to ponder. Le Brun could not be cajoled into revealing the solution. Instead, he said, "I was thinkin' on my way over here about my niece. Wife's sister's child. She's a pretty thing, but way too persnickety when it comes to men. Probably because she's smarter than most of them. Went to that new state college in Savannah. She's a schoolmarm, with a good salary. That makes a woman mighty independent. She's twenty-five, and I'm afraid she'll end up an old maid. Can you think of any eligible young men, say your age and educational level, who might be interested in meetin' her?"

"What about me?" Warfield bit.

John scowled. "I'm talkin' about somebody who wants to stay in the area."

"That's me. I do." Warfield dug into his pocket for his billfold. He pulled out $132. "I'm well on the way to a down payment for a little house. What's she look like?"

The murders were tabled through the entrée as the sheriff extolled his niece's virtues and had the young deputy salivating over more than the exquisitely prepared and presented food. As their desserts were being served, Warfield suddenly snapped his fingers.

"B of M! Not a railroad at all. The Bank of Manchester! You make reservations for a train or coach trip to New York. You 'book to arrive' if you're traveling by boat!"

"About time," John replied. "Let me tell you, I am very impressed with Mr. Pulitzer's staff. I telegraphed several questions off to them in the middle of the night, and before noon they had the answers back to me."

"What were your questions?"

John held up his right hand and wiggled one finger after the next. "What was the history of the Bank of Manchester's dealings in the United States in the early 1880s? Second, what relation a man named Saye had to the bank. Third, what happened to Saye. Fourth, what the initial S stands for in Dr. Thomas S. Russell's name."

"And?"

"Gonorrhea!"

The shocking word fairly echoed through the dining room and created a predictable stir. It had escaped from the lips of G. W. Hosmer, who could not wait to be seated before reporting to John Le Brun. He threw himself down onto the nearest unoccupied chair at the table.

"Andes is very annoyed with you," Hosmer told the sheriff. "He thinks you've inspired me to a new life as a forensic chemist. I told him nonsense. He's stuck with me for life."

"There's no doubt about the gonorrhea?" John asked.

"None whatsoever. Right there under the microscope. The double bean-shaped gonococcus. And I found evidence of poison as well. I strongly suspect curare."

"What are you talking about?" Warfield demanded.

Hosmer set his chin on his hand and regarded the chief deputy with perfect calm. "James Sage, of course."

"Curare," John said. "Isn't that the stuff some South American Indians use on their arrows?"

Hosmer pointed his finger at Le Brun. "Indeed! If Sage had eaten it, nothing would have happened. You can ingest ounces of it without risk, because it's digested by the gastric juices. One scratch, however, can cause paralysis of the motor nerves that command the striated voluntary muscles. The heart muscle keeps pumping, but the chest muscles shut down. Nothing happens to the brain, either, so the victim is fully awake as paralysis sets in and he slowly suffocates."

Le Brun nodded at the notebook. "Make a note, War. We'll want all the medicines in the cabinet analyzed, to see what Dr. Russell brought with him."

"You may find the curare clearly marked," Hosmer said. "It's a well-known adjuvant in anesthesia. As the medieval physician Paracelsus correctly observed, poison is generally a question of quantity. Foxglove can save a heart or destroy it, depending on the quantity administered."

"James Sage had gonorrhea and was poisoned?" Warfield asked, visibly bewildered.

Hosmer stood. "Absolutely. I found a small mark under the upper left arm when I was drawing fluids. Russell convinced Sage to let him be injected. The 'cure' was cur-*are*." He laughed, harder than a well-balanced person would have. "I really must get back to Andes. He's truly afraid I'll jump ship on him. See you at eight!"

Warfield fished his damaged watch from his pocket and consulted it. "I'll never make it until eight o'clock."

"Yes, you will," John answered. "Enjoy the meal. It's probably the last one you'll ever eat at the Jekyl Island Club." To emphasize his words, Le Brun picked up his dessert fork and dug into the tortoni cups with strawberry ice cream.

"I don't want to be as ignorant as the others," Warfield pleaded. "Tell me."

"All right. If you can answer me one thing," Le Brun said. "Have you been completely forthcomin' with me?"

Warfield looked the sheriff straight in the eyes. "In every matter having to do with these murders I swear that I have been completely forthcoming. Does that satisfy you?"

Sheriff Le Brun picked up the notebook and began thumbing through it. "It does not. You just tried to get away with a verbal evasion. I did not ask you merely about 'these murders'; my question was general. It also referred to this." He held the book down at the edges with his thumb and forefinger, so that the page he had selected would not turn. "There's a little piece of that torn-out pages I asked you about, the one you said was used to write a note to Dr. Russell. And on the next page?" Le Brun had run a pencil lightly over the page's entire surface, making the impressions that had been pushed into it from writing on the page above visible.

"You have a very heavy hand when writin'," the sheriff observed. "Must be those bulgin' muscles in your arm, or maybe a habit from the days when you were so angry. At any rate, I believe there is little chance of mistakin' what you had written down there in an approximation of John Pierpont Morgan's hand and then decided to tear out. A proper name, a date, a dollar figure, and a person."

Warfield Tidewell had been shaking his head since John displayed the page.

"I tore out that page to protect us both. *We* could be murdered over that."

"You should have shared it with me and let me help make the decision," Le Brun said pointedly.

"Do you realize how big the implications are, John?"

"Oh, I definitely realize how big. Mr. Morgan himself told me. It's the big picture. In order to understand the big picture better, I asked Mr. Pulitzer's researchers a fifth and sixth question: exactly who the person on your torn page was, and whether there were any interestin' changes in his finances durin' the first quarter of 1898."

"And?"

"He was one of the ordnance officers. Killed, of course. Almost everyone was. On January 16, he deposited the sum of five thousand dollars in his New York bank account."

Warfield smoothed down his moustache nervously. "We *must* leave this alone, John. This doesn't have anything to do with the murders."

"Oh, but you're wrong. It's all tied into one big picture."

Warfield snatched the memo book away. "Why do you keep saying that? What are you talking about?"

John took his fork and mashed it into the dessert. He pushed the plate away. "Too rich for my blood anyway." He stood. "You'll understand what I'm talkin' about at eight o'clock. You and I are startin' to trust and appreciate each other. Do not retard that growth by keepin' me in the dark about anythin' remotely related to a case. I'm retirin' to the smokin' room to collect my thoughts. Why don't you do likewise . . . somewhere else." He took a last mouthful of wine and walked out of the room, leaving his chief deputy too astonished and crestfallen to rise from his seat.

SAMUEL DEXTER and Charles Deering were enjoying cigars in the smoking room when John Le Brun entered. They were sitting side by side in enormous wing chairs, under a blue-white cloud, with their backs to the sheriff.

Dexter hawked loudly from his throat, expectorated into a nearby spittoon, then addressed his companion. "So this little Jew cigar maker says to Mason, 'And why are you a Republican?' And Mason replies, 'Because my father and my grandfather were Republicans.' To which Gompers says, 'And if your father was a horse thief and your grandfather was a whoremaster, what would you be?' Quick as a wink, Mason says, 'Why, I guess I'd be a Democrat!' "

As the two men were guffawing, John stepped into their lines of sight. "I have a riddle for you," he said. "Why are there so many more horses' asses than horses?" The club members stared at him, dumbfounded. Before they could recover, Le Brun had quit the room.

John took a peek at his watch and headed out the clubhouse's side door toward Sans Souci. Waiting for him was his chief deputy, silent and chastened looking, finishing a cigarette. Mr. Isherwood stood in the lower hallway, extremely alert. He gestured toward the stairs. The lawmen climbed. When they reached James Scrymser's apartment, the door was open. They entered.

At the far end of the room, a mirror of Versailles proportions hung on the wall, greatly expanding the perceived size of the space and visually doubling the number of occupants. On one side of the parlor stood or sat J. P. Morgan, Charles Lanier, James Scrymser, and Francis Lynde Stetson. On the other side sat Joseph Pulitzer, with G. W. Hosmer standing directly behind his chair. Between them, on a low table, sat a cigar humidor; bottles of rye whiskey; scotch, bourbon, and sherry; glasses; a seltzer siphon; and ice. All of the men but Morgan and Pulitzer held partially filled glasses, and a glass filled with amber liquid sat on a side table within Pulitzer's easy reach. No one was speaking. Neither had anyone been speaking when John and Warfield entered the room. The atmosphere was cold and ominous. Warfield moved to the Pulitzer side of the room. Sheriff Le Brun closed the main door and leaned against it.

"I had toyed with the idea of invitin' Judge Tidewell," Le Brun began, "but I do believe that the fewer the number who hear all this the better. And this is the fewest I could invite. Good evenin', gentlemen."

Somber nodding answered his salutation.

"Messrs. Claflin, Fabyan, and Eames have left the island," John reported. "So has Mr. Reed and just about everyone else. The one small mercy in this affair is that it occurred at the end of the season. I will also tell you that I am reasonably sure Mr. Deering and Mr. Dexter, their wives, and a few others I have observed do not know about the death of Mr. Sage, the attack on Mr. Morgan, or Dr. Russell's flight. You have done a remarkable job of containing awareness of the trouble in paradise."

Morgan allowed himself a small smile. He bent to the humidor on John's last words and extracted a cigar.

"Clearly your club has been left without a resident physician," John continued. "Dr. Hosmer has graciously volunteered to act as substitute, and Mr. Pulitzer has graciously volunteered to postpone his departure for two more days, until virtually every member and guest has left."

Morgan had concluded his ritual preparation of the cigar and was putting fire to it.

"No smoking!" Pulitzer exclaimed. "I'm not having my lungs polluted by those stinking weeds."

"I *will* smoke," Morgan proclaimed. "And why do we need this gadfly here anyway?" he complained to Le Brun.

"Because he has played an integral part in all of this," John replied. "Please put out the cigar, Mr. Morgan."

Morgan made no further protest. His apparent stratagem had been to annoy Pulitzer. Having succeeded, he was willing to sacrifice one of his very expensive smokes. He walked over to the side table where Pulitzer's glass sat and dropped his cigar into it. Before it had stopped hissing, G. W. Hosmer had snatched it up. Morgan crossed back to his camp's side of the room.

Le Brun shook his head with both misgiving and warning. It was clear that claws would not be sheathed this evening. He took a step away from the door, stuck his hands deeply into his trouser pockets, and began his slow rocking from heel to toe.

"Let us begin by asking why a man like Dr. Russell would commit murder. This is someone who has never previously been in trouble with the law, a man who is spoken well of by all his colleagues, who has devoted his life to preserving other people's lives. The answer lies in who he is and what happened to him years ago. As this sorry series of events draws to a close, I am reminded of two things recently said to me. The first was by my chief deputy. He quoted an Irish author who has written something like 'The husbands of very beautiful women are all members of the criminal classes.' The second was by Mr. Pulitzer. He guessed that Mr. Springer died because he had provoked a powerful emotion. Keep both observations in mind as I speak.

"We start in 1876. Dr. Arthur Russell arrived with his wife and two daughters from London. He began his chief residency at the New York College of Physicians and Surgeons. The next date is October 2, 1880. This is the day Thomas Curzon Saye arrived in the Port of New York City from Manchester, England."

Le Brun began to perambulate the room, moving in a clockwise motion that brought him first behind the Morgan camp.

"England. Junius Morgan, Mr. Morgan's father, was then the director of J. S. Morgan and Company in London. He had developed a virtual monopoly over stock and bond trading between the United States and Great Britain, particularly regardin' the English passion for investin' in American railroads. Are you sure you don't care to sit, Mr. Morgan?"

"I'll stand," Jupiter answered.

"Very well. Father gets a message to son that Mr. Saye will be arrivin' in October. Now, Thomas Curzon Saye is a risin' vice president of the Bank of Manchester. This particular non-London bankin' firm wished to establish its own investment connection in the United States, cuttin' J. S. Morgan out of any commissions. Thomas Saye arrives in New York as the Bank of Manchester's representative, along with his son, Thomas, Jr. Perhaps he knew the Russells from the old country. More likely, they became friends in New York. The English aren't any different than my people; the French have been stickin' together in Georgia for generations. That is, unless they're cheatin' each other on land deals."

As Le Brun passed close by a credenza in order to avoid touching the chairs Lanier and Stetson sat in, he brushed several sheets of loose paper onto the floor. He bent, neatened them up on his thigh, and placed them carefully back on the desk.

"I have no idea what happened to Thomas Saye's wife. They may have been divorced or perhaps she was dead before he was sent to America. There was probably a governor or tutor for the son, who was then ten. At any rate, it's obvious that Morgan the Younger's task was to sucker Saye into bad investments and sour the Bank of Manchester on its foray into the New World. This, of course, could not be done directly. After all, the Morgans were the known rivals. A young lawyer named James Sage was brought into the scheme, undoubtedly to gain Saye's confidence. Erastus Springer was already feedin' Mr. Morgan information on the Denver and Rio Grande from the inside. It was one of those railroads purposely doomed to failure. Investors in the railroad—Saye bein' one of them—smelled a rat durin' the late summer of '82. They hired a railroad construction engineer to investigate. He went to Colorado and looked at the track, the rollin' stock, everythin'. When he returned, the man estimated that the railroad should have cost between thirteen and fifteen million. Somehow, the other fifty-five million that had been raised had been misused or stolen."

"Damn you, Joseph," Morgan cursed softly.

Le Brun raised his hands. "I am not accusin' anyone in this room of those actions. Only of capitalizin' on them. By September 1 of that year, even though it was fully operational for months, the Denver and Rio Grande was failin' to earn even its interest charges. It was estimated that every man, woman, and child in Colorado would have to be ridin' day and night for it to break even. Spurs had been built where only sagebrush grew. Word got out. The stock plummeted. Of course, the millions the Morgan firm had put into the railroad in the beginnin', when it was low, came back out long before the collapse. The Bank of Manchester was not so well informed and, consequently, so swift."

The sheriff had timed his walk so that he had come up beside J. P. Morgan. The banker stood close to the mirror, so that Le Brun saw his profile facing in two directions simultaneously, like the Roman god of doors, Janus.

"Thomas Curzon Saye took his life."

"That was his decision. No one else can be blamed for that," Morgan defended. "Certainly, no one could have predicted it."

"Really?" Joseph Pulitzer said. "Jay Gould used the good name and credit of one of his early partners to speculate wildly. When he'd lost all the money, the man committed suicide. We can all name half a dozen men who have taken their lives in situations similar to these. Washing your hands of any blame is sheer hypocrisy."

"And so thought Saye's son," John hastened to say, to control the cross fire. "Of course, he was only twelve when his father died. His father must have left enough information behind to link Mr. Springer, Mr. Sage, and Mr. Morgan to the plot but not enough to satisfy a court of law. For whatever reason, Thomas Curzon Saye, Jr., remained in New York. He was adopted by the Russells. Out of gratitude, he eventually took his adoptive parents' last name, but he kept his own last name as his middle one."

Le Brun resumed his stroll. "Were you aware that Saye had a son, Mr. Morgan?"

"Of course not. I don't make rivals' personal lives my business. However, I do make their *business* my business. I know absolutely that Thomas Saye made several bad investments, totally on his own."

"You didn't know about the son, so you never suspected that Thomas Russell might be such a person?"

"Exactly. Which is why I couldn't help you."

"Well, he knew you three existed. As the years passed, Thomas Russell never forgot his hatred. If he had thought of revenge at any time, he must have despaired of ever exactin' it. He follows Arthur Russell's footsteps, also becomin' a surgeon. He's recruited by Johns Hopkins, as a teachin' surgeon and to serve the Negro charity wards. By a twist of fate, your usual resident physician gets in trouble with the law in Rhode Island and cannot fulfill his contract down here. The Jekyl Island Club appeals to the most prestigious medical school in the country for a replacement. Dr. Russell hears about this. Just as my esteemed colleague reads the society columns"—John nodded to the chief deputy—"so must Dr. Russell have. He knows both J. P. Morgan and Erastus Springer will spend part of their late winter on the island. He sees at last an opportunity for revenge."

Le Brun reached the door again and leaned back against it. "He has no worries of shaming his parents or adoptive parents in case he is caught. They are all dead. He has no wife or children who depend on his support. He volunteers for duty, bringin' along poisons and a rifle. But you never called upon him for medical attention, did you, Mr. Morgan?"

"No."

"Nor are you ever alone. Mr. Springer, however, delivers himself directly into Dr. Russell's hands. Every mornin', as he's being examined, he tells the doctor of his habits and proves his neurotic punctuality. The rules of the club help Russell as well. Every man who hunts must sign up the day before and specify what and where he is huntin'. Russell learns when Mr. Morgan will be near Springer's walkin' area and contrives to kill Springer that day."

In dispassionate, well-chosen words, the sheriff related the same theory of Springer's death he had given his chief deputy.

"Long years of hatred as well as much experience with death have made Dr. Russell extremely cool," John went on. "He participates in the investigation with professional calm. When it seems that Mr. Morgan's luck and power will put him beyond suspicion, Russell leaves me a letter in the clubhouse, urgin' the investigation forward. His purpose, I would guess, is to keep the club in an uproar as long as possible and to make Mr. Morgan as uncomfortable as possible."

"That old nigger must face trial," Jupiter Morgan declared, of Friday Cain.

"I think not," John countered. "That would only keep this wound open that much longer, and who knows what would fester out." He looked around the room and assured himself that the very intelligent men there understood and agreed with him.

"We could have solved this a whole lot sooner if we had paid more attention to the Negroes," Le Brun told the group. "The problem is that we tell them not to speak until spoken to, to hurry off the road if we're comin'. We don't want to see them, so we don't. But that doesn't mean they don't exist and don't see and hear things. We also might have solved this a whole lot sooner if we had thought of Dr. Russell as a man and not as an accessory to the membership's health and safety. He fell through the cracks because he was neither member, nor family, nor guest, nor servant, nor normal staff member. He also became invisible, and that invisibility allowed him more latitude than one would imagine. I saw this operetta by Gilbert and Sullivan over at the L'Arioso Opera House last year. In it, the emperor of Japan says that someone's to be killed, and even though he's not, they all say he is. Because the emperor said it should be so. Y'all *expected* that Dr. Russell should keep himself like a dog chained to the infirmary day and night, and members were outraged when he wasn't there and left a note. Y'all *expected* that he was sittin' in the infirmary when the murders occurred, and your expectations rubbed off on me. Truth is, he had the least number of people observin' him on the island and, consequently, the most opportunity. All it took was two well-calculated risks that no one would show up at the infirmary needin' his help for a matter of minutes. Shame on me for overlookin' that.

"Now, to Mr. Sage's murder. I believe Dr. Russell would have considered gettin' away with Mr. Springer's murder and Mr. Morgan's embarrassment a coup and would have felt satisfied at that. He couldn't have anticipated President McKinley's visit and Mr. Morgan calling James Sage to the island as an advisor. He probably didn't even *know* that Mr. Sage was here, owing to his isolation. But Sage came to him. He had gonorrhea, as verified by Dr. Hosmer. This all came to me only after Dr. Russell's motive was established. I saw Mr. Sage get off the club steamer after a fifty-minute ride in visible urinary distress. I later heard about his frequentin' of whores from Randolph Rasher. The two facts suggested venereal disease. If that was the case, he would have taken pains to visit the doctor in private. Better yet, he would ask the doctor to visit *him*, in secret, after dark. Sage was summoned here by Mr. Morgan, who everyone knows to be a very religious and morally demandin' man. The last thing Sage would want known was that he'd contracted a social disease. He leaves his porch door open. Dr. Russell visits without comin' in through the hallway. They share a couple drinks. Russell assures Sage that he can indeed relieve the fire in Sage's groin. He injects him with curare and watches calmly as his longtime enemy loses his ability to move and breathe."

"Which explains the look of horror on his face," Warfield interjected.

Le Brun nodded. "Unlike Mr. Springer, who he merely put to sleep. Sage probably had a note delivered to the infirmary, which gave Russell time to steal a steak knife from the dinin' room that evenin'. After Sage is poisoned, he lays him on the floor next to the bed, rollin' him onto his front. He feels around for the space between the ribs, sets the knife's point and drives it home. Sage would have seen the knife and felt it."

Lanier and Stetson both winced.

"Russell is kneelin' beside the body," the sheriff went on, "so the knife goes in at right angles to what would be normal if he'd stabbed Sage standin' up. Sage is all but dead by then and barely bleeds. On the way out, Russell locks the door behind him, hopin' we'll decide the murderer had to have been inside this buildin'.

"Time is now on Russell's side. Even if Mr. Morgan can't get Judge

Tidewell to dismiss a second murder, the powerful members won't allow themselves to be shut up on an island with an unknown person who's murdered twice. Everyone flees, leavin' the club in turmoil and with a sincerely sullied reputation. The nearly invisible Dr. Russell follows them.

"It doesn't quite work out as he would have liked, however. Various questionin' we have done makes Russell suspect that his exposure and capture are imminent. He notes that the rowboat that had been used to help explain away Mr. Springer's death is now at the bottom edge of the Village, not far from the infirmary. He determines to escape . . . probably late in the afternoon to get through the marshes and swamps by dark and to prevent pursuit. But then he sees Mr. Morgan ridin' south, with only my deputy at his side. His blood lust is up from two successful kills, and he cannot resist takin' a last shot."

"How could he have gotten away?" Morgan demanded.

"He may not have," said Le Brun. "As far as we know, he had no skill with boats. He may have sunk it or capsized it. He may have dragged it out of the water too early and set across the marshes on foot. Plenty of mud holes, plenty of varmints could have gotten him. If not, my deputies will."

"If they don't, I shall personally see that he is hounded to the ends of the earth," Morgan proclaimed. "And I will see that that old nigger is fired immediately." Not losing a beat, he turned on Pulitzer. "You supplied all that information against me, you bastard!"

"I supplied the sheriff information to solve a murder," Pulitzer countered. "A great deal of what he's learned I had nothing to do with."

"Oh, bullshit!" Morgan exclaimed.

"I tell you, I am frankly in awe of what he's pieced together," Pulitzer confessed.

Morgan pounded on the wall behind him. "I'm not having any of it. Your memberships are in jeopardy. And stop denying, because Sheriff Le Brun specifically said he invited you here because of your part in it."

The words flying between Morgan and Pulitzer encouraged the others to speak and to rise from their seats to prevent physical violence. A jumble of sound and motion filled the room.

"Enough!" Sheriff Le Brun cried out. "I have more to say, but only to Mr. Morgan and Mr. Pulitzer. I wish—"

"Whatever else you have to say," Morgan burst in, "you'll have to do it in front of my lawyer."

"And then Mr. Pulitzer will rightfully ask to have Dr. Hosmer stay," said Le Brun. "I assure the both of you: You will not want anyone else in the room."

"Wait for me in my apartment, gentlemen," Morgan said to his group, after a few moments of huffing and muttering.

"Go wait downstairs, G. W.," Pulitzer directed.

Everyone left the room except for Morgan, Pulitzer, and the two lawmen. Morgan and Pulitzer sat directly opposite one another, with Le Brun near the mirror and Tidewell near the door.

John gestured for Warfield to close and lock the door. "When I said I invited Mr. Pulitzer here because he has played an integral part in all of this," John said, "I was talkin' about what Mr. Morgan calls the big picture. Specifically, the issue of imperialism. That is a large part of why the president was coaxed down here, was it not?"

"I won't deny it," Morgan said.

John clasped his hands behind his back and began a second trip around the edge of the room. "Even more specifically, the questions of imperialism in the Caribbean and Central America and whether or not we should consider annexin' the Philippines."

"The ink-slinger has nothing to do with this," Morgan affirmed.

"Don't I? Does public opinion have nothing to do with it?" Pulitzer riposted.

John asked, "Mr. Morgan, would you say that after Mr. McKinley's visit, the president is more apt to abandon his aspirations for a Far Eastern colony?"

"This has nothing to do with Dr. Russell," said Morgan. "Either get to your point or I'm leaving."

"But I need to learn from you two," Le Brun insisted. "All the while I've been here, you've both been eager to educate me to your ways of thinkin'. United States imperialism has been a major topic. Indulge me for no more than five minutes. Last year, when the battleship *Maine* blew up in Santiago harbor, the *Oregon* had to make a mad and hazardous dash all the way down the Pacific side of Central and South America and back up the Atlantic to insure that we had enough firepower to beat the Spanish navy. Just last week, the *Oregon* had to dash back around the Horn to help put down those riots in the Philippines. This wouldn't be necessary if that canal the French started in the Isthmus of Panama were built. We might even be able to protect annexations in the Caribbean and the Pacific if a canal were there, not to mention absolutely control commerce and tax the rest of the world for its use. Did you speak to Mr. McKinley about a canal, Mr. Morgan?"

"I must agree with Pierpont," Pulitzer said. "This has nothing to do with the deaths."

"Doesn't it? The very reason Mr. Morgan pushed along the resolution of Mr. Springer's murder was the president's visit. You, Mr. Pulitzer, told me how McKinley was invited down last year, but the blowin' up of the *Maine* halted the visit. In your opinion, was McKinley invited with the intent of convincin' him to declare war on Spain?"

"Mr. Morgan does not confide in me, but I do believe so."

"However, once the *Maine* was sunk, the visit was no longer needed."

Morgan snorted. "Joseph and his *World* saw to that. 'Remember the *Maine*' in the three-inch letters. Front-page sword rattling day after day. Flaming editorials. Drawings of American women being stripped naked and searched by leering Spaniards."

"That last was in Hearst's *Journal,*" Pulitzer corrected.

"Only trying to outdo you. And your yellow journalism."

"Are you saying you objected to that war?" John asked Morgan.

"Of course not. It was a just, a necessary, and a splendid little war."

"You both agree that the Caribbean is 'our pond.' "

Morgan nodded forcefully.

"Better us than England, France, the Spanish, or the Dutch," Pulitzer declared. "They've carved up five continents among them; let them leave the New World alone. Is the lesson over, Mr. Le Brun? May we leave?"

"Three more minutes, sir." John addressed J. P. Morgan. "Mr. Pulitzer very graciously gave me carte blanche to borrow his vast investigative network for one day. It proved of inestimable value. One thing I learned about was a certain ordnance officer who served on the *Maine*." Both Morgan and Pulitzer blinked at the words. "An officer who received the sum of five thousand dollars in late January, via a check drawn on an offshore bank. You were doin' an investigation last year on the *Maine,* Mr. Pulitzer?"

"Of course. The U.S. Navy failed to get to the bottom of it. I had operatives both in Cuba and the United States investigating who might be responsible."

"And, because of the huge sum of money and the strange nature of its origin, this one ordnance officer attracted a good deal of your attention."

"For a time."

"Why didn't you continue the investigation?"

"For one thing, the man was dead. Blown up with the other two hundred and sixty men who lost their lives. For another, we despaired of learning the ultimate source of that money."

Le Brun again regarded the flaxen-haired, strawberry-nosed old titan of finance.

"What if I had proof that the source was Mr. Morgan?"

"Ridiculous!" Morgan exclaimed, without moving.

"Really? Mr. Tidewell tells me that you know he was in your study onboard the *Corsair III* last night. Do you also know that he was inside your safe?"

"I don't believe it. You're bluffing."

"Would you wager seven thousand dollars on that? Mr. Tidewell says you have that amount of cash in the safe, in two piles of twenties and two piles of fifties. You should place your trust in more than G-O-D."

The locomotive headlamp eyes grew huge.

"Who . . ." Morgan's nimble mind struggled for an answer to the rape of his safe.

Sheriff Le Brun looked with pride at his chief deputy. "You really should have hired him. He has a very sharp mind. Got the joke about the Morgan silver dollar. Guessed the combination from the coin's motto."

"What did you find, Mr. Tidewell?" Pulitzer asked, leaning toward the door.

"Mr. Morgan has kept two record books on his most secret dealings. In his notes for early last year there is a memo with the names of the ship and the ordnance officer, a payment of five thousand dollars, and the date."

"My God, Pierpont!" Pulitzer gasped.

"It wasn't me. I'd heard it was happening and noted it," Morgan said.

"Can that be true?" Sheriff Le Brun asked, his tone dripping with doubt. "Perhaps you should use your superlative investigative force to pursue it more deeply, Mr. Pulitzer."

Pulitzer sat stock-still and stared at Morgan with his dead eyes.

"If you do pursue this," Le Brun said with conviction, "it won't be any more forceful than your published report on Mr. Springer's death. Am I right?"

Pulitzer looked weary. "I already explained that to you. The club had to be protected."

"And you will protect it again," said Le Brun, "will you not?"

"There is no scandal that can come of this, Joseph," Jupiter pronounced, reclaiming his composure. "They broke into my study and safe illegally. Even if they carried out that book, a few notations mean nothing. I shall never divulge the persons behind the bribing of that officer, but I will tell you what was intended. We had to have a war. That idiot McKinley was about to negotiate a settlement, and the people of Cuba would have remained under the thumbs of tyrants."

"The people of Cuba, your plantation in Santa Clara, and your numerous other holdin's," John remarked sarcastically.

"I am speaking with my peer now, little man," Morgan said calmly. "So long as you hold your tongue, I will allow you to listen. Joseph, the man was hired to incite the country to war by sinking his ship. That is true. But his orders were to do it when the bulk of men were on shore leave and when no one was on the bottom deck. He must have been assembling the bomb near the forward magazine, and he bungled it."

"Two hundred and sixty-two men," Pulitzer said.

Morgan nodded. "A terrible tragedy. But their sacrifice was not for nothing."

"He's lying, Mr. Pulitzer," Warfield broke in. "It was him. In fact, he felt so guilty over all those deaths that he gave the navy *Corsair II* to outfit for the war."

"Save your breath, Mr. Tidewell," Sheriff Le Brun said. "Mr. Pulitzer will do nothin'. He knows we can't do anythin' either. We have no real proof. And he knows that exposin' the culprit won't bring back those men. But most of all, he agrees with Mr. Morgan. The sinkin' of the *Maine* allowed us to push the Spaniards out of the Caribbean. We assert the Monroe Doctrine and make sure no country ever competes with us there again. Next, Mr. Morgan and his cronies get to work on that canal. Just like they did financin' that revolution in New Granada. They established a puppet democracy in the new Colombia so they could secure the railroad and bridge contracts. Now they'll turn around and finance the overthrow of the Colombian government in Panama and establish a puppet regime that will sell us the rights to build and own the canal. I'm bettin' that was the subject of Mr. Morgan's little party with the president on board the *Corsair* the other day."

Morgan shook his head in wonderment at the Cracker lawman's depth of knowledge of his activities. His hands went to his temples and began rubbing.

Tidewell shook his head in disagreement. "No. The British have a treaty with us over ownership of any canal that's built. Clayton-Bulwer it's called. Mr. Morgan would never risk enraging all his British banker buddies with a coup."

"Don't you read anythin' but the society columns in your newspapers?" Le Brun chided. "The British are in trouble up to their eyeballs in South Africa and the Far East. Mr. Morgan will get the government to quote them a price, rattle a few sabers, and they'll have no choice but to draw up a new deal."

"Wild theories," Morgan avowed.

"No, sir," answered Le Brun. "It's your big picture at work. You are the king of American capitalism. Mr. Pulitzer is the champion of the common man. You two are often at odds over domestic issues, but in matters of foreign policy you are joined at the hip. If your visions of the American dream were not fundamentally the same, Mr. Pulitzer would not have applied to the Jekyl Island Club for two memberships, and you would not have let him join."

"You've had your five minutes of insult and innuendo, Sheriff," Joseph Pulitzer said. "What more do you expect?"

"Not much. We can't really do more than tell our story to some other newspapers, and then Mr. Morgan would sue us for slander. But his name would be dragged through the mud yet one more time. I ask only two things. The first is that you leave poor Mr. Cain alone. Allow him to keep his job here, with no harassment."

"And the second?" Morgan asked.

"That if we fail to discover Dr. Russell's body or fail to capture him, that you do not hire professional detectives to 'hound him to the ends of the earth,' as you have vowed. So far as we know, in this entire world there were only three men he wanted dead, and two of them now are. Thomas Russell is not a natural killer. He is no danger to society. I do not seek to play God as so many of your members do. Nor do I seek to play judge and jury, as Dr. Russell did. However, as Mr. Pulitzer has so colorfully stated, 'If amoral behavior were rewarded by death, this club should resemble the Little Big Horn.' For a time it did, but that's over. Dr. Russell will be punished even if he escapes. He can never return to his job. Fear of apprehension will prevent him from ever practicin' medicine in any state. If the world is lucky, he will leave this country and help the citizens of some more backward country with his skills."

"Do I infer from your words that we are not to declare this man a murderer and fugitive?" Morgan asked, bristling.

"Precisely. Erastus Springer was killed exactly as you declared; he was shot by a poacher. We all saw the . . . how did Mr. Lanier say it . . . abundant evidence. Mr. James Sage died of a massive heart attack on one of your private trains back to New York City. Dr. Russell took a boat out for some well-deserved recreation, and he is missin' and presumed drowned. And you, sir, were never shot at." The sheriff smiled at the nation's most powerful financier. "Ain't it the most exhilaratin' thing bein' shot at and survivin'?"

Despite himself, Morgan smiled.

"*Now* are we quite through?" Pulitzer fumed. "I'm starving."

"Yes. We're quite through," John said.

Warfield opened the door. "I'll take you down to Dr. Hosmer, sir," he said, offering the crook of his arm to the near-blind newspaperman.

On his way out the door, J. P. Morgan picked up the humidor and extracted two cigars from it. He offered one to the sheriff.

"You two are a formidable combination," Morgan commented. "Like a queen and a rook at endgame. You have won this match as well, Mr. Le Brun. Don't try to win a third time." He walked through the door without a look behind.

John waited a few seconds, until everyone had disappeared from the hall. Then he dashed into the bedroom where James Sage lay, folded into a fetal position inside a waterproof bag, surrounded by melting ice inside another waterproof bag, and all inside an opened steamer trunk laid lengthwise on the floor. The sheriff ignored the makeshift coffin and strode directly for the pince-nez glasses lying on the writing desk. He picked them up, slipped them into his inside jacket pocket, then wended his way quickly out of the Scrymser apartment.

I THINK YOU'RE CRAZY for bringing up that *Maine* business," Warfield Tidewell said, as John exited the apartment building. "We still might be killed."

"Naw," Le Brun replied, whisking the idea away with a flick of his hand. "Once Morgan sees his record book is intact, he'll forget about us. He has contempt of the president and chief justices; he knows we're no threat to him."

"Neither, unfortunately, is Joseph Pulitzer."

"Oh, they'll continue their war, but not over the *Maine*."

"I see you're smoking Morgan's cigar."

"It's a damned good cigar. I played that gambit for Mr. Cain's job and Dr. Russell's hide, should he escape. And for one more reason which Morgan and Pulitzer did not hear."

"What's that?"

"For your edification and my selfish needs. I wanted you to see just how nasty the big boys play, so you'd never get a hankerin' to head North again. That's all this ignorant country sheriff could salvage. When *you* become sheriff, I shall enjoy watchin' you eclipse me." He turned toward the dock and the old police launch that bobbed in the Jekyl River's gentle waves. "Tonight, I shall enjoy sleepin' in my own bed. Do you play chess, Warfield?"

"A little."

"Then we shall play, by all means. Nothin' sharpens a man's mind like the game of chess."

"Nothing sharpens a man's mind like working with you," Warfield countered as they walked, simultaneously using his powerful grip to give the sheriff's game shoulder a good, affectionate massage.

TUESDAY

APRIL 1, 1913

WARFIELD TIDEWELL picked up the Savannah newspaper from the porch, read one of the headlines at the bottom of the front page, and rushed back into the house.

"Aura, we're going down to Brunswick!"

His wife leaned into the hallway from the kitchen.

"You and I?"

"That's right."

"I can't do that, take off the day in the middle of the week. What about my job?"

Warfield had come to a stop in the hallway, reading the story.

"There's been a death."

Aurelia Tidewell headed down the long central corridor. "Oh my Lord! Who?"

"John Pierpont Morgan."

Aurelia hit her husband with the towel she was holding. "I thought you meant somebody important in our lives."

"Not important to yours, but to your uncle John and me he was. John's not going to last much longer either. It's past time we visited, and this will be a day filled with memories for him. You know he'll be disappointed if you're not with me."

"Oh, for heaven's sake," the school principal said. "I suppose I have a day coming to me." She looked over her husband's elbow as he continued to read, herself scanning the article. "The end of an era," she remarked.

"Perhaps," her husband replied.

Aurelia went to the foot of the wide staircase. "John! Claire! Get moving! Your father and I have somewhere to go, and we want to be on our way."

WHILE THE CONDITIONS of the roads from Savannah to Brunswick left much to be desired, the condition of Warfield's car did not. It was a new Model T Ford, just delivered to his business the week before. Warfield owned three mechanical garages in Savannah, Brunswick, and Waycross that sold automobiles. The horseless carriage had not yet made him a millionaire, but he was well on the way. Since quitting his job as sheriff of Brunswick six years earlier, he had ventured into several businesses that turned the new inventions of the day into products. Never once had he lost money.

As he motored along with his wife at his side, Warfield reflected on the fabulous resort on Jekyl Island. He had faithfully followed the news of it in the local and the New York newspapers. In the fall of 1899 the haven of the blessed had reopened with lavish parties, bearing no scars or stigmas from the murders of Erastus Springer and James Sage. Joseph Pulitzer added a wing to his cottage. In 1901, thanks to J. P. Morgan, Thomas Edison fully electrified the village, when only three major cities in the entire country had lightbulbs in their streetlamps. A new chapel was built in 1904, rustic in design and with cedar shakes but also with stained-glass windows designed and personally installed by Charles Comfort Tiffany, of the famed New York design firm. New cottages were added. New millionaires conspired to memberships.

Soon after the turn of the century, the bank failures, depressions, and panics of the past decades convinced the most powerful politicians and financiers that the United States needed a central banking authority to oversee commercial bank reserves, make loans, and issue notes to control the supply of paper currency. In the autumn of 1910, a few weeks before the Jekyl Island Club officially opened, a group calling itself the "First Name Club" booked the island for a week. The group consisted of J. P. Morgan; Rhode Island senator and chair of the Senatorial Banking Committee Nelson Aldrich; president of the National Bank Frank A. Vanderlip; Morgan's right-hand financial advisor Henry P. Davidson; Kuhn, Loeb and Company's Paul W. Warburg; and assistant secretary of the Treasury Abram Piatt. Ostensibly, their purpose was hunting. Warfield and John knew better. The mighty men of Wall Street and Capitol Hill were hammering out a first draft of what would later become the Federal Reserve Act. Nothing had changed; while the Jekyl Island Club's official rule dictated that no business was to be conducted at the ultraexclusive resort, the unofficial rule was precisely the opposite.

Warfield thought about Thomas Russell. The physician had not been found and was considered dead until John Le Brun turned a corner in London one evening and ran squarely into him. John had been on a celebratory retirement trip and, ironically, had become involved in a series of murders at one of London's most exclusive men's clubs.

When he sold his first automobile, Warfield had taken a photograph of it. He had the photo prominently attached to the dashboard of his new car. As he glanced at it, he remembered Joseph Pulitzer's scheme to have G. W. Hosmer photograph Morgan, McKinley, and the other powerful men taking a launch out to the *Corsair* to discuss the highest level of political business. Given Thomas Reed's presence at the Jekyl Island Club during the same period, Warfield reflected, it had probably been precisely to bargain over the issue of annexation of the Philippines that Pulitzer had expected. Direct annexation had not happened. But then again, the whole presidential visit might have been over the other issue that John Le Brun had brought up: the Panama Canal. The one thing even the multimillionaires could not create was a professional army backed by a recognized nation, so that the full blessing of the commander in chief would have been needed to accomplish that scheme. Panama had indeed declared its independence and was immediately recognized by the United States in 1903, paving the way for U.S. building of the canal. But all that had occurred more than two years after McKinley's death, when a photograph taken on Jekyl Island could no longer inhibit such dealings. McKinley had been assassinated, even though he had had much more protection than was afforded him on Jekyl Island. Hobart, Hanna, and Reed were all gone within five years of visiting the island. A quarter of those who had memberships in 1899 were dead. But the club endured.

By the time they drove into the limits of Brunswick, Warfield had been in private reverie for the better part of an hour. His wife had honored his silences, doing no more than rub his shoulder lightly. As she did, Warfield thought of Joseph Pulitzer. The self-righteous champion of the common man had returned to Jekyl Island faithfully every year. He had built his soundproofed yacht as he has promised, named it *Liberty,* and had it painted as stark white as Morgan's *Corsair III* was stark black. He had died in mid-October of 1911, on board the *Liberty,* vainly trying to outrace the Grim Reaper to his beloved island.

Warfield pulled the Ford onto the modest lot at the edge of Brunswick. He and Aura entered the equally modest home that John Le Brun had lived in for nearly three decades, through a front door that was never locked. They found the owner on the back porch, reading the newspaper. On the bridge of his nose perched stronger prescription glasses than the pince-nez he had appropriated from James Sage's writing desk. He looked every bit of his sixty-seven years. He had lost weight, making his creases and wrinkles all the deeper. His hair was silver-white. He did not bother to rise from his rocking chair.

"Hey!" he greeted, a grateful grin breaking out across his face. He received his niece's peck on the cheek and Warfield's handshake, then said, "The old bastard's dead."

"I know," Warfield answered. "I brought you the Savannah account."

"His last words were 'I must go up the hill,' " John reported. "He sure wasn't thinkin' about Jekyl Island at the end."

Aurelia wandered out to Le Brun's garden, leaving the men to reminisce.

Warfield handed over his newspaper. "This article says he died of a broken heart."

"How can you break somethin' you never had?" John remarked.

"Oh, that's not fair. He had something in there. His passion was for great ideas, great endeavors. He loved art and books."

"I suppose. Loved humanity; hated people."

"That Pujo Committee investigation killed him," Warfield declared.

By December of 1912, the era of the muckrakers and trustbusters had reached its zenith. J. P. Morgan's cavalier ways of doing business had finally caught up with him. He had been summoned to Washington to answer to the Pujo Committee as to the nature of his grasp into virtually every major financial, industrial, and transportation venture in the country. He had fought like an old, cornered lion, using every ounce of his guile. Again and again, he conveniently forgot events. He denied that, although the money trust which he commanded held 341 directorships in 112 corporations, he had any control. He had no power, he asserted. The only reason he was allowed to direct so many great ventures was because of his character. The press used his words like harpoons. The skilled prosecutor Samuel Untermyer, champion of the new order, failed to deliver a killing blow, but where he failed, the American public succeeded. Day after day, the press carried stories and man-on-the-street interviews that proved the average man placed no trust at all in John Pierpont Morgan's character. He fled the country, sailing to Egypt and finally Rome, where it was said he died of a loss of will to live.

"I have no pity for him," John declared.

"Even though he sent you that lovely note?"

On opposing walls of the ex-sheriff's front entry were two items under glass. One was a list of the rules and proscriptions for the Negro employees of the Jekyl Island Club. The other was a sheet of yellowed stationery with the embossed legend *On Board the Corsair III.* In an aggressive hand, with the *of*'s looking very much like ampersands, Morgan praised Le Brun lavishly for his genius in solving the crimes and for his discretion in concealing them.

"He didn't send that note; you did," Le Brun said. "You stole some of his paper while you were in his study."

Warfield kept the possum face that the sheriff had taught him. "Oh, really?"

"Yes, really. He never would have admitted in writin' that there had been murders on the island, even to me."

"Then why did you frame it and hang it on your wall?"

"Because you went through so much trouble. Besides, the paper's genuine, at least."

Warfield laughed. "I don't think I ever managed to put one over on you."

"Well, I wouldn't know if you did."

"I've got a spanking new automobile out front. What say Aura and I drive you down to the Oglethorpe Hotel and treat you to lunch?"

"And a game of chess on the veranda?"

"Sounds good."

John rose from the rocking chair with a deep groan. "Mighty kind of you, War. Let me change into something more presentable." He disappeared into the house.

Aurelia returned from the garden.

"I never told you how I scraped together the money for our first house, did I?" Warfield asked.

"No. Tell me."

"When I was on J. P. Morgan's yacht and going through his most secret record books, I came across plans he had with the House of Rothschild to corner the champagne market. I took the money old Jupiter had paid me to guard him, along with a few dollars more, and invested it in champagne. I convinced John to take a portion of his retirement money and do the same. Well, Morgan never did corner the market, but he drove prices up so high for a time that we both made a small killing. Enough for John to retire two years ahead of schedule and take a royal trip to England; enough for me to buy that little bungalow."

Aurelia smirked and tousled her husband's sandy hair affectionately. "Warfield Tidewell! That's not like you. What would possess you to do such an unscrupulous thing?"

Warfield smiled. "The Jekyl Island Club."

About the Jekyl Island Club

The ultra-exclusive club existed largely as it is described in the novel, although no murders ever sullied its reputation. The visit of President McKinley was just one among several events of national historical significance that occurred during the club's heyday. It fell out of favor during the Depression and World War II, and was sold to the State of Georgia in 1947. Many of the "cottages," as well as the chapel, still survive with their furnishings and can be toured. The clubhouse has recently been converted into a luxurious resort hotel. During the era of the novel, the island's name was spelled with one '*l*'. Before then, and since, it has been known as Jekyll Island.

About the Author

Brent Monahan lives in Yardley, Pennsylvania. He is the author of six previous novels. He collects chess sets and hardly beats anyone.